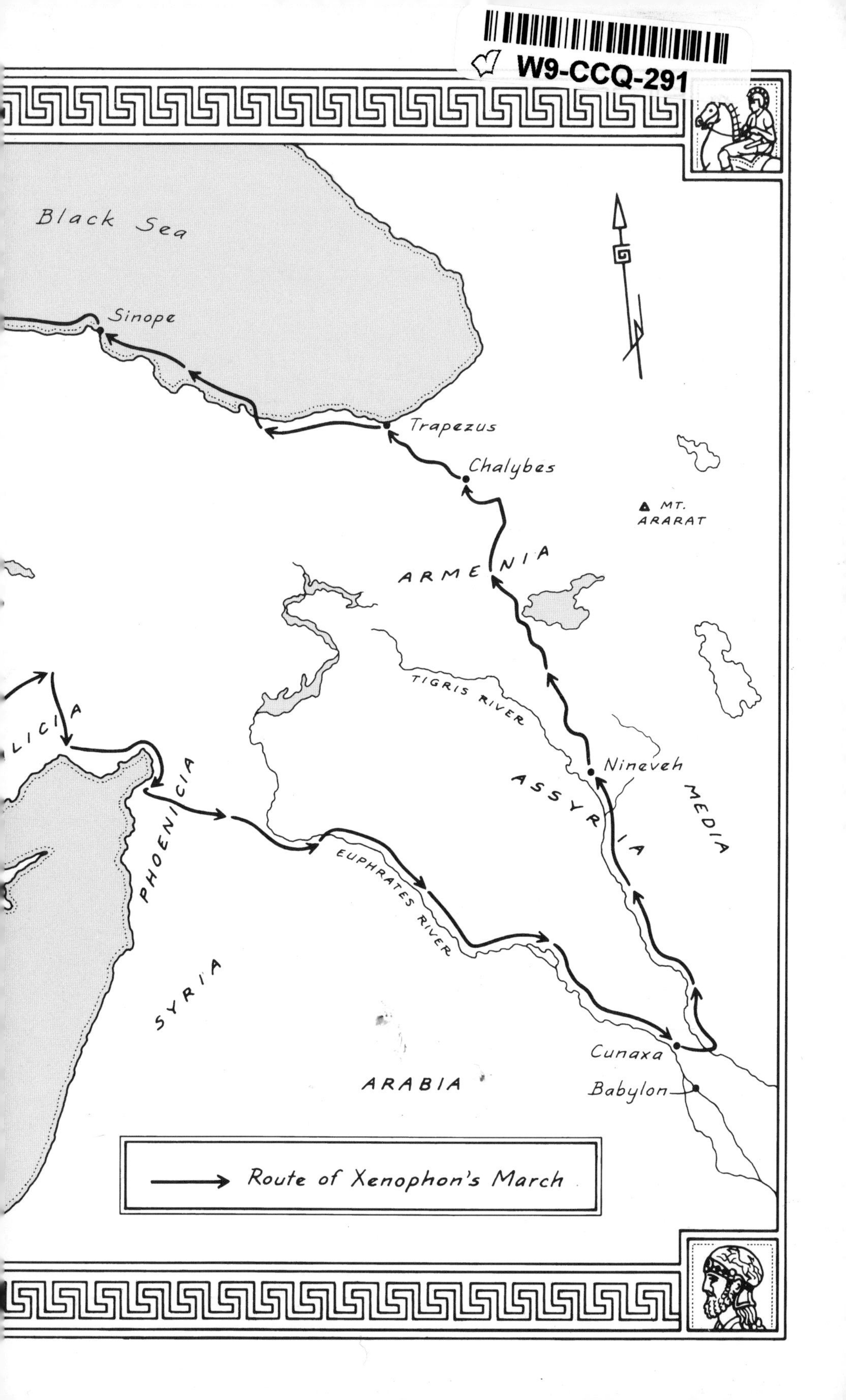
Black Sea
Sinope
Trapezus
Chalybes
MT. ARARAT
ARMENIA
TIGRIS RIVER
Nineveh
ASSYRIA
MEDIA
PHOENICIA
EUPHRATES RIVER
SYRIA
ARABIA
Cunaxa
Babylon
Route of Xenophon's March

THE TEN THOUSAND

THE TEN THOUSAND

A NOVEL OF ANCIENT GREECE

MICHAEL CURTIS FORD

THOMAS DUNNE BOOKS
ST. MARTIN'S PRESS NEW YORK

THOMAS DUNNE BOOKS.
An imprint of St. Martin's Press.

www.stmartins.com

Book design by Michelle McMillian

Endpaper maps by Jackie Aher

Library of Congress Cataloging-in-Publication Data

Ford, Michael Curtis.
The ten thousand: a novel of ancient Greece / by Michael Curtis Ford.—1st ed.
p. cm.
ISBN 0-312-26946-3
1. Greece—History—Expedition of Cyrus, 401 B.C.—Fiction. 2. Xenophon—Fiction. 3. Soldiers—Fiction. I. Title.

PS3606.O74 T4 2001
813'.6—dc21

2001017426

First Edition: July 2001

10 9 8 7 6 5 4 3 2 1

For Eamon, who was once found on the shoulders of a giant,
and for Isabel, who loves Homer

HISTORICAL NOTE

The late fifth century B.C. brought bloodshed and upheaval to the Western World. During the previous hundred years Athens had been experiencing a Golden Age, a magnificent flowering of culture and thought culminating in the establishment of the world's first functioning democracy under Pericles, the vast literary achievements of Sophocles and Euripides, and the construction of the Parthenon. Enormous maritime fleets brought untold wealth from every corner of the Mediterranean, and Greek military prowess had become the envy and dread of the ancient world, through two important innovations: the heavily armed and highly trained citizen-soldier known as the *hoplite*, and the impenetrable massed block of charging infantry known as the *phalanx*. Athens had become the very center of Greek culture and the greatest imperial power in the Mediterranean—yet all was brought to a shattering halt in 404 B.C. when the city was disastrously defeated by Sparta in the twenty-seven-year Peloponnesian War.

Now the monumental city of marble had been brought to its knees—its massive fortifications toppled, the powerful navy by which it had ruled the seas destroyed, its fields burnt and poisoned, its population impoverished and plague-ridden. A murderous and vindictive puppet government remembered as the Thirty Tyrants was installed by the victors to rule the defeated city, prompting cycles of rebellion and reprisal and further complicating an already chaotic political landscape. Thousands of battle-hardened soldiers from both sides in the conflict simply remained abroad after their discharge, seeking to satisfy their lingering taste for blood and plunder by hiring themselves out to the highest bidder for mercenary assignments. The rest of Greece, indeed the entire Western World, looked no longer to the vanquished Athens for political leadership—but rather to the secretive, xenophobic military state of Sparta.

The upheaval had shaken the moral foundations of society, and new leaders were needed, ones who could put the horrors of the internecine war behind them and look to rebuild Athens and restore Greece's preeminence in the world. Other centers of power, however, would not let Athens rise again so easily. Persia, in particular, an enormous empire sprawling from India to Egypt, had much to gain. Twice in the past century its plans for world domination had been thwarted by humiliating defeat in Greece—yet its ambitions continued to smolder, and it bankrolled the Spartans in the final years of the Peloponnesian War in an effort to prolong the fighting and prevent the Greeks from recovering their unity. Nevertheless, Persia was beset by difficulties of its own, not the least of which was the power struggle between the Great King Artaxerxes and the pretender to the throne, his young half-brother Cyrus.

The Greek city-states of Thebes and Corinth also had legitimate claims to leadership, and Syracuse, which in alliance with Sparta had destroyed Athens' formidable navy, remained a powerful force as well. Even the Spartans, though nominally the rulers of the eastern Mediterranean, were only reluctant leaders at best, fearing the sea and unwilling to open their own society and economy to the corrosive influences of the outside world. The various competing forces had effectively neutralized each other, creating a balance of impotence.

Within this milieu of chaos, oppression, and past glory following the Peloponnesian War, Greece would be unable to regain its position of political leadership and greatness for another five decades. During the intervening period, which was haunted by moral and economic devastation, when the humble philosopher Socrates was developing his marketplace ruminations that would soon form the very pillars of Western thought, a young man named Xenophon came of age. He was a member of the first generation of a new, post–Golden Age Greece, one that, though brilliant in many ways, would struggle mightily to overcome the destructive legacy it had inherited. It was a task that would cost much bloodshed and many lives—but in the end, it would also create heroes as great as any that have come down to us from antiquity.

Give me but a little leave, and I will set before your eyes in brief a stupend, vast, infinite Ocean of incredible madness and folly; a Sea full of shelves and rocks, sands, gulfs, Euripuses, and contrary tides, full of fearful monsters, uncouth shapes, roaring waves, tempests, and Siren calms, Halcyonian Seas, unspeakable misery, such Comedies and Tragedies, such absurd and ridiculous, feral and lamentable fits, that I know not whether they are more to be pitied or derided, or may be believed, but that we daily see the same still practiced in our days, fresh examples, new news, fresh objects of misery and madness in this kind, that are still represented to us, abroad, at home, in the midst of us, in our bosoms.

—DEMOCRITUS MINOR

PROLOGUE

It was the dragons of Phyle that defeated us in the end.

They and Thrasybulus, that rebel, that madman. As a general he had dined at our own table in Athens more times than I could count, but after running afoul of the wrong politicians, he had been banished to Thebes. There he had smoldered and fumed, his hate and contempt festering like a boil, and he had gathered about him a small band of like-minded men, Athenian exiles and mercenaries, each with his own debts to collect. Now, in an act of unbelievable gall, he had led his force of seventy picked warriors silently through the gorge, cut the throats of the outposts in the dead of night, and captured the fortress of Phyle that guarded the mountain pass a mere fifteen miles from Athens. To be sure, in the confusion after the city's surrender to Sparta, circumstances had practically invited him to do it—the fort's garrison had been undermanned and demoralized for months. It is of no use to cast blame on the stupidity of others, however, for that is the last refuge of losers. Now that Thrasybulus had taken Phyle, it fell to us to remove him.

Critias was charged with assembling the army and leading us in the assault, but Critias was no soldier; he was a politician, the leader of the extreme faction of the Thirty, precisely the sort of man Thrasybulus most despised. A fine show he made even in the pouring rain, all bombast and bluff, ordering his foot soldiers here and his archers there, posing with a new sword while his fine Carthaginian charger pranced beneath him. Admittedly, the fact that he kept himself surrounded by a squad of silent, scarlet-cloaked Spartans lent him a certain authority. But the canny Thrasybulus had blocked our main road to the fortress with huge rocks, forcing us to ascend through the torrential rain along a winding goat path that at one point veered perilously close to the fortress's outer walls. When iron met iron and leather met mud, this would not be Critias' assault to make; even cavalry was useless on that rock-strewn mountainside, and his own parade horse soon snapped its forelimb, toppling him ignominiously into the mud. Climbing the path up the gorge was a task for soldiers, pure and simple, and while Critias in his bespattered finery railed at us from below, Xenophon dismounted with the rest of his cavalry company, threw aside his cloak, and began slogging up the mountain on foot. Our force was three thousand strong and pissed as hell that we were out there. We would rout Thrasybulus' pitiful gang before nightfall and return home by the next morning, for the war was over now, it was beginning to freeze, and we were weary.

Our first assault was repelled with losses. The ancient fortress's barbican, the single narrow entry passage through the outer wall, was barely wide enough for three men to pass abreast, flanked as it was by two thick towers with sloping bases, squatting toadlike and malevolent on either side of the access. Window slits pierced the stone walls of the towers fifteen feet above the ground, through which the defenders emitted a murderous hail of arrows across the entry, point-blank into our faces. Grinning and hooting rebels up on the ramparts, backlit by the iron gray sky of the premature twilight and shimmering in the driving rain, heaved bricks and building stones onto our heads, from which we could not protect ourselves because of the arrows sweeping our lines from the front. Even after we turtled up with our shields and rushed between the towers in a box formation, the huge oak and bronze-sheathed door barring the passage stopped us cold, and we retreated in disarray, leaving behind wounded and dead.

Still, we were not discouraged, because we had anticipated such obstacles. On our climb through the driving rain up that miserable mountain path, we laboriously hauled a dozen thick planks of oak, each cunningly worked with a tongue-and-groove joint on the sides and fitted with wrought-iron handles and strap slots. In the shelter of a retaining wall on a slope in front of the fort, the last protected area before emerging into the hell of arrow fire under the towers, the men now assembled the boards with their frozen hands and hurriedly lashed and braced them together into a tight, peaked roof. It had a rain-soaked weight that would stagger five men, but which ten could easily carry when arranged beneath in two columns of five, gripping the iron handles and support braces. Thick wicker screens were hung from the sides to complete the shelter. The structure would protect not only those hoplites actually carrying it, whom we jokingly referred to as "pallbearers," but also several in the center between them, who rolled the battering ram.

The ram itself was not of cunning manufacture, and in fact was almost comically crude. It would have been impossible, though, to haul the usual bronze-sheathed logs up that tortuous pathway. We improvised with the material at hand—a rounded boulder six feet across which had been blocking the road near the top. With mason's chisels and axe heads we roughly chipped away its irregular corners and outcroppings, then bored two deep holes into its opposite sides. Into these we inserted stout iron bars to be used as handles, like an axle on an enormous, spherical wheel. This crude contraption we humped up the last few feet of the rise to the retaining wall, and set it on the path that would lead directly to the massive oaken door. Fortunately, the approach to the door was level, even sloping slightly downward. We calculated that with four strong men pushing the boulder from the axles, sheltered from the missiles by the sturdy plank roof overhead, it would attain enough speed to weaken the bar and hinges when it collided—with luck it might even bring down the entire door.

The first pass was made without the ram, as the ten pallbearers dashed out with the roof while another six "pickers" scurried beneath, slipping in the mud and the frozen slush to clear away rocks and obstacles in the path to the door. On their return run, they picked up the dead from our previous attack, whose bodies had been almost torn apart from the arrows and rocks raining down on them. Strangely, the rebels above did not impede us in this task—a few desultory arrows landed on the planks and skittered harmlessly off to the side, but otherwise they limited themselves to shouting out obscene taunts.

This we accomplished by dusk, leaving us time for only one more pass. The rain had now become a driving sleet, and the gloom of the weather and darkness of the approaching night made it impossible to see more than a few yards ahead. As the pushers took their position under the roof, the army massed behind, stretching out far down the hill because of the narrow confines of the space. The stone was given a slight shove from the top of the rise; it tipped ponderously forward, and the hands of the four pushers lent it strength, until it reached the speed of a slow walk, then of a trot. The men carrying the heavy shelter eyed it nervously, lest it veer to the side and crush them beneath its implacable course, but the slope was true and the boulder well rounded. Sweating and cursing, the pushers bent their backs and thighs into the iron rods, relentlessly gaining in speed. The army behind trotted, then ran, then sprinted toward the towers, their voices mounting in a roar that resounded off the approaching walls in a rising chorus of encouragement and anticipation. By the time the boulder neared the gate the pushers were struggling to keep up with it as it leaped and bounded over the path in a fury. Fifteen yards from the gate the pushers released their grip on the axle. The pallbearers skidded to a stop and the boulder shot out from beneath the roof. Behind them stormed the lead phalanx, a crack tribal regiment of Hippothontis who had fought and bullied rival companies for the honor of leading the charge, shields raised above their heads for protection and bellowing the battle cry. The huge stone surged forward, sending sprays of frozen water and mud to the sides, and at the last, just before reaching its target, it hit a small rise and flew into the air, slamming into the door dead in the middle with a huge crash.

The stout bar inside snapped with the force of the direct hit, and the enormous slab of oak was knocked askew on its hinges, opening a gap of a foot on the top and sides, with the outer corner leaning drunkenly against the ground. The impact splintered the wood across the waist of the door and sent an enormous crack running its length from top to bottom, threatening to fold it inward like a caved shield. The collision caused a tremor that dislodged stones from the battlements above, a groan in the walls that could be felt even in the ground beneath our feet. The Athenians emitted a roar of triumph, and the pallbearers tossed away the heavy roof and rushed to seize their shields and weapons that had been stowed in the framing beneath. Howling the battle cry, the phalanx surged forward to throw itself against the weakened door and force it wide before the rebels had a chance to barricade themselves again.

But closing the door was not the rebels' intent. Even before the hoplites reached the entry, the door shuddered and lurched, and with great and ponderous effort creaked open as if of its own accord. The defenders on top of the towers stood silent and unmoving, peering down at us through the sheets of thickened rain, and the cheer from the Athenians rose up even more fiercely at this sign of the rebels' surrender. We raced up to the entrance, half blinded by the sleet and the spattering mud thrown by the thrusting feet of the men in front of us, and the huge door swung wide inward, revealing the shadowy blackness of the vault within the ten-foot-thick walls of the Fortress of Phyle. As we rushed into the gap, the dragons came to life.

Horrendous balls of flame leaped out from the darkness, the stench of sulfur overpowering us as the black, stinking liquid blasted onto the men's faces and bodies, setting them afire and sending them screaming and stumbling in blindness. Murderous streams of flame roared out thirty feet, forty feet or more, three in succession across the width of the opening; each paused momentarily in turn like creatures drawing their breath, and then they again resumed their hellish blowing. In the darkness behind we could see the faces of Thrasybulus' rebels, gleaming and ghastly in the light of the flames, their eyes empty black holes in the pits of their helmets, their teeth gleaming yellow and fierce as they threw back their heads and grimaced at the strain of their terrible task.

Screams of agony and the stench of burning meat filled the air as men fell flaming beneath the onslaught, and those foremost in the charge were roasted alive in their very armor, charring black and writhing where they fell. Their hands curled into fingerless claws and their limbs contracted as they fell dead and shriveled at our feet like spiders dropped into the flame of a lamp. Farther back, my throat constricted and I choked and gasped on the sour black smoke produced by the burning of my comrades' flesh. I could feel the heat of the deadly blasts on my face like a furnace suddenly opened, and the thought of what a terrible death lay waiting behind that splintered and broken door was overwhelming. The troops panicked.

The narrow path behind us prevented a clean retreat. The men hurled themselves and forced their way through three or four at a time, as the inferno at their backs threatened a hellish death. Still-flaming victims raced crazily through the ranks, screaming at us to put out their fires, which we were unable to do as the burning substance ravaged without regard to water or dirt thrown upon it. The men were terrified, toppling and trampling one another in their haste to escape, and Thrasybulus' archers on the towers rained arrows down upon us, wounding dozens, further blocking our retreat. I peered back over my shoulder at the towers behind us, and saw the flames abate as the massive oaken door was slid and heaved back into position, the ghastly remnants of the dead and wounded left behind us in writhing, shrieking mounds.

The descent down the mountainside from the barbican was hellish, for the path which earlier we had navigated with difficulty even in daylight was now nearly impossible for troops injured and panicked, fighting downpour and dusk. The men clambered and dropped hand over hand, blundering their way down the rock-strewn hillside made all the more dangerous by the darkness of the shadows and of their own souls. The dead and injured were dragged and pushed, their heads and limbs bouncing over the rocks, while behind them disordered, confused troops bunched in terror. Men clubbed each other with fists and swords to push their way through faster. One terrified wretch leaped onto my shoulders and scrambled forward over the helmets of the soldiers ahead of me. He gained only a few yards before an enraged hoplite cracked him across the ribs with the rolled bronze edge of his shield, leaving him retching in the mud at our feet to be kicked and carried along with the mob. Speed was impossible, and not merely on account of the darkness; the switchbacks were so steep that one misstep in the dark would send a man crashing down onto the helmets, or spear points, of those creeping down the face below.

The route led around the fortress, passing over a shelf wedged between the outer walls and the steep gorge, where we were vulnerable to arrow fire from the ramparts above. Xenophon had been ordered to take over a company of archers whose captain had been lost in the assault, and here he deployed them to cover the army's descent by keeping up a steady barrage of arrow fire on any rebels that attempted to shoot or hurl stones on the retreating troops below. In so doing we killed several of Thrasybulus' men, who toppled from their positions on the rampart to land in a sodden steaming mass at our feet. Before we were able to clamber down the narrow path ourselves, however, Thrasybulus sent a detachment to barricade itself at the narrowest point between the outer walls and the gorge cliff, blocking our retreat and preventing reinforcements from coming to our assistance from below. Our hopes of threading our way past just before sunset were dashed when an enormous rebel wearing flame-painted Boeotian armor leaped out at our lead man from behind a boulder. With a powerful stroke of his long sword the rebel split through the man's helmet to the base of the neck, bursting his skull in a shower of brains and leaving the two halves of his head hanging by the neck tendons onto both shoulders. Xenophon thrust a spear into the throat of the rebel, who seized the shaft and attempted to wrench it out before toppling backward against the wall, cursing silently and spitting blood. He was immediately replaced by a swarm of enraged comrades, who flew at us from behind their barricade, driving us back with spears and rocks. We retreated to the shelter of the retaining wall hard by the towers, where we crouched, sodden and miserable, in the now complete darkness between the two enemy forces.

We were perhaps fifty in number, and we gazed in frustration at the passage in front of the barbican whence we had been routed only a short time before. The path was illuminated by dwindling flames still hissing in the sticky, noxious fluid that pooled among the bodies. So sudden had the initial blasts of fire been that the first victims were clustered in a single heap, some remaining upright and leaning against the mound of their comrades without room to fall, a phalanx still, even in death. One soldier in plain view, his charred head having fallen cleanly off his crispened neck like a withered grape off a vine, stood guard in the rain against a heap of his comrades, his corpse stiffened like a stump in his armor. Those in the ghastly stack who still lived peered at us desperately in their agony, imploring us with weakening voices to drag them from among the broken and bloodied limbs of their comrades before they suffocated or froze to death. There was nothing we could do.

"Lord Zeus," Xenophon muttered weakly as he swigged water from the flask I held out to him, "what the hell are we doing here? How can the entire army be thrown back by only seventy men?"

I glanced at him in the darkness, but was unable to see his expression. "When we get to Athens you'll be commended for bravery for leading these archers."

He grunted, and was silent. As I reached my hand out blindly to take back the flask, he seized my wrist and I found his grip unnaturally harsh, his hand trembling. I pried my hand away and seized his own wrist, feeling his racing pulse.

"What's wrong with you?" I asked, my concern mounting.

"Nothing. I'm wounded. I can't see it, I don't know."

"By the gods, you didn't say anything. Where is it?"

"Here—my leg."

I stretched out my hand and felt the arrow shaft emerging two feet out of his upper thigh, at an angle toward his torso, as stiff and implacable as if it had been fixed to his flesh by roots. On our retreat from the wall a few minutes before, he had been shot by an archer aiming down on him from straight above. I felt the angle of the shaft in the darkness, concluding that it had not embedded itself in the bone or pierced the artery. Neither, however, had it emerged from the other side, because of the terrible angle of entry—it had traveled through his entire upper leg, lengthwise.

My hand came away sticky with blood. He could not walk far, and even if this were possible, there was no place to walk to. We were trapped here until morning at least, and by that time his leg would have stiffened into a club, if he weren't already dead from loss of blood.

I had no belt with which to make a tourniquet, since we fought naked in our armor but for the stiff skirt of oxhide straps to protect the groin against sword thrust. Casting around blindly in the mud where our company lay, moans and gasps emerging out of the darkness from men bearing their own injuries, I came upon the leather flask I had just dropped. Seizing it, I pulled out my knife and pierced the skin, slitting it along the seam, then slicing it into a single pliable strip the width of a belt. This I tied about Xenophon's leg at the groin, placing my foot on his hip bone and pulling to fasten it tight before securing the knot. Xenophon grunted in pain.

"Are you mad?" he asked. "The leather will tighten even further in this rain. I'll lose the leg."

"Better that than die of bleeding. We have no surgeon here and I can't bind the wound with the arrow still in."

"Then you'll have to take it out."

"The hell you say. I'll do no such thing."

"You're a slave. You'll do as I tell you."

"I'm Gryllus' slave—not yours."

"You're my battle squire. Now grab the shaft."

I crouched for a moment, motionless, wondering whether this was truly what the gods had ordained. The men around us had fallen quiet, and I felt their eyes upon me, even through the darkness, though none volunteered to assist. The only sound was that of the enemy sentries on the tower less than a hundred yards away, calling out the watch. The rain had now hardened into a driving sleet, and I slithered through the frozen mud up to Xenophon's shoulders, facing the fletching of the arrow, then reached down and seized the shaft, again bracing my sandal on his hipbone to give me added purchase.

"No idiot, don't pull—*push!*"

"What?"

"Push the fucking arrow until it comes out the other side. You'll tear the muscle out of my leg if you pull."

Already his voice sounded weaker, and as I took my foot off his hip it splashed into a puddle beneath him, which was warm despite the sleet. The tourniquet was not stanching the flow.

I sliced off a piece of the leather strip hanging as excess on the tourniquet and gave it to him; he knew what was required. Folding it double he placed it in his mouth between his teeth. I twisted the toe of my sandal into the frozen mud behind me, making a small dent to gain purchase. In a single motion I seized the shaft again and pushed with all my might, in the direction of his knee.

Perhaps I was hesitant, for at first it did not move. Xenophon lunged in pain, arching his shoulder and throwing back his head, and his hand gripped the calf of my own leg like a vice. His chest heaved as he snorted air through his nostrils, and he grunted in agony as the arrowhead slowly cut its excruciating path through his yielding flesh with an audible tearing sound. I prayed that the gods would keep my strength true, that I would not waver or Xenophon jerk his leg, that the head would not break from the shaft. Though his body convulsed in pain he held his leg still, until with a slight pop and a sudden release of pressure the bronze head emerged from just above the side of the knee, slightly askew of the shaft, yet still secure.

I let go the shaft, my grip so tight I almost had to pry my fingers loose, and rolled back on my heels in exhaustion. Xenophon released his grasp on my leg and spit out the leather, panting and groaning. I reached out to touch his head and found that despite the bitter cold he was covered in a sweat.

"Now," he gasped, "cut the head and pull out the shaft."

I drew my dagger, and groping in the dark found where the long, narrow head protruded from the skin. The blood flowed unimpeded out the hole, and there was not much time. I sliced cleanly through the wooden shaft in two strokes, allowing the bronze head to drop with a small clink to the gravel between his legs, and then sitting up and resuming my squat in the mud at his shoulder, I grasped the fletching and smoothly and quickly drew the shaft back out the way it had entered. Xenophon did not lunge this time but merely twitched, and was silent despite the fact that he had not replaced the leather in his mouth. I seized a roll of bandage linen and stuffed shreds into the arrow holes, further securing them by wrapping the bandage around the wounds several times. In the dark, I could only hope for the best. The sheer pain had rendered Xenophon unconscious during the worst of it, though if I thanked the gods for this one small blessing it was premature, for they were not finished with us yet.

The sleet turned to hail, and the hail to snow, and when we stood to stamp our feet and bring warmth to our freezing limbs we found that it would not come, and we knew that we could no longer sit down that night. Fire was out of the question, for there was no fuel to be had on the rocky slope. Our jaws seized up in the cold and we found it difficult to talk, so we clopped woodenly up and down the muddy path in silence, our feet devoid of feeling. The entire night we tramped back and forth, blindly shouldering past one another, as the snow built on our helmets and shoulders and blew into treacherous drifts at our feet. We dared not venture further in the darkness for fear of falling off the cliff, or worse, running into Thrasybulus' men still lurking in the shadows. Xenophon, though awake and lucid, remained in excruciating pain. Throwing one arm around my shoulder, he limped along beside me in silence as best he could, as the skies opened up and the gods poured down upon us more snow in a single night than Athens had seen in two generations.

By the time the first feeble gray glow appeared in the east, three of our company were corpses, frozen to the stiffness of boards and covered with a dead man's shroud of white snow. They had been unable to move during the night because of their injuries. Xenophon, too, was in a dangerous state; the bleeding had stopped, but the foot was a terrible blue from the cold and from his inability to stamp it to move the blood. We could feel nothing, we could not grasp our spears, we could not talk, and though our armor provided some shelter against the driving wind and bitter cold, the feeling of the metal against our skin was unbearable.

"We leave now," Xenophon grunted, peering weakly through the thick snow as soon as he was able to make out the narrow ledge of the trail skirting the gorge. He held his palsied hands up to his face, blowing on them fruitlessly to warm them.

"And what if Thrasybulus' men . . ." I began.

"They'll be as frozen as we. Either we die here in the snow or we die fighting. I prefer the hard way."

Word passed along the line, and in an instant the men had assembled, limping and drawn, ready to depart. Litters were improvised of spear shafts and thongs to drag the dead and injured. We moved off, floundering through the drifts and steadying ourselves against the rocks with our frozen hands until our fingers bled and left bright crimson trails in the white to mark our passage, though we felt no pain in them. The men had left their weapons behind and stumbled along wraithlike, their hands in their armpits in the posture of madmen, peering fearfully through the snow and the semidarkness for any signs of attack.

There were none. Halfway down the mountainside we surprised a wild-eyed young sentry from the army who had hidden behind a boulder at our approach, thinking we were either the ghosts of those massacred, or Thrasybulus' men on a dawn raid. Astonished at learning we had lived through the terrible night on the mountain, he slid down the rest of the way to the camp, where he quickly organized a detachment of hoplites to climb up in the blinding snow and assist us in our descent.

Later that morning, as we shivered under thin blankets in camp while the snow continued to fall, several of Critias' Spartans returned from where they had been reconnoitering the fortress, attempting to determine how best we could lay siege and drive the rebels to surrender. They marched silently by our tiny fire, their tattered scarlet cloaks billowing and slapping in the wind, unperturbed by the powder covering their sandal-shod feet. Xenophon raised himself up on one elbow as they filed past to Critias' tent to report.

"Where are the rebels?" Xenophon called out to them. "Have they reinforced the entry? Did you see the dragons?"

They ignored his questions, staring straight ahead with faces as grim and stony as the mountain itself, not even bothering to disguise the contempt in which they held us.

Two days later, after the hellish return to Athens in a commandeered supply cart, during which three of the mules foundered and died in the bitter cold,

Xenophon was carried half-frozen and feverish into his father's house. Upon seeing his son near death for the second time in his life, steely old Gryllus openly wept. Later that night, after offering a libation of scarce wine to the gods and an entire cup to me in thanksgiving, he rewarded me with my manumission. I was a free man, at least in body.

I would later encounter the dragons and their keeper again.

BOOK ONE

A FATHER'S GLORY

In our mortal lives, the gods assign a proper time
For each thing upon the good earth.

—HOMER

I

LIKE THE GODS, or perhaps completely unlike them, I was always with him. My very nickname, Theo, reflects this fact. My earliest memories are identical to his, though my final recollections, I fear, have extended far beyond his own. I was present when he was born, assisting with his cleaning and attending to his tears. I will be there when he dies, no doubt engaged in precisely the same tasks. Throughout my life I tended him well, a guardian spirit, a muse, a scold, and a nuisance. Together we walked with shades and fought with Spartans, served princes and earned favor from kings. With him I entered hell and returned to the living. And with the exception of a brief interlude in a distant, muddy village on the Black Sea when my soul was not my own, or better said, when it was not his, I stood by him always. Having it otherwise would have been unthinkable for us both.

I was born, I am told, in Syracuse at a time when my people were involved in one of their numberless, dreary little wars with the Athenians. My parents and I were captured on the seas through circumstances unknown to me—whether by pirates, or through an attack by an Athenian naval trireme on the Syracusan merchant ship on which we were traveling, who can say? The little I have been told is that my soldier father was troublesome and my parents were sold as slaves, possibly several times, until they obtained positions in Gryllus' household while I was still a babe in arms. The only memory I retain of those times is a fragment of an ancient song in a language I do not speak, a discordant, tuneless chanting, which, though in days long past it may have brought meaning and even pleasure to those who heard it, to me remains indecipherable, even nightmarish.

My parents soon died of one of the terrible plagues that periodically swept through the city, one that unaccountably spared me. Orphans abounded in those times, of course, many of them born of pure Athenian stock, the children of parents who had been victims of the ongoing hostilities. These were raised by the State, lauded and praised at public events, and if their parents had died in the war, they were portrayed as heroes. Others, however, of nebulous ancestry, were subject to fortunes less clear—some prospered, if taken in by a kindly sponsor, while others were simply ignored and left to fend for themselves. So much the worse for those who, like myself, were born as slaves, or more ill-fated yet, as slaves from enemy peoples. I was mercifully kept on at the house, despite being only an infant unable to earn my keep. Possibly it was as a charity case in propitiation of the deities, or as a favor to the kindly old nurse who cared for me. My master, however, never concerned himself with my provenance, nor even seemed the least bit curious. It was simply another mystery, like the origin of the gods or the omnipotence of his father, that he accepted as a matter of course, forming, as it did, a part of his earliest understanding of life, one of those subjects it never occurred to him to question.

Those times were not easy. Athens was mired in a decades-long, self-destructive war with the Spartans, who after the defeat of the Persians by the Greek alliance had refused to submit to Athens' claim to leadership. Virtually every able-bodied man of means on both sides had been incorporated into the battalions of hoplites, heavily armed infantry troops that formed the core of the Athenian and Spartan armies. Each of these men, in turn, took one or more male slaves to serve as squires and baggage carriers, and this heavy commitment of resources to war left precious little manpower at home to do all such things for which men are needed, to keep a city prosperous and vibrant.

This made life difficult for the family of Gryllus, a wealthy Athenian landowner who maintained a rural estate in the *deme* of Erchia, twelve miles east of Athens. It was there that I was taken as an infant, and it was there that I spent the first years of my life raised by and serving a company of women. Most of the men, masters and slaves alike, spent the season at the front, with only a few months passed on the farm between campaigns, fruitlessly trying to make up for lost time and correct the ravages caused by neglect. Gryllus at one point had spent two years away from the estate, appearing at home only once for a single day before again returning to the front at the Council's orders. During that brief interlude, he managed to sire a son.

For Gryllus' wife, Philomena, however, a life of attempting to manage the rambunctious boy as well as the dwindling household and farm staff, while Gryllus battled the Spartans or served in the assembly at Athens, was too much. In the end, she threw up her hands, boarded up the house, sold most of the remaining farmhands, and moved in with her husband's widowed cousin, Leda, who maintained a house in Athens while her own husband's estate in Boeotia went untended. This city house had room to spare, though with the continued shortage of able-bodied men it was falling apart. Lamp and cooking oil was hard to come by in the city, even for the comparatively wealthy. Stove wood was hoarded and counted out splinter by splinter, and clothing was patched and repatched, made to serve long past the point that, in better times, it would have been given to the beggars. Only the plainest of foods were available, the staple consisting of a pasty lentil porridge. Figs, nuts, and olives were sometimes added for taste, and occasionally the family was able to obtain a bit of mutton or pork, smuggled into the city from the old sharecroppers in Erchia. Grasshoppers abounded in the vacant lots and were a handy source of protein for us slaves and kitchen staff, since even the most gristly scraps of meat were sucked dry by the patrons rather than left for the household help. Our only comfort was that Spartan food was known to be even worse. Gryllus often said that it was not surprising that the Spartans were so willing to die on the battlefield—death had to be better than living on food like theirs.

And so in Athens we made a new life, and it was while there that I was given permanent charge of the young urchin over whom I had been at least informally responsible since we were both barely old enough to walk. Gryllus' son, who until moving to Athens had never left the confines of the rural estate or been away from the watchful eyes of his mother or myself, viewed Athens as a paradise. To me, charged with monitoring his safety, the city was something else entirely. I close my eyes and can envision, as clearly as if it were today, walking through the stifling heat and dust of the streets of Athens during those years before its fall, surrounded by the shouts and curses of mule drivers and young street toughs gazing at them in admiration for their exquisite command of the colloquial; the constant stream of vagrants, who included not only the usual lot of the deformed, blind, old and rachitic, but also foreigners fallen upon hard times who were attracted by the city's glory; thinkers who relished and even sought out such hard times as a badge of pride and a source of inspiration for their various schools of philosophy; and idle crowds of able-bodied men, soldiers on leave and sailors awaiting their proximate consignment. I see the flurry of sundry musicians, snake handlers, acrobats, heralds, pickpockets, and prostitutes of both sexes or of not quite either; the assorted legitimate street-dwellers of all kinds, construction workers and shopkeepers, money lenders, food and water peddlers, scribes, fishwives, tattoo artists, tinkers and tailors; and the hair-plucking *paratiltrioi* from the baths, resting their falsettos and drying their tweezers as they sought a bite to eat. So, too, I see a hundred other colorful personages, actors, priests, bear trainers, soldiers, pimps, and midwives, shouting their individual calls, striving to be heard above the rest, contributing to the deafening uproar that was the excitement, the filth, the ambition, and the madness of this city that was the center of the world.

In my mind's eye I pass from these chaotic streets through a humble, unmarked doorway in the side of a long stone wall, into a dark, cool passageway. Upon closing the stout oaken door I hear the roar of the city muffled into a faint and distant throb. My memory's corridor leads toward a sunlit courtyard at the end, where the dominant sounds are the tinkling of water in the tiny fountain, the soft clinking and scraping of cooking, and servants' gentle laughter from the kitchen adjacent to the main house. Most incongruous of all is the sound of birds—dozens of them, for every corner is furnished with one or more cages filled with tiny, colorful songbirds, chosen for the exquisite designs of their feathers and the sweetness of their warbling. Rising above the household patter are the high-pitched voices of two young boys as they play in the dust at the foot of the fountain with a handful of marbles fashioned out of clay.

Ever since he had moved to the house, the younger boy, Gryllus' son, had filled the courtyard with his singing, matching the caged birds note for note in beauty and tunefulness. He was never happier than when sitting in the sun at his mother's feet, chanting children's songs and Homeric verses she had taught him by drill, striving to hold to the complex rhythms and sing-song stresses of her training.

Though not much to look at—he was short in stature and thin-chested for his age—he was talented. This much everyone knew, for he had sung already at a few of the banquets hosted by his father, attended by some of Athens' most renowned citizens and artists. The boy had received the highest of praises from both statesmen and poets for the clear, bell-like quality of his voice, and for his poise. To the boy, however, the compliments of diplomats were as water to a drunkard when compared to the praise of his father, which was rarely and grudgingly bestowed, for exceptionally fine performances only. Even then it was more from gratification at having pleased his guests than from any inherent pleasure he took in the boy's singing.

The boy had a name, of course, but his mother called him by it only when reprimanding him, and his father rarely addressed him directly at all. He most often answered to his nickname, one that had most naturally developed as a result of his skill. He was called Aedon, the songbird, and the unusual nickname seemed to auger further fortune for his developing talent. Not, of course, that such talent had any long-term prospects: His family was ancient and wealthy, and the life of a singer or poet was not something to which great families aspired for their children. Nevertheless, it was diverting, it garnered him a bit more attention from his father than he might otherwise have received, and it helped keep the boy occupied in the home until his formal education was to begin.

The older boy, Aedon's second cousin and two years his senior, was Proxenus, a squarely built little ruffian with an irrepressible grin and a swagger. Just as Aedon was a born poet and singer, Proxenus was a soldier from birth, and despite their different inclinations and interests, the two were fast friends, beyond a mere blood relationship. At least daily, Proxenus would startle Aedon out of his frequent reveries in the courtyard by whacking him on the head with his makeshift wooden sword, sending him into a chase that would end with the boys racing through the house, wrestling on the hard tile floors and getting underfoot of the long-suffering elderly servants who attempted to maintain order. Proxenus being the older and stronger of the two, Aedon invariably got the worst of their battles, but he rarely gave in to the bigger boy's repeated demands to surrender. When pinned, he preferred to disarm Proxenus by grinning spastically and singing faintly obscene ditties that would soon have his older cousin collapsed in paroxysms of laughter.

But even on the few occasions that Proxenus was not present, Aedon was never alone, for he played and talked animatedly with an imaginary friend, a being who, he said, was always with him yet whom he refused to name, saying only that he was a little god. This was a source of great hilarity to the family at first, as Proxenus and the slaves would sometimes pretend to trip and fall, saying that Aedon's little god had gotten underfoot, or they would blame missing articles on the covetousness of his little god. Over time, the godlet made his way into the pantheon of the family's household deities, at first as a joke, then more as an unconscious habit. Long after the boy had grown older and ceased to openly communicate with his mysterious friend, his mother and slaves still occasionally referred to the deity's presence in passing.

During this time we rarely saw Aedon's dour, distant father. Even during his brief forays home from his diplomatic or military duties, Gryllus had little time for boys, having constantly to attend to the comings and goings of strange men, men important and self-important, who would come to talk and argue with him far into the night. Gryllus' reputation as an officer was formidable, and he had thus far acquitted himself well in the war. He had even managed to retain most of his body parts, with the exception of the loss of an eye injured by a glancing blow from a Spartan spear point, which had become infected from, he swore, a quack army surgeon's treatment of it with plaster of cow dung and vinegar. The eye had to be removed, which Gryllus insisted on doing himself with a spoon, to avoid exposing himself further to the perils of the physician's science. The eye's cavity healed sufficiently, although it occasionally leaked a watery fluid tinged with blood if Gryllus engaged in strenuous physical activity, and the wound was a source of pride and wonder for the boy.

Occasionally Gryllus would take the boys and his old battle squire Leon back to the abandoned estate at Erchia, by this time practically a ruin. Gryllus retained a deep love for the land, and although his plans to make the fields productive had to be constantly postponed because of the exigencies of the war, he was nevertheless determined that his son not be deprived of familiarity with the earth. He maintained several fine horses, cared for by Leon's lame son, and would take them on long forays and hunts in the countryside. Even when Aedon was too young to ride by himself, he would sit up on his father's mount between Gryllus's strong thighs. Gryllus was so fond of riding that when his son tired he would take him back to the house for a nap, and then depart again immediately for the remainder of the day, without the slightest rest. He once took me along for company, lending me a smaller horse that he intended to give his son when he became older. Gryllus said that if the war continued, Aedon himself would serve as an officer, and that if I were to be his battle squire, I would need to have at least the same riding and military skills as my master. "I will be proud," he would say, "when my son kills his first Spartan."

Gryllus talked ceaselessly about the war, and his hatred for the Spartans and their destruction of Athens' prosperity was unfathomably deep. He despised their crudeness and lack of culture, and their swaggering, domineering attitude toward other Greek cities, allies and enemies alike. He ridiculed their blind devotion to their pathetic little mud-hut city, and their willingness to expend unimaginable effort to impose their overbearing system of police control on the grand cities they conquered. I vividly recall the time Gryllus used the Spartans as a lesson to Aedon, Proxenus and me, when he felt us to be lacking in diligence in some task or another.

"Aedon," he snapped after roughly lining up the three of us before him, "do Spartan boys shirk their duties? Do they argue with their parents?"

"No, Father," the boy automatically replied, but his voice lacked sincerity and his eyes were merry. Gryllus looked in disgust from Aedon's face, to Proxenus', to mine and back again, and his own expression took on a hard cast.

"Proxenus, what's that in your hand?"

"Honey cake, Uncle," Proxenus mumbled, his mouth full. Proxenus had chosen an inopportune time for his snack.

"Honey cake? Open your hand." Proxenus did, and Gryllus slapped the contents roughly to the floor and ground it underfoot. Proxenus flushed crimson, and his eyes welled up with hot tears, but he remained silent.

Gryllus looked at the boys sternly, his voice low and heavy with disdain for our pitiful softness. The sinews in his neck stood out in his tension. "Spartan boys your age get one meal a day. Watery black broth, not with their families, but on the ground outside, with their classmates. Spartans believe that a well-fed soldier is a poor soldier, so as children they are starved. If their classmates are caught stealing food, the entire class is beaten—not because of the stealing, but because they were clumsy enough to be caught. If they survive the beatings, they are taught to beat their comrades in turn. Do you understand?"

We all nodded, our eyes wide.

Gryllus again searched our faces, his one eye staring intently. After a moment he raised his gaze and stared off into the middle distance. We still stood at attention in front of him, expectantly, and as he looked back down at us he sighed. Then his face resumed its hard expression.

"They tell of a Spartan boy who once stole a fox cub," Gryllus said, "for to the Spartans even a fox is food. He was seen running away, and the owner caught him. Before the boy was seized, however, he had just enough time to stuff the cub into the front of his tunic. When the cub's owner demanded to know where the beast was, the boy denied any knowledge. That is what he was trained to do. The interrogation went on for some time, until the boy suddenly fell down dead where he had been standing. When his body was examined, it was found that the hungry fox had chewed his way directly into the boy's intestines, but the lad, in his mindless Spartan way, had remained quiet at the cost of his life."

Proxenus stood his ground, but Aedon's lower lip began trembling. As Gryllus coolly watched, he blanched, and suddenly whirling, ran out of the room. We could hear the sounds of his retching as he made his way outside. Proxenus and I stood silently watching Gryllus, who stared back at us impassively for a moment, then calmly strolled out, leaving us alone. For nights afterwards, I was wakened in the darkness by a trembling Aedon as he crawled into bed with me, terrified at nightmares of Herculean Spartans overpowering his house. Proxenus, however, remained in his own bed, tossing and turning, gamely taking on the attackers single-handedly.

II

AEDON RACED THROUGH the crowded streets, dodging porters and carts as he ran, merrily snatching samples of fruit and sweets from the baskets carried by the women and girls on their way to their market stalls. Racing up the hill of the Acropolis and through the Propylaean Gates, he stopped, panting and perspiring, at the newly completed Parthenon to inspect the progress being made on construction of the garishly painted marble temples in the vicinity. He came here almost every day, to converse with the stonemasons and builders, who knew him by name, and to ask endless questions of the chief architect, Callicrates, who only half jokingly would sometimes ask him to check a calculation or two.

After Aedon had closely scrutinized the footings for the new pillars to be erected in the Temple to Nike, I reminded him that it would soon be time for his afternoon lessons, which I attended with him at home. He nodded grudgingly and offered to race me back to our house. I declined, as always, but he ignored my refusal and sped off down the hill.

He was in his twelfth year of life, on the verge of manhood, and his vast ability was beginning to become apparent. Aedon was not only musical, but quick of wit besides—though of boys like this there were plenty, for Athens cultivated them like herbs in a kitchen garden. Even in the city's hothouse intellectual environment, however, he was a prodigy, a privileged child who could calculate sums in his head long before meeting his tutor and being whipped by him for the first time, whose speaking and reading skills surpassed those of boys much older. He could recite lengthy passages of Homer, Hesiod and Stesichorus from beginning to end, or from any point at which he was asked to start. He could identify the authors of every book and play for the past four hundred years, or cheerfully improvise a dozen lines of dactylic hexameter on any suggested theme. He could discuss Pythagoras' technique for measuring the hypotenuse and his ratio of musical consonances, interpret Hippocrates' theorem on the quadrature of lunes, and debate the obscurities of the basic identity of individuation, $X = T$. He admired Pindar, though he had to hide those scrolls from his father, who did not approve of Boeotian authors. And simply by wandering through Athens the boy found himself surrounded by matchless models on every side. Painting and sculpture had already scaled a height which no subsequent artist could ever surpass. The names of Zeuxis, Polycleitus and Praxiteles were on everyone's lips. Architecture was a matter of pride and beauty, and well-known architects collected as many fervent admirers and hangers-on as did famous actors. Mathematics was taught everywhere, and lessons in grammar and rhetoric had been freely given and studied in the city's *agorai* and plazas for a hundred years by itinerant scholars.

Just prior to this time, Aunt Leda had decided to return to Boeotia, to salvage what she could of her husband's estate from the grasp of greedy relatives. Proxenus had returned with her. Aedon was crushed at his cousin's departure, and all the more dependent upon me for companionship. Gryllus decided that the means of filling the hole in Aedon's heart was to keep him physically and intellectually active the entire day. With Gryllus absent in Athens' service and the boy's mother busy with household affairs, this task had been charged to me, and to the series of tutors that Gryllus had carefully selected and hired. Despite their strictness and my best efforts, however, when Proxenus left Aedon began exhibiting an uncharacteristic wild streak, intent upon demonstrating his independence. He was impatient with my efforts to rein him in, and my defense of Gryllus' strictures and demands left him angry and exasperated. His tutors and I gamely tried to fill his day with constructive activities, but at the least hint of drudgery or boredom he would sweep his scrolls and tablets aside and stride out of the house with scarcely a moment's preparation. On this particular day, as he sprinted and dodged his way through the crowded city, I, his irritated *paidagogos,* twice his size and half his speed, barely managed to keep up.

Racing through a narrow, jointed alley at breakneck speed, I stumbled over some loose cobbles and became separated from him. He continued on out of sight, much to my terror. This had happened once before, three years earlier, and the story is worth a brief digression. I had lost sight of him during a festival, when the streets were teeming with performers, vendors, and spectators. Gryllus was departing with the fleet the next day, and had brought Aedon to the festival with him that evening to take in the excitement. It was a rare treat for the youngster to accompany his father in public, but Gryllus had taken the precaution of bringing me with them, sternly charging me to watch the boy so that Gryllus could be free to greet his peers without hindrance. Aedon walked proudly by his father's side, politely responding to the queries and compliments of Gryllus' colleagues. Somehow, though, the careless boy slipped my watch, and we became separated in the throng.

Gryllus was deeply engrossed in a discussion with some politicians about the war's progress, and it was I who first noticed that the boy was missing. Gryllus saw me standing on tiptoes to peer over the crowds, and immediately realized what had happened. Scarcely breaking the rhythm of his conversation or the jovial smile on his face, he squeezed my upper arm so hard it made me wince, and bent down to my ear.

"If the boy is not back at my side in five minutes," he hissed, "you will be sold." Just that. Four words that even now, decades later, make my throat constrict in fear. I had five minutes or my life would be over, scarcely before it had begun. Gryllus had that power over me, and he stood back up and smilingly resumed his conversation with his oblivious colleagues.

Aedon had not meant to become separated, and when he realized what had happened, he panicked. Standing in the street crying, he was almost knocked down by an enormous, half-drunk, somewhat simian-looking actor, a street performer really, in full regalia: embroidered robe with bared chest, tragic mask, braided hair. Aedon was an extraordinarily handsome young boy—smooth olive skin, enormous round eyes so dark they were almost black, even white teeth—and he would not long go unnoticed wandering alone in the city. It was fortunate that the actor was not, like many in his profession, seeking a catamite, but was, rather, an honest soul. He no sooner saw the youngster than he squatted down and asked him his name. When he discovered through the boy's tearful sobs that he was Aedon, whose musical reputation was well known in dramatic circles, the man swaggeringly introduced himself as "Otus, renowned interpreter of the greatest Athenian playwrights," and swept him up joyfully onto his shoulders. Otus then pushed and careened through the jostling crowd, bellowing, "Gryllus! Lord Gryllus! I have a package for you."

Gryllus' colleagues heard the commotion first, and peering through the crowd one of them asked dryly, "Gryllus, isn't that your boy riding that ape's shoulders?" Gryllus looked up in dismay at his son's noisy arrival, accompanied by the tittering of the surrounding onlookers. The tear tracks still shone on Aedon's dusty cheeks as he smiled down at us in relief, his eyes glistening. Gryllus' expression, however, remained as stony as I had ever seen it. He gingerly reclaimed his offspring from Otus and tossed a piece of silver to the hirsute, malodorous giant, who ostentatiously waved it in the air like a victor's spear, bellowing out his thanks. Gryllus graciously took his leave from his peers and walked us straight home, nodding and smiling at passersby, but keeping a death grip on the backs of our necks. "Aedon!" I hissed. "Your father told me to watch out for you. Now look what you've done!"—but neither of us was able to pursue the argument further because Gryllus tightened his grasp on our necks. I received a sound thrashing from him that night, though the punishment was mild compared to Aedon's. To him, Gryllus offered not a word. Not a touch, not a gesture. Only a brief glance of disdain and disappointment, and in the morning he was gone, back to the war. Though it was my buttocks that burned, it was Aedon who cried himself to sleep for many nights afterward, despite my many attempts to convince him of his father's true concern for him.

But to return to the alley where I had tripped: My later questioning of Aedon told me precisely what happened after he had sped on ahead of me. When rounding a corner, he was suddenly brought up short by a cane held horizontally across his path. He tried merrily to dive under it, but the cane's owner deftly parried his move, and gave him a swat across the chest for good measure. Aedon tried to squirm around the tip of the cane, but the owner merely projected it further, impaling its tip in a crack in the crumbling mortar of the narrow alley's opposite wall. Having trapped the boy's forward progress, the cane was then used like a shepherd's rod to nudge him from side to side until his back was against the wall with the cane pressing him from the side against his belly. At his size and age Aedon could have easily pushed the tip away from his body and broken free, but suddenly, with a deft movement, the canesman slipped the rod behind his knees in such a way—I still wonder at the speed—that with a slight upward jerk of his wrist both the boys' legs slipped out from under him and he landed with a grunt, flat on his buttocks. Aedon looked with astonishment at the cane as it disentangled itself from his legs, and slowly followed its length up to the junction with its owner, who possessed a knotted, gnarled old hand like that of an ancient soothsayer. This in turn was attached to a burly wrist and a hairy, scarred arm—an arm that, in its day, must have seen a good deal of fighting, though with a sword rather than a thin wooden stick, and against Spartans and Thebans rather than cocksure young boys.

Aedon's eyes continued to travel up the cane-wielder's arm until he came to a most remarkable visage, that of a man he had often seen in the agora, talking to groups of young men. The face was the exact image of Marsyas the satyr, whose bronze image on the Acropolis I had often laughed at and pointed out to Aedon. The man's eyes were bulbous and protruding, his nose broken like that of a boxer, and his thick lips split his deeply creased face across the middle like one of those overripe Ephesian plums you sometimes find in the marketplace on festival days. His cranium was completely smooth and bald on top, with greasy wisps of white hair hanging down the sides and back in long strings. His tattered, ill-fitting tunic, the stains of which clearly showed the contents of his breakfast that morning and for the past several days, did little to hide the enormous belly that protruded over two spindly legs which were completely hairless, like those of some enormous, ungainly bird.

Like the old soldier that he was, the man paused to critically survey his catch, and his eyes, for all the homely aspect of the rest of him, twinkled merrily as he spoke. "Begging your pardon, lad," he chuckled, as if apologizing for having accidentally trapped Aedon in a narrow alley and tripped him flat onto his back with a wooden rod. "But I was wondering if you could tell me where I might purchase some turnips?"

The boy stared, astonished at this odd question. He considered the man's query carefully, looked around to see if there was any immediate escape, and resigning himself to the fact that there was none, he piped up in his sing-song voice, "Yes, sir. The first stalls as you enter the market from the south end sell all manner of fruits and vegetables. Surely you will find turnips there."

The man grunted in assent, but remained standing where he was, the cane hovering menacingly over the boy's head as he assimilated this response, slowly and somewhat densely. It was at this point that I came running up, panting and sweating, and stopped in astonishment at the sight of this fat, odd-looking gentleman standing over my ward. He looked deeply into my face, and I averted his gaze with a scowl, but then saw the man's eyes again turn to Aedon, who held his stare unblinkingly. A trace of a smile was beginning to form on the boy's lips.

"And where," the man continued, "might I find some of that good Attic peasant bread, the flat round kind, still warm from the hearth?"

This response was easy, for Aedon had just swiped some of the very same bread that morning, a crust of which, I saw, was still tucked into his belt for an afternoon snack. It was no doubt the view of this crust that had prompted the old man's query.

"Why, on the street of the bakers, of course," he replied. "Not all the shops sell the Attic flat bread you want, but the third shop on the left most certainly does, and you can be sure of its quality." He grinned, and this time the man openly returned it, ignoring me completely, and gazing in frank, almost fatherly admiration at Aedon for his quick and articulate reply. I saw passersby out of the corner of my eye, squeezing between the wall and the old man, glancing at us briefly and then smiling as they continued on their way, shaking their heads, in what? Exasperation? Pity? For the old satyr or for us? The man lowered his cane to its normal position, standing it upright next to him, and Aedon scrambled to his feet, though not without some degree of caution lest he again end up flat in the dust. I seized his forearm and spoke to him harshly.

"Aedon, let's go! Your father expects us to be at our lessons now . . ." and I began tugging him back out of the alley in the direction whence we had come. He started to turn, but at the mention of his father he impatiently shook off my hand and stood looking at the old man, his face open and full of expectation.

"One more question for you, youngster, if you have the time to spare," said the strange man. Aedon was already planning his response, prepared to show off his gift of speech as he so often did for his father's friends when they tossed him easy questions that he knew he could answer. "Where might men go to become good and honorable?"

Aedon's face clouded in confusion and then in disappointment, as he found himself at a complete loss for words.

"You don't know?" said the man. "Pity, a smart lad like you. Come with me, and I will show you."

That afternoon, the old tutor sat fuming in Gryllus' house, waiting in the gathering darkness for a student who did not arrive. Aedon and I had trudged to the agora with the strange old man, and spent the rest of the day there with him and his followers. The boy's education as a disciple of Socrates had begun.

III

ANTINOUS WAS A hulking youth, shoulders as broad as a temple column and as solid. Legs like tree trunks supported a thick torso quite unlike the artistic ideal, but the effect was not uncomely: His abdomen was the same circumference as his chest, lending him a stolid, almost sinister aspect considerably more unnerving than that of the sculptor's favored triangle-shaped taper. Though he was by no means tall, his girth seemed to lend him height beyond his actual endowment. This was complemented by a head and face in keeping and proportion with the rest of his build: a heavily ridged brow and jutting jaw, though not to exaggerated effect; and a nose of a surprising length and evenness, surprising, I say, because of his profession, which more often yielded a proboscis laying crazily to the bias, or one with odd bumps of cartilage skewing its balance.

The twenty-two-year-old athlete's expertise was pancration, the all-in, no-holds-barred wrestling that combined kicking, boxing, and strangling. The sport was fanatically popular in Athens, though of an incredible brutality—favorite maneuvers included breaking the fingers, kneeing the groin, or twisting a knee out of its socket. There was a whole series of moves devoted to strategic thumb insertions. Biting and eye-gouging were forbidden, but this rule was only sporadically enforced. Antinous' skill at the sport was such as to have once earned him a temporary exemption from military training, during which he had worked with the city's most renowned athletic trainers in a bid to win the laurel crown in this event at the Olympic games. Unfortunately, he had been disabled only days before the event when a clumsy servant girl spilled a pan of sizzling oil on the back of his right shoulder, disabling him for months and leaving a profoundly ugly, puckered pink scar, as broad as a man's hand. Despite a daily application of salves and poultices, the skin had never healed properly; the scar tissue had thickened and periodically cracked, like a horny callus on a foot, seemingly stretched too tight for the area it covered. Its extreme sensitivity precluded him from ever again becoming a champion wrestler, and this blow to his aspirations hastened his return to common barracks life—but not before catching the expert eye of Gryllus.

If Aedon was the son that Gryllus was surprised to have begotten, Antinous was the one he felt he deserved, and shortly after the wrestler's return, Gryllus, a former pancration athlete himself, hired him at a stupendous fee to visit the house thrice weekly to supplement Aedon's regular gymnasium training. A makeshift sandpit was constructed in a little-used back courtyard separated from the rear alley by a crumbling stone wall, and this became Aedon's small circle of torture whenever Antinous visited. Stark naked, they practiced, wearing only stout leather thongs wrapped around their fists to protect the thin skin of the knuckles, the boy's pale, hairless body contrasting harshly with Antinous' scarred, heavily muscled torso.

At first the athlete's training methods stunned Aedon—the conditioning exercises alone were enough to crush any mortal. Antinous stretched the boy's tendons and muscles to a point that left him gasping in pain, to just short of actually tearing the tissue, his vision blurring as he struggled to keep from fainting; Aedon felt as if his skin were being ripped like poorly woven cloth. Weight training left his triceps and pectorals quivering spasmodically, as Antinous taunted and cursed him.

"One more, you sniveling ass-wipe! My nine-year-old sister could press more than that. Push!"

Aedon would collapse on his belly during push-ups, the dust from the pit mixing with his spittle to form a dirty ring around his anguished mouth. Antinous would stand straddling him, lifting him from above by the chest, forcing him to do yet more push-ups with only three-quarters of his body weight, then with one-half as Aedon's arms weakened further until finally, at the point of complete muscular failure, the boy dropped flat again. Three minutes' rest, then another set of the same, and another, until he was unable even to rise, but lay panting and drenched with sweat, glaring at his trainer with hate-filled eyes while Antinous leaned against the wall, absent-mindedly scratching his bearish chest.

I performed the exercises with him, both in a show of solidarity and to strengthen my own limbs, but Antinous ignored me, a mere slave, and Aedon did too—this was a battle he preferred to endure alone. At night, after Antinous had left and Aedon had recovered somewhat through my careful massage of his tortured muscles, he would rail at his father's cruelty, to my calm protests as to Gryllus' genuinely good intentions. Aedon swore he would stay in the house not a day longer, that he would run away as soon as he was able to stand again—but the next day, as his burning muscles began to heal, he relaxed his determination to defy his father and simply set his face grimly to survive the next session.

Several months of such efforts left little visible effect on his body—he was still the slight, somewhat pretty youth he always had been—but considerably improved his tolerance for pain. When Antinous was convinced that the conditioning was beginning to have the desired effect, he advanced to the next stage: actual training in pancration.

For this he brought a helper, his younger brother, two years older than Aedon. This boy was much thinner than Antinous, and though strong and rangy, he lacked his sibling's rugged handsomeness. More simian in appearance, already showing a coating of dark body hair and a coarseness about the jaw line, he had long, swinging arms that draped almost to his knees when relaxed. The boy's brain was addled—his eyes stared dully, he spoke only with great effort, and he was forever sporting a foolish grin, despite the quantities of loathsome epithets his brother would rain down on him for his slowness and stupidity. Antinous refused even to call the lad by name, as if he considered him too stupid and animal-like to deserve one—he referred to him simply as Boy, seemingly unwilling even to acknowledge the blood relationship. At heart, Boy was a peaceful enough sort, believing his sole mission in life was to please Antinous, whom he followed like a puppy. He had little talent in the more refined techniques of the martial art; still, he was fast and strong and had assimilated enough to be dangerous, and he was useful for humbling beginners. As Boy pummeled Aedon unmercifully, Antinous watched with a critical eye, flogging them indiscriminately with his "donkey-beater," the stout rod used by referees to separate clinching opponents.

On one of Gryllus' short leaves from his duties, he asked to view a session to gauge his son's progress. He instructed Antinous to do nothing special, but to conduct the training in the usual fashion, while Gryllus sat quietly on a stool in the corner of the courtyard. Aedon glanced once at his father, then glowered and pawed the sand, bracing himself for the signal to begin sparring.

At the clap, Aedon stepped gingerly toward his opponent, and after two swift feints dove quickly in at Boy's knees in a two-legged take-down. The bigger boy sprawled, throwing his feet out behind him to deny Aedon a grip on his thighs, then leaned the weight of his torso on Aedon's shoulders, flattening him on his face into the sand. Antinous flogged Boy on the back to stop the match and disgustedly motioned for them to get up. Gryllus watched impassively.

Antinous again gave the signal to start the match. Aedon circled warily around Boy before again dropping swiftly to one knee and diving beneath his swinging arms for a one-legged take-down, hoping to trip Boy onto his back. Before he had even touched the other's leg, however, Boy brought his knee up sharply into Aedon's face, nailing him squarely on the jaw with a sharp crack and dropping him heavily like a sack of barley thrown by a stevedore. He lay motionless and I glanced over at Gryllus, who did not rise, but whose eyes narrowed as he watched his son closely. Antinous sauntered over and roughly jerked Aedon to his feet.

"You'll live," he said harshly, after briefly examining Aedon's eyes and swelling lip where he had bit himself. It was the most tenderness I had ever seen Antinous express.

Again and again Aedon dove for take-downs, and Gryllus watched as his son's face was driven into the dirt, or he was thrown onto his back, or suffered Boy's knee driven sharply into his kidney. Each time he lay senseless for a moment before again staggering gamely to his feet, his face bloodied and his eyes swollen almost shut. After shaking his head to clear his gaze, he would stare pointedly at his father, as if trying to memorize every detail of his face, before returning to his corner of the ring and glaring fiercely at Boy. Antinous began to worry that this was not the display of skills he had been hoping to show Gryllus, but rather a show of dumb, brute determination more indicative of pure stubbornness and stupidity than of any better quality.

"Lesson's over," Antinous grunted several times, hoping to see Aedon's usual slump of relief. Each time, however, the boy shook his head silently and resolutely returned to his corner for yet another round. Antinous stared at him in exasperation. "Keep your head up then," he would say, or, "You've got to get your hooks in before he throws you. I'll bust your nose myself if you don't start using your fucking brains out there."

Gryllus shifted restlessly on his seat as his son's face swelled beyond recognition. Boy grinned stupidly after each of Aedon's ill-fated forays against him. Antinous, however, had had enough. It would not do to have a student killed in front of his own father. I saw the trainer catch Boy's eye and nod to him slowly, in a signal with which both were familiar.

Aedon wavered unsteadily on his feet, but still moved gamely into the center of the ring and made a fierce lunge. Boy stepped aside deftly and kicked out sideways, and Aedon, his feet tripped out from beneath him and his hands grasping only air, crumpled into the dirt with a grunt and a dazed, confused expression in his eye.

Boy quickly made his move. Pressing his sweaty chest against Aedon's back in the ladder-grip, his legs wrapped around his opponent's stomach and his bicep around his neck, with his free hand he pressed Aedon's head forward, cutting off the air supply. Aedon's eyes bulged even through their swelling, and his tongue emerged from his split lips as his legs twitched helplessly. He flailed his arms wildly above and behind him, seeking to hook anything—hair, nostrils—in a desperate bid to remove Boy's arm from his throat. In his struggle, he somehow managed to seize Boy's earlobe with his fingernails, ripping it from its tenuous attachment to the side of his head. Howling in pain, Boy dropped him and backed away, his mouth working soundlessly in bewilderment, then his eyes narrowing in fury.

Aedon scrambled to his feet as well, suddenly energized by this unexpected success, and carefully circled Boy as the other eyed him ruefully and rubbed his bloodied ear. The two opponents locked eyes, Aedon's muscles quivering in fatigue and tension. Gryllus, I saw, had straightened up and was now watching the match intently, as the two boys froze momentarily, testing each other's reflexes, each daring the other to strike.

This time it was Boy who launched first, and in a swift, catlike maneuver he dropped to one knee, seized Aedon about the legs before he could sprawl out of reach, and lifted him high into the air. Aedon, however, having identified his opponent's weakness, began repeatedly clubbing his injured ear with his fist. The mauling staggered Boy, who dropped Aedon in a rage, his ear turning a lusty purple and swelling into a shapeless mass before our eyes. Before Aedon could rise to his feet, Boy took two quick steps forward and landed him a terrific kick in the ribs, sending him sprawling onto his belly at the edge of the ring, gasping for breath. Boy eyed him warily to be sure he wasn't feigning exhaustion, then straddled Aedon's back, a crazed expression flitting across his face, masking the pain that had been evident since the ripping of his ear a moment before.

Seizing Aedon once more with his arm across the neck, Boy dug the knuckles of his free hand into the side of his throat, against the carotid artery on the side of the trachea, in the choke that stops the flow of blood to the brain and can kill a man in seconds. Aedon's eyes glazed immediately as the sleep of death began creeping over him, and when he went limp, Boy released the pressure of his knuckles; but when Aedon regained his senses, Boy applied the pressure a second time. Gryllus leaped up in alarm and bounded over to his son, arriving just ahead of Antinous. Grasping Boy by the hair he pulled him roughly to his feet, allowing Aedon to drop to his belly in the sand, his eyes open but bereft of understanding. I carried him to his room, where I revived him with cut wine and a massage to the chest to increase the flow of blood to his head. Gryllus accompanied Antinous and his loutish brother to the door and summarily dismissed them, telling them in no uncertain terms that to return to his household would be their death.

That night, in an awkward gesture of reconciliation, Gryllus came into Aedon's room bearing a bundle wrapped in a greasy piece of fabric. "You'll never be a pancratist," he admitted grudgingly, "so you may as well at least arm yourself well."

He unwrapped the parcel to display a gleaming Spartan short sword, a *xiphos*, only slightly longer than a dagger but constructed of a tremendous heaviness, lending it a strength fit for years of battle. The weapon was not beautifully crafted—it was, in fact, rather crude in its finish—but it was well balanced and had a pleasing heft. The otherwise smooth, plain grip bore a primitively carved Greek letter κ. Aedon stared sullenly at the blade, his face reflecting the confusion he felt at this unexpected gift from his father. Gryllus remained silent for a moment as his son turned it over in his hands.

"It was given to me years ago, when I was a young officer accompanying an Athenian delegation to Sparta. All the Athenians and Spartans exchanged weapons as a gesture of good faith, and my counterpart gave me this piece."

Gryllus paused for a moment as his mind went back to the days before Aedon was born.

"I ran into that son of a whore many times over the years," he mused, "both on the battlefield and off. I learned the hard way that I couldn't trust him any farther than I could throw him in the pancration ring. That man's betrayals and broken agreements put ten years' worth of gray hairs on my head. Perhaps someday you'll be able to return the favor to a Spartan, by planting this sword in his gut. It's yours now; may you use it to good profit. I can't bear the sight of it."

After Gryllus left, Aedon and I lay in our cots, sleepless.

"Thank the gods your father stopped the match when he did," I commented. "Boy might have killed you."

Aedon stiffened and raised himself up on his elbow, ignoring the pain that screwed his face into a wince. "Thank the gods, my ass!" he spat. "It was Father who insisted I learn pancration in the first place! Do you think he was ignorant of Antinous' grinding on me day after day? I'm sick of you always apologizing for my father, Theo, justifying his actions. You are a slave! What loyalty do you bear him?"

Shocked at this outburst, I said nothing for a long while, until I sensed his breath had returned to a more even rhythm, that he had cooled down.

"Aedon, you are your father's son, and he loves you as a father should. He simply is not a man to openly express such sentiments. Tenderness, to you or to anyone, is not an art that Gryllus values highly."

"If he valued it any less highly I would be dead."

Aedon again fell silent and I hoped that the matter was ended, but he was still restless, tossing and kicking at his blankets, his mind troubling him so much that it kept him from sleeping, even in his exhausted state.

"What in the name of the gods possessed you to continue fighting today?" I asked him, attempting to lift him out of his doldrums. "You looked like you wanted to kill Boy."

Aedon drew a deep breath, and paused for so long that I thought perhaps he had finally dropped off to sleep. When I peered at him, however, he was glaring fiercely at the ceiling, and even in the room's dim light I could see that his face was contorted in silent rage.

"You wouldn't understand, Theo," he finally mumbled dismissively.

"Understand? What's there to understand?"

Another long silence.

"Look, I just imagined Boy was someone else. It helped to focus my concentration."

I pondered this warily, but my curiosity finally overcame my caution. "Whom did you imagine you were attacking?" As soon as the question left my lips, however, I regretted it, for I knew the answer as well as Aedon.

He glanced at me with a look of disdain for my denseness, then turned his face to the wall.

"Better I'd been born a bastard," he grunted thickly through his split lips.

IV

ON AN OTHERWISE silent evening two years later, when Aedon was fourteen, he was awakened by a sound he knew was not proper to the house. As his personal servant, I was the only domestic allowed to spend the night in that wing of the house, and I had been snoring at the foot of his bed. Gryllus had left on a diplomatic mission several weeks before, resignedly charging his son with care of the household, and Aedon, hoping to please his father, felt this responsibility keenly. The sound had awakened him before me, and peering through the slats of the window he spied an intruder in the moonlit courtyard, naked but for a loincloth. He was smeared with a dark, greasy substance, and scaling the wall to the dining room he left a faint smudge behind, a dark blotch on the white plaster. Aedon snatched the short sword Gryllus had given him, and slipped silently out the room, determined not only to preserve his family's honor and wealth, but to live up to the trust his father had placed in him. Stealing silently into the dining room, he glimpsed the felon's fleeting silhouette just disappearing into the other wing of the compound, and he recalled even in the tension of the moment wondering how the fellow could be so familiar with the house.

Feeling his way in darkness through the other door to head off the thief, he rounded the corner and collided with his adversary, who with his blackened, greasy skin and faintly gleaming eyes appeared like a creature from hell. They both yelped, but Aedon reacted first, seizing the other and muscling him to the floor, then rolling with him back into the dining room.

During the struggle the slippery intruder escaped his grasp and drew a knife from his belt, which Aedon could see faintly glinting, subtle and lethal, in the near-pitch darkness. He could sense, perhaps from the other's irregular panting and jerky motions, that the fear was rising within. Aedon made a conscious effort to slow his own breathing, to keep his own terror submerged and to think, think hard, of what his father would have wanted him to do. Circling the thief slowly and silently, his eyes straining to see the other's movements in the blackness, Aedon suddenly threw himself at his target with his dagger raised high. He miscalculated the position of a stool on the floor, however, for as he swiped at his enemy's neck, he stumbled, his shoulder smashing heavily into his adversary, and he felt a blinding pain in the ribs. Struggling to regain his balance, he slipped on some residual grease that had rubbed onto the floor, cracked his head against the stone wall, and lost consciousness.

I arrived just as Aedon fell, and was at first puzzled to hear nothing but the frantic twittering of the birds—hadn't I heard a heavy commotion in the room just seconds before? Feeling my way through the room, however, I tripped over a soft object, someone lying on the floor, and landed heavily on another. I felt the warm stickiness on my palms and bare knees, and realizing what it was an instant later, I raced out in horror, bursting into the cook's room and seizing the small oil lamp the cowering old lady had left burning for comfort. Leaving her shrieking in darkness, I tore back into the dining room, where the dimly lit scene left me aghast.

With excruciating pain and difficulty, Aedon had pulled himself into a half-sitting position against the wall, and was watching in silence as the bright blood frothed and bubbled from his side, hissing slightly as it mixed with air escaping from his pierced lung. The furniture in the room was upended, and the greasy black culprit lay prone on the floor, his neck half severed by Aedon's single, lucky dagger thrust. His blood pulsed thickly from the artery in ever-weakening spurts, like that of a ram being bled for the ritual sacrifice, conjoining with the sticky pond forming beneath Aedon. As often happens in my moments of stress or shock, the wordless Syracusan chanting of my early memory rose from the dark recesses of my mind where it lurks like a bat in a cave, pushing itself to the fore of my concentration, and it was only with great effort that I was able to force it back and focus on the task at hand. Aedon's mother burst into the room and began wailing in terror, and the elderly cook, her wits now about her, attempted fruitlessly to extract the thief's blade stuck in Aedon's rib, and splashed water on his face from a small bowl to keep him from passing out again. The caged birds had stopped their raucous chirping and now solemnly watched the proceedings, not without, it seemed, a certain clinical interest. Not a sound came from Aedon, apart from his labored breathing. He closed his eyes, and through his pain managed a half smile.

Because of Gryllus' position, though not without some misgivings, the family was able to secure the services of the city's most respected physicians. They soon had the blade removed from his ribs and prescribed a regime of poultices consisting of a concoction of ashes, spurge, and sour wine. For days afterward he was given to drink a beverage of bitter herbs that made him lightheaded and sleepy. I sent his father a hurried message by military courier, fearing that Aedon might die any day, and Gryllus returned home within two weeks, riding confiscated horses and navy vessels the entire way to speed his journey. Still wearing the dusty and sweat-begrimed clothes in which he had been dressed for the past week, he strode into the house without ceremony, pausing briefly to compose himself and to straighten his shoulders. With tears in his eyes, he entered the room where his son was recovering.

"Son, you truly are a man," he said, clasping Aedon's forearm in both his hands. "You have acted to the glory of the gods and our ancestors. Athens will be proud to see you serve her one day, as will I."

Aedon's face was expressionless, even wary, at this rare sign of his father's approval, but his eyes sparkled in a way I had not seen since he was a young boy. Gryllus was quick to allow the news of his son's bravery to be spread among his colleagues, and within days Aedon was swamped with offers for the services of the most renowned athletic trainers. His friends treated him as a god, or at least as a war hero, though he himself refused to discuss the affair, and shrank from all mention of it except by his father.

Why such reticence to accept glory? During those months lying in bed recovering from his wound, and particularly after Gryllus returned to his duties a few days later, Aedon had all too much time to reflect on the fact that the intruder he had killed was not, in fact, a vicious murderer. The thief, as it happened, was Boy, who in a moment of greater stupidity than usual, or at Antinous' urging, had sought to take advantage of his knowledge of the house to expropriate a few trifles for his own use, and who had died still wearing his habitual foolish grin. Though Aedon bore no love for his wrestling opponent, still the lad was an acquaintance of sorts, one whose skin and hair he had gripped with his own hands, and a messy death had never been a consideration. Aedon had at first been in despair at this revelation. His only recourse was to harden his heart, telling himself that the simpleton had received fair sanction, convincing himself of the wisdom of placing glory and his family's safety over mere sentiment.

I, too, had occasion during those months to reflect deeply on the event, and came to the conclusion that not one boy, but two had died by the knife that night; for in fact, young Aedon had not been revived by the splashing of cold water on his face after the stabbing. His cheerful soprano was never heard again in the courtyard after dinner, nor was his joking and flirting with the slave girls as they went about their tasks. His childhood toys and books were put safely away in a box. For in killing Boy, my master had also killed something in himself, something precious and innocent, a boy who in some ways was more orphan than myself. That boy was the only person my master ever killed who did not truly deserve to die, and for whose life of art and music he never ceased to despair in his moments of regret. Even his name was discarded by everyone, seemingly unanimously and simultaneously, as if a blood oath had been sworn, as if the deceased were not to be mentioned.

Aedon was dead, and Xenophon was born.

V

THE FIRE BURNED hot and bright, enough to make those closest to it wince when they faced it directly. A hundred pairs of young eyes gleamed from the darkness around it, some still blinking from the sleep from which they had just been roughly roused. Around us the light of the flames reflected blood red on the roughly cut stone walls against which we had been lined up, in a small amphitheater on the edge of camp that was used for harangues or weapons demonstrations. The flickering shadows cast by the squadron of newly inducted *ephebes* against the wall were strangely distorted—a black row of round heads and narrow, squared shoulders. They resembled nothing so much as a line of pegs on which to hang clothing, or a row of pins in a children's game, oddly swaying or jerking now and then as one looked to the side to gaze questioningly at his neighbor.

We stood in silence. The day before, Xenophon, as a boy of eighteen who was now of age to serve in the military, and I as his designated battle squire, had marched under Gryllus' stern, proud gaze to the barracks built hard by the city walls. Now we had been awakened in the middle of the night. Xenophon and the other ephebes had been made to put on their newly issued *chlamydes,* the knee-length black cloaks that signified their status. We had been led here in silence by a burly instructor, his own face obscured in a full-faced hoplite battle helmet, his bushy beard emerging from beneath the cheek plates like some nocturnal mammal peering from its burrow. Only his eyes, gleaming from deep within the blackness of the visor, distinguished him from a shade risen from the underworld. For perhaps an hour we stood motionless and silent before the fire, watching as it burned down to glowing red coals. Our faces around it slowly faded into darkness until the only being wholly visible to us was the hoplite, who stood frozen in an erect, spread-footed guard stance, his eight-foot spear placed butt-end to the flagstones and held straight out in a ready position. Since arriving here, the man had not moved a single, hard muscle, and after the first few minutes before the fire, all our own rustling and movement had ceased as well. We trained our eyes expectantly and wonderingly at him, his armor glittering strangely in the firelight as if it were the living skin of some enormous reptile.

Without warning, we were startled by a sudden blast of a *salpinx,* a war trumpet, directly behind us, and twelve more hoplites in full panoply, each bearing a flaming, spitting torch, marched in precision to line up before us at the glowing fire. They, too, stood motionless for a moment, as if surveying us, and we them. Then, as if on queue, they turned to the side, stepping away and stationing themselves at equal distances against the perimeter walls, surrounding us and bathing our faces in the lights of their sputtering torches. We eyed them nervously and unconsciously shuffled closer to each other in the middle, herdlike. Again we waited, in utter silence but for the low sizzling of the flames surrounding us. The ceremony, if that indeed is what it could be called, was one of tension and suppression, of silence and waiting. Despite the open sky over our heads, I felt smothered and claustrophobic. Finally, one of the bronze-clad hoplites, taller and broader than the others and apparently their leader, stepped forward. His bearing and the tone of his voice indicated that he was a seasoned warrior.

"Ephebes!" he bellowed in a gravelly voice, so loudly I could almost feel his hot breath, though I myself stood several rows back. "You have been called to commence your training as defenders of the *polis*. You are about to embark on a sacred mission which, after the requisite period of time, will have hardened you into hoplites worthy of the name, and of the black cloaks you now bear." I could almost feel the wave of excitement and anticipation as it rolled through the mass of boys now warily inching closer to the speaker.

"Over the next two years you will train until your muscles ache and your body screams for rest. You will learn to march in phalanx, shoulder to shoulder with your comrades, straight into the teeth of the enemy, though fear gnaws at your gut and urges you to sidle into the shadow of your brother's shield. You will learn to stand firm, javelin in hand, though threatened by enemy spears and assaulted by Spartan curses, because you have taken a sacred oath to abide by the hoplite ethic, to not abandon the man standing next to you in the battle lines. This you will swear on your life!"

The boys rustled and murmured in anticipation at the glory that awaited them.

"But you are not yet worthy to call yourself hoplites! Before you can be trusted to fight alongside a man whose life depends upon your skills, you must prove yourself alone. As ephebes, you will be stationed to defend the outermost frontiers of the polis. You will skulk in the night and prowl through the woods at the very edge of civilization, to engage lone thieves and solitary attackers before you are allowed to fight in open combat on the broad plains with the phalanx. You have a sacred duty to learn to protect yourself and your comrades from the enemy! Does that mean being the strongest?"

We stared at him in eager silence.

"I said, does that mean being the *strongest,* you piss-ants!?"

"Yes!" we called, though with some hesitation. The instructor stood in the shadows, seeming to glare at us with disgust, until he pointed to one of the larger ephebes standing in the front row. I had unconsciously flexed my knees in an attempt to make myself appear shorter in case he should look in my direction. The chosen boy walked uncertainly into the firelight.

The instructor nodded to the smallest of the several hoplites who had been standing motionless to the side. The soldier whipped off his helmet and stepped forward, slowly and stolidly, until he stood directly before the boy and crouched in a wrestling stance. The boy smiled faintly and he too crouched, as if eager to demonstrate his skills against his much shorter opponent. At the instructor's clap the hoplite shot forward and in a move that was barely visible to us in the semidarkness, he tripped the ephebe onto his belly in the dirt. The boy's arm stretched straight out behind him with the soldier's foot planted squarely on the shoulder joint. The man paused for a second before leaning back slightly against the arm, eliciting a loud "pop" as the joint pulled out of its socket, and the boy screamed. An audible shudder ran through the crowd and we all took a half step back in horror, as the hoplite roughly assisted the sobbing boy to his feet, his arm hanging limply, and gestured for him to step back into his place in the darkness.

The instructor stepped forward again.

"You were wrong!" he growled. "There will always be an opponent stronger than you. Even great Hector fell to one who was stronger. He who relies on strength alone endangers himself and his *polis.* Does that mean, therefore, being the most skilled with a weapon?"

Silence.

"Sons of whores. I said, does that mean being the most *skilled* with . . ."

"No!" a hundred voices shouted.

"Need I demonstrate?" he asked in an evil tone as he drew a sword and began scanning the faces of the ephebes peering fearfully at him from the darkness.

"No!" we shouted again, in rising panic.

"You learn your lessons quickly," he said dryly. "Tell me then, does it mean having the fastest reflexes?"

"No!" came the automatic response.

He chuckled hollowly. "I believe I will demonstrate this one," he said.

The crowd of boys shrank back away from him as he began peering at their faces. Unaccountably, his gaze rested directly on me. "You," he said, "the big one. Let us test your speed."

I stepped forward warily, memories of the training bouts with Antinous still fresh in my mind though they had occurred over six years before. The instructor looked me over, with what seemed almost an expression of disappointment behind the shadows of his visor.

"A squire," he said in disdain, noting my lack of a *chlamys.* Hawking his throat he spat an enormous, glistening gob on the ground at my feet. "Blindfold me, squire." He took off his helmet and breastplate and stood before me, massive, his bare chest and shoulders dark in the torchlight under a layer of curly hair. I hastened to obey, using a black linen cloth one of the other hoplites handed me. I then stepped back, and the man faced the boys, though unable to see any of them from behind the fabric.

"Now, squire, attack me, from any direction, however you see fit."

At this, the other hoplites began clanging their spears rhythmically, in unison, against their shields, setting up a racket that would obscure any sound that my feet might make as I circled around him seeking the optimal angle of attack. The beat was taken up immediately by the ephebes, who clapped their hands and stomped their feet in the same rhythm. As I looked around, however, I saw only fear on the faces of those around me. I stood motionless for a moment, gazing at the instructor and summoning my courage, listening to the rhythm of the beating hands and clanking spears. I then began moving slowly around him in concentric circles, drawing ever nearer, fixing my eyes steadily on him, wary of any trickery. The man stood erect and immobile, not a muscle twitching, his jaw thrust forward in utter concentration.

As I moved closer I made several feints toward his body, once almost touching him, to test his senses, experimenting as to whether he was able to see my moves from under the blindfold. All these maneuvers were met with a rising volume of din from the ephebes, who in their excitement increased the speed of their stomping, losing the sense of the steady beat until the noise was no longer a distinct thumping but rather a prolonged roar. Again and again I dove in, stopping just before committing to a full-fledged attack, while the man stood as if frozen.

Suddenly, sensing that his concentration must have flagged, I leaped forward, plunging my fist with all my strength directly into his exposed belly. Scarcely had my knuckles met the hair on his skin, however, than he whirled, catlike, stepping to the side and throwing me into an off-balance stumble, augmented by an iron fist clubbing down across the back of my neck. I slammed jaw-first onto the flagstones, half senseless, and heard vaguely, as if from a distance, the sound of metal sliding on leather as he drew his sword and pressed the tip against the middle of my back almost before I had even hit the pavement. I opened my eyes and peered through the semidarkness into the crowd of now silent ephebes. I could make out Xenophon's face staring straight at me, his eyes wide in surprise and terror.

"You were wrong again, shitworms," the instructor said in a low, menacing voice. "It does indeed mean having the fastest reflexes."

We endured two years of training in hoplite weaponry, archery, javelin-throwing and maneuvering of the catapult, I performing the same drills as Xenophon, as well as serving as his foil and weapons bearer. For two years we were roused from bed before sunrise to submit to conditioning exercises that surpassed anything Antinous had put us through, and to suffer the relentless reflex drills designed to make our defensive responses unthinking and automatic. We dined in the common mess with the officers and men and practiced parade drills before the entire city. In those two years we became men. Upon successful completion of the regimen, Xenophon was awarded a fine shield and spear and formally inducted into the Athenian army. Through Gryllus' manipulations, however, young Xenophon would not serve as a mere foot soldier. His father, now retired from the military but maintaining a heavy presence in the city's political life, fitted him out with a fine horse and all the cavalry equipment needed by a young nobleman. He presented him with a commission as squad leader, the same position in which Gryllus himself had started his illustrious career many years before.

In this role, Xenophon cut a fine figure. He had grown to a man of medium height, but quite muscular, his broad chest tapering to a slender waist and well-defined thighs. Gryllus even had to order a special cuirass made for him, to be more comfortable around his collar and shoulders. His glossy black hair was cut short and left curly, military style, and unlike many heavily bearded officers, he kept a clean jaw. His eyes were still as round and limpid as they had been when he was a boy, but since his recovery from the chest wound years earlier, they had lost their sweetness and innocence, and instead glinted with a hardness that belied the boyishness of the rest of his face. When introduced for the first time to his men or to other officers, his features often gave the initial impression of a young man promoted too quickly to a level beyond his experience. This view was corrected as soon as he issued his first orders in a deep and commanding voice, and fixed his eyes on their recipient with an expression that brooked no dissent.

I regularly attended morning gymnasium with Xenophon and cared for his animal, reporting to Gryllus on his son's whereabouts and traveling with him as his squire to his postings at Athens' dwindling garrisons. He was a model officer, possessing not an ounce of frivolity, the ideal of his father's virtue. Yet during his infrequent leaves he would disappear for days on end, spurning both his fellow officers in the barracks and the comforts of Gryllus' house, where his father vainly awaited his arrival, eager to trade camp stories and discuss military tactics. Only I know the hours he spent in drab civilian clothes, quietly accompanying Socrates as he made his rounds throughout the city, and how Xenophon would discreetly scratch cryptic notes of the philosopher's words on a small travel tablet and transcribe them at night. Only I know the days he spent with a bitter, discredited old general named Thucydides, who was busy writing a history of the war, and who occasionally used Xenophon as an aide to check his calculations and organize his notes. Only I know these things because Xenophon told them to me, and swore me to secrecy. Gryllus considered Socrates a frivolous charlatan, and Thucydides a revisionist madman, and though he would have raged at Xenophon for frequenting the former, he would have disinherited him for assisting the latter.

The city's military situation progressively worsened, and over the next few years Xenophon found himself increasingly occupied in defensive activities more befitting a besieged provincial garrison than the center of the Hellenic world. He was in Athens the night the vessel *Paralus* arrived, bearing shocked sailors carrying the terrifying news of the Spartan admiral Lysander's sacking of Athens' colonies. He remained in the besieged city that year, riding the walls in its defense against the gathering land and sea forces of the Spartan alliance. He heard the tragic moaning of the people, both for those lost and for their own fate; and he watched as the city's fortresslike Long Walls were destroyed to the rhythmic wailing of the reedy *auloi*, played unceasingly by weeping young girls whom Lysander had ordered to accompany the city's dismantling.

Thus the war's dismal end, and in the shadowy, shifting political alliances that emerged to rule Athens immediately afterwards, Xenophon's star began to wane. His wound at Phyle was the least of his worries, for he soon recovered full strength in the injured leg. When the Thirty Tyrants were overthrown by the democrats, Xenophon, who never outwardly supported any regime but merely followed the orders of his father and his superiors, found himself in actual disgrace, if not in outright danger of his life. The cavalry were disbanded and Xenophon's wages rescinded. There were even calls in the assembly for former cavalry troops to return all payments that had been made to them over the past two years. Gryllus fiercely stifled this motion and others, in a determined rearguard action to protect Xenophon's, and his own, declining reputations. Athens' new leaders eventually came to their senses and reconstituted the cavalry corps for the city's defense—but prohibited former officers, Xenophon included, from joining, on account of their past association with the Thirty. Xenophon's political viability was in jeopardy, and his very patriotism had been called into question.

It was around this time, when his morale was at its lowest and he had confided in me his fears that he would soon be forced into exile or imprisonment if the regime did not stabilize, that a fortuitous event occurred, one of those few occasions that make one lift one's eyes to the heavens in wonder at the impeccable dramatic timing of the gods. A letter arrived, borne by a runner from the port whence it had just been taken off a tramp grain ship from Ephesus. Xenophon unrolled it suspiciously, for little news he had received of late was in his favor, and was startled to find that it had been written by Proxenus, from whom he had heard nothing since his return to Boeotia twelve years before.

Proxenus, who had been elected to the rank of general in the Theban army and had inflicted considerable damage on the Athenians in the war, had now found a position in Sardis, commanding a Greek mercenary brigade in the employ of the Persian prince Cyrus. Cyrus had generously bankrolled Sparta during the war, and was now raising an army to dispatch some troublesome neighboring tribes in Asia Minor. Proxenus was seeking able-bodied recruits for the campaign.

"Xenophon," he wrote, "past political affiliations are of no consequence. Previous history is ignored. The war between Sparta and Athens is a thing of the past. Cyrus' only requirements are a stout heart, strong arms and a willingness to fight." Did Xenophon know of anyone who might fit those qualifications?

His eyes clouded over in thought as he considered the proposal and his own current prospects in Athens. Holding the letter in his hand, he slowly turned away and began walking absent-mindedly to his father's study, as if to seek his advice. I caught my breath, then quickly strode over and placed my hand heavily on his shoulder. He stopped and looked at me in puzzlement.

"Xenophon," I said. "Wait, before you talk to your father; think about this. Proxenus is your cousin, but he is also a Boeotian, an ally of Sparta, and therefore in Gryllus' eyes no friend of yours. He is a mercenary now, an irregular, employed by Sparta's biggest backer, a Persian no less. Is this really something you wish to present to your father?"

He fixed his eyes on mine for a moment, and then again glanced down at the letter. I could see the paper trembling in his hand, and I recalled the agony he had felt when Proxenus left. "Perhaps it would be better to speak first to Socrates," he muttered to me under his breath.

I wondered aloud at this, too, despite what I knew of his deep admiration for the old philosopher. "Xenophon, you're going to ask advice from a man your father can't abide, about a project that would kill him if he knew you were even considering it."

He flared for an instant. "Always protecting him, aren't you, Theo? Why don't you look to my side for once? Gryllus is my father, and for better or worse, I am his son. But his war is not my war." He looked away, seething, and I waited for a moment while he struggled to gain control of his emotions. Finally, he took a deep breath and pointed sadly to the long-unused saddle blanket neatly folded in the corner of the room, and to his army-issue shield, both gathering dust. "What would you have me do, Theo? What would you have me do?"

VI

SOCRATES MEANDERED THROUGH the stalls of the thronging agora, poking his head into the shops of the vendors he knew, gently handling pieces of fruit or sandals or ceramic lamps and commenting favorably on their quality. He nodded and smiled at everyone, even those who, he knew, disdained his lack of regard for worldly goods, or found his thinking on these matters dangerous. He was accompanied in his apparently aimless wandering by a small knot of young men, most of them from the best families, by the look of their clothing. Noticing our presence, however, which had been rare of late, Socrates brushed past the others and practically skipped up to us. He was surprisingly agile for his age and the extent of his belly, which had not grown any smaller over the years. The man had hardly changed since we had first met him, unless his eyes could be said to have even a merrier twinkle than before.

After a polite greeting Xenophon, who after five years in the military had little patience for chatter, broached the subject of Proxenus' letter with Socrates. The old man frowned unhappily.

"Xenophon, you have many reasons to stay," Socrates said after a moment of thought. "Regimes come and go. The Thirty were in power for only two years, and now the democrats rule. They too will pass soon enough, or at least the indiscretions of those who served under them will soon be effaced from memory. But even admitting this—or perhaps that your true problem is that you are bored and have a desire for adventure and for wealth—is Cyrus' banner really the one under which you should march? Your service under the

Thirty will be forgotten six months from now. But joining with Cyrus, who financed the Spartans to destroy our city—that is a different matter, and the adventure you gain may be very dearly won."

Xenophon stood stiffly, a soldier's posture, facing his mentor. His eyes were directed toward Socrates, but were focused on the middle distance, like one whose mind has already been set. Socrates noticed this too, and paused, searching his face. He sighed.

"Xenophon," he said gently. "One thing more: You are not yet married, and you're not likely to find a suitable wife among Cyrus' camp followers. Your father will be expecting a grandson soon. You have a family here, friends, a fortune, a future ahead of you and an Athens that will soon be reconciled with itself again." Socrates smiled sadly. "I know that Proxenus is your blood relation and your friend, and there are ties between you that I can never loosen. But please, consider your position carefully. Talk to your father, or if you feel that his opinion is a foregone conclusion, at least take the trouble to sacrifice to the gods, and ask the oracle at Delphi for guidance in making your decision."

We walked back to the house in silence. That afternoon we rode, still in silence, to the old family estate at Erchia, which he had not visited in years. The weather was cold, windy and rainy, and as soon as we arrived Xenophon strode through the dusty hallways to his old room, closing the door behind him. For two days I scarcely saw him as he remained shut inside, reading the books he had brought with him, writing letters, working assiduously on his notes. I cannot say this was unusual—ever since losing his commission he had been in a state of depression, sleeping late, neglecting to shave, writing volumes of work that no one ever saw and which he destroyed by fire in a brazier in his room or carefully filed away in a locked chest. This time, however, I was concerned, because there was a finality about his actions, a determination in his expression, like that of someone set on completing a task, and because I knew of the decision that was hanging over his head like a leaden weight, one that would affect me every bit as much as him.

On the morning of the third day he burst into my room, bathed and well-rested and with blood-stanching cobwebs still dangling parasitically from his jaw as the result of his hurried shaving. The transformation in him was so dramatic that I was momentarily startled, though at the same time delighted to see him having returned to himself. Xenophon was not in the mood for idle chatter, however.

"Pack up, Theo," he announced. "We leave in an hour."

BOOK TWO

THE ORACLE

He arrived at Krissa beneath snow-peaked Parnassus,
Where a foothill turns to face the west: A cliff overhangs it
From above, a rugged hollow glade lies hidden beneath:
There the lord Phoebus Apollo resolved to build his glorious temple.

—HOMERIC HYMN

BLOODY BATTLE AND homecoming embrace, lightning-studded skies and Arcadian pastures, riddles, mirrors, smoke, illusion, the love of a woman, the wrath of the gods. Life is drama, a tragedy and comedy both, and we the actors. A trite observation, one decidedly inspired by some other man's muses. Yet for all the horrors and triumphs of the stage, I have found that the arts of Dionysus offer little to compare with the struggles and achievements, the lives and deaths of real men, or at least men of thought and action, men who renounce the apathy and ignorance of those who pass through life as if they were mere temporary visitors, gawking occasionally but for the most part simply following the meaty desires of their bellies and loins. Sophocles said as much when he wrote a few years ago,

> *Numberless are the world's wonders, but none*
> *more wonderful than man.*
> *His is the power to cross the storm-driven seas . . .*
> *His are speech and wind-swift thought . . .*

But there is little that can be recited on the stage that can match any true story of men who have sought to rise above base passivity, men who have taken their lives into their own hands, shaping other men and their surroundings into something more amenable to their own desires, and in the process irrevocably changing their world. Men truly live just as passionately as in the great dramas. They die just as brutally; they love just as fiercely. But in the real world they do not wear plaster masks that are hung on the wall at the end of a performance. Men's actions endure beyond their faces and names, and their effects are not finite and temporary, but encompass their descendants and the descendants of their fellow protagonists in widening yet ever fainter rings for all eternity. How odd that we seek through drama to depict, or to escape from, our own world, the infinite variety and cosmic timelessness of which puts even that of the gods to shame.

My pen rambles and the impatient Muses urge me to move on with my tale.

I

THE TRIP TO DELPHI was long, though not without interest. Xenophon was the perfect pilgrim, stopping at every roadside attraction, keeping a purse full of *obols* to tip the young guides importuning us to visit this or that sacred spring, never letting a table of fruit set up outside a farmstead be passed by without a sample. The roads were crowded with men and women, merchants, shysters and prostitutes, all traveling to Delphi to attend the annual festival celebrating Apollo's departure to the northern Hyperborean regions for the winter, and the arrival of his mad brother Dionysus. The ceremony was to begin with the usual dissipation in just a few days. We were rushing to consult the Pythia, the oracle of Apollo, before the festival began, but were hindered by the mobs of other travelers heading in the same direction. The closer we came to our destination, the more frequented the roads became until at length it was impossible to pass the other pilgrims, so heavily traveled was the route. We dismounted and led our horses, to stretch our legs and converse with some of the other travelers, since like it or not, we were condemned to travel with them in this fashion all the way to Delphi.

As it happened, Xenophon had carefully chosen the pilgrims near whom he had dismounted. He quickly struck up a conversation with a cheerful, heavyset country girl named Aglaia, who was traveling to Delphi for the first time, to ask the oracle for guidance on choosing a husband from among her three suitors. Oddly, she was traveling unaccompanied by any male guardian, a fact that would have raised disapproving eyebrows among the other travelers had it not been for the formidable, glowering old crone she was dragging in tow, who turned out to be her grandmother. Though dressed in the rough clothes of a village lass, a goatherd really, Aglaia was plump and lovely, with strong, fleshy arms tanned from her daily exposure to the sun, and full, soft breasts which, even without her calling overt attention to them, nevertheless drew men's gaze to their mesmerizing ripeness. Her eyes sparkled as do those of young maidens before clouding over with the cares of the house and the pain of childbearing, and her bell-like laughter carried far above the deep-voiced din and tramping of the mostly male crowd. Although I appreciated her beauty, she was lusty and demonstrative, just the sort of trollop I disdained, and she had taken an immediate liking to Xenophon, admiring his horse and gingerly touching the jeweled hilt of the short sword he carried at his belt.

"Xenophon!" I said under my breath. "Don't be an idiot! Can't you see she's got you pegged to be suitor number four?" I tried to elbow him over to another group of travelers heading in our direction.

He shot me a black look. "What am I, Theo, an ephebe?" he hissed. "Are you still Father's stool-pigeon slave, guarding my morals from the evils of the world? I'm of age now. I don't need your handwringing."

I felt my jaw tense in anger at his insults, but forced myself to remain silent, and to keep looking straight ahead. After a few moments he seemed to regret his hasty words, and he excused himself from the girl and drew me aside. "Theo, relax. It's been months since I've even spoken with a woman. I just want to chat a bit with someone better looking than you. Believe me, I'll be better company for it afterwards."

I remained staring straight ahead as I walked, determined not to give him the satisfaction of a response. He shrugged, and stepped back up to Aglaia's side, and I resignedly lifted the elderly grandmother onto my horse, on which she rode stiff and trembling, grasping its mane tightly with both hands in her terror at sitting so high. I then walked behind Xenophon and the girl, casting my large shadow over their shoulders.

Aglaia had done her homework before setting out on her journey, and had collected quite a number of stories concerning the oracle, a few from good sources, most from the most spurious origins imaginable. She regaled us with what she had learned, her peals of laughter making men smile for yards around, even if they were unable to hear her actual words. Xenophon traded her story for story, to her great delight. She was most moved by the tale of King Croesus of Lydia, which Xenophon had learned from his mother as a young boy.

"Croesus," he recalled, "learned that the Persian king was becoming more powerful by the day. This worried him, and he began to wonder whether he should attack the Persians before they became too mighty. He decided to consult an oracle.

"In those days, Delphi was not the most famous oracle in Greece, it was simply one of many. Since Croesus didn't know which was the most truthful, he sent runners out from Sardis to every one, including the Pythia of Delphi, with instructions to wait until the hundredth day after their departure from Sardis. On precisely that day, each runner would consult the respective oracle and ask what King Croesus was doing at that moment. All their answers would be recorded and brought back to the King.

"At Delphi, just as the King's messenger entered the oracle's sanctuary, before he had even had a chance to sacrifice and make his inquiry, the oracle spoke in perfect hexameter verse:

I know the number of the sands, and the measure of the ocean;
I have ears for the dumb, and hear those who cannot speak;
Behold, there striketh my senses the savor of a shell-covered tortoise,
Boiling on a fire in a cauldron, with the flesh of a lamb—
Brass is laid beneath it, and brass the cover placed over it.

"All the messengers returned with their answers, and Croesus began reading them, but no sooner did he read the reply from Delphi than he himself was nearly struck dumb, and he discarded every other response. As it happened, when his messengers first left Sardis months before, he had wracked his brain to think what impossible thing he could perform that no mortal could guess by chance, and then, on the hundredth day, he took a tortoise and a lamb and cut them to pieces with his own hands, and boiled them together in a brass cauldron with brass lid. The oracle had described this perfectly.

"Because of this test, Croesus showered gifts on Delphi, to gain favor for the crucial advice he needed. He sacrificed thousands of animals and donated a huge pile of riches, golden goblets, statues and purple vestments. He even levied a huge tax on his own people, melting down all the money he collected into solid gold ingots."

Here the girl interjected a comment with her tinkling laughter. "I hope I'll be able to see some of the statues and drink from the cups! I've heard that even the dung-sweepers in the street use gold-handled brooms!"

"Herodotus," Xenophon said, "says that most of the riches are kept locked in the treasury, but that he himself had seen Croesus' enormous offering bowls, and a statue of a golden maiden, adorned with his wife's necklace and girdles."

Aglaia shrieked with laughter as Xenophon grinned and winked at me. "What happened next?" she asked.

"Well, Croesus asked the Pythia whether he should declare war on the Persians. The oracle's response was clear enough: 'If you make war on the Persians, you will destroy a mighty empire.' Croesus was overjoyed when he heard this, and marched his army from Sardis all the way to Persia—where his own troops were demolished. He retreated back to Sardis, pursued the entire way by the king. After a long siege, Sardis was taken and Croesus fell into the Persians' hands. He spent the rest of his life complaining how he was so cruelly deceived by the oracle, which had led him to believe he could wage war against the Persians."

Aglaia was silent for a time, puzzling this over. "But why did the Pythia deceive him?" she finally asked. "I thought the oracle always told the truth!"

Xenophon laughed. "You're falling into the same trap as Croesus—you guess the response even before you ask the question, and then you have ears only for the answer you've decided upon! The oracle was right. She said Croesus would destroy a mighty empire, and he did—his own. The Pythia's response was in the form of a riddle—it almost always is—but Croesus had no right to complain. If he'd been wise, he would have asked the oracle which empire she meant, the Persian or his own. He should have been more careful when formulating the question and receiving the answer." Xenophon looked slyly at the girl. Her face was wreathed in smiles.

"Well," she said finally. "I see now how dangerous it is to ask a question of the Pythia that is too vague. I was simply going to ask which of my three suitors was the best man. A question like that would never do—it's far too open-ended. How could the god possibly know what their best qualities would be, to me? Gods have their idea of good, and—well, I have my own."

We walked along in silence for a few moments, thinking on this, and as she turned her head to look at Xenophon, I could see a half-smile slowly forming on the girl's face.

"It's settled, then," she finally said. "I'll just ask the oracle to tell me which man is the richest."

II

LONG BEFORE ARRIVING at our destination, we saw glimpses of mist-shrouded Mount Parnassus towering over its neighboring summits, with its sheer, snow-capped peaks, storm-wracked trees, and above the timber line, its naked slopes. As we approached, the wind sometimes stirred the boughs of the trees, revealing the village of Delphi high above, a shiny cluster of garish color and gleaming white set against the huge flank of the mountain, glittering like a tiny jewel worn on a matron's plump breast. There, part way up the south flank of the mountain famous throughout the world for being sacred to Apollo, his mad brother Dionysus, and the Muses lies a sort of a natural hollow, like an enormous theater built for Titans but populated by nymphs. It is surrounded on three sides by the sacred mountain itself and two enormous upright crags, the Phaedriads or "Shining Ones." Their sheer cliffs seem to catch the summer's burning sunlight and intensify it across the deep, echoing gorge. Here, as if suspended in space over the river valley, exposed to the wind, air, and penetrating light, is Delphi, the most venerated place in all Greece, the place chosen personally by the god Apollo for his domain.

There are signs of the god's presence everywhere, and the forces of nature seem almost magnified by the deity's startling closeness. The light is brighter there, almost blinding, and at midday the luminous air seems to lift the very rocks from the earth until they burn in a blaze of holy light. At dawn and dusk, the magnificent colors that paint the landscape to the distant horizon are so pure and clear that sky and earth no longer seem to have any definable boundary. Earthquakes often rock the low-framed houses nestled into the cliff, and after dark, when nature seems to be at its most raw, thunder from distant mountain storms rolls and echoes through the gorge and across the mountainside.

Instructors of rhetoric teach that it is not wise assume equal knowledge on the part of both reader and writer. A word of explanation is in order here, in the event that these scribblings someday fall into the hands of distant readers in lands unfamiliar with the Pythian oracle, though I can hardly imagine how far one must travel not to have heard of this wonder. It is said that in ancient times, when gods alone roamed the earth, the site of Delphi was occupied by a terrible dragon known as the Python, which from its dark lair guarded Gaia, the ancient earth goddess, and her powers to foresee the future. After man was created, Apollo, the god of art and enlightenment, wished to communicate with the mortals, but to do so he had to find a place to enter into contact with them. An ancient hymn we often used to sing in his honor during festivals tells how the god traveled from Crete riding on two dolphins until he arrived at Delphi, where he slew the dragon with his arrow, and took the oracle for his own use. From then on, he was the Lord of Delphi, known as the Pythian Apollo. He was later joined by his younger brother, the mystic god Dionysus, who resides at Delphi during the three months of the year when Apollo is taking the winter months in the northern regions. The holy oracle never speaks to human petitioners directly, but rather through the Pythia, a local Delphian priestess, usually of peasant stock, who is chosen by the temple priests at a young age and who spends her entire life in chastity and dreamlike prayer in the god's service. It was to the Pythia that Xenophon planned to address his question, and if Apollo found favor in his sacrifice and in his pureness of heart, then it would be from the Pythia's lips that the answer would be received. The legendary ambiguity of her responses, however, which were often couched in the form of riddles, usually required written interpretation by her attending priests, the *prophetai.*

Upon our arrival that evening Xenophon and I immediately began the task of searching for lodgings, a difficult task in this crowded season, and obtaining care for our horses. After arranging a room at a small, timeworn inn, and treating ourselves to a quick splash of water from the inn's tiny, bubbling fountain, we left to wander the enchanted streets of the holy town, guided by one of the street urchins gathered outside our inn. Xenophon had been in almost a trancelike state since arriving, in awe and wonder at being so close to the gods, and it was all I could do to keep him from walking off the edge of the cliff in his utter distraction. His eyes seemed permanently fixed on the summit of the peaks or the tops of the temples, as if expecting Apollo to arrive at any moment in bodily form to answer his query personally.

The town of Delphi itself is as much a wonder as its setting. I had always thought Athens to be the most beautiful city in the world, but Delphi is a worthy rival. Under the late-slanting autumn sun reflected from the glowing cliffs, the temples and public buildings shine and even glow with their polychromed surfaces. Xenophon and I were entranced by the contrasts between the blinding white of the building stone in the few places where it was left unadorned, and the soft pastel shades of pink, blue, and green used so effectively by the Delphians elsewhere, to emphasize the contours of the pillars and stonework. The graceful structures of the temples and gymnasiums, the porticos and fountains, the art galleries and treasuries, and even the more modest houses and inns, were all designed and constructed with the subtle elegance of a holy city.

Most eerie in the moonlight of our walk were the hundreds of bronze statues, gifts from grateful suppliants and cities, which were adorned with a delicate blue and green patina produced by the moisture-laden air constantly blowing over them. Along one side of the sacred approach to the sanctuary stood a row of monumental bronzes erected by the Athenians; standing directly opposite them and casting hostile stares at their carved enemies was another series of bronzes erected by the Spartans. Every temple was surrounded by statues, which spilled onto the street corners, public fountains and gardens. There were the usual portraits of the gods, of course, but also a surprising number of sculptures of animals, which added an almost barbarian aspect to the city. Horse statues abounded, donated by winning generals from their share of the battle loot, or by winners of the chariot races at the festival of Delphi. I saw a bronze bull, offered by the people of Corfu in return for a miraculous haul of tuna during a famine several years earlier; several goats, one of them from a small tribe in thanksgiving for its delivery from the plague; and near the great altar outside the main temple a bronze wolf offered by the Delphians themselves, in honor of a beast that had killed a thief who had stolen some of the sanctuary's gold. There was even a statue of a donkey that was said to have alerted its people to an ambush. The gods apparently cherish our beastly companions as much as they do us ourselves.

The day after our arrival, and the day prior to our scheduled appointment with the oracle, we came upon Aglaia walking along a side street, her aged grandmother in tow along with a small retinue of admirers whom she had already collected. Her face was beaming and she greeted Xenophon warmly, as if they were two old friends separated for months.

"I've just come from the oracle," she announced. "I asked the Pythia exactly what you told me to ask, rather than 'whom should I marry.' And wouldn't you know it—the man that Apollo said was the richest was the very one I most wanted for a husband anyway!"

"Unless the Pythia had told her that another one was even richer," the dour old woman muttered.

Xenophon congratulated her on her good fortune, and after listening absentmindedly to her chatter for a few moments, he politely excused himself, and we continued on our stroll.

"Xenophon!" Aglaia called after we had moved on only a few yards. "We'll be leaving tomorrow morning at sunrise, so if you'd care to visit tonight to wish me well . . ."

She blushed at this display of forwardness, which must have been extreme even for Aglaia, and hurriedly turned away down the street. Xenophon stood staring after her for a second and then, reluctantly it seemed, continued his stroll with me through the streets.

We trudged along Delphi's steeply inclined flagstones for an hour without a word passing between us. I stopped at a stall, eager to purchase a memento of our visit, for who could know when, or if, I might return. I selected a small, antique brass figurine of Apollo, sword in hand, holding by the hair the head of a man with a vaguely Persian countenance, his beard long and pointed. The shopkeeper was unable to tell me to which event it referred, but I purchased it anyway, as it seemed like a good omen, and besides, it had caught my fancy. Though tiny, the faces and expressions were of a realism that made one think that the original castings had been modeled on individuals known to the sculptor, and the god's stance and posture suggested utter fearlessness, trust in the strength of his body, and confidence on the sculptor's part to depict such a scene with seemingly no reference to any actual story of Apollo. What might the world have been like, I wondered, when men were as certain of themselves as that? Xenophon ignored the colorful shops, the stalls being set up in the street for the coming market, the frankly appraising gazes of the local girls eyeing the handsome stranger walking obliviously among them, even the magnificent vistas of the rocky mountains and temples that sprang to our sight around every corner. I finally broke the silence.

"Xenophon, I don't mean to belabor this, but you could have your pick of a thousand young virgins from good families in Athens. I just can't understand seeing you bedazzled by this roadside trollop Aglaia."

He stopped in the middle of the street and stared at me. I feared I had again spoken too bluntly, and I braced myself for his violent reaction. After a pause, however, during which I could almost see his mind working furiously in response to my complaint, he burst into a loud laugh and clapped me on the back. The men around us looked up briefly from their tasks at the sudden sound.

"Poor Theo, is that what you think has been weighing on my mind this whole time? Aglaia? Go to her inn tonight yourself, if you like, she's clearly looking for a quick roll before she marries her town's rich man, who probably has three obols to his name compared to his rivals' two." He winked at me, and I cringed in distaste.

"You're right, though," he continued. "I was thinking of Aglaia, but not the way you expect. I was just considering how satisfied she was at having asked the oracle her precise, narrow question, and at receiving the answer most useful to her. There are hundreds of stories of men blinded by their pride and ambition, asking an open-ended question of the oracle and receiving an open-ended answer. They ignore the ambiguity, and hear only what they wish to hear, taking the wrong course of action and suffering for it. Is Aglaia wiser than those old kings, in not trying to tempt or confuse the god, and in seeking only an answer she is capable of obeying?"

Xenophon resumed his stroll, but now he was agitated, his mind working faster than he was able to speak, a troubled expression on his face. "I can't understand why Socrates didn't advise me on this before we left," he went on. "I see the wisdom of Aglaia's solution, and the satisfaction she feels at the answer she received, which is actually the answer she would have wanted all along. But if you narrow your question as she did—restricting the range of the god's answers, which you could take so far as to eliminate the god's every choice but the one answer you wish to receive—are you not still trying to deceive the god, and thereby deceiving yourself? And if you are deceiving the god—well then, does the god know that? I mean, do the gods really see into our hearts and minds? Can they read our souls? Do they even care to, or is it enough that from their heights on Olympus they see only our physical actions, the outward evidence of our thoughts?"

He continued speaking, becoming more excited, gesturing with his hands as we walked and ignoring the sidelong glances of the passersby.

"The problem is, Theo, if Apollo knows he's being duped by being asked a staged question from which his choices are limited, why would he meekly accept this, and cause the oracle to provide the truly best answer? Because of the goat we sacrifice in his honor beforehand? Is the god so easily bought? If the truthfulness of his answer is conditional upon the size of the sacrifice, next time I'll bring an elephant! If Croesus, with all the wealth he donated to the oracle's treasury, was given an answer calculated to lead him astray, even though the god knew of his ambitions to conquer Persia, what hope did penniless Aglaia have of receiving a straight answer from the god? At least Croesus asked an honest question!"

Xenophon fell silent for a few moments, as we finally approached the inn. He looked longingly back at the streets, as if reluctant to go inside, though I myself was exhausted from our long ramble up and down the steep flagstones.

"I'm speaking gibberish, Theo, forgive me. But I was much more confident of my prospects with the oracle before we met Aglaia. She's put more doubts in my mind than Socrates ever did."

I was at a loss what to say to my troubled master. The faint echoes of the ancient chanting had begun repeating themselves in my mind, like an irritating buzzing of which I was unable to rid myself, and my feelings for the success of our venture had begun to darken.

III

THE DOORKEEPER CHALLENGED us as we passed through the entrance to the inner temple, demanding our names and business. "Xenophon of Athens," my master replied condescendingly, "and my freedman Theo. . . . Themistogenes of Syracuse, who will assist me." The custodian coolly appraised us, then turned to a scroll containing a list of names. This was the last day the oracle could be consulted this year, and though the list was short, containing only two or three names, the guardian pursed his lips self-importantly and made a considerable effort to maintain the protocol of his position. At last finding our names on the scroll, and verifying that we had already paid the consultation fee, the guardian grudgingly waved us through the narrow door into the huge temple grounds.

Before us was a broad, square courtyard, paved with flagstones worn smooth by the centuries of sandal-clad and bare feet that had trod its surface. It was completely abandoned, except for a half dozen acolytes lethargically mopping the stones in the corners with hand rags, in preparation for the dedication of Dionysus' arrival the following day. At the front of the courtyard stood a small altar, with a lamp burning on either end. A stone trough had been placed to the side of it, into which flowed a trickle of water from one of the many sacred springs located on the mountainside. We walked cautiously up to the altar and waited in silence, wondering whether we were expected to seek a guide, or to call out and announce our presence.

The wall above the altar was carved with the wisdom of the responses emanating from the oracle over the generations. *Know Thyself,* and *Nothing Too Much* were placed in prominent locations directly over the entrance to the inner temple. Other sayings too, all conveying the spirit for which Apollo stood, adorned the side doors, even the entrance to the stone barn where the sacrificial animals were kept for the ceremony: *Curb Thy Spirit, Keep a Reverent Tongue, Observe the Limit, Glory Not in Strength* and my favorite in consideration of its effect on Aglaia: *Keep Woman Under Rule.* The impact would have been lost on her in any case, as I doubted she could read.

Suddenly a side door opened, and a bald, elderly priest in white robes shuffled out, accompanied by a young acolyte leading a magnificent ram. The ram followed docilely as the trio calmly approached the altar. Upon reaching it, however, the ram determined not to stop, but rather to continue on with its stroll, and it took all the boy's strength to tie the beast to an iron ring set into the stone wall, where it continued to strain against the tether with might and main.

Xenophon had studied the customs of the oracle in advance, and knew that at this point we were expected to sacrifice the animal, which had, in fact, been paid for as part of the consultation fee. The procedure was to sprinkle the creature with cold water taken from the sacred trough, to induce a shudder. This could not be merely a quick tremor, but rather had to consist of a trembling and a shaking throughout the animal's entire body, to the tips of its hooves. The animal's very bones must rattle, the point being to obtain its nod of assent for the sacrifice. If this were achieved, the occasion would be deemed propitious, and Xenophon allowed to make the sacrifice to the god.

With the boy's help, I held the squirming animal between my legs, uttering calming words until its thrashing had subsided and it stood still. Looking down on its face from above I could see my own head and torso reflected in the ram's large watery eyes, until my legs disappeared into the edge of its long eyelashes. I wondered if the gods, too, saw their reflections when looking down into men's eyes from the heavens, and whether, if one were careful and closely observed the Pythia while communing with Apollo, one might not catch a glimpse of the god himself in her eyes, even if the reflection were upside down. Xenophon scooped up a handful of water and sprinkled it gently on the ram's brow. It snapped its head in irritation and snorted, but gave not the slightest semblance of a shudder. Xenophon stepped again to the trough, scooped up more water in his cupped hands, and this time, rather than sprinkling it, dumped it straight into the ram's face. The beast bleated in rage and spit, nearly bucking me off as I struggled to immobilize it between my legs, with my hands tightly grasping its horns. Still no shudder.

In exasperation, Xenophon looked around and spied one of the temple slaves continuing to mop on his hands and knees in the corner, pretending to ignore the whole proceeding while his shoulders shook in silent laughter. He stalked over, grabbed the boy's bucket, and before anyone could react, strode straight to the trough and slopped an entire bucketful over the doomed beast, soaking it and me in the process.

If ever I heard a ram roar, this one did: a deep, lengthy bellow of protest at this ill treatment of its august self. It kicked up its hind legs, tripping me and causing me to flip over its body flat onto my back, knocking the wind out of me. One of my hands slipped free of the horn, and the squirming ram flopped around on top of me with its wool in my face and its sharp hooves flying, while with my free hand I struggled to gain purchase on one of its limbs. I grasped at its wool, which kept tearing free in my hand, and then finally clamped down hard on its soft flesh with my entire fist. The animal stiffened like a plank, and I realized I had seized it by the testicles, causing it to freeze in terror and pain. I cautiously struggled to my knees and secured the grasp of my other hand on its horn, until I was finally able to let loose with the offending hand and assume my original position, straddling its back, with my hands pulling its head up by the horns. As I cautiously let go its balls, the ram heaved a tremendous shudder of relief, and the priest nodded in satisfaction. Xenophon leaped to with the sacrificial knife, I muttered a short prayer under my breath, and in an instant the task had been successfully completed.

"Xenophon of Athens," intoned a voice from behind the thick curtain. Two slaves drew it back along the rod on the rings from which it hung, revealing a small, shadowed room, the central temple, the *adyton,* wherein mysteries older than mankind itself had been perpetuated. Before us was the most sacred object in Greece and the most ancient, the *omphalos,* the marking stone of the world's navel, the center of the earth. On either side of it stood two solid gold eagles, commemorating the finding of the earth by Zeus' eagles. The stone itself was unremarkable: Cone-shaped and perhaps a foot high, it was worn smooth by a hundred generations of Pythian hands and by the daily oiling they devoutly applied to it. Remarkable as this object was, however, my eyes scarcely lingered on it a moment before being drawn to the side, where a withered, monkeylike creature sat immobile and silent, pale as a larva. The voluminous folds of her white gowns were tucked around and behind her, the purity and newness of the starched linen fabric contrasting sharply with the rough, papery skin and wispy strands of hair it enframed and enveloped.

Xenophon stood silent, staring at the tiny, ancient woman as she sat motionless on her *holmos,* her bowl-shaped tripod seat, with her feet dangling down and her face turned toward him expectantly. Her eyes were closed, but even so one could see that she was blind, and not merely blind but blinded—the eyelids closed flat behind the darkened shadows where her eyes would have been, evincing not the slightest hint of the normal convex bulge of the eyeballs. The lids were withered and wrinkled, lacking lashes, and gave the impression of having been fused shut to permanently conceal the empty sockets. On her lap was balanced a plain wooden bowl, on which a small pile of the laurel leaves that had been burning on the altar continued to smolder, sending a small plume of smoke floating lazily upwards and enwreathing her face with its astringent scent. A crown of laurel had been placed on her head, and she held a small branch in her right hand. Thus sat the Pythia, the two prophetai on either side waiting to interpret or otherwise assist her in speaking for the god, all staring back at Xenophon, ready for his query.

"Thou may pose thy question to the lord Apollo, through the person of the holy Pythia," the voice again droned in the ponderous accents of the ancient Delphian dialect, which caught me by surprise. It was only with some difficulty, by recalling the sentence again in my mind, that I was able to understand what our interlocutor had said, whom I now saw was a small, potbellied scribe seated on a high stool just behind the Pythia, his stylus poised over a fresh wax tablet.

Xenophon's eyes flitted from the Pythia to the two priests and back again, but he remained silent. Perhaps he had failed to understand the scribe's order to begin? I prepared to step forward out of the shadows to assist him with a quick, prodding whisper in the ear. The priest facing us on the left wore a sour, irritated expression, glaring at Xenophon as if resenting him for having dragged him out of bed for this duty. The other priest, however, the senior of the two, bore a benign, grandfatherly expression, and waited patiently. Finally, the elder priest nodded at Xenophon kindly, as if reassuring him that he was permitted to speak, and he opened his mouth slightly as if to utter words of encouragement. Before he did so, however, Xenophon seemed to snap to, and without even taking an introductory breath, launched into the question he had so carefully prepared over the past few days.

"Mighty lord Apollo, I entreat thee, hear my question," he intoned quietly, but deliberately and confidently, in his best imitation of the ancient dialect. He stood stock-still and straight as an oar, his eyes fixed on the sightless, sealed face of the Pythia. "Pythian Apollo, god of the Muses, I beseech thee to tell me whether it be thy will that I journey to Sardis to accompany my friend, Proxenus, on his expedition with Cyrus. . . ."

From the moment he began speaking, the old woman had been trembling and showing signs of agitation, rocking back and forth and thrusting her chin up in the air, her feet kicking and heaving like a toddler wishing to be let down from a high chair. Her breath came in a series of short gasps, and before Xenophon had quite finished, she raised her face straight up to the ceiling, flinging the branch she was holding and clapping her hands fiercely to her ears. She uttered a short shriek, as if from pain, flecks of spittle glistening on her chin. The two priests, their expressions as unflappable as hers was frenzied, quickly placed their hands behind her shoulders to prevent her from tipping backward off the tripod.

Suddenly she leaped forward off the seat, landing unsteadily on the floor. Taking a crouching step toward Xenophon, her twisted face pointed directly at his, she paused, then began pacing shakily to the side, still supported by the priests, and mumbling in her dialect so quickly and disjointedly that I was able to pick out only the occasional word. Her arms flapped wildly in gesture, as if she were inebriated or entranced, and her utterances, now repeated over and over, were punctuated rhythmically by the same little shriek with which she had first interrupted Xenophon. She seethed and foamed, ranging back and forth before the altar, appearing to ignore our presence, and jerking her head as if to rid herself of an insect that had crawled into one of her ears and was tormenting her. The scribe followed close behind the old woman and the two priests, rapidly scratching out her words on his tablet. Xenophon stood dumbfounded, his hands hanging limply at his sides, and he glanced at me with a look of utter bewilderment. Nothing we had heard had prepared us for this reaction from the priestess.

After a few moments, the old woman again stopped directly in front of Xenophon and peered up at him, her ancient fingers knotted in tight fists, and her shriveled eyelids seeming to stare straight into his face. Xenophon held his ground and moved not a muscle, for the crone's aspect and behavior were terrifying.

Suddenly she seemed to slump, with her face still staring into his. The two priests half carried, half dragged the Pythia two or three paces backwards, and lifted her again up onto the tripod, where she took a deep breath and reassumed the calm and expectant posture we had seen upon first entering. The priests cautiously removed their hands from under her upper arms, and when convinced that her turmoil had passed, quickly stepped behind her to the scribe, where all three conferred in whispered tones. Moving back to their positions after a moment, the scribe stood up, looked at Xenophon and spoke, reading from his tablet.

"He of wisdom unsurpassed,
Whose words with venom must compete,
Knows that which rules old men and fools,
Though not thyself in thy self-deceit."

"Xenophon of Athens: The Pythian Apollo knows what passeth in thy heart."

At this, Xenophon blinked, and seemed to recoil slightly in silent confusion. He quickly recovered, and again stood at immobile attention while the scribe continued.

"Attempt not to deceive the god with thy mortal lips. Peer deep within thyself, and ask not questions to which thou already knowest the answer, seek not advice which thou dost not intend to obey. Though thy sacrifice has been found worthy, Apollo has rejected thy question and refuses to answer. Ask only that which is of significance to thee."

At this, Xenophon's confidence appeared to flag for an instant. His shoulders slumped, and he gazed over at me again in bewilderment, until I gave a slight shrug, and looked away. He stared down at the floor for what seemed like an eternity. Everyone present in the room, the priests, the scribe, and most especially the Pythia herself, had fixed their unblinking faces on him, again maintaining the utmost silence. Finally he looked up, straightened his shoulders, and stepped forward a pace to stand once more directly in front of the ancient, leathery creature.

"Mighty lord Apollo, I entreat thee, hear my question," he began again using the stock formula. He paused slightly, then continued, his voice hoarse and croaking. "To which god should I sacrifice to make my intended journey to Sardis successful, to fare well upon it, and to return in safety?"

This time the Pythia remained calm, her wrinkled face as expressionless as a dried apple. After a moment, what appeared to be a smile crept across her lips, revealing the black, rotten stubs of her two front teeth. Apollo the double-tongued was filling her being, surely weaving a web of words on her lips that would leave us wondering in our confusion, words that would coil and uncoil and meander tangentially to their meaning like a water snake through a bed of reeds. Suddenly, she flung open her dead, frozen eyelids, revealing behind them not eyes, nor even the watery whites of the blank eyeballs as the blind often show, but what was worse, pure nothingness—black, empty sockets where eyes should have been, like those of a plaster mask worn by an actor, but without the actor's living eyes peering from behind to humanize the eerie, dead quality of the blank surface. Her vacant, cavernous holes penetrated deeply into Xenophon's face, and in reply to his query, she uttered merely one word, in a croak imitating, or mocking, his own voice:

"Zeus."

She continued staring at him as the curtains were drawn back together by the slaves, hiding the leering Pythia from our sight, her empty sockets remaining focused on him until she finally disappeared behind the folds. The attendants stepped forward and took our arms, leading us out from the cool, silent dankness of the temple to the blinding sunlight and raucous shouts of the street vendors setting up their stalls for the festival.

IV

SEATED ON A LOW STOOL in the semidarkness of Socrates' single room, Xenophon seemed scarcely aware of his surroundings in his agitation.

"I wasted my chance," he groaned, his shoulders slumped, his back curved like that of a whipped dog. I had not seen Xenophon this wretched in twenty years. "My one chance to ask the god to guide me in the most important decision of my life, and I asked the wrong question. I can't even tell my father what the oracle said, much less what I am now to do with my life."

Socrates was silent for a moment, puttering about the room, arranging papers and scrolls here and there. As always, there was nothing of reproach in his silence; only thoughtfulness and comfort, like the presence of a beloved grandfather. Xenophon did not stir, nor did I from the corner to which I had retreated, trying to remain as unobtrusive as my large frame would allow.

"You attempted to deceive the god," Socrates said finally, his old satyr's face expressionless. "You asked the question that most closely suited your desires."

"But Socrates," he interrupted, standing up and pacing, "I tried to ask the question you told me to ask. The Pythia stopped me and wouldn't let me proceed! As the gods are my witness, I tried!" He glanced at me, and I nodded slowly, but Socrates did not even bother to look up from his chores.

"Do you know what true wisdom is?" Socrates finally asked, and this time he stood squarely in front of Xenophon, demanding with his posture that the younger man pay complete attention to his words. "Do you truly understand what it is to obey the dictum carved on the temple wall at Delphi, *Know Thyself*? Listen to me now, and do not interrupt. For once this is not a dialogue. Men call me wise, and you apparently believe I am, or you would not be here now, before even speaking to your father. I will give you advice, as far as I can, and you may do with it what you will.

"Wisdom is far more," Socrates continued, "and what is most important, far less, than you might think, and to that extent men are right—I am indeed wise. But you need not take my word for it. You could, if you wished, look to your friend the god at Delphi as witness to my wisdom, such as it is."

Xenophon looked up in interest, for none of us who had accompanied Socrates in the agora were aware that he had ever consulted the Pythia.

"It was not I who consulted her," he said, as if reading our thoughts, "but rather my boyhood friend, Chaerophon, who many years ago asked the oracle if there was anyone wiser than Socrates. To this the Pythia had replied that there was no one."

I could see in Xenophon's eyes that the same thought had flashed into his mind as into mine: *He of wisdom unsurpassed* . . . What was the rest? . . . *whose words with venom must compete* . . . That had nothing to do with Socrates; the Pythia's words remained obscure. The old man continued, instructing his fools:

"When Chaerophon told me the oracle's answer, I asked myself, 'Why does the god not use plain language? I realize I have no claim to wisdom, great or small; so what might he mean by saying no one is wiser than I? He cannot be telling a lie; that would not be proper for a god.' After turning this about in my head for some time, I finally resolved to check the truth of it in the following way: I went to speak with a man famous for being wise, because I felt I would then succeed in disproving the oracle and demonstrating to the deity that here was a man wiser than I. Well, I gave this man a thorough examination—I will not tell you his name, but he was one of our politicians at the time—and in speaking with him I concluded that even though in the view of many people, and especially in his own, he appeared to be wise, in fact he was not.

"Xenophon, real wisdom is the property of the gods alone, and the oracle tells us that human wisdom has little or no value. I finally decided that the oracle was not referring literally to me, to this man Socrates, but had rather taken my name as an example, as if to say 'the wisest man is he who, like Socrates, realizes that he truly knows nothing.'

"You know, I once attempted to study the writings of Heraclitus the Obscure. What I did understand of them was excellent. I believe also to be excellent that which I did not understand." Socrates smiled at his little joke. "Heraclitus," he went on, "once said that you cannot step into the same river of time twice, and in this he was correct. You cannot have a decision both ways.

"The god saw inside your heart, Xenophon, and the wisdom you thought you had, by trying to second-guess him, was worthless. You had already made up your mind what to do, regardless of the oracle's answer to your intended question. Do not be ignorant of yourself, nor make the same mistakes as other men, who are so busy looking into the affairs of their rivals that they never turn to examine themselves. Go now. You received your answer from the oracle, and you have talked it over with me. The die is cast, and there is nothing I can advise you to do, except the god's bidding, now and always."

At this Xenophon, who had been staring morosely at the floor, looked up at Socrates and saw the old man gently smiling at him, without a hint of sadness or reproach. There were no tears, not a trace of hesitation on his face, and he clasped Xenophon to him for an instant like a son, and then released him, swatting him on the arm as if to shoo him out the door. He then fixed his gaze upon me—the first time I believe he had ever even noticed me—and clasped me as well, but upon releasing me looked me straight in the eye with a twinkle and said softly, "You, Theo, I perceive as being among the wisest of men. May the Fates be on your side." Given Socrates' definition of wisdom I wasn't sure whether to take this as a compliment or an insult, but I gladly accepted his blessing and followed Xenophon out the low door.

The sky was darkening early and the wind blew bitingly cold. Athens was still recovering from the poverty into which the recent war, and the subsequent peace with Sparta, had thrown it, and there was little activity in the streets after dark. Few boarding houses were open, and the noises of any activity issuing from the windows of the inns were rare. Xenophon stood in the street a long time, watching the dry dust blow cold along the gutters, seeing the windows of the houses grow dark and turn black, as few people in Socrates' quarter could even afford oil for lamps. The squalor and filth that are part of any large city had never been readily apparent in Athens, perhaps disguised by the beauty of the buildings and monuments on every street corner, masked by the natural vivacity of its citizens bustling about their daily activities. On that evening, however, the stench and the rot gathering in the gutters and against the sides of once-pristine public buildings were overwhelming. It was the dominant sensation in a city that was otherwise practically abandoned to its ghosts until the dawn's light returned to rid it of its specters. Xenophon stood and watched the darkness descend, and saw his future in this city to be as black as the shadows that were relentlessly invading it. Several weeks before, he had ordered me to mark with red ink on his chest the position of his heart, in case, he said, he had to take recourse to it with his dagger to avoid falling into his enemies' hands. I had laughed it off at the time, though somewhat uneasily I admit, dismissing it as nothing more than excessive dramatics on the part of an overwrought young man. Nevertheless, I had resolved to keep a close eye on him, and his mood tonight made me wish I had misapplied my red brush.

That evening Xenophon sacrificed an ox to Zeus in the main temple, and early the next morning we boarded a merchant ship carrying heavy-fleeced Attic sheep, bound for Ephesus. As we pulled away in the tender, we looked back and saw that old one-eyed Gryllus had appeared on the rain-soaked beach, pushing his way through the fishmongers and loincloth-clad porters in a belated effort to intercept his son before departure. We sat in the boat, frozen at the sight of Gryllus standing knee-deep in the receding surf, shaking his fists in rage and howling curses that were mercifully dissolved in the wind by the gods before reaching our ears. In one final, futile gesture of fury at Xenophon's betrayal, Gryllus hurled stone after stone at us, which splashed harmlessly into the water far short of our vessel. It was for no man's sake, least of all Proxenus' or Cyrus', that Xenophon had embarked on his journey toward the Persians, but rather in search of a road that led to Zeus. In seeking out one immortal, however, he left others behind, for he never saw Socrates, or his father, again.

BOOK THREE

THE WARRIORS

Hoards of wealth have I, left behind when I departed
On this ill-starred journey, and yet more shall I bear
home from hence,
Gold and ruddy bronze, and lovely, fair-sashed women,
And gleaming gray iron, all that fell to me as spoils . . .

—HOMER

I

TO THE ACCOMPANIMENT of the groans and rattling chains of the sweat-drenched slaves wielding the oars, the ship bumped to the wharf at Ephesus, the closest port to Sardis though still more than fifty miles distant. I seized our gear, and Xenophon and I leaped onto the quay, not even bothering to take leave of the ship's brutish captain. We quickly wolfed down a few hunks of steaming flat bread slathered with a spicy lentil sauce that I purchased from a nearby vendor, and after a bit of haggling, I bought two healthy Cappadocian asses to carry ourselves and our baggage. In the echo of our journey to Delphi, we spent three days traveling the "King's Highway," the road that ultimately led to the royal city of Susa, on which Sardis was the most important way station. Climbing up from the coastal route, the road passed over bleak, desiccated hills as barren as Aphrodite's marriage to lame Hephaestus. It descended finally into the Cryon valley before taking up the left bank of the Hermus River, which led us directly into the city. Our original plans had been to inquire immediately into the whereabouts of Cyrus' army, but the sights and sounds of this oriental metropolis, the largest city we had ever seen, were so beguiling that we decided to find an appropriate inn and spend a day or two touring before leaving to visit Proxenus.

Sardis did not disappoint. Surrounded by the fertile vineyards and farms through which Xenophon and I had passed while riding into town, the ancient city rose towering from the flat plain, a massive, rock-walled fortress with battered turrets soaring into the sky. Its clamorous markets, the overwhelming odors of the spices and herbal potions sold on every street corner, and the exuberant, thronging citizens from every nation of the world reminded me of Athens in my childhood, before its devastation and impoverishment. It was so long since I had enjoyed the pleasures of a prosperous, optimistic city that even when alone in our rooms, listening to the muffled street sounds outside, I was exhilarated at the prospects waiting just outside my door.

Some three hundred years earlier Sardis, even then a great city, had been overwhelmed by hordes of pale-skinned barbarians who had swept down from the north in endless numbers like packs of ravenous wolves, devouring all its riches and mingling their wild barbarian blood with that of the refined and delicate natives. It was said that so many men and women were killed during the barbarians' brutal sweep through the city that when the carnage was over, thousands of children were left wandering the streets, homeless and wailing. The offspring of royalty mingled with those of the lowest cowherds, and the children's identities were obliterated through the effacement of their outward customs and manners as they scrounged for scraps in the gutters. It was finally decided that no one could determine their origins with certainty, for every child claimed to have been sired by the king, and so they were simply lined up in the market like so much chattel and auctioned to the highest bidder, as slaves of the barbarians or for adoption by surviving Sardesian adults. Since that time, each baby has been imprinted with a tiny, discreet tattoo shortly after birth, usually along the hairline on the nape of the neck, depicting an identifiable family symbol such as an animal or a letter. When walking through the streets, I enjoyed noticing these small signs on young babies riding in slings on their nurses' backs, with their soft, hairless heads slumped forward in sleep.

Under King Croesus, who was said to own as much gold as Midas but who had been cursed by the gods, Sardis was restored and became even more wealthy than in the past. In the last century Sardis, like the rest of Asia Minor, passed over to Persian control, and despite sometimes heavy-handed governance by the king's satraps and descendants, the most recent of whom was the young Cyrus, the city had over the years continued to prosper.

It was from Sardis that Darius and Xerxes had launched their expeditions against the Greeks almost a hundred years earlier, the former's culminating in his defeat at Marathon, the latter's being fatally delayed by the

Spartans at Thermopylae. From here, battles famous in Greek history had been commanded and planned, and soldiers in all three Ionian wars had been drawn chiefly from the region of Sardis and had made their last stand here against Athens' retaliatory raids. We wandered the city's libraries and monuments by day, its taverns and theaters by night, and before I realized how fast time was passing, Xenophon noted that we had spent three weeks, and a considerable quantity of our dwindling supply of silver.

We packed the next day, reclaiming our mules from the stockyard where they had been kept, and within two hours of leaving the city saw the first stockades of the army, fencing thousands of pack animals and their forage, and after that mile after mile of neat rows of military tents, most of leather, some of the cheaper yet more durable canvas now becoming more common among armies. The numbers of troops that had assembled on the plain were astonishing. Proxenus had said in his letter that Cyrus was raising a force to be led by Greek mercenaries to put down an uprising of the Pisidians; but the Pisidians were a backward, barbarian race, and surely their defeat did not require the massive army we saw gathered here before us. This was not the ragtag bunch of worn Spartan mercenaries and hangdog Persian slave soldiers we had expected to see. An indefinable feeling, one of tension and unease, sat low and heavy in the pit of my stomach as we rode through the camp, surrounded on all sides by heavily armed, bearded Persian soldiers who did not even bother to disguise the hostile glances they shot our way.

Xenophon asked the first officer he saw where we might find Proxenus of Boeotia. He looked at our dusty garments in frank appraisal of our intentions, and cautiously directed us toward the center of camp, to general staff headquarters. We wound for an hour through the narrow alleys of tents and thronging soldiers, a camp that was no less an independent and wealthy city than Sardis itself, with its own markets, taverns, baths, and residential sections. We were finally stopped by two enormous Ethiopian guards, wearing leopard skin tunics and carrying eight-foot spears, who informed us in camp Greek that we could not pass into Cyrus' compound without his permission.

Xenophon inquired after Proxenus, and they pointed us to a tent alley nearby, which I found later to be the Greek quarters, and the first officer we encountered, in the first tent we passed, was Proxenus.

Had I simply passed him in the streets I would never have recognized him, but when he locked Xenophon in that familiar bear hug and flashed his old grin at me, I knew that he was still, at heart, the Proxenus we had known years before.

"Xenophon!" he shouted heartily, and gestured to some of his captains to come meet us. "Are you shaving yet? By the gods, look at those shoulders! Gentlemen," he said to his gathering mates, "this handsome young devil is the cousin I've been telling you about. I babysat him in Athens years ago when he still needed his nose wiped, and now look at him—he's on the verge of growing up!"

The men laughed heartily, for Xenophon had indeed grown since Proxenus had last seen him—he now stood half a head taller and twenty pounds heavier than his boyhood friend. Proxenus himself seemed much smaller than I remembered, or perhaps his own growing reputation in my mind had simply not kept pace with his physical stature; but his years fighting with the Spartans had made him into a wary, hardened soldier, tanned and scarred. Much to my amazement, he was also the general of a battle-tested troop of two thousand utterly devoted men whom he had recruited primarily from among his former brigade in the war with Sparta—fifteen hundred hoplites with their attendants, and an additional five hundred light infantry, all of whom looked to him unquestioningly as their leader.

Xenophon grinned happily, slipped the strap supporting his luggage on the mule, and tossed the heavy bundle to Proxenus, who mock-staggered under its weight. "Thank you for the warm welcome, cousin," he said, glancing around at the tents surrounding him. "Conditions are a mite shabby, but I'm sure you'll correct that. Meanwhile, my quarters, please."

Proxenus feigned an expression of insult and ostentatiously dropped the bags on the ground, but then laughed heartily and clapped Xenophon on the back again. "You are truly welcome, cousin, and you too, Theo the Giant," he said, addressing me. "I thought Xenophon had grown, but by the gods, I'd hate to face an army of Syracusans if they're all built like you!" Then speaking seriously to his friends, "I've known Xenophon since he was a boy, and have followed his military career for years. I'm proud to say he is one of the finest cavalry officers ever to be dismissed from Athens' service, and in this day, it is a compliment to have been dismissed by those rump-humpers now in charge over there. Welcome to our campaign, Xenophon; the prince will be pleased."

At this, the men laughed even harder, to Proxenus' consternation, since he was trying to provide a formal introduction to his friend. The irony soon became apparent, however, when he looked away from Xenophon, whom he had just presented as a fine cavalry officer, to the animal on which he had just ridden in—the dusty, swaybacked mule who just at that moment was attempting to uproot a tent peg. Proxenus grinned. "Come with me," he said. "You can wash up and rest from your journey. I have to see to some affairs with my troops tonight, but we'll catch up on old times tomorrow." He led us to the officers' baths, a serious affair befitting the army of the satrap of Sardis, where we spent the rest of the afternoon washing and dozing until one of Proxenus' orderlies arrived to take us to the tent to which we had been assigned.

The next day, Proxenus gave us a tour of the enormous encampment and explained his role in the army. He had served Boeotia energetically during the war, and was especially well known for his expertise in the construction and use of the Boeotian engine. This consisted of a long, straight log, split in two lengthwise, with the two halves carefully hollowed out, lined with iron or tin and then fitted back together into a hollow tube. An enormous bellows was attached to the nether end, and a large iron cauldron containing a blazing mixture of sulfur and pitch hung from the front. The entire contraption was mounted on a cart covered with a heavy plank roof to protect its drivers from enemy arrows and missiles, and when it had been brought sufficiently near the opposing army or its palisades, the bellows were worked, forcing a stream of air through the long tube over the flaming cauldron at the other end, throwing a murderous, sticky flame over its target. Xenophon and I glanced at each other knowingly. This, then, was the "dragon" that Thrasybulus had applied to such murderous effect against us at Phyle. Since its initial use during the war, Proxenus had managed to make numerous improvements to the engine's design, increasing its efficiency, and had even developed portable models that could be taken on campaign, a formal demonstration of which he was eager to give us.

We rode several miles out of camp to a barren place Proxenus used as a testing ground for his engines, far from the stares and comments of the other troops and the city's onlookers. There, a handpicked group of thirty men were responsible for maintaining and firing the engines, the latest version of which consisted of a barrel about twenty feet long and one foot in diameter. They rolled it to the edge of camp, where a training palisades had been set up in imitation of an enemy fortress or barricade. At Proxenus' count, the bellows were expertly inserted and the cauldron hung. While a wooden cap was placed on the front end, the bellows crew pumped a dozen puffs or so into the log to build air pressure. When the pressure had built up sufficiently, it blew the cap off, and as the forced air rushed out, a terrifying stream of flame shot forty feet across the field to the barricade, setting it on fire and scorching the grass along the way, to the bare earth.

Proxenus grinned. "What do you think?"

I was as amazed as I had been the first time, at Phyle. With three or four properly trained and armored troops handling it in close combat, the engine had the destructive force of thirty men.

Xenophon, however, remained skeptical. "But the war is over. What do you intend to do with it—and with your two thousand men? Cyrus surely doesn't need all your Greeks, along with a hundred thousand of his native troops, simply to put down a local uprising?"

"This is just the beginning," Proxenus replied, evading the question. "With a half dozen of these dragon machines, no enemy force will be able to hide from my hoplites behind shields or palisades, especially after they've been softened up a bit by the targeteers. As for the war—you don't think I brought you all this way just for a demonstration, do you?"

As we watched the maneuvers, Xenophon pressed him for more details.

"Prince Cyrus engaged my troops to take on the Pisidians, who are wreaking havoc in the western regions of his province. And we aren't the only Greeks he's recruited. Xenias is already here with another four thousand men-at-arms, and Sophainetos, Socrates the Achaian and Pasion are coming soon with a few thousand more. The 'war with Sparta,' as you call it, did nothing but impoverish us and destroy our morale—and our alliance won! I can't imagine the effect it had on you Athenians. By marching on the Pisidians, with Cyrus and his Persians at our side, we Greeks will have a chance to put aside our past enmity and regain our honor—and we'll fill our pockets besides." Proxenus winked at us, and eyed our mules. "What do you say? Looks like you could stand to capture a new horse, and Theo the Giant here probably wouldn't mind snatching a Syrian dancing girl or two. And you can be sure of getting a proper introduction to Cyrus if you stick close to me."

Xenophon pursed his lips thoughtfully and watched Proxenus' grim, tight-muscled Boeotians maneuvering their engines. He gazed at the hillside in the far distance whence we had ridden that morning, the upper slopes hidden in the dust raised by a hundred thousand head of cattle, horses, goats and sheep, the gently undulating foreslope black with the tens of thousands of the army's massed tents. The destructive potential of the vast array of troops was overwhelming. Cyrus had assembled an enormous mercenary force of battle-hardened and war-hungry veterans, and he was preparing for glory.

As we trotted back to camp in the blazing heat, so different from the damp chill of Athens on the day we had left, Xenophon questioned Proxenus more closely about the prince's intentions.

"As it turns out," Proxenus said, "Cyrus does have one weapon that puts even my engines to shame. Did you know he recruited Clearchus?"

Xenophon looked surprised. "Clearchus—the Spartan general? I'd heard the Spartan Council had sentenced him to death."

"It appears Cyrus has rehabilitated him," Proxenus said dryly.

"Is he at Cyrus' camp now?"

"No, he's collecting additional troops farther east." Then noticing my puzzlement, Proxenus volunteered further information on this mysterious character.

"Clearchus is an exiled Spartan general whom Cyrus much admires for his military skills. He's a military genius, but the biggest asshole in the army. You'll find out why when you meet him. Physically he's a giant, bigger than you, Theo, and is in an evil mood that never ends. He spends all his time stalking about camp and takes pleasure in punishing violations of military discipline. He looks like hell and smells even worse—he munches garlic cloves like grapes and always keeps his pockets full of them. 'Clears the head and fends off the plague,' he says, and the stench of his breath could color the air around him. Before a battle, he spends half a day braiding and oiling his hair, which hangs to the middle of his back. I can't say it improves his appearance any, for all the work he puts into it."

"War isn't a beauty contest," Xenophon chided his cousin. "I don't care if he looks like a Cyclops, so long as he frightens the enemy."

"No need to fear there," Proxenus continued. "The enemy will be pissing on their sandals if he comes within a hundred yards of them, especially if he's upwind. As repulsive as he is, there's no man on earth as competent in battle."

He rode on in silence for a few minutes.

"You think I'm fond of war," he continued, "because I signed on with Cyrus without even a pause after Athens and Sparta made peace. Well, Clearchus has been moving from war to war for the past thirty years. The man can't live without war. He eats war and sleeps it. His men are terrified of him, but they follow him blindly and defend him to the death against any comments by outsiders, so watch what you say about him in front of others. You should thank the gods you'll be serving under me—Clearchus and his officers refuse even to use tents. They sleep in the open in the foulest weather, live on rancid bread and that disgusting Spartan 'black broth,' and ignore women, whether camp prostitutes or their own wives. His men use their shields as pillows and sleep with their spears, and each other, for comfort. I asked him about that once, thinking he was putting himself through hardship just for show, to keep up that insufferable Spartan image. He's Cyrus' top general, after all; he doesn't need to sleep in the mud. He scoffed at this. 'Shit,' he said, 'every lame-assed water boy with a grudge and every harem wench pissed off at Cyrus for sleeping with a different harem wench knows where to find him at night. That's why Cyrus needs thirty guards around his tent. And who can trust the guards? Thanks, I'll sleep in the mud.' "

"So how did Clearchus fall in with the prince?" Xenophon interrupted. "From what you say, there are no two men on earth more unalike."

"It's a bit complicated. Believe me, there is no love lost between those two, but they exploit each other for their own purposes. Clearchus approached the prince a year ago, about the same time I did. He was looking for a patron, and Cyrus knew that he was a brilliant soldier, and even better, that he was an outlaw—no chance of him losing heart and running back home to Sparta for his mother if things got tough. Cyrus gave him ten thousand *darics*"—here both Xenophon and I gasped, as this was a huge fortune—"to recruit a mercenary army, and Clearchus didn't spend an ounce of it on himself, although the prince would hardly have minded if he had. When word spread that he was paying good money for veteran soldiers, recruits began showing up in droves from every corner of the Greek world—every exiled, disillusioned, disgraced, hard-bitten Greek veteran that wanted a new start in life applied to Clearchus. He picked the cream of these men, paid them in advance, and trained an army, supposedly to suppress the Thracians, who had been marauding some of Cyrus' cities in the northwest. The Spartan elders sentenced him to death for pursuing an unauthorized war in disobedience of their orders—in Sparta that's a charge tantamount to treason. Clearchus didn't give a shit. He's like a hound tearing at a boar, he's unable to stop making war, and Sparta doesn't have enough wars to fight to keep him busy anymore.

"In any case, you've already seen some of his troops. He outfitted them all in new bronze helmets with horsehair plumes and scarlet cloaks—they all look like Spartan Peers. He armed them with those wicked short swords, new bronze shields and breastplates, and imported some drill sergeants from Sparta to put them through field training. Damn near killed them, and half of them were mustered out as being unfit. But within six months Clearchus had whipped the remainder into the strongest standing army in the Greek world short of Sparta's itself, and you can bet that young Cyrus is pleased. Everywhere the troops march the people fall on their knees and call them 'Cyrus' Greeks.' Well, Cyrus' Greeks whet their blades by destroying the Thracians, and now Clearchus is up-country collecting more soldiers. We'll be meeting up with them later on the march."

We rode along silently, digesting this portrait of our future colleague. I knew that Xenophon would be torturing himself with the irony of the situation. He had enlisted in the only viable Greek army short of Sparta's, at least partially with a view to redeeming his and his father's names—only to find himself serving with a man who was one of Athens' most hated enemies, a man whom Gryllus would sooner have spit on and cursed to three generations than have his son fight under. How strangely the gods ordain things, that the destinies of men as disparate as Clearchus and Xenophon are made to cross paths. One wonders whether Zeus had such a circumstance in mind when he offered Xenophon such favorable omens for traveling to Sardis. It is difficult to imagine that it was not foreseen.

Within three days of our arrival at Cyrus' camp, Proxenus had officially enlisted Xenophon as an officer and his personal aide-de-camp, and I was fitted for light cavalry armor and weaponry, and assigned the duty of bearing his brigade's pennant, a black flag depicting a snake shooting flame from its mouth. It was a role with which I was very pleased.

II

PROXENUS, XENOPHON, AND I entered the prince's compound, warily eyeing Cyrus' fierce-looking guards. Some thirty of these giants, seemingly chosen as much for their aesthetic qualities as for their strength and fearsomeness, were on duty at a single shift. Precisely half consisted of Ethiopians, with skin so black as to be almost blue, their huge heads shaved bald and polished by beeswax into shiny knobs decorated with a patterned system of raised tattoos. They carried enormous Persian scimitars and wore baggy pantaloons in the Persian style, and kept their massive chests bare, emphasizing the preternatural darkness of their skin. The other half of the guards, who were arranged in alternating order with the black Ethiopians around the tent, were enormous Scythians, pale of skin to the point of pinkness, almost albino, with shaved jaws and long, drooping mustaches. Twisted ropes of yellow hair hung to their waists, bound with colored strings, and they wore long, straight swords with wrought hilts, and gold-plated, snake-patterned bands on their biceps. Though both races were astonishing to look at, even to cosmopolitan Athenians like ourselves, the Scythians attracted particular attention, even though members of that tribe had long been employed in Athens as a mercenary police force. Scythian soldiers had been known to drink the blood of the men they killed in battle, and to take the scalps of their enemies by making a circular cut around the head above the ears, grasping the hair and then simply shaking the skull out the bottom, leaving the victim, whether dead or yet living, with a bloody, smooth-domed caul. Such scalps were required to be presented to their king for a share of any plunder, and were then tanned and hung from the soldier's bridle rein as mementos. If they were sufficient in number, they might even be sewn together into cloaks or arrow quivers. Such a fate was a terrible prospect to a Greek, who could not imagine presenting himself to the Boatman after death absent his hair, and possibly with skin from other parts of his body flayed and mounted in unspeakable fashion on a barbarian's kit. These men, alternating ranks of Scythians and Ethiopians, were Cyrus' personal bodyguard, and they eyed us suspiciously as we shouldered past them into Cyrus' tent.

Having heard so much about the prince, I was curious to meet him. Only twenty-four years old, Cyrus spoke flawless Attic Greek and Persian, as well as a half dozen other languages of the countries under his domain, and he was as well versed in the writings of the philosophers and men of science of both east and west as many others who had spent their entire lifetimes gaining such knowledge. His appearance was a study in contrasts: He was slight of build, beardless, and kept his chestnut-colored hair long and flowing in an unaffected style, quite unlike the pompous and effeminate, carefully coiffed nobles who served as his advisors and senior officers. The natural handsomeness of his face and the even olive color of his chest and arms was marred by a series of deep scars which Proxenus explained had been given him by an enraged she-bear in a hunt several years before. On the day of our audience with him, he was dressed quite plainly, even severely, in a short ceremonial robe with a military tunic underneath, a combination that would allow him to meet with anyone from diplomats and generals to the lowest private without wasting time changing clothes. This unpretentious demeanor greatly endeared him to his troops as well as to his civilian subjects. His arms were bare, exposing a long white scar running the length of his left tricep—whether from an earlier battle or from his brush with the bear I do not know. His robe was simple, with barely an inch of purple embroidery along the border, but was of the finest-combed Milesian wool. His sandals, though dusty, were of polished and stamped Egyptian leather with gold clasps. Cyrus' plain though elegant dress was that of a man who knows only one stall in the market—the very best.

The prince had been born after his father Darius had come to the throne as Great King of Persia, and so Cyrus ascribed to the ancient Persian tradition that he outranked his brother Artaxerxes who, though thirty years older, had been born while his father was still a mere subject. But the Great

King, for reasons to which I was not privy, thought differently. He had arranged for the succession to revert to Artaxerxes, leaving Cyrus in the comparatively minor position of satrap of Ionia, equal in rank to a wily old scoundrel named Tissaphernes, who governed farther south in Asia Minor. Cyrus and Tissaphernes went back a long way—Tissaphernes had married Artaxerxes' daughter, making the old man a sort of relative to the prince, a nephew by marriage. He had also been a close advisor to King Darius, a constant presence in the courts and even in the royal family's living quarters, and Cyrus had detested the sway that the unctuous and crafty counselor held over his father. Three years earlier, sensing that the prince's power and influence were growing, Tissaphernes had denounced him on trumped-up charges to Artaxerxes, who had Cyrus arrested and ordered executed. Cyrus' mother saved his life and arranged for his removal from the court and his satrapy in Ionia, but the rage and humiliation Cyrus experienced from the episode had never left him. He now perceived the quest for power as an obsession, and the elimination of Tissaphernes and Artaxerxes as a ruling passion.

After entering Cyrus' tent with Proxenus and Xenophon I lingered near the door, while the other two advanced to Cyrus' chair and table. Cyrus amiably asked them to stand at ease, while he finished up some current business he had with his advisors. Since this was the first time I had ever visited the quarters of a wealthy Persian, I glanced around curiously, taking in the rich carpets and brocaded drapes, which kept the tent refreshingly dark and cool, and the heavily armed guards standing at motionless attention on either side of the door.

A tall, aquiline beauty slouched languorously behind Cyrus, gently fanning him with a large wicker screen and occasionally whispering orders to various serving girls and guards who kept up a never-ending parade of activity in the shadows between the table and a low rear exit, which communicated with another chamber of the tent. This consort, though breathtakingly beautiful, looked completely bored, and did not deign to make eye contact with any other person in the room.

I heard a rustling in the shadows in the opposite corner, though, and when I looked more closely, I noticed two dark, almond-shaped eyes peering at me with interest, coolly appraising me, and not averting themselves from my gaze as the eyes of Persian women usually did. I held their stare for long seconds, and was finally rewarded by the flashing of white teeth in a quick, shy smile as the girl silently giggled at her own audacity. She leaned forward slightly, her face emerging from the shadows into a thin beam of sunlight invading the tent through a open flap, and my heart stopped at her beauty—she was perhaps eighteen years old, her skin fresh and seemingly unmarred by any additional cosmetics, her only adornment being a bright yellow feather threaded carefully through her hair. Her face revealed an innocence and joy of expression that belied her inexplicable presence in Cyrus' tent, surrounded by fierce-faced Ethiopian guards and the bustling of military couriers. She smiled at me once more, then turned back to her task in the shadows—which I now saw involved handling a thick scroll. This astonished me more than anything else about her, for never before had I seen a woman reading.

Cyrus' advisors left after a few moments, and Proxenus stepped forward casually to the prince's table, informing him that he had brought a friend who was joining the expedition.

"Well done, Proxenus," the prince exclaimed. "Between you and Clearchus I'll have half of Greece fighting for me before we're through!" He flashed a friendly grin. "Xenophon of Athens, son of Gryllus?"

Xenophon seemed momentarily taken aback, but quickly recovered and stiffly replied, "Yes, sir."

Cyrus stood looking at him for a moment in some amusement. "At ease, my man! By the gods, who do you think I am, King of Persia? I've heard much of your father—all reports of the very highest order, I assure you, though I don't imagine he would say the same about me." The prince chuckled and stood up to walk around his table to where we stood. I was surprised to note how short he was. I somehow always imagine men's influence to match their height, and never fail to be disappointed at how modest in stature most great men are, or for that matter, how tall I am.

"I understand you're a follower of Socrates of Athens?" Cyrus asked. Xenophon glanced questioningly at Proxenus, surprised again to find how much Cyrus already knew of him, but Proxenus gave a slight shrug as if to say that he was on his own with his responses. "Indeed, you have company here among us," continued Cyrus. "One of my Athenian generals, Menon, is also a disciple of his—perhaps you know him? I regret never having had the opportunity to sit at the great man's knee myself, as I have never been to Athens and Socrates has refused all invitations to visit me here in Sardis. But Menon has been kind enough to repeat for me as much as he can recall. Indeed, I was most impressed with Socrates' justification of a soldier's life, and I am told that Socrates himself is an old veteran, and a well-regarded one, besides. As I recall, he said that to fall in battle is in many ways a desirable thing. A man is granted a splendid funeral, worthy of an *archon,* even if he dies poor, and though penniless, he is praised by great orators, who do not offer compliments lightly."

Cyrus paused for a moment to murmur something to his tall consort, who slipped away through the rear flap without a word, and then he turned back with his broad grin. "In any event, there will be no danger of any of my men dying in penury," he laughed. "And," he said, looking straight at Xenophon, "I'm delighted to have a man of culture in my camp. The Spartans are the most dour, ignorant mob of bullies you can imagine, and frankly, Proxenus, your Boeotians are a bunch of country jackasses, though I'll admit your engines are a marvel. Xenophon, I hope your duties won't be so heavy that you can't find the time to join me for some good Greek wine in the evenings, to tell me what your friend Socrates' latest outrages are that have your city's leaders so riled up." Cyrus began to walk us to the door of his tent.

"I'd be delighted to join you at any time, your lordship," Xenophon replied stiffly.

"So," said Cyrus with a wry smile, "I presume that Proxenus has found an appropriate position for you in our little army? Something that will loosen you up, I hope, before you turn into a Spartan yourself. I can't promise more than a daric or two a month as pay, but you can count on wealth beyond your imagining in the form of booty, if we are successful."

Xenophon considered how to respond as the three of us left the tent together, but hearing the sound of steel sliding on leather, I turned to find that the prince, with a playful grin, had drawn his sword and was brandishing its tip under Xenophon's chin. Proxenus looked on in barely controlled alarm.

Before anyone could move, some passing, mischievous godlet, some playful spawn of a satyr who was eavesdropping on our conversation, triggered the defensive reflexes I had developed during the long ephebe training in Athens. Without thinking I stepped in front of Cyrus and gave him a tremendous blow to the wrist with the heel of my hand. His sword went flying high in the air, impaling itself in the roof of his tent and eliciting a small, frightened shriek from within, and as I finished my swipe, I placed a hammerlock with my forearm around the prince's neck. In a trice, eight enormous Ethiopian guards had locked their spear points into position inches away from my face, but I fixed my eyes on Xenophon's, as I had been trained to do, as if in a trance, waiting for him to give the word before I broke the neck of the Prince of Persia. It was only then that my reasoning caught up with my body, the nasty satyr scampered away chuckling, and I realized with horror what I had done.

Xenophon was petrified and hoarsely ordered me to let go, with visions of spending the rest of his life in a Persian dungeon before he had even started on his adventure; but Cyrus, after the initial moment of shock, burst out laughing.

"Well done!" the good-natured prince exclaimed as I let him go. Proxenus was white as a sheet. Cyrus rubbed his wrist and babbled incomprehensibly to his guards, telling them in their barbarian tongue not to skewer us. "I asked for that one! I meant to show you that if you're going to do battle against Asians, you'll have to get used to treachery. I should have known that the Spartans aren't the only fighters in my camp. If you surprise the enemy as well as you did me, you'll be a general before the year is out!"

Proxenus glared, but I could see a wave of relief wash over his face at the happy outcome of the mock attack, and perhaps a glimmer of pride. Cyrus clapped his hands on the two men's shoulders as he walked us back to our quarters, while I walked alongside, and Proxenus kept a wary eye trained on me to be sure I didn't further endanger his livelihood.

"Proxenus, we're marching in three days. Find Xenophon any armor and weapons he needs, and make sure he has a horse to ride instead of that mule I'm told he straggled into camp on. And don't neglect our touchy friend here," he said, nodding at me. "If there's anyone in this camp I want to keep happy it's him!" And flashing another of his grins, he strode off through the tent alleys, to the approval of his men and the exasperation of his trailing counselors and bodyguards.

That evening, after the day's business was complete and Xenophon, Proxenus and I were washing up in the officers' bath, I mentioned the brief vision I had had of the lovely girl in Cyrus' tent. Proxenus looked at me strangely for a moment, then sighed.

"So you're in lust with Asteria. Line up behind the rest of us."

Xenophon looked questioningly at him, and then quietly admitted, "I saw her too. Reading, no less."

Proxenus grunted. "She's a rare bird all right. Cyrus keeps an entire harem, of course—even travels with them on campaign, and it's usually that tall Phocaian bitch, the one standing behind him, that keeps his dog happy." He smirked for emphasis. "But it's Asteria the Milesian, the one you noticed, who is his favorite. She stays in his tent all the time, I hear, though not for the reasons you might think. And she's not a concubine—remember that at all costs. Cyrus once had a steward flogged for calling her one. Men say she's the daughter of one of old King Darius' satraps, and that she's somehow related to Cyrus as well—a niece or a cousin. She was raised in the harem in Persia along with the king's own children. She speaks Greek better than I do, recites Homer aloud when the prince wants to relax, and plays the lyre like a goddess. She also knows the medical arts, from studying with the king's physicians. I'm told she nursed Cyrus back to health after his bear adventure, when his own doctors had given him up for dead. Go ahead and admire her, but take care it's from a distance. If Cyrus catches you even looking cross-eyed at her, you'll be joining the ranks of his eunuchs faster than you can say, 'Bless me Uranus.' I have yet to meet a woman who's worth that."

Thus my first contact with Asteria, a girl who could read Homer, and who was to have such an impact on the rest of my life. Had I entered Cyrus' tent twenty minutes before or later, or had I not peered curiously into the dark corner, it is entirely possible I never would have looked into those kohl-lined eyes. So much of the future hangs upon the most ephemeral of webs spun by the Fates, the remote likelihood that one of a thousand possible results will be chosen by the deities. If a man were ever able to unravel such threads, he would have finally solved the mystery of the universe and attained the wisdom of the gods. In so doing, however, he would be struck down by those very deities in defense of their existence, as was Icarus upon approaching the sun.

Perhaps it is best to resolve not even to try to unravel those threads; but such resignation flies in the face of one's own humanity. It is a quandary.

III

OUR DEPARTURE FROM Sardis on the ninth day of March was splendid, a day of sunshine and confidence, and the entire city turned out along the route to view the spectacle. The men began marching at first light, and by midday not even half the enormous army had taken to the road yet. The tremendous cloud of dust raised by the tramping feet obscured the sun so that no one could see the entire army in a glance, but watching the thousands upon thousands of solemn faces as the troops passed by in their wide columns gave sufficient indication of power as to impress even the gods. Only Clearchus and his most recently recruited troops were absent, as they would be joining us later on the march.

The procession was led by long trains of surly pack camels, followed by herds of goat and sheep for the daily sacrifices, to obtain the gods' favor before battle and hazardous river crossings. These were followed by big-eyed, lowing oxen trailing enormous wagons laden with the troops' heavy equipment and supplies. The animals' early lead would allow them and the gear to arrive at the daily campsites first and begin seeking forage, and would allow the quartermaster's slaves to start setting up tents and cook sites for the arriving troops. The oxen were followed by forty elephants, which Cyrus had acquired from Indian traders. They were the first such beasts I had ever seen, and were fearsome, seemingly holdovers from the age of the Titans. They stood as tall as a small tree and were hairless and wrinkled, from a distance appearing to have a tail at both ends. If one didn't know better, they would seem to be walking backwards, although I soon learned that the large, flapping ears were a reasonably accurate indicator as to the location of the head. These creatures, however, were merely for show during the grand departure from Sardis. The forage they would have required would have been too difficult to support during a normal march, so after the grand review was finished, Cyrus ordered them to be circled back to the city to continue assisting in the construction of its defensive works.

Cyrus' native troops followed next: a hundred thousand Persians, Lydians, Egyptians and even Ethiopians, bedecked in their own country's armor and clothing, each with their individual drummers and pipers to keep the marching feet in rhythm, their native officers shouting orders in barbaric tongues. The pennants and standards of the native brigades flew proudly, and each unit tried to outdo the others during this lead march out of Sardis before the prince's watchful eyes.

Behind the infantry, led by the prince himself, rode the Persian cavalry, thousands of identical white Arabian stallions, prancing and snorting, their proud riders sitting erect and motionless, wearing pointed bronze helmets and chain mail that glittered in the sun like the squamae of fish. Surrounding them were ranks of pantalooned Medes marching in perfect precision, bearing gilded and bejeweled lances topped with silken banners woven in the form of dragons; as the breeze blew through their gaping jaws, they seemed to hiss with rage, their long tails fluttering behind them on the wind. Following the cavalry, in the place of honor usually reserved for the general's bodyguard, came the proud Greeks, marching in unison, their scarlet cloaks fluttering in the breeze and the long, oiled braids of the Spartans among them carefully dressed and flowing down their backs. It would have been wonderful to roll out a walking display of Proxenus' Boeotian engines, but the crowd was too pressing for it to be safe, and Clearchus, who detested the machines in any case, had vetoed any discussion of the matter among his captains, even during his temporary absence. Proxenus and Xenophon, along with the other officers, rode alongside the columns of marching troops, though not so much to keep them in order as to keep the crowds contained. So enthused were the onlookers by this time that it was difficult to restrain the women and girls from flitting into the columns to plant kisses on the men's faces, or the male bystanders from thumping our Greeks stoutly on the shoulders in a jubilant display of well-wishing and hope for success against the upstart Pisidians.

Following close behind were Cyrus' six hundred cavalry bodyguard, his "Immortals," in demeanor and discipline every bit as fearsome as the Greeks. These men were handpicked from every nation under Persian dominion, but were uniformed and armed identically, and had been trained for years to serve no personal desire and to favor no master before their duty of protecting Cyrus. They were somewhat put out at having to march behind the Greeks in the army's column, but during the course of the next few months, Clearchus made special efforts to ingratiate himself with them, as far, at least, as he was capable, given his lack of social skills. Eventually the Greeks and Cyrus' Immortals gained a grudging respect for each other.

The rear of the column consisted of more native infantry and the army's twenty "scythe chariots," the curved blades on their hubs sheathed for safety but still cutting ominously through the air, to the delight of the crowd and the utter disdain of the Spartans, who loathed any such gimmickry. Behind this was Cyrus' personal retinue, an enormous mob: the quartermaster general, with his ninety subalterns, responsible for billeting and feeding the troops; a company of haughty horsemen, couriers for the prince and the senior officers; and carriages bearing dozens of Persian seers, priests and their assistants. They were accompanied by an equal number of vehicles loaded with their supplies: lavish robes and other garments, ceremonial knives, chalices, incense, scrolls, and vessels. Next were the covered wagons bearing the royal wardrobes, which despite their size were dwarfed by those bearing the wardrobes of the Persian generals, much to the scoffing and hilarity of the Greeks. The importance of the marchers and goods declined rapidly from this point: fifty empty carriages and wagons used for reserve, an entire herd of unmounted horses, each led by a Persian boy in pantaloons and slippers, and an unending parade of vehicles reserved for the prince's concubines, valets, physicians, barbers, footmen, apothecaries, scribes, porters, tailors, laundry women, the head cook and his fourteen assistants, the prince's taster and two replacement tasters, engineers, historians—one's head spins.

After this came the real show—the enormous, straggling, jeering and cheering crowd of camp followers—leather tanners, con artists, prostitutes, water sellers, musicians, jugglers, seamstresses, money changers, laundry women, wives and children of the soldiers themselves, and a horde of beggars and tramps trailing behind, a complete representation of the entire lower strata of Persian and Greek society, a veritable city of thousands, half again as many as the soldiers themselves, who made their living serving and fleecing the army by day and entertaining it by night, or perhaps the other way around. They were despised by the officers and army regulars, but ultimately tolerated and even protected, because otherwise the services they provided would have to be rendered by the troops themselves, and trained fighting men were too valuable to be wasted on mundane camp tasks.

I shall not go into excessive detail regarding the daily progress of our march. For the most part the routine was uneventful. Cyrus had arranged for sufficient provisions from the outset, so we were not dependent upon foraging from the countryside as we passed through. Consequently, our arrival in each city and village was not feared by the inhabitants, but was instead an occasion for cautious celebration. The prince traveled with an ever-present chest of copper coins, which he would toss in handfuls to the crowds on either side, with the expansive gestures of a benevolent father. The crowds would mill frantically around the caravan, competing with the native company of beggars from Sardis, and create an uproar as they scrambled in the dust for the tiny coins that became trampled underfoot. Cyrus and his minions rode past, solemn, imperious, only the occasional tight-lipped smile breaking the gravity of their demeanor, watching as their subjects rolled in the filth at the feet of their horses.

Thus we traveled steadily eastward across the length of Asia Minor, in good weather and order, the men challenged every day by Cyrus' insistence on readiness and drilling, and by daily inspections of our equipment and weapons. We tramped straight into the heart of Pisidia—though contrary to our expectations of battle and plunder, we fired not a single arrow nor captured any enemy territory. The prince disdainfully ignored the barbarian warriors lined up warily along the ridge tops, watching our enormous trains of baggage, our servants, and our camp followers in awe. Five weeks into the march, we stopped at one of the Great King's palaces on the River Meander, which we used for a month as a way station to regroup and retrain, and to resettle the baggage. It was here, legend has it, that Apollo punished the leering satyr Marsyas, who had challenged the god to a music match. Apollo played his lyre upside-down and demanded that Marsyas match this feat with his flute, which of course he was unable to do. After flaying the foolish satyr alive, Apollo hung his skin on the wall of a nearby cave, whence comes the source of a small but wild local river fittingly named the Marsyas.

It was here, too, that the long-awaited Clearchus joined us with the remaining core of the army he had raised earlier with Cyrus' darics, a thousand fierce and silent scarlet-cloaked Spartan men-at-arms, each with two or three *helot* slaves to carry their heavy armor and weapons. He also brought eight hundred broad-shouldered Thracian targeteers who had defected to his forces, and two hundred Cretan bowmen. These were to form the hard-muscled center of Cyrus' Greek army, over which Clearchus himself was general, the counterpart to a Persian named Ariaius who commanded Cyrus' native forces. Clearchus was as terrifying an individual as Proxenus had led us to believe, and worse. His face was so homely and pockmarked as to be almost comical, but he had an evil, jagged scar running halfway down the side of his temple, which he was constantly picking at, keeping it inflamed, perhaps intentionally, for effect. His beard was so ragged and lice-infested as to raise eyebrows even for a Spartan, and he never smiled—in fact, he hardly even talked except to cuss out his men, and could barely chew for the rotten blackness of his teeth. He rode disdainfully among his troops, scarcely deigning to show obeisance to Cyrus, but his new recruits marched in perfect unison, without a single wasted movement or word, showing little concern and even less curiosity at the hundred thousand native troops gathered to watch their arrival. They followed Clearchus' smallest gesture and command as closely as if they were a single machine—a war machine, one begotten in turn by a determined god.

During the army's reorganization here at the Meander, Clearchus, surveying the situation, flew into a fury and demanded that the quantity of baggage and camp followers be drastically reduced—the Spartans refused to fight to protect clothing wagons, flute girls and kitchen staff. Cyrus resisted for a time, although when Clearchus threatened to march away with the troops he had just brought, the prince acquiesced in part, cutting the baggage train and followers by half, and paying the latter in gold to return to their homes. He insisted, however, in the face of much Spartan grumbling, on keeping a small coterie of slave girls and attendants—the prince was Persian, and had appearances to keep up.

In view of what the Fates had in store for me, I cannot say whether the prince's stubbornness in this affair was to my benefit or not, though his decision had as great an impact on my life as any decree from the gods, or from the Spartans, for that matter.

Clearchus be damned.

IV

THE RAGGED, BAREFOOT BOY sat on a boulder at the side of the trail, staring steadily into the distance as he methodically reached into the leather pouch at his hip, picking out grubs he had collected from beneath logs and roots, and munching them one by one. Not that I had ever been especially fond of the grubs and grasshoppers I myself had eaten as a slave in Athens—they filled the belly, barely, and that was about all one could say in their favor—but the fact that this boy was eating them so systematically indicated that they were a mainstay of his diet, not a supplement as they had been for me, and I sympathized with him.

For an hour Xenophon and I had been riding through the narrow gorge of the Meander, picking our way carefully upriver along a rocky trail ripe for twisting a horse's knee or laming its foot. We were seeking a crossing point that our guides had said was to be found nearby, but had seen nothing but the ruins of two rope-and-log bridges that the locals had recently cut, apparently in an attempt to hinder the army's progress. In fact, the army was not even following that path—Cyrus had no interest in pursuing minor tribes of nomadic herdsmen into the interior mountains. Still, our herds had been harassed lately by Pisidian raiding parties, and Xenophon had volunteered to go out in search of a path by which a more heavily armed band of hoplites might later be sent to frighten them away. Proxenus had consented, and assigned to us an interpreter named Cleon, and two Boeotian scouts.

We had to speak loudly to be heard above the roaring of the water, which rushed in a torrent through the narrow gap it had been cutting for the past several miles. On our right was a steep, gravelly hill, almost a cliff, unclimbable, riddled with the holes of an enormous colony of rodents that had constructed a vast network of tunnels beneath the surface. Small spills of flaking shale and debris occasionally tumbled down in front of or behind us as we passed, startling us into thinking that someone must be above us at the top of the ridge; yet whenever we looked, we saw only the pock-marked gravel and the occasional small furry head peaking stealthily out of a hole.

Seeing the boy sitting out here alone, I signaled for Xenophon to stop, and we pulled our horses up alongside, looking at him curiously. He ignored us completely, or feigned unawareness of our presence. He could not have been more than nine or ten years old, and I wondered how he had come to be here, for I saw no signs of any Pisidian encampment nearby. His cheeks were drawn in hunger, and his eyes hollow. The skin around his mouth was filthy, as if he had gorged on honey some time before and neglected to wash afterwards, allowing the dirt to collect around his lips and mingle with the steady stream of snot from his nose that he seemed to have no inclination to wipe off.

Xenophon and I looked at each other. "Is the boy right in the head?" I asked. He shrugged, and called over Cleon to help us communicate.

Cleon was a tall, rangy fellow with weak eyes and odd, bushy hair, a Pisidian who had been captured in a Persian raid years ago, but had become thoroughly Persianized since. He looked at the child disdainfully and barked a question at him. The boy showed no inkling of understanding, neglecting to even blink or glance at him; he merely continued to stolidly chew and pop the glistening white larvae. The interpreter asked something else, to equal effect, then shrugged his shoulders.

"He is an imbecile," Cleon said. "Either that or deaf and mute."

"It would be useful if we could get him to talk," said Xenophon, thoughtfully gazing at the urchin. "He clearly knows the country, or he would not be sitting here so comfortably. He must know if there are any crossings close at hand."

He swung off his horse and I did the same, welcoming the chance to stretch my legs. Xenophon sat down on the boulder beside the boy, rummaging through the pack he carried slung across the horse's haunches.

Removing a chunk of roast boar left over from a hunting expedition two days before, he held it out to the famished child.

The boy's eyes flickered as he caught the scent of the meat, and he turned his head slowly to look into Xenophon's face. Almost faster than I could see, his hand shot out, and without even looking at the meat, he snatched it and in one swift motion stuffed it into his leather pouch. He intended it for later consumption, I suppose, because he then turned his gaze back to its previous target over the river, and resumed his slow chewing of the grubs.

"I'm not sure what that tells us," said Xenophon, puzzled. He motioned Cleon down from his horse too, and he looped the reins of all three over the twisted branches of a small shrub. The two Boeotians waited patiently fifty yards behind us along the trail, making their own snack and chatting quietly with each other.

"Speak to him more kindly," Xenophon said. "Don't demand to know where the crossing is. Just ask him what he is waiting for."

Cleon scowled, then with great effort softened his expression to a resigned grimace. He squatted beside the boy and questioned him for several minutes, but again to no avail. Just as he was standing up, however, the boy said something briefly in his language, only two or three words. Cleon stood looking at him motionless, as if waiting for more, but the boy had evidently said his piece and would speak no further. He shrugged.

"The boy says he is waiting for Death."

Xenophon looked more closely at the boy's face. "That's strange," he said. "He looks hungry, maybe, but nowhere near death. I wonder what he meant."

Just then, another trickle of gravel slid down and landed at our feet. We had learned to ignore these small slides, but the boy glanced down nervously at the rocks that had fallen before us. The small quantity of gravel was followed by a more substantial fall, this time involving several rocks of a size that could bruise a leg if they were to make a direct hit. I looked up to the top of the ridge, but saw nothing. The boy, however, had hopped down from his perch on the boulder and stood facing us, shifting from foot to foot.

"He looks as if he's about to say something now," I said, for he had opened his mouth and begun to speak, but his words were suddenly drowned by a crash and a deafening, sickening roar. When I looked up I saw that the entire shale cliff-face had split from its underlying structure, like bark sloughing off a rotten tree, had broken into enormous chunks, and was hurtling down upon us.

There was no time to seize our weapons, or to even think—one could only move. Xenophon and I leaped to the trail and raced forward, unthinking, seeking only to beat the crashing rocks we could hear tumbling down from the precipice above us, tearing out shrubs, boulders, everything in their path. Showers of dust, gravel and small rocks were falling about our heads and shoulders, and we seemed to be running impossibly slow, as one does in a nightmare. Within seconds we had skidded around a sharp bend, where the path clung closely to a corner of the cliff, and we realized that barring a collapse of the entire mountain, we were out of the course of the slide and were safe. We pressed our faces and chests against the rock wall, digging in with our fingernails, panting and gasping not from exhaustion, for the run had only been a few yards, but from the soul-purging effect of sheer terror.

For several minutes we listened as the rocks roared down the wall around the corner beyond our vision, slamming into the trail with a deafening crash. Hitting the flat ledge of the trail, the boulders paused briefly, as if to consider their position, then continued their frantic journey, crashing over the side of the lower wall and tumbling into the river below with a great splash of yellowish spray and foam. After a moment the roaring stopped as quickly as it had begun, and we stepped gingerly around our protective corner to witness the destruction.

The trail had been completely obliterated. No sign of life or human activity was evident, and the place where Cleon and our horses had been standing a moment before was piled twenty feet high with huge boulders. Dust hung heavily in the air, making it difficult to see and even to breathe, and the cliff face, which had before been a steep, almost vertical angle, now exhibited a great depression or cave, the depth of which could still not be clearly seen through the dust.

Over the steady throbbing of the river, however, we heard voices—not those of our own party, as we thought at first, but rather young voices—and looking up to the top of the ridge, we saw a line of perhaps fifty figures standing on the crest. The angle of the sun silhouetted them, so we were unable to identify their clothing or appearance, but from their build they looked to be boys—some as young as the one to whom we had spoken, others slightly older. Peering down from the ridge top, they cheered and waved at the destruction, which we now saw had been their own device. Several of the bigger youths were still holding the stout poles they had used as levers to force down boulders from the top and start the slide. The effect must have been even greater than they had originally hoped.

"Pisidians," Xenophon spat. "They ambushed us. We should have listened to the boy. He was waiting for death, he said. Ours. Look!"—and pointing halfway up the hill we saw the same boy energetically leaping and pulling himself from rock to rock up the side of the face, apparently having taken shelter from the slide under his boulder and emerged no worse for wear. How, I wondered, does a boy practice for something like that?

By now, the ruffians on the ridge had seen us, and were howling in outrage at their failure to destroy us with their onslaught. Half the band immediately disappeared, no doubt to take one of their secret trails down the side to finish us off where we stood, while the others began probing frantically with their levers, loosening more rocks and gravel and threatening to send another shower of boulders raining down on us.

Xenophon quickly pushed past me and skidded back around the corner where we had first taken shelter, to see what our options were in that direction. The trail behind us, from which we had come, was impassible. The trail forward was already filling with the shouts of angry boys descending to where we stood. An ominous trickle of gravel was beginning to fall on our heads from above. Xenophon looked at me, wild-eyed, and without a word we both began ripping off our armor, while at the same time half-scrambling, half-tumbling down the steep slope below us, hoping to ease into the river before we were crushed by another avalanche.

"Easing in" was not exactly what transpired, for at that point the river was flowing through a narrow defile with sheer rock faces extending twenty feet above the surface of the foaming water. We paused briefly at the lip, and with a quick prayer to the gods to recall to us the swimming skills we had learned as boys at Erchia, we leaped.

Eight hours later, to the astonishment of the sentries, we limped into camp, naked but for our sandals, covered with deep cuts, bruises, and thorn scratches. Half an hour of battering and near drowning in the roiling river had brought us four miles back downstream, safely out of reach of the

Pisidians, but a long trek still from our camp, which we did not reach until dusk. Proxenus had already set about sorrowfully making funeral preparations for us, having been told in great detail by the two terrified Boeotian scouts of our gruesome deaths. He was overjoyed at our return and feted us far into the night with meat and uncut wine, begging us over and over to relate how we had leaped into the river to escape. Word of our adventure even made its way that evening to Cyrus, who had also been told of our untimely deaths, and who stopped by Proxenus' tent to congratulate us on evading this fate.

"Your return is a good omen for the army!" he exclaimed. "I have told the quartermaster to issue you new horses—you can arrange that in the morning. Meanwhile . . . by Zeus, Theo, take a look at that gash!" And he spent the rest of the evening with us, comparing his own scars with ours, and laughing at the likely reaction of the Pisidian boys when they descended their mountain and found we had disappeared.

About poor Cleon nothing more was ever said; but his loss was not a great one, for he was only an interpreter.

After leaving the Meander, we marched another one hundred and fifty uneventful miles further east, Cyrus celebrating and entertaining local dignitaries as we passed, until we arrived at the vast Plain of Caystros, where the army gathered like a huge flock of noisy crows, wheeling, strutting, and shouting orders and insults at each other. The pause was necessary to rest and regroup, as we had been on the road for over three months now, the weather had become deadly hot, and the Greek troops were slow in becoming acclimated. The Persian contingents in our army—Ariaius' troops and Cyrus' handpicked personal cavalry guard—ribbed the Greeks unmercifully about their complaints, saying that they themselves felt quite refreshed, since after all, we were still traveling through the relatively cool Pisidian mountains. "The best is yet to come," they taunted. "You soft-assed Greeks are going to wilt like flowers in the Syrian desert!"

Morale had begun to drop as well. The men had been complaining for some weeks now that they were owed back wages. The prince had allowed no looting on the way, nor plunder to be captured, and since he had paid the troops no stipends since we had left, the men were feeling the pinch every time they passed through a market town and were unable to buy even basic supplies, much less purchase trinkets or gamble. This distressed Cyrus greatly, for he had always been justly proud of having treated his men fairly, and he placed great stock on retaining their loyalty, particularly in view of the size of his army and its isolated position. Just as the grumbling was beginning to be of concern to the officers, we spied a short wagon train approaching in the distance. Cyrus did not seem at all surprised—in fact, he appeared to have been expecting it.

I was sitting my horse next to Proxenus when it arrived, and we both watched it with interest. The coaches were richly appointed, with well-dressed horses and heavily muscled guards and liverymen garbed in fine silks and gold chains. "The train belongs to Queen Epyaxa of Cilicia," he said. As the woman carefully stepped down before the eyes of the gathering troops, I could see that she was past her youthful prime, though had not yet lost a certain flush of the beauty she had once possessed.

"She's the wife of King Syennesis, one of Cyrus' allies. He is an old man, who was a satrap to the prince's father as well."

"Where is the king?" asked Xenophon, riding up to us. "He didn't send his wife out alone to meet us, did he?"

"Ha! That's a story in itself," Proxenus replied derisively. "This king hasn't left his palace in ten years, out of shame at the way he was handled by the Pisidians when they captured him during one of their petty little wars. Rumor has it that the treatment he received resulted in the loss of his manhood, though I can't say whether this was something physical or a form of madness imposed by the gods as punishment for some act he committed." Proxenus paused and looked around carefully to see if anyone was near. He then broke out in a broad grin. "But if his virility was mislaid somewhere, they say that ever since, the queen has spared no effort looking for it among lucky candidates."

Indeed, I do not know precisely what transpired in Cyrus' tent during the queen's state visit, for it was one of the few times that Proxenus was not invited to be present during an official reception. Even Cyrus' favored concubines were summarily turned out, to the amusement of the Greek officers at seeing the indignant pouts the girls affected during their temporary exile to a neighboring canvas.

I do know, however, that the queen brought Cyrus an enormous sum of money, several chests filled with silver, part of which he used to pay his troops four months' wages on the spot, plus a bonus for their patience. The men shouted their appreciation to the queen, blessing her in the name of the god Priapus and waving their drinking horns in salute to her absent husband. The queen, being too dignified to show offense, merely nodded and smiled at the men demurely as she exited Cyrus' lodgings and ducked back into her own travel tent of hairy, untanned leather.

BOOK FOUR

UP COUNTRY

It is shameless how readily mortals cast blame on the gods.
From us, they say, come all their sorrows, from us their misery,
But they have no one to blame but themselves—
Themselves and their own blind folly.

—HOMER

I

GOOD QUEEN EPYAXA accompanied us in march for some weeks, and at Tyriaion, the first major city we encountered after her arrival, the army was called to halt for three days. The queen had become ever bolder in her displays of affection for Cyrus, and had begged him to arrange a review of his army for her. Thinking that it might be a good opportunity to impress the city's inhabitants with his military might, and thereby continue the supply of easily gotten provisions, Cyrus readily agreed.

The men grumbled about the extra work required to polish their shields, wash their linens and their bodies, and dress their hair, but I believe that in general they were pleased at the opportunity to perform for the awestruck population. It was a welcome break from the routine and drudgery. Tyriaion was by no means a grand city—a sprawling collection of low mud hovels with a dusty square in the middle, inhabited by the local governor and a small garrison of troops, and supported by a large population of abject-looking farmers and slaves. The place was pestilential—an open sewage line ran straight through the middle of the dust-choked streets, stinging flies tormented the men, and the stench was suffocating. Proxenus noted, out of earshot of Clearchus and his men, that it bore a close resemblance to Sparta. In fact, the Spartans did look much more at home there than they ever had in the oriental splendor of Sardis, or the grandeur of Athens.

The Greeks were ordered to align themselves in battle array, each according to the custom of his unit and country, and each captain commanding his own men. Thus we marched on the parade ground four deep, with Menon the Thessalian and his thousand heavy infantry and five hundred targeteers holding the right wing, Clearchus and his terrifyingly blank-faced Spartans the left, and the rest of us in the center. The men had polished their bronze helmets to a luster that gleamed in the bright sunlight, set off by their greaves and scarlet capes, and they left their shining shields uncovered. To anyone facing them as they marched toward the sun, the reflection was almost unbearable. Cyrus and the queen first inspected the Persian troops, who marched past in regal splendor on horse and on foot. The royal couple then climbed into a chariot together, and rode slowly past the central line of Greeks, who all stood motionless and at attention, a low cloud of dust settling at our feet and steam rising off the sweaty flanks of the officers' horses.

As Cyrus and the queen passed the last of the Hellenic lines and were returning back to the prince's native troops, the prince gave a quiet signal behind his back to the Greeks. There rose from behind our ranks the mournful, five-note fanfare of the call to arms blasted on the salpinx, the Greek battle trumpet whose resonant sound Aristophanes attributes to its being shaped like a gnat's anus. Pikes were presented, the bronze-tipped points filed to a deadly, needlelike sharpness. The front ranks of troops gripped the smooth ashwood staffs in a horizontal thrusting position, while those marching behind snapped theirs into the vertical ready position with Spartan precision, and the Greek force advanced in a single unit toward Cyrus and the native troops at double time, as if readying an attack. Proxenus' infamous Boeotian engines, prepared in advance for an effective demonstration, suddenly began spewing forth flame at the empty air along our troops' flanks. The Persian officers stiffened and glanced quizzically at each other, and their men began shifting nervously in the ranks. The salpinx blasted again, the urgent, raucous call to attack, and ten thousand throats broke into a deafening roar. Shields held high, razor-sharp spears throbbing menacingly before them in rhythm with their steps, the Greeks burst into a mad sprint, surging like a bloody, scarlet wave directly toward the center of Cyrus' astonished native troops.

The Persians bravely stood their ground for a moment as their officers stared in amazement at the murderous Greek onslaught, and then, as if at a signal from their commander, all but the prince turned and ran like rabbits. The horrified queen vaulted out of the chariot like a mule driver being called to breakfast, and the entire population of the city fled the field. Cyrus signaled for the Greeks to halt, which they did immediately, raising an enormous cloud of fine dust as they skidded to a stop, lowering their pikes butt-end to the ground. The sound of their terrifying roar died to a distant echo and then disappeared completely. The only sound to be heard, carrying across the field and reverberating through the silent, windblown streets of Tyriaion, was Cyrus' hooting laughter as he stood alone in his chariot, tears streaming from his eyes.

"By the gods," I whispered to Xenophon out of the corner of my mouth as we stood motionless in the dust with our eyes locked on Cyrus. "Did you see them run?"

"Don't gloat, Theo. Remember, they're supposed to be on our side."

"Let's hope the barbarians we fight against are just as cowardly, or we don't stand a chance," I said.

Xenophon merely grunted, but I could see that he had gained little pleasure from the display.

The men were angry, and the tension in the blazingly hot, dusty camp was palpable. After dropping off the now tiresome queen in Tarsus, where her long-suffering husband maintained his palace, the army had dug in its heels and for three weeks had refused to march, to the mutual consternation of both old King Syennesis and Cyrus. The troops had heard rumors that the prince's true goal was to conquer his brother, King Artaxerxes of Persia, and for this, they said, they had not been hired. Mutiny was at hand, and disaffected leaders had risen among the men. "Greeks are men of the sea!" shouted one budding orator. "The sea! As long as we are near the sea we are near our homes! The same waters that lap our feet on enemy territory also wash the beloved shores of our homelands!" The thought of facing the enormous forces of a powerful king hundreds of miles from the sea, across burning desert sands and sun-scorched mountains, among strange gods and men ignorant of the sea, was incomprehensible to the soldiers. With the exception of Clearchus' Spartans, they refused to take further orders. When a group of officers led by Proxenus stood before the troops and tried to reason with them, they were pelted with rotten food.

Xenophon returned to our tent bewildered and astonished, wiping egg from his hair. He had no time to rest or explain, however, as Proxenus burst furiously through the tent flaps a moment later.

"Don't even clean up!" he ordered, his face red and his jaw clenched in fury, his own tunic fouled with rotten fruit. "I want Clearchus to see this!" Grabbing Xenophon, he stalked over to the general's quarters, meeting along the way the other officers who had been present, and who were equally outraged.

When he heard their account Clearchus was livid, raging up and down the tent in front of his officers, and muttering threats of death against the mutineers. He finally stopped, glaring at the officers, and took a deep breath, holding it for a moment. The scar on his temple stood out from the surrounding skin, angry and painful. He let his breath out in a great sigh, and then slowly and consciously, he composed his face with the calm air of an actor performing the lead role in a tragedy by Euripides in the Great Theater of Athens. Taking Proxenus to one side, he whispered to him for a moment, gesturing to him tensely with his hands in tight little thrusts and chops as Proxenus nodded grimly. Then striding impassively out of his tent, Clearchus stepped up to a large boulder, shouldering aside an angry sergeant who had been shouting epithets against Cyrus to the growing ranks of rebellious Greeks. The sergeant at first looked behind him in fury at this rough treatment, but when he saw Clearchus glaring at him, he flushed white and hurriedly took his place among the watching mob.

Clearchus recomposed his face, and cleared his throat as the men began quieting themselves to hear him. He was a man of authority, a Greek like them, yet one they were not sure they could trust. And then he began to weep.

"Comrades!" he shouted, tears streaming down his cheeks. The troops went stone silent at this unexpected display of emotion. "We have fought and marched together since pummeling the Thracians in the snows of their own mountains a year ago. Some of you have been with me even longer, in the war between Sparta and Athens. Since that time, I have been privileged to lead veterans from every Greek polis, in service to my benefactor Cyrus. The prince gave me ten thousand darics to convince me to join his forces—and not a copper did I spend on myself! All of it has gone to you, to recruit the most skilled, the most experienced, the most battle-hardened sons of bitches that have ever marched on earth!"

Scattered cheers went up at this, which he refused to acknowledge, his eyes cast downwards as if in shame. He held the men in his hand, dropping his voice for effect, and they crowded closer to hear his quavering words, as his tattered crimson cloak whipped around him in the hot desert breeze.

"I know as well as you that the prince has not played straight with us," he said, looking back up at the men. "Cyrus feared we would refuse to march with him to the Euphrates, for that is his intended goal—not to fight his brother the king, as you may have heard, but to thrash an ancient enemy of his, Abrocomas. I, too, feel betrayed. Yet I still value the prince's friendship. That is why I now find myself so hard-pressed to respond. Since you, my comrades in arms, are refusing to march with me, I must now choose between deserting you and keeping his friendship, or betraying him and staying with you."

The men watched in growing agony as their commander pondered his dilemma, his emotions pouring out.

Clearchus sighed deeply and looked up at the men, his eyes red and glistening. "Can you have any doubt what my choice will be? Let no one say that I led my men—my Greeks!—against barbarians, and then chose to desert them and join the barbarians. I am Greek first and foremost, and only then am I Cyrus' general. If it comes to a choice, I throw my lot in with you, to hell the consequences! You are my country! You are my friends and comrades! With you I am honored, without you I am empty, for friendship even with a man as great as Cyrus is worthless if I have betrayed my men."

At this the troops broke out in a lusty cheer. Clearchus seemed lost in reverie, his gaze directed down toward his feet, his shoulders shaking as if wracked with emotion. After a moment he looked back up at his men, his eyes clearing as he gazed at the faces of those who only a few minutes earlier had been prepared to lynch him, yet who now honored him with wave after wave of rolling cheers. I watched the scene as a poor student does a master sculptor, awestruck as the artist breaks off a lump of clay and begins kneading it, pummeling it to warm it and soften it, and then begins to expertly fashion it to his designs.

Clearchus again sighed in misery, then resumed. "The good wishes of Greek soldiers warm my heart as nothing else could. However, after breaking my oath of loyalty to Cyrus, it is impossible for me to remain in command. I cannot remain a general expecting other men to follow me. Even as I stand here, Cyrus is calling me to explain myself to him. I beg of you, elect a worthy man to lead you, and I will take my place in the ranks alongside the most humble goatherd. With the gods' help, your new leader will take us back to our beloved homes, through the hostile lands of the Cilicians and Pisidians."

Hostile lands? The mutineers had unaccountably failed to consider this, and the men fell to muttering. Finally, someone stood up and shouted, "Clearchus is right! We buy provisions and return to Greece, before Cyrus decides to slaughter us!" Someone else shouted him down. "No! Ask Cyrus for ships to carry us back by sea, or to at least assign us a guide!" Some hollered that they would never ride in a ship of Cyrus' for fear of treachery, while others protested that they would never follow one of his guides. The meeting degenerated into chaos, yet Clearchus stood silently on his rock, his head hanging in shame, his massive shoulders slumped. Suddenly Proxenus stepped forward to his side, gesturing the men to silence. I looked at Clearchus and saw him glancing sidelong at Proxenus out of the corner of his now dry eye, a small smile seeming to appear at the corner of his mouth, if ever Clearchus was capable of one.

"Greeks!" Proxenus shouted, and the men became silent. "We are arguing about the fate of an army of ten thousand, but we are ignorant of the facts! We have no idea what Cyrus' reaction might be, whether hostile or friendly—we only know that he will not be indifferent. Let us send Clearchus to Cyrus to ask him directly what he intends. The prince is honorable, he can either persuade us to stay and accompany him against Abrocomas, or we can persuade him to let us depart honorably, as friends, with a promise of safe conduct. We can then decide based on his response."

The men muttered their assent, and Clearchus clambered down from his perch. Accompanied by Menon and Proxenus, he left the men on the parade field and walked slowly across camp to Cyrus' headquarters, where they passed the guards and entered the canvas tent. There they remained for two hours, while the men's fears at the thought of returning, without Cyrus and his native troops to protect and guide them, grew and festered in their minds. Xenophon remained silent, apart from the rest of the men. He ignored the efforts some of them made to divine his opinion, offended that they would so readily turn for advice to someone whom they had pelted with filth such a short time before. Shadows lengthened and the men's patience stretched to near breaking, when someone finally shouted that the officers were returning, and we saw Clearchus and the others emerge into the sunlight, salute back into the dark entrance of the tent, and walk stiffly back across the camp to the anxiously waiting men.

Clearchus climbed back up onto his rock and looked out over the men, this time with his shoulders thrown back and his great bearlike chest thrust out in his customary arrogant Spartan strut. There was no need for him to quiet the men with his hand, yet he stood still, drinking in their expectant silence for a long moment before beginning.

"Men!" he bellowed. "The prince tells me he intends to march to the River Euphrates twelve stages away and engage his enemy Abrocomas. If Abrocomas is there when he arrives, he will destroy him and disband the rebel army. Cyrus invites us to go with him, though if we refuse, he will let us depart as friends and will give us a guide for an overland march. To sweeten our decision, he offers every man half again as much pay as before—instead of one daric per month per man, one and a half . . ."

The men broke out cheering even before he had finished, and there was no hesitation as to what the decision might be. The troops disbanded happily back to their units.

That evening, in response to Xenophon's questioning glances, Proxenus laughed and told us that he was bound by oath not to disclose the conversation that had taken place in Cyrus' tent. I later found out, however, that the prince had not even been present in the tent—he had left camp the day before on a boar-hunting expedition, and had not returned until after sundown the following day.

II

IT ALL STARTED WHEN my old rooster died," Nicarchus said, his eyes bleary in the firelight but with a sly grin spreading across his face.

That night, unable to sleep amidst the sounds of singing and celebration surrounding us, Xenophon had awakened me for company. Approaching a fire that had been built high and was particularly well attended, Xenophon was hailed by the men, who invited us to join them and have a swig or two from their wineskin—they seemed to have already spent the extra darics Cyrus had promised them.

Nicarchus the Arcadian, one of Proxenus' sergeants, had been laughing so hard at a joke that I thought he would burst his gut. When he saw us approach, he gained control, clapped Xenophon on the shoulder, and ceremoniously dusted off a space on a log for us to sit down. Normally a reserved, even rather morose individual who spoke slowly and with the drawn-out vowels of his native country, his face was ruddy from the unaccustomed wine and he was feeling especially voluble tonight.

"What a pleasure you're able to join us, Cap'n," he drawled, overcompensating in formality to offset his lack of concentration, and passing me the dripping skin. I looked around the fire and saw twenty faces in various states of inebriation grinning at me, and I wondered if I might have better spent my time that night continuing to try to sleep. "We was just singin' a few old songs and discussin' the glorious history and culture of my dear native land." He reached back over to reclaim the wine.

"Don't listen to him, sir," said Gellius, a hard-bitten old veteran who alone among the others seemed to be maintaining his sobriety. "As if Nicarchus ever had anything to contribute to Arcadia's glories! He's just a drunk old farmer too much into his cups to even tell a story straight."

Nicarchus drew himself up in indignation. "A drunk old farmer, you say?" His eyes struggled to focus. "I'll have you know, I was the biggest egg producer in all of Arcadia, and would still be livin' the good life there today 'stead of settin' here on my arse with you lice-bitten pig turds, if it warn't for that damned rooster." He looked around the campfire expectantly, waiting for someone to take the bait. I saw a few of the men smiling and shaking their heads in exasperation.

After a few seconds of silence, my own curiosity got the better of me, and against my better judgment I asked Nicarchus, "What rooster?" Several of the men groaned.

"Well now, sir," he said thoughtfully, "it's quite a story, and I might add, an instructive one at that." I began to think we might end up seeing sunrise out here, but the men were happy, the wineskin continued to be passed, and I made myself comfortable.

"Y'see, I had a large farm, with the biggest hen coop in those parts—a hundred and eighty laying hens, I had, at least they *were* layers, until a fox got my rooster. I depended upon those eggs for my livelihood, y'see, so I go into town to the poultry dealer, and ask for the best cock he has, because I have a lot of hens that need servicing.

"The dealer reaches into his cage and pulls out the biggest rooster I ever seen. He has a huge red comb, muscles bulging on his legs, and a Spartan *lambda* tattooed on his shoulder, which was shaved. Shit, if Clearchus were a rooster, this would be him. 'His name is Leonidas,' the dealer tells me, 'and he'll cost you a bundle, but he'll keep your hens satisfied.' "

The men chuckled, and Nicarchus leaned forward to poke at the fire.

"Well, I take Leonidas home and throw him in with the hens, and sure enough, he struts around like the overgrown sack of chickenshit he is, picks out the hen he wants, jumps on her, and before she can even let out a squawk, he keels over dead. I pick him up by the neck and think, 'What the hell did that bastard sell me? This old buzzard barely got it up once before he fell down cold.'

"That same afternoon I take my dead bird back to the dealer and show him what happened. Well, I have to admit, the dealer was nice enough about it all, even apologizin' for Leonidas' sorry-ass performance, and I almost begin to feel sorry for the feller. So then he reaches back into his cage and takes out another rooster, even bigger than the first. This one has a bright yellow comb and blue eyes—looks like a fuckin' Scythian—and I'll be damned if he isn't wearin' a spiked leather band around his neck like Cerberus the hound, and kickin' the shit out of the other roosters in the cage. Well, I take him home and throw him in the coop with my hens, to see if I can get my money's worth out of this one.

"That blond rooster, I swear, he don't even strut around. He just jumps on the first hen he sees, does his duty quick-like, jumps onto the second one and nails her to the wall, goes for the third and isn't even breathing hard, when all of a sudden—he just up and dies too, like old Leonidas. I'm beginnin' to think there's something wrong with my hens."

At this, Nicarchus sighed sadly and reached out for another swig of wine, as if to quench his sorrows.

"Well," Nicarchus finally drawled, "I grab that old blond giant of a rooster and drag him back to the poultry dealer and shout, 'Listen you son of a bitch, my business is going to hell in a handbasket, all because you can't sell me a bird that can keep his peter straight for two hours before he dies on me! You give me a working cock right now, you camel-jawed ape, or I'll burn your piece-of-shit store to the ground.' So the guy begins to look a little worried, and he reaches into his cage and pulls out the scrawniest, wrinkled old bird I ever seen. His comb is drooping down over one eye, he don't have more than two feathers on his entire body, and he can barely stand because of the kicking he received the day before from the Scythian bird. But that sorry-ass old rooster still has a bit of life gleaming in his eye, and the dealer says, 'I wouldn't inflict old Polyphagus here on anyone, but you're desperate, and he's my last bird, so here you are.'

"Polyphagus. Wretched name and pathetic bird. I'm furious, I can tell you, but I see no other choice, so I just take that pitiful old fowl home and toss him in with the chickens, without a lot of hope. I'm not even goin' to bother to stay and watch—don't think I can bear it—but then just as I'm turnin' to leave I see old Polyphagus stand up straight and tall, and I tell you, I am amazed to see that the old brute is hung like a donkey. He looks all around hisself at my one hundred eighty hens, gets a evil grin on his beak, and goes through every one of them chickens like there is no tomorrow, and then the dumb bastard musta lost count, because I'll be damned if he doesn't go back through every one of them a second time. There's hens layin' around on their backs everywhere with silly smiles on their faces, and when I go to look for Polyphagus I find he's punched right through the wall of the chicken coop and is trying to rape my dog.

"Well, you can bet I'm amazed. I grab him by the neck and lock him in the woodshed that night so's the hens can get some rest, but the next morning I go fetch him and throw him in the coop again. Old Polyphagus is practically frantic at having been kept celibate for, what, a whole twelve hours? and before I can catch him again he's gone through every hen, my boarhound, a prize sow and two of my cows. I finally seize that priapic son of a bitch, give him two smacks upside the head to calm him down and throw him back in the woodshed so's I can patch up my animals.

"The next morning when I go to get Polyphagus again, I find the old bastard has drilled right through the wall of the shed and escaped. The chicken coop is a shambles, a hundred eighty hens lying around everywhere panting and worn out, the hound trembling in the corner, and my old sow sitting in her water trough trying to cool down. I'm afraid Polyphagus has taken off to the neighbor's farm, so I go grab my mule, who's staggerin' around bowlegged, and I take off to catch that bird before he does any more damage.

"You can imagine, at least his trail isn't hard to find. Shit, the road is littered with casualties. Limping goats and sore-assed sheep. A quivering tortoise climbing back into its shell, three lame quails. I even find a big old hairy-assed boar tryin' hard to stifle a smile. Finally, I come around a corner, and there's old Polyphagus lyin' flat on his back, motionless, his tongue hangin' out, while two vultures are circlin' low overhead. I guessed Polyphagus had finally had enough, and the best rooster I ever had was now one with the gods.

"I yell, 'Polyphagus! Nooo!' and I slide off the mule onto my knees.

"But damned if that old rooster doesn't open one beady eye to look at me, nod over toward the vultures and whisper, 'Stop shouting! You'll scare them away!' "

The men roared, and I reached over to claim the wineskin again. Xenophon had just taken a swig, although unfortunately it was precisely at the story's conclusion, and he was now alternately laughing and gasping as he spattered wine from his nose over the feet of the man next to him.

"A fine yarn, old man," he choked hoarsely, tears streaming from his eyes. "I'll think of you whenever I eat eggs!" As we took our leave the first pink rays of dawn began arching across the eastern sky.

Trudging back to our tent, Xenophon gazed at the vast expanse of glowing sky, and we paused on a small rise to view the entire extent of the camp. The thousands of tents were laid out in neat rows almost to the horizon, a city sprung from nowhere, as if commanded into existence by the very hand of Zeus. Men were beginning to emerge, scratching and yawning, stirring up their fires from the night before. Smoke drifted lazily, hovering shadelike in low pockets or in hazy swirls, before meandering almost reluctantly to tree-height where it dissipated in a breeze as yet unfelt by those below. The stifling heat of the previous day was only a distant memory, or a faint worry of the harshness to come, and the crispness of the air, the wafting scent of oil simmering over a fire, and the stark beauty of the vast desert emerging from the night filled us with a sense of elation.

In Cyrus' compound at the side of the encampment I saw several of the women emerge from their tent, cloaked head to foot in the veils they wore for modesty when in the presence of men, even at this hour of the morning. They chattered gaily with each other as they bustled about their tasks, though I could not make out their words, and presently I saw Asteria, whom I recognized from her graceful movement and slight build even without seeing her face. As she emerged from the tent she stood motionless for a moment, gazing up in our direction, though I could not tell whether she was looking at us, or at the streaks of pink light arching across the sky. I gestured to her faintly with my hand, not enough as to draw the attention of others, but sufficient that if she were looking at me, she would notice. She stared motionless for a moment longer, and then turning away briskly she skipped cheerfully over to the older women nearby, from whom a moment later I heard peals of laughter.

Turning back to Xenophon I found him already facing the same direction as me, his thoughts focused on the same sight. He looked at me and smiled.

"A fine sight to start the day," he said. "Dawn and her attendant goddesses."

And he raced me down the hill, just as we had done on those warm summer days in Athens so long ago.

III

THE MIGHTY EUPHRATES. The two words are inseparable, like twins joined by the rib cage, like the Great Nile, like Olympian Zeus. Even here, five hundred miles from its mouth, the river was a half mile wide, larger than any flow we had seen in our lives, a king among rivers. The flood plains extended for miles on either bank, and the irrigation channels alone, which had been built by men generations earlier, could each have served a city the size of Athens. How far must this river have traveled, from what distant rainy lands or glacier-studded mountains, to bring such quantities of water to this desert, otherwise bereft of any moisture? The locals showed us fish they had caught, ancient creatures longer than two men together, fearsome things with reptilian snouts, from which the men would remove the eggs for their own consumption, then release back into the stream. Such monsters would have given men pause even if found in the vastness of the sea. Here in a fresh-water flow, their presence was terrifying. The river at this point could be crossed only by a long pontoon bridge, but we saw that the one that had once been there had been recently burned. The two ends were still smoldering from the fire set only days before. Abrocomas had decided not to keep his date with Cyrus at the intended place, and had fled with three hundred thousand men across the river to combine his forces with those of King Artaxerxes.

The army camped here for five days while Cyrus pondered his next move, and on the fourth evening the prince assembled the Hellenic officers in his tent compound for a feast and a council of war. Xenophon invited me to accompany him, and I gratefully accepted, even if I was not permitted to do other than stand quietly in the shadows near the doorway, with the other squires and guards. The enormous tent had been decorated inside as a monumental battle trophy, a brilliant move by Cyrus designed to hearten and bring out the warlike spirit of his guests. They had scarcely settled on their couches when Cyrus stood up.

"Captains," he said, eschewing the typically flowery speech Persians reserve for such formal occasions. "I will not mince words. Ordinarily, in order to gain power, the second son of a great king, like myself, either resigns himself to some minor satrapy or resorts to an assassin's skills. His position is nebulous, he remains always at the mercy of others. I prefer war. In war, a man either wins or loses. The outcome is clear. The gangrenous member is lopped off cleanly, the wound does not fester.

"Abrocomas fled before us in fear, his tail between his legs, even though his forces outnumbered ours by a factor of three. It is his misfortune that combining his army with those of my brother the king will not increase his strength; a company of cowards only makes those around them more cowardly. We will now have a million men to rout, instead of three hundred or seven hundred thousand. Tell your men to rest their sword arms with special care—the killing we have before us is much more than we had any right to hope for."

Cyrus then sat back down at his place, and calmly sipped from his goblet. All in the tent had fallen to stunned silence at this display of bluster. Hardly a man moved but for the slaves padding softly among the diners, filling their cups. Xenophon shot a cautious glance over at me where I stood in the shadows.

Certain of the captains, namely Clearchus' Spartans, nodded their heads and began banging their fists enthusiastically on the table in front of them, shouting their approval. Others, however, muttered under their breath, despairing as to how they would break the news to their men, who were already pressed to the limit by the long march and unwilling to venture any farther from the sea than they already had. After a few minutes, Proxenus stood up, and the room fell silent again.

"Prince Cyrus, permit me to speak openly, anticipating the reactions of our men." Cyrus nodded in assent.

"We have loyally followed you this far, first in our belief that we were to punish the Pisidians, then the Cilicians, and finally Abrocomas here at the Euphrates. Each time we pushed the men farther from Ionia. But pushing Greeks away from the sea is like herding cats from a plate of fish. The men will say that your true intent all along was to engage the king's army, and that you hid this from them; that you prevented them from returning weeks ago when we were camped in Cilicia; and now that we have advanced as far as the Euphrates you have deceived them again, as it is even more difficult to return home now. Prince Cyrus, I tell you with all respect, it is at your own peril that you attempt to cross the Syrian deserts and fight the king with a Greek army, unless you make amends with the Hellenic troops and convince them that it is in their interest to continue following you."

I held my breath at Proxenus' audacity. Cyrus, of course, was not dense. Proxenus' hint was so broad as to be bordering on extortion, but the prince did not flinch. He gazed evenly at Proxenus, who remained standing, staring back at the prince impassively, as the other officers shifted uneasily at their places. Finally he smiled, and standing up he raised his cup to Proxenus.

"And I thought I was a man of direct words," Cyrus said as the men chuckled tensely, though in some relief. "Proxenus, you know my circumstances as well as any man here. For practical reasons I cannot carry wagonloads of gold to distribute to the men each month. But I acknowledge that the men may have had . . . other expectations." The officers nodded at this, and Cyrus paused for a moment as if thinking, his eyes still locked on Proxenus.

"Let us strike a bargain, then, which you will carry back to your men. When we reach Babylon, each man will be entitled to five *minas* of silver." A general buzzing started up among the men in the tent, and even the slaves paused in their tasks to listen more closely. The sum was huge. "And," he continued, "I shall double their current wages to a full three darics per month until their safe return to Ionia."

The officers gasped. Proxenus, inscrutable as always, paused briefly before raising his cup to the prince in return. "A generous offer, your lordship. I shall convey it to my men, and though I cannot yet speak for them, I feel confident that under those conditions they would follow you to Hades and back."

The officers erupted in loud exclamations, standing up and raising their goblets to the prince, and clapping each other on the shoulders. Xenophon, however, was slow to raise his cup and stood quietly in place beside

Proxenus, saying not a word while the men around him chattered enthusiastically with each other. He would tell me later that he imagined that the sorceress Circe had cast her weird spell on the greed-blinded men and turned them to swine. I wondered what old Gryllus would have said, when told of a war fought by Greeks not for pride or principle, but for three Persian darics a month.

The banquet proceeded in a merry way. Cyrus' slaves poured copious amounts of pine-aged, resinous Thasian wine carried all the way from Greece for the enjoyment of the guests. Steaming stacks of roast fish were brought in fresh from the river, drenched in syrupy pomegranate and peach juices and garnished with leeks and other greens, followed by thrushes served on steaming beds of asparagus. Just as the guests' appetites had been whetted, a chorus of oboes sounded and six men staggered into the tent carrying a roasted ox spit between two poles. Laying it carefully upon a wide, flat board, one of them drew a scimitar, and with three enormous blows split open the beast's belly from sternum to crotch. The attendants leaned their arms into the cavity up to their shoulders, for what we expected to be the removal of the viscera, only to proudly emerge with a roasted sheep, steaming and dripping with onions and herbs, the sauces pouring from its sides. The man with the scimitar then split this open, spattering the nearby guests with fragrant juices. A roast pig emerged from the mess, its own belly neatly sewn up. The scimitar man gave a sigh of mock exasperation, to the delight of the guests, and with another blow split open the pig. It had been stuffed with a kid goat, the empty spaces filled with baked apples that had been simmering for hours inside the entire concoction, lending their perfumed fragrance to the meat of all the animals surrounding them. The scene continued, each animal containing another one smaller—a fat goose, a chicken, a partridge, an ortolan, a nightingale, and several animals more, no doubt down to a final grasshopper or grub, though I was too far in the back of the tent to see what precisely the cook was displaying. The servants soon ensured that every man was happily gnawing a favored limb, and watched carefully that no empty space appeared on a guest's plate without another slab of steaming meat or a chunk of flat, toasted bread being heaped on.

A banquet by Cyrus would not have been complete without entertainment, and this he provided in abundance, from the talent he had brought with him or later recruited among the camp followers. The Spartans looked on in dumb amazement and no little consternation as jugglers and tumblers, whose services they thought they had banned months ago from the army's presence, pranced through the tent, sometimes performing several acts at once for various groups of eaters. Clearchus, because of his fierce countenance, was a favored foil of the jesters and magicians, though amazingly, he took it in good humor. Lovely, nude flute girls from Syria supplied even more active entertainment, dancing and contorting their limber bodies through ever-spinning series of hoops tossed into the air and caught in time with the music, or juggling small, razor-sharp swords, glittering in the lamplight. One girl danced and writhed on the floor with an enormous trained snake, and it was remarkable the things she had taught it, or perhaps how she had drugged it.

Suddenly, however, at a signal from Cyrus, all the slaves simultaneously snuffed out the lamps along the walls, to the consternation of the always tense Clearchus and his captains. The callipygian beauties then danced wildly with flaming torches, threatening constantly to set the tent or the Spartans' long hair afire, but never failing to complete their intricate steps in perfect precision. The cheering for their performance was deafening. On their way out, they stepped delicately among the diners, seeking spare coins, pausing here and there to good-naturedly slap a wayward hand that had accidentally worked its way too high up a slender, brown thigh.

To the surprise of all, Clearchus then stood up with a serious expression, pounding the table with the flat of his hand for attention until all were silent. He expressed his thanks to Cyrus in a gravelly voice, and swaying slightly on his feet, moved seamlessly into what we soon perceived with dismay was a military harangue.

"Fellow officers: These girls have proven that they have no less natural ability than men, but lack only judgment and physical strength. No one who witnesses these amazing feats of swordplay and fire can deny that courage is a trait that can be taught, when these fragile girls throw themselves so daringly onto the sharp blades. Just so, we Spartans must also teach our troops, by rote if necessary, to heed the call to arms and to exhibit such courage that . . ."

Cyrus, exasperated at this unexpected and unwarranted interruption of his celebration, tossed a hunk of hard bread at Clearchus, striking him in the throat and stopping him in mid-harangue. The Spartan looked up, shocked at this violation of protocol and military solemnity, and peered fiercely through the darkness and haze of the tent in an attempt to see the source of the offense. Cyrus' cheerful voice rang out through the silence.

"Sit down, Clearchus, and shut up. Tonight I don't give a damn whether you are a Spartan general or my old grandmother. There is a time to show courage, and a time to be merry. No one questions your superiority in matters of war. But if you persist in demonstrating your inferiority in matters of sociability, I will not hesitate to throw you bodily out of the tent!" With this he clapped twice and two enormous Ethiopians stepped to his side, all but invisible in the dim light of the tent but for the whites of their eyes and gleaming teeth, who stared avidly at the astonished Clearchus. The men roared at this unprecedented slap to the fierce general, and he sat back down on his couch with a sheepish expression. The Spartan captains, unused to the quantities of wine they had been drinking, spontaneously broke out in a Spartan victory song, clumsily attempting to make up for Clearchus' awkward digression, and the musicians gamely accompanied them as the other officers joined in.

As the dancers and flute girls drifted back toward the rear entrance, Cyrus began looking expectantly toward the front, barely able to maintain his concentration. The officers' table conversation had resumed, and the tent was again filled with raucous laughter, the boasts and taunts of happy men. Finally, the prince was rewarded as the tent flap was pulled aside and Asteria stepped into the room, looking for all the world like Artemis or golden Aphrodite, her small lyre under one arm, her eyes cast demurely down to her feet, a shy smile on her face. She wore a diaphanous gown that allowed fleeting glimpses of her girlish profile as she passed in front of the lamps. Her waist-length black hair had been elaborately braided and coiled about her head, with an assortment of colorful feathers threaded through the locks, forming a lovely contrast to her bare, unadorned neck and arms. She was barefoot and wore only the lightest of rouge on her cheeks, for her naturally olive complexion already lent her a radiant glow in the lamplight. She was heartbreakingly young and beautiful, though the gentle swell and quiver of her breasts visible through the thin fabric of her backlit gown betrayed the fact that she was a grown woman, and one who was fully aware of the enervating effect she was having on the room.

A eunuch silently drew a low chair onto the carpet in the middle of the tent, gleaming in the torchlight with its inlaid whorls of silver and ivory. The master craftsman who had made it for Cyrus' ancestors centuries ago had added a low footrest under the seat, mortised into the very frame, a perfect design for a musician to rest a foot while plucking the lyre. Over it all was draped a heavy fleece for comfort. Asteria gently sat down on the magnificent chair, and the room went silent.

From the first, single pluck of the lyre's string she held the men captive and breathless, entranced by her beauty and by the sweet, crystalline purity of her voice. She fingered the instrument's strings almost randomly at first, as if searching for a motif or attempting to identify mood and pattern, then suddenly seemed to be completely absorbed by the music she was playing. Her fingers tumbled over the strings like a vessel floating down a current, pausing here and there to explore eddies and avoid shoals, picking up speed along the straight rapids and then vacillating over the still waters of a heavenly lake shimmering in the moonlight. The girl sang in flawless Greek, a love ode set to a melody undoubtedly of her own device, for it had elements of Persian intervals quite unlike what one might have heard sung in Athens, which were in striking counterpoint to the song's utterly Grecian mood and lyrics. Her face assumed an expression of such utter concentration as to be almost unbearable, like one of those ambiguous masks used in the theater, on which pleasure and anguish meet and coexist, seeming to break over each other alternately like waves against the outgoing tide. I was astonished to find, or perhaps I merely imagined, that as Asteria's gaze swept calmly about the room from man to man while she sang, it seemed to linger on me, so that I felt as if she were addressing me alone. No doubt every man felt the same, for she was trained in the ways of pleasing an audience, and what better measure of success than for each man to feel as if he had been the recipient of a private performance? Still, I was certain her gaze had stayed on mine longer than her childhood music instructors might have dictated.

There is an ancient Greek word, a strange and lovely word rarely used anymore in its earliest sense, which describes the gradual return of a vibrating lyre string to its point of rest and equilibrium after the instrument has ceased to sound. In modern times, a more sinister meaning has overtaken the original. As Asteria's last, sweet note died slowly into silence, calling this ancient word to mind, every man, slave and general alike, held his breath. Then looking up at us, she smiled shyly, stood quickly with a deferential nod to Cyrus, and skipped out the rear of the tent to join her companions. The men's conversation again began filling the room, though more subdued this time, as the raucous mood had been broken and reverie had taken its place. Once touched by the gods, it is difficult for a mortal to return so soon to the toils of the earth. The banquet broke up shortly afterwards, as each man excused himself, thanking the prince and pledging his own assistance in the forthcoming venture. Xenophon and I walked slowly back to our camp, each in our own silent thoughts, each undoubtedly thinking the same thing.

The word, my Muses prod; what is the ancient word I mentioned, with the two-faced meaning? A word connoting aspects of both art and brutality, life and death, beauty and terror, a strange word in its ability to encompass such things simultaneously, a word tragic in the loss of its benign significance in favor of one more searing. Such a word, so fitting in many ways to my own little tale, this word I gingerly lift and expose from its grave one last time, in the hope that its earlier meaning, that of a peaceful resolution of a gently sounding chord, might thereby not be forgotten without at least a wake.

The word is *katastrophe.*

IV

ONE AFTER ANOTHER the muttering, swaying seers stood up from their crouching position, their arms bathed in blood to the elbows as they finished examining the entrails of the sacrificed goats and conferred with each other on their meaning. The prince had gathered the entire army at the makeshift drill grounds on the riverbank to watch the omens being taken for crossing the enormous river and proceeding on to Babylon. The men craned their necks, peering at the mysterious doings, their hearts heavy at the thought of either outcome. The seers finally nodded at Cyrus to approach, and with somber expressions they explained to him in low tones the results of their omens. A hundred thousand pairs of eyes were fixed on his face as it slowly broke out in a grin, and he raised his arms in triumph.

"The gods are with us!" he cried. "The omens are good, we cross today!"

Scattered cheers broke out among the troops, and those on the outer edges began to disperse, some separating into the crews that had already been organized and for several days had been working to repair the bridge, while others returned to their individual units to begin breaking camp. All stopped their departures, however, when they noticed what Cyrus did next.

Gathering together his elite bodyguard of six hundred cavalry, he calmly and deliberately rode down to the bank of the river, and without pausing, urged his mount in, followed closely by his troops. On they splashed, as the broad river became gradually deeper, to the horses' knees, to their bellies, to their withers. The men stood silent, some muttering questioningly to themselves as they wondered how the prince would swim his horse safely across the fast-moving stream, and even if successful, how he would expect a body of a hundred thousand troops, most of whom could not swim, to follow him, laden with weapons, armor and the enormous baggage train.

The horses continued wading forward, and had now reached the middle of the brown river, the water swirling about their flanks. Even at this distance we could see the desert-trained Persian ponies hesitating, their eyes rolling in terror, but the disciplined cavalry soldiers, sitting bolt upright and looking straight ahead at the opposite side, kept a firm grip on their reins. Suddenly, with all eyes upon Cyrus, we saw that his horse's belly had emerged from the current—then its tail and its hocks. With a final flourish the prince urged his mount into a canter and the entire six hundred pranced through the shallows on the other side, frothing the water in a cloud of spray and raising a distant cheer that we could clearly hear over the din of a half mile of water flowing in front of us.

We reciprocated with an ear-splitting roar—every man raising his fists, his spear, his helmet, in jubilation at the most remarkable omen we had yet seen from the gods: the mighty Euphrates, considered by the locals as being impassable without boats, had given a sign that Abrocomas' vicious burning of the bridge had been a wasted effort. Even the river itself had made way for the prince's army.

As we marched, we kept the Euphrates on our right, though at times because of the roughness of the terrain we were forced to divert ourselves away from its course for miles, even days. For a month after the crossing we picked our way silently across that accursed terrain, where the Persian sun god Ahura-mazda tormented the land with a blinding light and oppressive heat by day. By night, he was replaced by some evil lunar deity who took advantage of his colleague's temporary absence from the skies to send darkness as gelid as a Scythian winter to torment the troops in their sleep. The wood of the wagons grew so dry and shrunken that pegs and joints fell out of their own accord, and the spokes rattled and spun dully in their hubs, unless tied with green hides or secured with pebbles wedged into the gaps. The land was as flat and hot as an armorer's anvil, the heat rising in waves on the horizon, forbidding even trees from growing, for nothing could survive save twisted, stunted little shrubs not sufficient even for small cooking fires for the army, and pitiful, ground-hugging little herbs.

For thrice a hundred miles even this sparse forage failed us completely, and dozens of baggage animals starved to death. The ground was bare, and the men ran out of grain. The market that Cyrus' camp followers maintained charged exorbitant prices—certain of them had a knack for business, and were wiser in the ways of provisioning than our own quartermasters. Even a rancid donkey's head could scarcely be bought for sixty drachmae. We were beggared long before we emerged from the desert, and most had resorted to gnawing the thin, stringy meat of the mules and pack oxen that died of starvation or thirst along the way. Only the camels in Cyrus' train appeared content, if camels can ever be said to be so, evil-tempered creatures that they are.

Xenophon was philosophical about the situation, and once I even caught him smiling as he listened to a Spartan captain, Chirisophus, complain bitterly about the price he had just been forced to pay for wheat.

"What are you laughing about?" the officer asked, astonished.

"I was thinking about a friend of mine in Athens, Charmides," Xenophon replied.

"I remember him," interjected Menon, who was passing by and had stopped to listen, "from Socrates' chats in the agora. The man actually used to boast of his poverty—said he was so proud that he was no longer a slave to his wealth."

"He was a fool," Chirisophus said. "How could anyone imagine it better to live like a pauper than a rich man?"

Xenophon laughed. "It was just for the sake of argument, really." The notion of argument for argument's sake was way beyond the ken of the impatient Spartan. "Socrates praised the notion of poverty. 'A most worthy asset,' he would say. 'It causes no jealousy or rivalry, requires no protection to keep it safe, and it only improves from neglect.' "

Chirisophus simply stared at us uncomprehendingly. "Who in the hell is Socrates anyway?" he asked, and stalked away, shaking his head at our ignorance.

It was Cyrus' habit to consult with each of his senior officers individually when he anticipated a major encounter, knowing that they would feel freer to express their true opinions to him singly than they would in a group. When his scribe was incapacitated one day by illness, Proxenus asked me to accompany him to a meeting called by Cyrus. Entering the prince's tent, with which I was now familiar, I waited a few minutes for my eyes to adjust to the darkness, and then began glancing around eagerly, but unobtrusively, for a glimpse of Asteria. I was promptly rewarded by a quick smile from the corner, where I spied her sitting quietly on a cushion, engaged in sewing a delicate bit of embroidery with her needle. She was almost invisible in the shadows, her olive complexion blending almost seamlessly with the smoke-darkened canvas of the tent walls. Only the whites of her large, limpid eyes occasionally betrayed her presence, as she intermittently focused them alertly on the conversation at the front of the tent before turning them back to her work.

"I understand, Proxenus," said Cyrus, after some preliminary banter, "that you had occasion to battle some Persian mercenaries on one of your Ionian campaigns. Was there anything you learned then that you think might be of use against the king?"

Proxenus thought for a moment, as I divided my attention between rapidly scribbling notes on my wax tablets and glancing at Asteria behind the prince. "With all due respect, sir," he said, "I didn't really fight the Persians, but rather interrogated one we had captured, who happened to be a former member of the king's personal bodyguard, one of his Immortals. He had been disgraced for some reason or another and was hiring himself out for service as an officer. We actually became friends, to a point."

Cyrus straightened in interest.

"As you know," Proxenus continued, "the king's Immortals are highly trained—possibly the best trained guards and horsemen in the world. That's both their strength and weakness, however. According to this fellow, the Immortals are so disciplined, they are inflexible. They are paralyzed without explicit commands from the king."

Proxenus let this sink in for a moment. Cyrus was familiar with the Immortals, of course, having himself been trained and raised with them, and having his own band of them as bodyguards, but this was an aspect he hadn't considered.

"The entire world is terrified of the Immortals," said Proxenus, "and King Artaxerxes has six thousand of them—utterly loyal to their master, ready to die for him at a moment's notice. The only way of dealing with them is to kill the head, the king himself. One bold strike to take out the king—even by a smaller force, perhaps one carrying out a suicide run—

and the entire band of Immortals will be immobilized, and seeing that, the whole Persian army will turn tail."

Cyrus sat frozen, deep in contemplation. Asteria's needle was working more slowly, her eyes now fixed unblinkingly on the prince, much to my irritation. Proxenus was not yet through, though.

"The same goes for the king's general, Tissaphernes," he said. Cyrus started, wrenched out of his reverie by mention of the hated name. "I understand that for all his bluster, he's basically a coward. He likes to take credit, to look good, but when faced with a determined force, even a smaller one, he cringes like a boy facing his father's belt."

There was a sudden movement from the corner behind Cyrus, and I saw Asteria ruefully sucking her finger where she had pricked it with the needle. Her concentration was broken, but before she returned back to her sewing I saw her shoot a glance not at me or at the prince, but unmistakably at Proxenus, who was standing to Cyrus' side. Even through the partial darkness of the tent, I could see that her eyes were full of venom.

The prince remained thinking in his seat for a long time without uttering a word. Asteria did not look up from her sewing again, however, and Cyrus finally dismissed us.

V

OUR ANIMALS SUFFERED tremendously on the march, dying in droves, though the desert somehow provided sustenance for thousands of wild creatures. It would have been a hunter's paradise, though few of us had the energy to stalk the beasts. We were constantly watched, and even accompanied, by troops of fleet-footed wild asses, bustards and gazelles, as well as ostriches, which the men avoided after one of them was killed by a kick to the head. Our native guides even told stories of a mysterious village of pig-faced people in the desert, from which lost travelers never returned sane. Such peasant myths I ignored, but several times I gave chase to the asses, which would appear to be the easiest target of all the local beasts. They ran much faster than our horses, however, often so outstripping me that they would suddenly stop and stand still for a moment, as if laughing and daring me to approach closer. As soon as I did, however, they would streak off again, remaining just beyond bowshot. By hard trial and error, we found they could be killed if horsemen positioned themselves at intervals and hunted in relays, until the ass being targeted simply dropped from exhaustion. In the process, however, we would also exhaust five or six of our own horses and men, hardly an effective means of obtaining meat for the army.

One such chase after a troop of wild asses led me miles away from the main body of the army, into rugged terrain and down a steep ravine, where my horse tripped in a hole. Her leg snapped like a straw and she threw me over her head onto some sharp rocks. I must have lain unconscious for some time, for when I awoke the sun was low in the sky and my companions were nowhere to be found. We had strung ourselves out in the relay hunting technique and they had probably not realized until hours later that I was not among them. My head was pounding like a hammer on an anvil, from both my fall and the heat that had been beating on me all afternoon, and in one very ill-considered moment, I emptied my entire water bag, swilling greedily for a minute and then pouring the rest of the brackish Euphrates water over my aching head, to little relief.

The horse was lying on the ground nearby, screaming like a child and in spasms from the heat and pain of the compound fracture in her leg. She had to be killed, which I did regretfully and with some difficulty, by crushing her skull with a rock. I then climbed to the top of the ridge to take my bearings, and in the last light of the day, I thought I could discern the cloud of dust raised by the army in the distance as it marched across the desert. I struck out in that direction at a trot, accompanied by my ever-lengthening black double, and doggedly kept up the pace for most of the night. I guided myself by the stars, pausing only briefly for rest near the half-buried skeletons of three mules from an earlier party of travelers, the bones so white and clean that they seemed almost incandescent in the moonlight.

The next morning, as the sun rose, I saw again the cloud of dust—but realized to my dismay that it was at the same distance as the night before, and that in reality it was not dust at all, but only the normal smudging of the horizon caused by the waves of heat rising from the sand and rocks. By now I was afraid, and deathly thirsty, for after trotting all night I still had not drunk anything since swigging my last water the previous afternoon. Toward midday I felt I could go no farther, and finding a sparse shelter from the fierce sun in a small rocky ditch, I sank down and prepared to die.

The next morning I awoke to the faint tinkling of bells. My mouth tasted foul and wool-like, and my skin hot and sensitive to the touch. I realized vaguely that I was suffering from fever, and that I must have been for some time, perhaps hours, for in my delirium and irritation I had scratched off the scant garments I had been wearing and they lay shredded in the dust beside me. I stared for a time at the vast, sterile sky, trying to clear my mind, to gain my bearings, wondering why I was not yet dead, when I heard the sound again, the distant tinkle of bells.

Rising shakily to my feet I looked around but could see little from my cramped position in the ditch. My knees wobbling, the impulse to retch rising up in my throat, I consciously and carefully placed my feet in natural toeholds in the slope and pulled myself up to the top. The distance was no higher than a man's head, but for all my weakness it seemed the summit of Mount Olympus. Flopping there on my belly, I rested for some minutes, my eyes struggling to focus, until I was able to lurch to my feet and blearily scan the surrounding area for the source of the sound.

It was not difficult to find. Thirty yards away milled a small flock of yellowish sheep, their filthy coats deeply encrusted with the dust and burrs of the desert, their eyes peering dumbly from beneath unsheared locks of fleece falling over their faces as they meandered calmly down a barely visible trail in the gravel. The powerful, musty smell of their unwashed fleece wafted toward me, an oddly comforting sensation. The sheep were unaware or uncaring of my presence, and continued their soft bleating and clanking of tiny bronze bells as if I were of no greater account than a stump or a wizened desert bush.

Not so their mistress, however. The young girl, who was wearing a flowing and dirty garment the color of her animals, with a thin linen rag tied loosely over her head as shelter from the sun, could not have been more than twelve or thirteen years old. She had been accompanying her flock on the side parallel to my ditch, and now stood no more than fifteen feet away from me, staring in dumbfounded astonishment at the enormous, glassy-eyed giant who had reared up before her stark naked, seemingly from the ground itself. I had not even the presence of mind to cover myself with my hands, or to gesture to her for a swig of water from the sack I saw hanging across her shoulder, for the blackness closed in on me in a rush from the sides of my vision, inexorably narrowing my sight to a mere pinprick of a tunnel, a tiny circle centered on the sweating water bag before me. I stumbled toward her blindly with my hands outstretched, hearing her gasp and scream as if from a tremendous distance, and then even my needle-eye view of the bag went black and disappeared.

I woke as if returning from that same impossible distance, the girl's wail of anguish still ringing in my ears, and I lay motionless for a long time, my eyes closed, attempting to judge my location by the feel of my shoulder blades beneath me and the weight of the fabric covering me. My mouth felt as if mice had nested in it, given painful birth, and died. The wailing continued and I cautiously opened one bleary, bloodshot eye.

The greased leather tent was small and bare, and I could see through the open flap that it was just becoming dusk. A low fire of dried sheep patties smoldered just outside, and I heard the comforting sounds of people shuffling about slowly and chatting as they moved between their chores. The wailing was not a sound of fear or anguish, as I had first suspected when coming to my fever-charged senses, but was rather the serene humming of the girl, who sat calmly in the far corner of the tent, gently pounding some substance with a small stone pestle. I stared at her in the dim light without moving, this time noticing her long black hair braided in a complicated pattern and wrapped around her head, and her loose-fitting robe, the same as I had seen her wearing earlier. The garment completely covered her shoulders, back and legs, so unlike the light and airy *chiton* Athenian women wear on summer nights. The girl's face was just beginning to show the leaner lines of the woman she was becoming, yet she still retained the soft, trusting innocence of a child. Her expression, as she softly scraped and pounded, was one of deep absorption in the simple task she was performing, and contentment at her progress. I rustled slightly, and her humming stopped as she looked over at me, staring for a moment as if startled for the second time that day to see me before her. This time, however, her face broke in a delighted smile, and she quickly stood up and approached me, kneeling by my side on the floor. She picked up the water skin lying nearby, and pulling out the bone plug, she held the opening up to my mouth in offering. I seized the skin and gulped greedily, but she pulled it away from me with a laugh, exclaiming softly in what sounded like remonstration, and then took the skin with her as she slipped out the door.

I heard excited voices outside and then the tent flaps were lifted open and several people stepped into the tiny room. They were short and thin, and all of them, men and women alike, wore garments of the same rough, dirty weave. Most strangely, their hands and faces were completely covered in stained rags, as if in protection against the heat and dust of the desert. Only their dark, piercing eyes were visible through the complicated wrappings. They chattered softly in their incomprehensible, guttural language as they stared down at my body prone beneath the blanket. An old woman entered, the only one with her face uncovered, displaying a visage at first glance as wrinkled and prunelike as the Pythia's. As she bent over me in the dim light, however, and I peered at her more closely in my feverish fog, her face took on a horrifying cast: dark, glittering eyes set not over a nose, but rather over two open nostrils, like the end of a boar's snout, and teeth bared in a hideous grin, as if protruding so far that the narrow lips were unable to cover them. I clenched my eyes shut and willed myself to regain lucidity, to emerge from this vision of pig-people, as does someone who is dreaming, yet knows he is dreaming, and in his dream commands himself to awaken.

The woman passed her hand over my face and forehead, just above the surface of my skin but not touching it—feeling, I suppose, for signs of my fever. When I anxiously opened my eyes again, however, I saw not a woman's hand, but rather the rounded, stumpy foot of a pig, discolored and misshapen, passing in and out of the shadows over my face. She apparently detected the feverish heat emanating from my skin, for turning to the girl who was hovering at her shoulder, she said something in a sharp tone that sent the girl scurrying out. Next the old pig-woman gently drew the thin blanket off my body, leaving me again exposed in a state of nature, to the evident amazement of the observers in the tent, whose eyes ranged up and down my limbs as their voices dropped to whispers. I sat up and feebly attempted to pull the blanket back over me, but a sudden wave of dizziness and nausea swept over me, and I lay back down quickly, resolving simply to endure the nightmare until the comforting light of morning.

The girl returned a few minutes later with an earthen jar bearing a substance redolent of vinegar, but with a sharper, ranker odor. This she proceeded to pour liberally on some freshly laundered rags produced from a basket in a corner. Oblivious to my feeble protests, the girl gently swabbed my entire body with this potion, lifting limbs and mopping out folds and crevices, as the pig-woman gave her instructions. The mysterious healing substance left my irritated rashes feeling cool and comforted, as when you climb wet out of the bath and feel a chilling breeze on your damp skin. They chatted quietly to each other as they performed their task, the woman pointing out places the girl had missed and laughing softly at her wondering questions, while I alternately clenched and opened my filmy, swollen eyes in fear and curiosity, trying desperately to recover clear vision. I finally resorted to my other senses, my ears particularly, attempting to divine what the women might be saying. The girl repeated a word constantly while looking at the woman, a vocative I took to mean "grandmother" or something of the sort, while the old woman repeated a word back to her in return: the girl's name, Nasiq.

Thus I lay for two days and two nights, though I know this to be true only because I was informed later by my comrades. My own reckoning of time was confused, floating as I was between delirium and lucidity, terror and exhaustion. Nasiq faithfully dampened my body with the cooling substance several times a day, while two of the men, whom I took to be Nasiq's father and brother, peeked in occasionally to check on my progress. Sometimes their faces were covered, other times their own boar-snouts were exposed, as they asked questions of me in their tongue, to which I was unable to respond, and offered pieces of charred lizard or coarse flat bread. Grandmother scolded them away in irritation, enforcing on me her regimen of small doses of water, supplemented by spoonfuls of a kind of gamy broth administered by Nasiq. The grandmother's kind yet brusque method of healing, nurturing yet never touching, contrasted with the girl's lingering glances and cool fingers resting gently on my forehead after my bathing. Several times, however, the old woman spoke to her sharply, causing the tears to well in her eyes as she stood up and left the tent to do her grandmother's bidding. Weak and confused as I was at the time, I am hard pressed now to know how much of what I remember is true, and how much a mere feverish dream.

The afternoon of the third day I awoke to the pounding of hooves and shouts of men. This first flurry of activity outside the tent, however, was followed shortly afterwards by further shouts, this time of dismay, accompanied by the sound of the quick departure of the horses who had just arrived. My fever had broken by now and I was feeling much more alert, yet terribly weak, when I thought I heard Proxenus' gravelly voice calling me from a distance. With great effort, I raised myself to my elbow. The tent flap flew open and Nasiq rushed in with a worried expression on her face. Feeling my forehead for fever and peering into my eyes for a sign that I had regained my senses, she seemed satisfied for the moment and helped me to drink from the water skin. After that, chatting softly in her language, she motioned to me to rise, which I did painfully and trembling. I was surprised to observe, as if I were an outsider objectively viewing the scene, that I had lost all traces of my former shyness at being naked in the young girl's presence. She, however, stared at my body as if noticing it for the first time, and clucking as if in reproach, snatched up my blanket and wrapped it modestly around my chest under my armpits, securing it with a bone pin she pulled from her hair. She then motioned for me to stoop down and emerge from the tent.

Shakily I made my way out and stood blinking in the bright sunlight, still unable to see clearly through my sun-damaged eyes. Nasiq led me slowly to a small, thorny tree a few steps away, propping me against it as the world spun dizzily around me. This was the first time I had been out of the tent, and as I sluggishly examined my surroundings, I was surprised to see that Nasiq's tent was not the only such shelter, but rather formed part of a small nomadic village of perhaps twenty such structures, all of the same greasy hide, with small fires smoking in front of each. There were no signs of any other inhabitants, however, pig-people or otherwise.

Suddenly a man emerged into view from my side, a man familiar to me, yet oddly timorous and cringing. I recognized him as one of Cyrus' native interpreters, on whom we had relied heavily in recent days, since he was from this desert area and spoke the languages of several of its tribes. He stood apart from me and in rapid babbling sharply ordered Nasiq back from me as well, which she obeyed, reluctantly it seemed. He then addressed me, in broken Greek.

"Theo, Proxenus is here, we have found you. You come now?"

My jaw dropped. So that *was* Proxenus' voice I had heard a few minutes before, calling me. I looked at the interpreter in confusion.

"Where is he? I don't know if I can walk," I said with effort. "Ask Proxenus to come, or have the girl's father help me to go to him."

The interpreter looked at me wide-eyed, and began wringing his hands as he struggled for words. "Proxenus say you come, he not come, must not touch these people, these . . . sick people."

I painfully pushed myself to my feet, scraping my back up the rough bark of the tree, and staggered after the man. I glanced at the other tents, wondering vaguely why I saw no people, recalling the sounds of children's laughter and household chores outside Nasiq's tent during my days of convalescence. Rounding the last of the tents in the small compound, however, I stopped dead, swaying in my exhaustion. Every person in the village had been rounded up into a small, milling clump. Men, women and sobbing children stood in a tight circle, their faces contorted and their limbs in various stages of wrap. They were guarded by three Greek archers with their bows drawn and arrows aimed straight into the terrified group. Proxenus was overseeing the operation, while Nicarchus stood nervously nearby, holding the reins of several horses in his hand and impatiently glancing at the village from which I had made my painful shuffle.

"Theo, are you alive, or are you a shade?" Proxenus shouted, yet he did not run toward me in greeting as I would have expected, nor make any move to assist me in my progress. "Make your way around the lepers as quickly as you can, and go to that horse tied to the bush."

Lepers? I started in horror, wondering whom he could mean, and then with a growing sense of understanding, I looked more closely at the pig-people of the village, now clearly visible in the bright sunshine. Nasiq's grandmother stood in the front of the wretched knot of wailing women, she alone silent, almost defiant. As before, she refused to cover her face, challenging me to stare at her absent nose, the cracked and sloughing lips that refused to cover her teeth, the thin hair, missing in entire clumps from her scaling scalp. Looking straight at me, she raised her arm in a blessing or a curse, and I recoiled at the rounded stump of her forelimb, bereft of all fingers, the skin raw and bleeding.

"Move, Theo!" Proxenus shouted at me, startling me from where I had been rooted in my repulsion. I staggered to the horse Proxenus indicated, and one of the archers quickly ran over to me, ordered me out of my ragged blanket, and tossed me a clean loincloth from his own kit. I stepped out of the blanket and put on the new garment, as the entire population of the village, now silent, watched me. The soldier laboriously helped me climb onto the horse's back, to which he tied me in a prone position, my face resting against the back of the animal's neck to prevent me from slipping off in my weakness. He then walked back to the rest of the horses.

Proxenus gave an order, and the archers relaxed their guard, gesturing to the village people to return to their tents. I heard him gruffly tell the interpreter to thank Nasiq's father for his trouble and saw him flip the man a gold daric, which landed in the dust at his feet. Nasiq's father looked up at Proxenus on his horse, and then down at the coin in confusion, and I realized that he was unable to pick it up with his rag-wrapped stumps. He called to one of the boys who, like Nasiq, appeared not to be affected by the blight. The child came running over, and at the man's instructions solemnly picked up the coin and pocketed it. Both then turned without a further word or glance, and walked slowly, and with great dignity, back into the compound.

Only Nasiq remained standing, seemingly transfixed at the sight of the Greek soldiers, their horses, and my sudden departure. After warily appraising the archers while they packed their weapons and remounted, she walked calmly over to the horse on which I lay miserably blinking in the blinding sunlight, and took my large hand in her tiny one. She patted my limp paw as would a little girl comforting a doll, smiling gently and chatting to me in her language, confident that I understood her or that I someday would. As Nicarchus walked over to tether my horse to his own animal to lead me, Nasiq reached up to stroke my forehead once more. As she did so, however, I noticed for the first time the small white blotch on the otherwise flawless skin of her hand. I involuntarily shuddered and jerked my head away. Nasiq, following my gaze, instantly dropped her hand and thrust it into her robe, her eyes welling with tears. She stood watching motionless as my horse set off at a painful, bumpy trot. It took no more than two hours to ride back to the Greek camp, where my arrival in this degrading position was obscured by nightfall.

Among my people I recovered quickly. Cyrus sent a message congratulating me on my survival, and good-naturedly threatening to return me to my mule as this was the second of his horses I had lost. He also arranged for my recovery to be monitored by his personal physician, a Persian well versed in the ways of treating desert sicknesses. The physician once came to visit me accompanied by Asteria, who behind his back shook her head in silent contradiction of the learned doctor's diagnosis. As he was leaving my tent, she lingered and stealthily slipped me a small earthen jar of a bitter herbal substance with her own wax seal upon the cap, pouring me the first dosage administered in a large goblet of water, and indicating that I should ignore the physician's suggested remedy of daily bloodletting. In return, I presented her with a small ostrich plume I had come across in the desert on an earlier outing, which I had been saving for the appropriate occasion.

Since that time, not a day has gone by that I have not taken a quiet moment to ask the gods' blessing on gentle Nasiq, forever virgin Nasiq, and to request forgiveness for my treatment of her. As a libation, I offer a cup of pure, cleansing water, the most sacred substance known, savoring the sensation of its flavorless coolness, marveling at the notion of its somehow containing, in reduced or distilled form, the ancient elements from which the earth was formed, the holy rain from the heavens, perhaps even some vague essence of immortality.

VI

THE MEN'S NERVES WERE already on edge when the riot broke out. For days our scouts had been reporting signs that the king's forces had recently passed along the road before us. The forward troops were soon tramping through the droppings of several thousand horses, which were so fresh they had not yet even been coated by the layer of fine dust that settled on everything from food to a sleeping man's face if left exposed for more than a few hours. Villages and orchards we encountered were still smoldering from having been recently torched to prevent our procuring supplies. Deserters from the king's forces began appearing in increasing numbers, but interrogating them yielded contradictory accounts. Clearchus was of the opinion that they had even been sent purposely by the king with orders to exaggerate the numbers of his forces to create alarm among our troops. The men maintained a state of heightened alert, which combined with their growing anxiety at being hundreds of miles from the sea, and their physical exhaustion, greatly raised the level of tension in the army.

When a fistfight broke out between several of Menon's and Clearchus' soldiers, Clearchus broke it up; after hearing their dispute, he decided that Menon's men had started it and had one of them severely flogged. This did not sit well with them and later that day, when Clearchus was trotting his horse through the camp, one of Menon's men threw a hatchet at him. The blade buried itself to the haft in the horse's flank, causing the lamed horse to rear in pain and spill Clearchus to the ground. Uninjured but furious, he stood up stiffly, and was astounded to see that several other men from Menon's troops had gathered, not to assist him, but rather to stone him while he was down. Clearchus bellowed like a bull, seized an enormous stick lying nearby and swinging it like a cudgel, nearly killed one of his tormentors with a tremendous blow to the neck, even further infuriating Menon's men.

Fortunately for Clearchus, who though unrivaled as a fighter was no match for the number of gathering Thessalians, one of his captains nearby heard the tumult. Thinking that a skirmish had broken out with a squad of the king's soldiers, he summoned some Thracian infantry, who rushed over in battle formation. They linked their enormous oak shields in a phalanx behind Clearchus, while a detachment of Spartan cavalry stormed into Menon's camp just behind, cornering the now-terrified Thessalians against a rock wall with their skittish mounts, lances poised to kill.

Proxenus, Xenophon, and I, who were nearby, came running up unarmed and surprised, as did Menon, who flushed pale in his fury at seeing forty of his troops on their knees begging the Spartans for their lives. Clearchus was in a rage.

"Did you see these madmen?!" he roared, stalking back and forth before Proxenus and me, spittle flecking his beard and an enormous swollen blue vein throbbing visibly on his forehead. "These fucking traitors?! By the holy gods, I'll dice their balls like apples and send them home in a dung-cart before they betray the entire army in its sleep some night!" He raised his cudgel as if to strike and all forty of Menon's disarmed Thessalians simultaneously winced and cowered in terror.

Proxenus, though subordinate to Clearchus, assumed a commanding air. "Let go the club, Clearchus, and call off your men. Let's settle this privately between officers, not here in the presence of camp followers and knot-headed Persians." He glanced over at the growing number of native troops gathering on the side, watching expectantly, attracted by the prospect of seeing the Hellenic troops beat each other into the dust.

Clearchus was in no mood for discussion. "I was practically stoned to death by these stinking, camel-lipped bastards!" he sputtered. "They lamed my horse! They were still in diapers when I was killing their goat-fucking fathers in Thessaly, and I'll be damned if I'll allow the entire god-damned army to have its throat slit in the night by these cowering dogs who attack unarmed officers . . ."

Just then Cyrus and eight of his bodyguard came thundering up, roughly pushing the onlooking men to the side with their horses and forcibly shouldering past Clearchus' steady-eyed troops, still with lances poised to slaughter Menon's entire company the second their general gave the word. Cyrus' face was flushed with anger as he surveyed the scene in silence. Clearchus slowly lowered his club, but retained his defiant expression.

Finally the prince spoke, in a voice that was steely, yet so soft the men went silent and instinctively leaned forward to hear what he said. "Clearchus and Proxenus, and all the rest of you—you have no idea what you are doing. I have over a hundred thousand men under my command, but if I lose my ten thousand Greeks I have nothing. If there is any dissension among your ranks, the unity of my entire army is threatened. You'll see then that the wrath of the king will be nothing compared to that of the men surrounding you now." We looked up to see that thousands of Persian troops had gathered, and were continuing to flock to the site of the dispute in expectation of some dreadful event.

At this Clearchus' eyes lost their fanatic gleam, and he came to himself. He sullenly ordered his men to dress arms and return to camp. The terrified Thessalians stood up and shamefacedly made their way back to their individual tasks, and the crowd began to disperse. Cyrus looked at Xenophon and me, and shook his head warily, as if clearing his mind of a dreadful dream. "I'm glad the Greeks are ready to fight," he muttered as he climbed back on his horse. "I think we'll be able to make use of some of that excess energy in a day or two."

VII

SHE WAS SOMETHING MORE than a slave but less than a peer, more than a consort but less than a sister, educated as a man yet wise in the ways of the harem. Her role in Cyrus' lodgings and heart was vague and undefined, a source of intrigue and curiosity to those living without, yet as accepted and comfortable as that between cousins for those inside. The time has long passed for me to define Asteria's place, to formally introduce her into the narrative, yet I have resisted until now, whether for lack of skill and objectivity or from pure ignorance—may the reader be the judge.

I came to know her over the course of several months, yet racking my brain as I have, I am utterly unable to define precisely when, or on which occasion, that defining moment of familiarity occurred. I have related already my first sight of her in Cyrus' tent in Sardis, yet when talking with her much later she swore she could not recall that portentous meeting, much to my disappointment. The vision I had created and developed in my own mind, through hours and days of refining that single memory until it glittered like a gemstone fresh from the polishing of the sand wash, had for her been nothing more than a chance encounter, a brief glance at one of the dozens of visitors her master received in his quarters every day. A shining recollection was shot out of the sky like a grouse by a slinger, leaving a small residue of surprised feathers drifting lazily down, briefly marking both the height the bird had attained in the air, and its final point of impact with dusty reality.

Yet by the time of my disastrous, and somewhat humiliating near-encounter with death in the desert, we had somehow come to know each other. Of this I am certain, because during my two or three days of recovery she was sufficiently confident as to actually visit me in my tent, arrayed like all harem dwellers in gauze and veils from head to toe, and to leave me mementos of her affection—or at least that is how I perceived those stray touches, the unnecessary but welcome hint of jasmine scent in the medicinal water she gave me, the longer-than-required glances through the anonymity of the facial screens. When, then, did this familiarity develop?

As for me, my own recollections have already been fatally discredited by her utter failure to remember my first sight of her. In fact, she herself suffered from the same inability to remember the precise instant when her attitude toward me changed from one of indifference or, at best, mild curiosity, to something more. What I can say is that during the course of those months of the desert march, I became a zealous student of the hunt, not so much of ostriches and asses, but of pinfeathers woven intricately into dark strands of hair, of kohl-lined eyes with lightly hooded lids, of a slight, girlish form tripping gracefully over the matted grass or scrub of the campsite, unable to be disguised by the voluminous folds of the robes and veils. Like a trapper, I sought my quarry where it would be most likely to be foraging away from the secure enclosure of her tent, surrounded by the glaring Ethiopians: among the physicians' quarters on the edge of the army's encampment, where she spent hours discussing the medical arts with the learned doctors; at the deserted edge of the camp, where she would stroll quietly with the other denizens of her harem colony; at bookstalls in the markets of the cities through which we passed, lingering in conversation with the scribes, while being tugged impatiently at the sleeve by her uncomprehending attendants. My hunt, however, was clandestine, and went unperceived, I believe, by observers. I had taken Proxenus' original warning about her to heart, and was determined to keep intact every valuable cell of my nether anatomy.

Given my secretiveness, did she notice me as I pursued her? I personally have no doubt that she did, and in fact once, in a moment of weakness on her part, I even gained her grudging admission to this effect, though she gave no indication of it at the time. A hulking, brooding foreigner, standing a full head above the surrounding crowds, and seeming to be present whenever she emerged into view from her lodgings, would be a hard sight for her to miss. Here the hunter and hunted metaphor breaks down, for if she had indeed been some sort of human prey and I the pursuer, it would not have taken her long to learn to avoid me, to post watchful and giggling sentries, to keep a sharp eye out for my stalking approach and thereby to passively dishearten me in my unwanted attentions. As it happened, she did not do so, and so by default gave impetus to my chase, even casting a smiling eye of encouragement to me now and then when my patience seemed to flag.

Who, then, was the hunter, and who the hunted?

Even today it is a question I cannot answer.

BOOK FIVE

CUNAXA

The victor's cause is pleasing to the gods,
But girls prefer the vanquished . . .

—UNKNOWN

I

THE PERSIAN SCOUT GALLOPED furiously up to Cyrus on his frothing horse, his beard wiry and dusty from the sprint, a wild expression in his eyes. He shouted in Persian and in camp Greek, sometimes intermingling the two, his tongue tripping over itself in his hurry.

"The king . . . the king is marching toward us in battle array! Today is the day, Lord Cyrus! The hour of your glory is at hand!"

Word spread quickly down the line, raising panic among the camp followers and confusion among the men. Officers marching in the front, near Cyrus' party, immediately wheeled and began racing back to their units, colliding with the troops advancing behind. Concerned that we might be attacked at any moment, and on unfavorable ground, the prince dispatched officers the length of the army's march to begin making order out of the chaos and to provision the troops. Other riders he sent up into the surrounding hills to observe the king's forces, and to identify favorable terrain for a battle. Cyrus himself hastily donned corselet and greaves.

Within a half hour the army had arranged itself into full battle formation along the crest of a low range of hills running perpendicular to the river. We were just outside the tiny hamlet of Cunaxa, six months and a thousand miles distant from Sardis, a mere three days' march from Babylon itself. The Spartans anchored the pivotal right line against the Euphrates, with Proxenus' division beside them, along with a thousand Paphlagonian horsemen from Cyrus' native troops, all of whom would be commanded by Clearchus. Menon held the left wing, adjacent to Ariaius, while the remainder of the native troops were positioned in the center. Behind the long ranks of soldiers the motley thousands of camp followers had gathered in shuffling order, bearing gap-toothed grins of anticipation and wielding makeshift weapons they had assembled from broken remnants of the drilling field. All carried sacks or baskets, for they did not intend to return empty-handed from their task. Behind them the quartermasters worked frantically, arranging the supply wagons into a compact, organized array, leading the vast herds of beasts into temporary enclosures, and setting up field hospitals and officers' quarters. The five hundred Lydian guards Cyrus had posted over the camp arrangements, in continued punishment for their sorry performance before Queen Epyaxa, stalked impatiently among the chaos, irritated at being assigned to camp detail. Sitting his horse motionless in the middle of the front ranks was Cyrus, easily recognized by his bare head and flowing hair, surrounded by his six hundred cavalry, their polished armor glittering in the blinding sunlight.

We stood in silent formation, facing the hills to the east whence the king's troops would be arriving. Hardly a man stirred. The only movement was the occasional distant rider galloping from or toward the army, retrieving messages from the outposts and carrying Cyrus' orders to his far wings. The moment was otherworldly and eerie, tens of thousands of men motionless and silent—that brief moment before engagement when the lines are orderly, the troops confident, the horses calm, and the Homeric glory of battle is most apparent and anticipated.

The distant hills facing us began shimmering in the mid-afternoon heat, becoming hazy and ill-defined. Small flies buzzed about our faces, and sweat trickled down my sides under the corselet. My scalp burned and itched under the helmet, the felt caul lining my head underneath already drenched with perspiration. The initial tension, the sharp knot I had felt in my stomach while making my preparations, had given way to a dull, throbbing ache, a weight in the lower belly and knees, a pervasive background presence of anticipation and fear. Some men, even officers, became restless in the heat, shifting on their feet, gulping fetid water from their skins and chatting idly with their companions. A few set the rims of their heavy shields on the ground leaning against their knees, to free up their hands while they wrung out their caps. Others simply sank down into the dust where they were, grunting loudly as they sat, concluding that whatever repose they were able to afford their tense limbs was worth the difficulty of standing up again under the weight of their gear.

The sun beat on us relentlessly, turning the outside of our armor and helmets hot to the touch, steaming our bodies inside like loaves of bread in an oven. The haziness increased, and we had almost begun to doubt we would be seeing action that day at all, when we noticed the distinct outline of a brownish cloud floating up from the horizon. At first it was so distant and faint that when I pointed it out to Xenophon, he simply dismissed it as the effect of heat waves on the sand as the sun burned hotter. After a few minutes, however, we saw that the cloud was drifting closer, becoming denser and more ominous as it approached—the dust raised by the million marching feet of Artaxerxes' army.

The horizon at the top of the distant hills darkened to black, and then thickened in a wavy line, from the downstream course of the Euphrates at the right of our present location, in a wide arc almost to the farthest left of our view—and then the line began spreading and thickening like the dark shadow of a cloud, moving toward us, inexorable and plaguelike, as the massed forces of five times a hundred thousand men and horses approached us in formation. Certainly no sight ever seen by mortals, not the sacking of Thebes nor the destruction of Ilium, surely not even the war between the gods and the Titans, was a match for this sight of the king's enormous army, for pure, destructive splendor. Here and there shone sparkles of light as the sun reflected off glittering armor and polished bridle bits, and within moments the occasional shouts of officers' orders, the whinnying of horses and the thunderous, rhythmical tramping—above all the tramping—were carried floating and wafting to our ears by stray gusts of wind.

Earlier in the day Cyrus had warned us not to be unnerved by the battle cries of the barbarians. As a Persian himself, he was well accustomed to their practiced technique of trying to break their enemies' concentration even before coming to blows, by emitting an ear-piercing shriek that would carry for miles, designed to strike terror into the hearts of all who heard it. But this time the prince was wrong: The barbarians came marching in complete and utter silence, without a sound from their men other than the insistent tramping. In its own way, this was even more unnerving, making them seem more like shades or gods than creatures of flesh and blood.

I glanced at Xenophon, who stood transfixed by the sheer wonder at seeing in this barren, empty landscape the vast multitude of men and animals suddenly appearing from nowhere. Only Clearchus seemed unmoved by the spectacle. He trotted ceaselessly up and down the lines on his enormous, frothing war-charger, fine-tuning placements here, berating an officer there, his long, carefully dressed braids flying out behind him from under his full-faced Spartan battle helmet—a terrifying sight, only his glittering eyes and bushy chin exposed from beneath the polished bronze.

Cyrus pounded up to our lines, searching out Clearchus, who calmly finished bellowing orders to his captains before he turned to the prince, waiting impatiently on his skittish horse. "Your highness!" Clearchus exulted, a murderous glint flashing through the deep eye sockets of his bronze helmet, "*This* is your Greek army! These are the men who will lead you to victory!"

Cyrus ignored Clearchus' boasting. "Victory! Victory over the enemy's auxiliaries perhaps. The false king and his Immortals are marching against us in the center of their forces—if we defeat them there, the battle is won. You are on the wrong end of our lines, General! Fall back and cross with your men to the left!"

Clearchus gaped at Cyrus in astonishment, then scanned the approaching forces more carefully and saw that what the prince said was true—the enemy was so numerous that the king's center actually faced our far left, so much did the king's lines overlap and extend beyond ours. Still, the value of shifting his troops to the other end of the line at this late hour was dubious, and the prince's implicit questioning of his tactical skills was intolerable. He whipped his helmet off in a rage.

"Wrong end, my ass! The first rule of battle, *Prince,* is to position your strongest troops to anchor the right. Absent us, the king's cavalry will cut through your right like butter and fold you up from behind. With our forces hard against the river, we can't be outflanked on this side at least. Believe it—I've been doing this since before you were born. As long as I command the Greek troops they stay on your right."

Now it was Cyrus' turn to gape at his subordinate's direct challenge, and after an astonished pause, he lit into the Spartan with a barrage of oaths and insults that made my hair rise, even under the soaked helmet and caul. Proxenus, Xenophon, and I froze as we watched Cyrus and Clearchus rant at each other, shouting and gesturing as the vast forces of the enemy continued their inexorable march toward us across the plain. Artaxerxes would not wait for our tactical dispute to be resolved before launching his troops into battle. I despaired at seeing the two generals at the point of coming to blows, but Clearchus remained unyielding. There are few men more stubborn than an old soldier, and none more stubborn than a Spartan. The prince finally raised the palm of his hand sharply, cutting off Clearchus in mid-sputter.

"I have staked my life and my fortune on defeating the false king in this battle," he seethed, in a voice barely audible to the rest of us, "and I will not be stymied by a petty autocrat. You have resisted my orders, but I do not have the time to enforce them. The enemy is almost upon us! If you will not take on the king, by the very gods, I will myself! And we shall see this matter through again after the battle, Clearchus, I assure you."

Wheeling his horse with an angry jerk of the reins he cantered off, his chestnut hair flowing freely behind him, and Clearchus angrily jammed his own helmet back on his head. His long Spartan braids, oiled and black yet streaked with the gray of his years, draped over his shoulders like the snakes of the gorgon.

"Stupid, vain son of a whore doesn't even wear a battle helmet," Clearchus spat, not bothering to lower his voice to prevent the rest of us from witnessing his insubordination. "If he wants to feel the wind through his hair he'd do better to ride without his pants. At least then he wouldn't be jeopardizing the whole fucking army."

Proxenus spoke up for the first time, pressing his horse against the side of Clearchus' nervous animal to calm him, and looking straight into the face of the furious Spartan.

"Clearchus, your position is correct, but this is no time to break with the prince. Whether Cyrus is right or wrong, you disobeyed his direct order, which you would never tolerate from us. For the sake of the army and our future, send an olive branch before battle commences."

Clearchus stared at him in a fury, and I thought he might even strike Proxenus with his sword for second-guessing him; but after a long moment he glanced away in silence, the cords in his neck working furiously as he clenched his jaw and surveyed the rapidly approaching enemy. He coughed harshly, clearing his throat of the thick, acrid dust, and then turning his head to the side he seized his nose between thumb and forefinger and blew two arching strings of snot to the ground, narrowly missing Proxenus' horse. He then twisted in his seat the other way to locate the prince, who by now had stationed himself at a more favorable viewing area several hundred yards away. "You," he said, glancing at Xenophon. "Run a message to Cyrus over there: Tell him I will take heed, and all will go well." With that, he wheeled his horse contemptuously and galloped off to make further preparations. Xenophon and I raced over to Cyrus' position, anxious to deliver the message and return to our own forces before the battle commenced.

The two sides were now no more than a quarter mile apart, and we were able to distinguish the Persians' various units. The black cloud of marchers separated into individuals. Cavalry in white, silk-decked corselets supported the heavy infantry in the enemy's left wing facing us, and Clearchus passed word down the line that these riders would be led by Tissaphernes himself. He was proven right a moment later when the enemy commander's personal banner—a golden, winged horse on a black pennant—hove into view. "A gold daric to the man who kills that donkey-faced son of a bitch!" Clearchus bellowed to all within earshot. The men's excitement visibly increased.

Within minutes, we were able to identify the king's vanguard to our left, the fearsome Medes, marching in disciplined silence with their rouged faces, bright purple pantaloons, and bejeweled necks and ears. They resembled Cyrus' effeminate eunuch slaves, but their chain mail vests, plumed bronze helmets and tanned, muscular arms added a sinister effect to their otherwise delicate appearance, which was intended to strike terror into less disciplined forces, as does the ambiguous face of a clown to a small child. They were followed by troops from the dozens of nations over which the king of Persia held sway, and from which he had forcibly conscripted his forces: Phrygians, Assyrians, Bactrians, Arabians, Chaldeans, Armenians, Kurds—the list was endless. Even the most expert among our troops were, in the end, unable to tell one from the other, much less recall each of their peculiar fighting styles, weapons, and special penchants for killing. Most astonishing of all was the variety of weapons and defensive devices arrayed before us—from the light wicker shields carried by the Cissian archers, so different from our own thick oak and bronze bowls, to the thin, reedlike spears carried by the Egyptians, which were deadly when thrown at medium range, but which were too light for close-in sparring. Perhaps most unnerving to all but the Spartans were the sixty Persian scythe-chariots pulled by white stallions. Their drivers grinned murderously beneath their visors as they surveyed our lines, waiting for the opportunity to charge into the fray with their axle-mounted knives, slicing in half or running down any soldiers who might stand in their way. To Clearchus the range of men and techniques was of no consequence. He held all enemy forces in equal disdain, convinced that the superior Spartan discipline and endurance of his troops were capable of overcoming any number of enemy forces he might face.

As the enemy steadily approached, Clearchus dismounted and strode over to the seers waiting before the front lines of troops. Like Euripides, he believed that it is with the gods' favor that wise commanders launch an attack, never against their wishes, and so he ordered a goat sacrificed to Zeus and then to Phobos, God of Fear and Rout, seeking to avert the latter's eyes from our men and to focus them instead on the Persians. Clearchus himself began the ritual, and despite the relentless advance of the enemy troops, he carefully and deliberately followed the prescribed protocol, slicing his blade through the beast's exposed throat and letting the blood spurt and gush, placating the gods. As it fell, it soaked into the hot, parched earth, leaving only a dark, steaming stain which itself would be effaced within minutes by the stifling dust, as the earth healed itself of the scars and stains inflicted by men in their puny affairs.

Clearchus had not yet called his troops to attention. Though they carefully watched the advancing hordes and the sacrifices, they feigned nonchalance, glancing out of the corners of their eyes, their shields leaning against their legs and the gripcords exposed, some of the men still sitting down. Xenophon and I had been warned in advance by Proxenus of this unsettling habit of the Spartans, a calculated effect designed to indicate their scorn for the advancing enemy. It was not until the Persian archers, some 200 yards distant, finally began finding their range that the men casually stood up and mounted their shields.

At a signal from Clearchus' trumpeter the Greeks bellowed the watchword we had devised, *Zeus soter kai Nike!* "Savior Zeus and Victory!" clanging their shields and increasing the volume of their roar with each repetition until the very earth seemed to shudder. After a moment, the reedy, high-pitched wailing of the battle pipes soared over our voices, an otherworldly top-note rising in arrhythmic counterpoint to the bass of the hellish chorus. The rising, rolling beat of the oxhide drums, which we felt as a thumping tremor in our bellies, resonated through the ranks, and as the throbbing beat suddenly doubled we broke as one into the chanted war hymn, the paean to Apollo. The thunder of the massed ten thousand voices and the explosive clanging and crashing of spears on shields rolled over the field between the opposing forces, and seemed to hit the Persians almost physically, like a wall. The enemy companies directly across the field from our right wing faltered and their front visibly wavered as the troops behind them began to cluster in bunches. At another deafening blast from the salpinx we broke toward the Persians' left wing in a trot. Our hoplites maintained a flawless, tight phalanx formation on the slightly downward sloping plain, while the light infantry followed close behind, fitting their arrows on the run, forever chanting the bloody hymn. As we approached to within fifty yards of the enemy lines, the heavy infantry broke off the rhythm of the war chant and commenced a full-throated, wordless wail, a howl as if of pent-up rage, summoning Ares, the implacable god of war, with the deafening cry, *"Eleleu! Eleleu! Eleleu!"* They snapped their spears down in perfect unison to full horizontal, the freshly sharpened edges and tips glinting their promise of painful death in the blinding sun. The mouths of the terrified enemy soldiers before us worked soundlessly, contorted in fear, and their officers' horses rolled their eyes wildly and reared their heads to the side in an effort to escape the bellowing wall of men and metal fast approaching.

The enemy line faltered, its front ranks stopping dead. The rearward Persian marchers, unable to see what was happening uphill beyond their leading comrades, kept pushing forward, tripping over those who had halted in front, and in turn being pushed by their fellows in the rear. Encouraged at this sign of hesitation, the Greek heavy infantry picked up its pace to a full sprint, armor and shields crashing madly. The discipline of the Greek forces was heart-stopping—men prepared against those unprepared, good order against disorder, troops surging forward in absolute, deadly precision, as tight and as uniform as the scales on an asp.

As for what happened next, it is impossible to say whether the gods were responsible, or whether no enemy could resist a tide of men as determined as ours. The Persian ranks collapsed without a struggle in the face of the Greek hell-storm, unable to muster even the deafening crash one usually hears as the lead warriors of the opposing forces collide and fold into one another in a chaos of metal, body fluids, and screams. The front line broke and we plowed over them as if they were so many molehills, neglecting even to kill those we ran over, but simply trampling them and moving on to the next rank, a seething, roaring wall of iron and death. The frenzied camp followers swarming close behind us stripped the dead of their valuables and food, using clubs and discarded spearheads to make short work of any enemy soldiers who remained twitching or sobbing after being mowed down by our surging hoplites. The Persians in the front lines tried desperately to wheel and run to the rear, but their comrades behind, fifteen or twenty ranks thick, marched doggedly forward like the slaves they were, under the whips and threats of their sergeants, blocking the path of the panic-stricken front ranks and hindering their retreat. Slaughter ensued, panic fed upon panic. Even those few Persians originally inclined to take a stand and fight lost heart when they saw they had been deserted on all sides, and then they themselves joined the terrified mob.

Our archers took special aim at the enemy chariot drivers, who had held slightly back behind their heavy infantry, waiting for a gap in the fighting to open up through which they could drive their lethal scythes without cutting apart their own men. The Spartans loathed such machines, and had not used them in their own forces for a hundred years. They did, however, relish the thought of facing them, for they had mastered the trick of calmly opening up gaps between which the chariot drivers would charge harmlessly, while one or two Spartans darted in from the side and stabbed the horse or driver. In his youth, Clearchus was known to be well accomplished in this trick.

The Spartans were to be disappointed, however, for not a single Persian scythe-chariot even made it to the Greek lines. Our bowmen toppled several of the drivers, and in the ensuing chaos none of the Persian infantry even bothered to pick up their comrades' reins. The panicked horses raced about aimlessly among their own men, the razor-sharp blades violating the sanctity and virginity of fragile skin, lopping off an arm here, a head there, gouging through men's breastplates and ribs as if they were cheese, exposing the gods' secrets to the eyes of leering and terrified onlookers. I watched as two Boeotians from Proxenus' battalion, brothers as it happened, each took charge of a runaway chariot and began lending method and discipline to the general carnage they were wreaking, turning the Persians' most terrifying weapons against them with devastating effect. They cut a bloody swath through the most densely packed of the enemy lines, and then calmly drove their captured trophies up to Proxenus, grinning, with odd pieces of bloody flesh and dripping helmet leather still hanging off the murderous tines. Socrates once said that to peer inside a human being, you can make him laugh or observe him in love; he neglected to note that you can also use a blade or a spear point. The latter method proves beyond a doubt that people are more alike inside than they are outside, and in fact are scarcely different from pigs or asses.

Xenophon galloped back and forth the length of our immediate line, wheeling his mount in tight circles at the end of his range, and observing Tissaphernes' forces closely for any indication of an attack or an attempt to outflank our troops. The exercise was useless, however; Tissaphernes' cavalry were helpless in the chaos, and they assembled nervously far to the rear of the battle, awaiting the outcome. I glanced at Proxenus, who was darting in and out of the slaughter on his horse, trying to maintain order among the fury, and at Clearchus, who after having led his men directly to the enemy lines, had backed away to monitor the situation, and was now sitting his horse impassively on the edge of the fray, watching as his men mowed down the enemy as if harvesting wheat in a field.

Finally the Persians' surviving middle and rear ranks reversed their march and began a general retreat. The Greeks ran them down as they went, tripping over the bodies of the fallen and slipping in the gore on the ground as they churned it into an ankle-deep slurry of mud and piss, salted with shattered weapons and the detritus of dying men. The Hellenes' spears, both the throwing point and the *sauroter,* the bronze-tipped "lizard-killer" used for standing the weapon in the ground when at rest, had long since broken and shivered on the fragile spines and skulls of the Persians, and our men were now reduced to a frenzied, blind hacking with their short swords. Mobs of Persians threw down their shields and weapons in their panic, forgoing any protection, forgetting even to fight, but doing everything to assist in their own slaughter. The enemy dead numbered in the thousands, while our troops had scarcely lost a man, suffering only from the weary numbness in our limbs from the strain of the relentless killing.

Clearchus at last roused himself from his apparent boredom at the appalling carnage, and ordered his trumpeter to sound a halt. For what seemed an eternity, nothing happened. The horrifying bloodbath continued unabated. Finally, however, after further trumpet blasts, Clearchus resorted to riding into the slaughter himself, swinging and beating at his own men with the flat of his sword to drive them back, to force a respite. The mad blood-trance lifted and the Greeks staggered, gasping, to a halt. The shattered men slowly lowered their arms and stood trembling in place, dropping their weapons in exhaustion. The terrible roar of battle died away to a mere echo in our heads, which was gradually replaced by the moans of the injured and dying. The troops' appearance was hellish, godlike—so slathered in gore from helmet to greaves they might have been wallowing in it like dogs, their eyes glittering evilly through the darkness of their visors, the muscles in their shoulders and thighs swollen and taut. Their chests heaved, quaking legs collapsing in exhaustion, some crumpling into the steaming, fetid muck, kicking aside corpses and unclaimed viscera to make room for themselves. Moans of agony filled the still, heavy air, the death throes of bleeding Persians who had not yet been dispatched by the pitiless camp followers. The ground was purple with blood, it flowed in rivulets into puddles and pools and collected in hollows, corpses lay mingled with each other, shields pierced, spears splintered, daggers unsheathed, some on the ground, most stuck in bodies, some still in the hands of the dead. The hardiest of the Greek troops struggled to remain on their feet, their hands shaking from the shock of the slaughter and the intensity of their effort, and they sought out comrades, even strangers, to lean against in their exhaustion and to feel some human comfort.

It was only now that the men realized the extent of their accomplishment, and of the danger they had faced. For all our awesome bluster, our attack was a precarious one—the men had kept their shields in an even line out of sheer discipline, but the unintended effect of this was to hide the enemy's view of what lay behind our front. We had, in fact, stretched ourselves so thin, in order to cover the entire length of the massed Persian forces facing us, that our phalanx was only four ranks deep—half the normal depth. We had had only one chance to break through the enemy, and against all odds, we had succeeded.

Clearchus dismounted and walked solemnly among the dazed men, lending a shoulder to one on which to lean momentarily, helping another to rise from the spot where his knees had given way in the shock of the killing. I was astonished to see him offer calm, quiet words of encouragement, amazed at the visible strength he lent to each man as he strode among the ranks. The groups through which he passed stood noticeably taller and stronger than those whose shoulders he had not yet touched. This, I reflected, was the source of Clearchus' own strength, his fierceness, this restorative and inspirational effect on the men at his command. After a few moments, he found a small boulder on which to stand, and throwing his helmet back from his face and raising his blood-encrusted sword to the heavens, he lifted a heart-stopping cry to the gods: "Lord of the Gods, Protector of Armies, these men—these men are *Greeks!* Savior Zeus and Victory!"

The troops leaped to their feet in triumph, clanging their swords upon shields with deafening effect, repeating the terrifying war chant. Hearing a strangled *"Eleleu, eleleu,"* voiced with great effort from somewhere nearby, I glanced behind me and realized it was coming from the parched, constricted throat of Xenophon as he too stared at Clearchus, an expression of murderous triumph in his eyes.

The men settled back down to rest for a moment, silent in their exhaustion and gratefulness at remaining alive, and gulping watered wine from their skins. At Proxenus' request, I galloped atop a small rise for better visibility, peering through the heat waves rising from the earth to where Cyrus' cavalry and the Greeks' left flank stood awaiting the outcome of our skirmish. The dust was still heavy in the air, but as it slowly cleared, I could perceive the outline of our other troops, a mile or so distant. I raised Proxenus' battalion flag and waved it in mad circles, and as I did so I saw their pennants lift high in jubilation, men raising their weapons above their heads. A moment later I heard their throaty cheer come rolling toward me over the plain. I glanced at Proxenus, and his eyes smiled beneath the uptilted brim of his visor.

The most imminent danger was from the king's right wing, which extended to our front as far as the eye could see, far overlapping Cyrus' relatively short left line. The king himself had maneuvered to face Cyrus, and had apparently ordered an encircling movement, for his hyperextended right wing was now folding in and around the prince's left side. Even the most ignorant battle squire could see that unless immediate action were taken, Cyrus' troops would either be surrounded, forced to retreat leaving our group separated and vulnerable, or driven back toward its right to the river, leaving all of us to our own fates, trapped between an enormous army in the front and an impassable river in the rear.

Seeing the prince's quandary, Clearchus ordered the men up and in battle order, and we wearily began a forced trot in the blazing sun back across the field whence we had just come, to support Cyrus' forces. Tissaphernes' cavalry, however, was nowhere to be seen, and when I pointed this out to Xenophon, he looked up, startled. Proxenus had assigned him to observe their movements, but in the exhaustion and glow of our rout over the Persians facing us, he had neglected this task for several minutes.

Cyrus was not about to wait for us to arrive, and for his own forces to be encircled, before he attacked. Astonishingly, he sounded a trumpet and began charging toward the king's heavy infantry, his own six hundred horsemen beside him in close formation, struggling to keep up with their racing leader, screaming the horrifying, ululating Persian battle cry as they sprinted. The king's men halted their march immediately, standing stock still in amazement. These were well-trained troops, not about to turn tail at the first approach of the adversary like those we had met; yet they were not so foolhardy as to continue advancing in the face of Cyrus' flying cavalry.

The king shouted an order, and his ranks of bowmen launched their arrows, forming a thick cloud as of evil birds, whizzing and humming through the air. Some struck home among Cyrus' lead horses, tripping them up, throwing their riders and creating chaos as those behind them stumbled over the writhing bodies of the fallen. Another volley of arrows was launched, this time more of them finding their mark; still Cyrus raced on, his long mane of hair streaming behind his helmetless head like a torch in a stiff wind.

With a roar of frenzied men and horses and a ringing crash of metal on metal, the prince's cavalry hit the king's armored troops in what seemed an explosion. Terrible screams rose from men and beasts, as the first ranks of the Persians were mercilessly trampled and Cyrus' lead horses were run through with javelins, or their legs hamstrung by enemy swords, toppling their riders into the dust. We were now running as fast as our fatigue would allow, determined to support the prince in his impossible charge against the king's hugely superior forces, yet also scarcely daring to believe what we were seeing: none of Cyrus' horses were retreating from the whirling cloud of dust, and that in fact a steady stream of broken and terrified enemy soldiers were flying toward the King's rear, shifting the cloud steadily back and obscuring what little we could see of the battle.

At this point my vision failed me for the dust and lengthening shadows of the day, and I shall have to rely on what I was told after the battle by Cyrus' comrades. Even by the light of day it is impossible for those doing the fighting to see everything, and in fact in battle, as in much of life, no one really knows anything more than what is happening right around himself. When we finally arrived at the prince's initial point of impact with the enemy, there was no one there still living. The battling forces had raced away, like rabid dogs rolling over each other down a street in a frenzy, and Cyrus' initial line of six hundred cavalry had been broken up and dispersed in the confusion into small bands that were running down Persians by the dozen. The prince had personally launched himself against the king's general, lancing the officer's horse through the haunches to trip him up and make him throw his rider, and then using the lance again to impale the man through the neck as he lay helpless on the ground.

The sight of their general pinned twitching and writhing by the broken lance point broke the nerve of the few enemy forces who were still maintaining order, and they began fleeing, singly and in small groups, across the wide plain, scattering to avoid being run down by Cyrus' marauding cavalry. His strategy was working, for as he routed the king's guard, the Persian right wing stopped advancing in its encircling movement as its officers tried to discern the outcome of the battle before committing themselves further to an attack against Ariaius' and Menon's forces.

After a frantic sprint across several hundred yards of the plain, Cyrus finally spied the king and the remnants of his guard attempting to maintain order in the retreat. "There he is!" shouted the prince. "Death to anyone who strikes the king before me!" Galloping up to Artaxerxes he struck him on the chest with the blunted end of his broken lance, knocking him off his horse. Just as he struck, however, one of the king's guards, throwing his own lance to ward off the blood-mad prince, struck Cyrus in the cheekbone under the eye, knocking him unconscious and off his horse. The king's bodyguards and Cyrus' nobles began viciously hacking at each other over possession of the respective bodies of their leaders. Neither side knew even whether the king and the prince were still alive, for they lay still as stones, brothers almost touching each other with their outstretched arms. After a few seconds, the king groggily arose, and himself actually began contributing to the fighting, which was no longer a kinglike affair on splendid stallions, but rather like one fought by common soldiers, on the ground in the piss and the mud, and the king was fighting for his very life.

Artaxerxes' men finally gained the upper hand, killing eight of the soldiers defending the prince's unconscious body. One of those soldiers, Artapates, a massive, scarred Scythian who had been with the prince since his boyhood and who was Cyrus' most trusted protector, leaped off his horse and threw his enormous body over the prince, shielding him with his own, and receiving the points of twenty lances in his back which had been intended for Cyrus. Even so, the man continued to live and breathe, and when the king ran over to where Cyrus lay, he was chagrined to find the old warrior still snarling at him through his broken teeth in hot hatred, shattered lance tips sprouting from his back like bristles on a boar and blood pouring from every orifice. Kneeling, the king pleaded with Artapates to roll off the prince's body, that the king would spare him, for the old Scythian had been his own boyhood instructor as well as Cyrus'. The warrior spat at him in fury, too spent and near death to even curse him with his lips, though his fast-glazing eyes still glowered at the king in a poisonous rage. Sorrowfully, the king drew Artapates' own scimitar from his belt, and muttered a quick prayer. He then brought it down hard, in one hasty stroke removing both the massive, battered head of the fearsome old fighter, whose eyes continued to glitter fiercely from their sightless sockets, and the small, smooth, almost childlike head of Cyrus, which rolled several feet along the same downward path, settling against Artapates' grizzled jaw as if still seeking the shelter and protection of his old tutor, in death as in life, like two plaster masks tossed carelessly in the corner after the performance is complete.

II

THE SIGHT OF THEIR STILL-LIVING king revived the Persians' hopes, and officers began forming them again into battle array. The king, now recovered from his fall, personally led a large contingent across the field, searching for the main body of invaders that he knew must be in the vicinity, but which in the chaos of the moment he had lost sight of.

Proxenus had ordered Nicarchus and me to gallop to a small hillock a mile or two distant from our troops, to survey the overall scene and attempt to determine where we could be of most use. Suddenly, from out of the dusty confusion, we saw several hundred Persian riders break away and begin streaking in the direction of our own camp. The realization struck us both at the same time like a blow to the face—Tissaphernes! The Greeks had left the camp unguarded in the rush to prepare for battle, assuming that the enemy forces would never be able to slip behind our lines, and that if we were forced into a retreat, we would simply fall back directly to the camp we had left behind, to defend our provisions and camp followers. We wheeled our horses.

"Ride to the camp!" Nicarchus screamed, as he raced his horse back down the steep slope. "Round up the camp followers behind the supply wagons! Do your best to hold!" He tore off to Clearchus' troops, hoping to intercept them before they had marched even farther from the camp, and tell Clearchus to turn around to defend our precious stores.

It was a contest I was destined to lose. Though the Persians and I were racing to the camp from opposite sides, the rough terrain I encountered hampered my horse, and I knew there was no chance of warning the camp ahead of the hordes about to sweep down on them. My horse descended a shallow gully and followed a dry stream bed for several hundred yards, during which time I lost sight of the camp. By the time I ascended several minutes later, I was too late—the cloud of dust had swept over Cyrus' followers and baggage train, and was now hovering there like a tornado stalled over the one spot where it inevitably does the most damage.

Some of Ariaius' native troops positioned near Cyrus had also rushed back to defend the camp when they realized the Persians were targeting it, but their heart was not in a fight to the death with their own countrymen. They were easily repelled, bouncing off of Tissaphernes' marauders like a ball thrown by a boy at a stone wall. They fled as far back as the previous day's camp, twelve miles down the trail, taking nothing with them but what they wore on their backs.

I continued riding, hoping to assist the hapless camp followers, and plunged blindly into the dust and chaos, ignorant even of whether I was entering the Persians' side of the fight or ours. Those in the camp were, in fact, acquitting themselves far more bravely than had Ariaius' troops. They had hastily arranged their meager defenses in a circle, surrounding their scant supplies and improvising the use of the Boeotian engines as they had seen the troops practicing. Amazingly, the ragged mass of sick men, prostitutes, cooks and mule drivers repelled Tissaphernes' attacking cavalry with frightening efficiency. Flames shot out in all directions from the terrorized mob, who had all gathered in a tight, wailing throng behind the engines, some hurling rocks ineffectually at the Persians, others desperately seeking shelter—behind tents, animals, and even fallen bodies—from the volleys of arrows and missiles raining down upon them from the riders. Mounds of Persians and frantic horses were stacked writhing in front of the engines, many burned black by the fire, some roasted alive in their heavy armor as the oily flames poured over the metal of their breastplates and helmets.

Dismounting to better pick my way through the chaos and slaughter, I saw a sight that chilled my blood to the marrow. Tissaphernes himself was among the marauders and had dismounted. Stalking through the rampaging troops in his heavy cavalry armor, he had seized Cyrus' beautiful Phocaian mistress by the hair as she ran terrified from Cyrus' flaming tent. The general handed her off to his battle squire to be taken behind Persian lines, then ordered three of his guards to race through the oily black smoke into the portion of the prince's tent that had not yet caught fire, to seize any battle plans or plunder they might find.

What they found was all the more valuable, and terrifying—for emerging a moment later, two of them carried scrolls and maps in their arms that they had blindly snatched up in a race against the flames, while the third was dragging Asteria by the collar of her robe. Tissaphernes froze as he watched her fight like a Fury, digging into the dirt with her bare feet and scratching the guard with her nails. She finally sank her teeth so deep into his wrist that he roared in pain and rage. He let go her collar momentarily and swiped her across the side of the face with his forearm hard enough to lift her bodily into the air before she landed, nimble as a cat, on all fours, spitting blood from her broken lips and glaring at him with hate-filled eyes.

Tissaphernes reacted in rage. He drew his jewel-encrusted scimitar and stormed to where Asteria crouched in terror and fury. Looking down at her, his face black and contorted with anger, he raised the glinting blade high above his left shoulder, and I felt the world grind to a halt. All the commotion and chaos around me seemed to freeze, as if time had become fragmented. The screaming of wounded men and terrified horses, which had risen to a deafening pitch, now thundered into silence, and the stench of the acrid black smoke and burning flesh was pushed into an odorless vapor in the back of my mind. The space between moments seemed to stretch, to become extended, and all my senses focused in utter concentration, to the exclusion of anything else, on the dream-slow trajectory of that lethal blade. It hesitated at the peak of its arc for an instant, quivering, and I held my breath, as the eyes of Asteria, the guard and myself all converged on its tip, each of us willing it with all the strength of our being in a direction to be ultimately decided only by Tissaphernes and the gods themselves. The world moved slowly, trancelike, as Asteria agonizingly raised her thin arms to ward off the blow and I involuntarily did the same, even though distant from the blade by many yards, by a lifetime.

My senses came crashing back to me with a roar, the mayhem that surrounded me bursting and flooding back into my consciousness and the din of the battle nearly knocking me off my feet by its sudden ferocity. My eyes did not waver from the blade. Tissaphernes, whirling quickly, slashed it viciously through the air almost faster than the eye could see, slicing off the head of the guard who had struck Asteria, as a gardener lops off a wayward branch from his fruit tree. Two thick streams of blood rose writhing and snakelike from the stump of the neck, crossing and twining about each other as they curved in a smooth arc to land with a spatter in the dust at Tissaphernes' feet. The dead guard stood upright for an instant, incephalic and spouting, stiffened and propped by his heavy cavalry armor, before his knees buckled and he slowly toppled into the dust, blood bubbling like black broth from the still-quivering flesh of the stump of his neck and mingling with the black, sour-smelling pools forming under his feet. Tissaphernes glared at the knoblike head lying several feet away, the helmet knocked askew from the impact, exposing the unfortunate guard's eyes and mouth, which were wide open in his now perpetual astonishment.

Tissaphernes then dropped his sword arm, and barely glancing at the cringing Asteria, shouted something to another of his guards standing nearby, and then strode back to his horse. The new guard roughly seized the girl by the collar and began dragging her again. She flopped jerkily like a fish being drawn in on a line, clawing desperately at her collar to relieve the pressure on her throat and keep from being garroted as she was finally forced behind the Persian lines.

Something snapped inside me, that instinct for self-preservation with which all men are born and which to a greater or lesser extent governs all our activities. At that moment, that instinct died, and I did things that no sane man should do. Throwing my shield up to my face to guard against the thrusting spears, I raced blindly into the Persian lines, slashing at any living being I could find, parrying and blocking in desperation. To my surprise, I suddenly found no resistance, as the enemy troops simply parted to let me pass through, a single maddened Greek being of little consequence to the Persians intent upon rushing the Boeotian fire and screaming camp followers. Each Persian soldier assumed that the man at his shoulder would dispatch me instead.

I did not let Asteria leave my sight, and although the entire lapse since she had been dragged kicking from the tent could not have been more than a minute, it seemed like an eternity to me as I hacked my way after her. When I had advanced to within several yards, her eyes fixed on me; though it is impossible that she could have known who I was through the helmet and nasal shrouding my face, and the sheets of blood and gore on my breastplate and limbs, a gleam of recognition seemed to spark in her eyes, reviving her from her half-strangled state. Suddenly summoning every fiber of strength remaining to her, her eyes bulging and her face an apoplectic red, she dug her feet once more into the ground, seized the silk fabric that had knotted and bunched around her throat in the guard's grasp, and pulled with all her might, ripping the robe from neck to waist.

The sudden release of her weight as she fell to her buttocks on the ground threw the struggling guard off balance, and he pitched forward onto his face. I was still several yards away, but just then was confronted by a Persian cavalryman who was startled to realize that a single, armed Greek was racing rampant through the middle of his lines. The man reined in his horse just in front of me, and with an evil grin raised his battle-axe, preparing to split my head like a melon. It was all I could do to tear my eyes off Asteria, who sat panting on the ground, ripping at the shreds of the long robe entangling her neck and legs. The guard who had been dragging her was struggling to regain his feet, hampered by the unwieldy cavalry armor he was wearing and the rushing mobs of men surrounding him and knocking him off balance.

I turned my attention to the rearing horse in front of me, and putting my head down, dove with every ounce of strength directly into the horse's belly. I felt the metal edge of my helmet crest bite deep into the soft solar plexus, and sensing, rather than hearing, his enormous gasp as the air exploded out of his diaphragm and lungs. I bounced back away from the horse from the shock of the impact and the rider's battle-axe cut through the air, shearing the crimson horsehair crest of my battle helmet. The animal stumbled in its pain, doubling over and writhing on its side, slathery strings of saliva trailing from its mouth and splattering onto my face and neck, its eyes rolling in terror. The horse's tongue, bleeding from having been bitten in the shock of the blow, lolled crazily out the side of its mouth.

The rider fell screaming beneath the animal, but I too tripped and fell, and spent precious seconds struggling to my own feet, trying desperately to dodge the flailing hooves. There was scarcely any strength left in my arms and legs, and I tottered like an ox after being poleaxed in a sacrifice. I turned frantically toward the spot I had last seen Asteria. There stood her captor, having finally gained his own feet, still clutching a long piece of silk in his hand like a torn banner, looking befuddled and searching for the girl where she had fallen from his grasp. There on the ground was the remainder of her robe, which she had finally disentangled from her flailing limbs and neck. And there, by now ten yards away and increasing the distance with every second, was fleet-footed Asteria, racing stark naked through the middle of the astonished enemy soldiers, wearing only the courtesan's ruby in her navel and an oversized wicker shield she had snatched from a dead Persian, protecting her from both blades and intemperate stares.

I leaped over the panting horse I had just felled, landing full in the face of its still struggling rider with my hobnailed leather sandals, and tore after her, laboring to slash with my now-deadened right arm, as she burst out of the Persian lines and scampered nimbly through a gap in the flames of the Boeotian engines like a spooked rabbit. I was not so fleet myself, preferring instead to assume my tried-and-true posture of putting my head down and barreling straight through, hoping for the best. Miraculously, the best occurred, and I too was unscathed by the flames.

With my last bit of remaining strength, I raced among the mob of followers, who grasped at me as if I were their saving god, as I searched desperately for where Asteria might have run among the chaotic defenses. I finally found her, against all likelihood, and without a thought for her tattered modesty, assisting a line of women with the bellows powering an engine. I rushed up, threw my blood-soaked and torn scarlet cloak over her shoulders, and then assumed my own place among the line of defenders.

The single rider's thundering hoofbeats had startled Clearchus' troops out of the mechanical marching rhythm into which they had fallen in exhaustion after their battle.

They were miles away from the camp, seeking the site of Cyrus' battle, and believing themselves to have been victorious on all fronts. Most were praying that they might avoid further engagement that day, for victory in surfeit can drive a man trembling to his knees as much as can defeat, and the men's only wish now was to return to camp, remove their armor, and rest. No one knew of Cyrus' fate, save those who had witnessed it firsthand, and the Greeks simply assumed that he had been successful in the general charge and was marauding and plundering to exhaustion.

The horseman, blood-soaked and caked with dust and grime, came racing in among the men and tumbled off his mount in his haste as he shouted for Proxenus. As it happened, Proxenus' squire was immediately at hand, and even he took several seconds before recognizing Nicarchus under the layers of dirt and blood.

"The Persians!" Nicarchus gasped. "The Persians are plundering the camp! Fetch Proxenus!" The astounded squire could not believe his ears—the king was in our camp? Had we been defeated after all? But what of Cyrus? The squire raced through the milling infantry, bellowing at them to continue marching, and found Proxenus and Clearchus riding together, calmly discussing whether to pursue the Persians further or return to camp for the night. Nicarchus came running up and sputtered his news to them without so much as a greeting. Their eyes widening in disbelief, they galloped over to the troops and found them already shifting their direction toward the camp and picking up their pace to a trot even before being ordered. Clearchus ran on foot at the head of his soldiers, brooding darkly on what this might mean.

When they arrived, the camp was a smoldering ruin. The camp followers wandered about like wraiths, seeking what shelter and food they might salvage. The king's troops had managed to burn or plunder over four hundred wagons of supplies, including most of the barley and wine we had so painfully dragged across the desert. Rather than the hot meal and sleep the weary soldiers had been looking forward to, they settled for filthy water, what few remains of stale bread had survived the plundering, and a blanketless rest on the hard ground.

But that was not the worst of it. For what Clearchus' reports soon confirmed to us was that Cyrus—the very reason for our long march, and our hope for guidance and supplies on our return back to Greece—had been killed. The Greeks had lost hardly a man in the battle, but we had lost our precious provisions, as well as our leader and benefactor. It was a long, cold night.

III

I FIRST SAW THE FAINT moving shadow cast on the wall, even before its source, as the intruder slipped silently into Proxenus' tent and moved cautiously toward my cot.

So many officers' tents had been destroyed in the attack that Proxenus had invited Xenophon and me to move into his own lodgings until better arrangements could be made. Though his tent had been clearly marked by its pennants as an officer's quarters, it had somehow survived the Persians' rampage, and in this way even seemed to the men to be a positive sign from the gods, one of ultimate hope and triumph. As Proxenus passed the night with the other officers at Clearchus' own makeshift quarters, sorting through the day's events and planning their strategy for tomorrow, I lay alone, trying to empty my mind of the myriad thoughts and memories that kept crowding in. It was a weakness of mine, from which I have always suffered. I do not know whether other men experience this as well, for I have always been too ashamed to ask, and if they do, I have no doubt but that they too are unable to mention it for fear of being thought mad. I find that just at those times when I most require a clear head—just as I consciously try to clean away the cobwebs, all those extraneous and unrelated passing notions constantly intruding upon my concentration—it is precisely at those times, as if at a signal set by an impish god, that every possible stray thought, every fear, every memory of childhood shame, every twinge of remorse for friends now dead, every haunting echo of the ancient Syracusan chant that drives me nearly mad, all come rushing back into my skull like wind into a void, shouldering each other aside to come to the fore of my thoughts, jostling and being tripped up and muscled to the back by one another. It is enough to drive one mad, and one can see from the careening and jolting of my syntax that I cannot even logically explain the experience. I had been lying there, my overheated brain at the point of driving me to panic, when I saw through the lashes of my half-closed lids that the tent flap had opened slightly and someone had stealthily entered.

My head instantly cleared. Anyone entering this tent could only have been searching for Proxenus, yet in the soft flickering of the tiny oil lamp perched on my table I could see that it was not Xenophon, as I first thought. Peering more closely, my breath stopped as I recognized the intruder, standing stock-still, profiled in the light in the small space in the center of the tent, her eyes still unaccustomed to the dimness. I pulled back my blanket to sit up, and Asteria, startled, whirled around to face the sound. Her face registered shock as she recognized me, and she stood motionless for a moment, staring at me before stepping silently over to my cot. She was wearing only a light shift and a leather belt, and was barefoot, trembling from the cold, or from the horrors she had seen that day, or from fear as to what would become of her now that her master was dead and she was alone. I could see the dried trails of tears that had streaked through the layer of dust still coating her cheeks as she lay down in my arms, pressing herself to my chest and burying her face in my neck as she emitted a sigh—a long, shuddering, wracking sigh that seemed far too deep for her tiny frame, as if welling up inside her from some secret place, from some time long before.

I held her tightly, pulling the blanket up over us both and feeling her cold, shivering limbs gently relax and respond to my own body's heat. After a time, the spasms of her sobbing gradually subsided, and she lay quietly in my arms, awake and keeping her own thoughts, her long eyelashes softly brushing my neck with her blinking, and the damp, steamy scent of her breath and hair rising up to my face in the silence. She lifted her head, her face inches from mine in the semidarkness, peering into my eyes, searching my thoughts. By the dim lamplight I could see nothing but the dark silhouette of her long hair, a faint halo of light glowing behind it, the odor of charred wood and crushed flowers from her skin and hair oddly comforting. I put my hands on either side of her face, my fingertips in her hair where I could feel the broken shaft of a small feather, like a shattered lance, which she had woven into the strands, painstakingly sifted from the ashes of her burned possessions in an attempt to salvage some last remnant of adornment. I shifted my body slightly and turned her face into the dim light, to discern her expression. As I did so, I looked intently into the flickering shadows passing before her and revealing her, watching as the penumbra lifted from the depths between her brows and cheekbones. I waited for her eyes to appear from the darkness as does a seer fearfully observing the emergence of the moon after an eclipse, and feeling the same tremors and uncertainty as he would in divining the gods' intent. Eyes like hers had never before been seen, at least not in this world, and in the darkness their coloring, whether blue, gray or green, was unknowable. The true color may have been any or all of them, depending upon the quality of the outer light, or of the inner thought they concealed. Later, in the days to come, I would see them turn as black and unfathomable as the ocean depths when one peers over the side of a ship, and in her sleep, under her half-closed lids, the orbits would gleam a brilliant, gelid white, like a sliver of ice on an eave glinting both refreshingly and deadly in the sun.

She seemed to be questioning in her mind, divining the oracle, and she apparently received a positive response from the gods, for suddenly she pressed her warm, sweet mouth to mine, harder than I would have thought possible for one seemingly so fragile; and then I felt her moist, flowerlike lips gliding lightly, but with increasing pressure, over my neck and chest as I slipped off her thin garment, which had been tied with a belt holding an enormous, sheathed dagger, and I wrapped my arms around her, and we gave each other much solace.

I lay awake most of that night, watching as the fear and worry gradually left her tense face and her features relaxed into a blissful dream, or perhaps merely into nothingness, into an empty place where the absence of pain and fear, even of love, is the greatest happiness of all. I drifted off for a few minutes at a time, waking at the slightest noise, the discreet coughing of a sentry pacing outside, and then falling back again into a fitful dream. I was asleep, or so she thought, when she finally arose an hour before the first hint of dawn had lit the eastern sky. I watched as if in a dream, through barely opened eyes, as she pulled her shift back down over her slender body and tightened the leather belt around her waist. To this day, I am unsure whether I continued to watch, or had slipped back into dreaming, when she silently drew her knife, considered it closely for a minute in the semidarkness, and then carefully, noiselessly, not daring to touch me with her hand or sleeve for fear of waking me, brought the razor-sharp tip up to the pulsing, blue vein in my neck just below the jaw. Whether truly awake or merely dreaming, I feigned the deepest sleep, fearing that the slightest gesture or flicker of my eyes, the softest catch of my breath, would cause the dagger to be plunged into my throat. She held the tip there for what seemed like minutes, as motionless as one who has seen a gorgon, staring into my just-closed eyes, daring the slightest response. My soul slipped away from my body and floated through her, behind her, to the ceiling of the tent, and I could see her from above, leaning over my frozen body, the tendons in her wrist tense and quivering from the strain of holding the knife in perfect stillness at my neck.

A small drop of blood appeared on my skin just below the tip of the knife, pure and clean, virginal in comparison to the gushing, grime-filled gore I had witnessed the previous day, and seemed just about to slowly make its streaked path down the side of my neck, when it paused, as if to consider whether this was the best course of action, and began slowly to coalesce and gel. This I could see, by all the gods I swear I could see, as if I were a third person in the room, watching helpless and voiceless from behind her back. The drop quivered and hung, like a bead on a necklace, its increasing inner weight straining against its thickening surface, and my eyes from above were unable to focus on anything other than that tiny, malignant, reddish black globe, reflecting, upside down, the wavering flame of the lamp and the oddly distorted and magnified face of the girl. I could see from the reflection that her eyes, too, were focused on the drop as if in a trance, considering all the implications to her life and to mine that were represented in that silently swelling little mass, that tiny, pregnant bulb, which itself appeared to be endowed with growing life, rather than merely reflective of it, and of death.

Without warning she straightened up, bringing the knife again to her eyes and examining the reddened tip for a moment in the soft lamplight, before shaking her head as one does when waking from a deep sleep, and slipping the knife quickly back into the sheath at her belt. She bent down again, silently licked the tiny red drop from my neck with her hot tongue, and just as silently kissed my dry and trembling lips. She then slipped back out to the cold coals of her campfire, as wraithlike as she had entered, and my soul came rushing back into my body, leaving me gasping for breath and shaking in cold perspiration, sitting up alone in the cot as if waking from a nightmare. We had said nothing to each other the entire night, indeed we had never yet spoken a word to each other, but I felt my fate as entirely in the hands of this woman as of the gods, and I realized what an extraordinary, and damnable thing that can be.

BOOK SIX

CLEARCHUS

His white head and gray beard in the dust, breathing the last of his strong soul, bloody entrails grasped in his beloved hands . . .

—LYCURGUS

I

IT WAS THE STENCH THAT finally roused me from my fitful dreams that morning—a smoky, sweet odor not unlike that of meat roasting for the sacrifice, but with an indefinable rankness, as of the burning of tainted flesh, of meat lacking in fat to absorb the heat and flame and allow the fire to cook the substance gradually, rather than rapidly charring it. I rose groggily from my cot, splashed a handful of water on my face from the skin hanging on a peg by the door, and stepped outside.

The morning sky, by contrast with the usual whitish blue palette that spawns and accompanies the desert heat, was today a glowering, malignant yellowish gray. The air was fouled by a vile, stinking smoke that hung low to the ground and drifted as if alive, swirling slowly in small circles, dissipating and coagulating, meandering serpentlike in futile paths that began in death and ended in reluctant oblivion. The churning haze effaced the life-giving rays of the sun, rendering it a dull scab-red in color, pulsing squat and malevolent in the sky, as if loath to make any greater effort to rise or to shimmer. For miles in all directions lay the flat, immeasurably dreary expanse of the desert, stretching unbroken to the horizon with hardly a tree or a range of hills to break the monotony. I had failed to notice earlier the dreadful endlessness of this terrain, forsaken of the gods, bereft of all interest, even as I had marched through it only days before.

As my eyes drifted away from the horizon to the nearer perspective, I saw that contrary to my first impression, the land was indeed composed of many features that had not been immediately apparent, like brush strokes on a painting, or the waves and currents of the sea as observed by the sailor, standing out in relief on the water's infinite flat smoothness. The earth was cracked and broken, split into random patterns that bifurcated and converged like a rash on the skin, strewn with gullies and washes, dry streambeds and low, withered shrubs. It was a foul terrain of pain and frustration, ground that had slowed my frantic return to the camp on horseback the day before. In the middle distance, just beyond a line of small hills that I could barely distinguish from its surroundings, I made out the vast expanse of the Persian army where it had halted in its retreat, massed like a milling column of ants stretching off to the horizon. The Persian battle pennants providing tiny spots of brightness and color on what was otherwise a drab, undifferentiated cloud of men and beasts. I shook my head to concentrate my thoughts, and focused my gaze on the specifics.

For miles around lay the detritus and destruction of the previous day's wide-ranging battle. Upturned wagons smoldered on their sides, their contents of grain and salted fish spilled and half torched, some still spewing a foul, greasy smoke. Spear shafts and javelins were spiked into the hard earth at crazy angles where they had landed, the ends swaying and quivering slightly as if curious, invisible desert gods were testing the depth and the strength of the shanks. My gaze ranged over the broad landscape, flitting sideways from fractured hill to withered clump of grass until I reluctantly, unwillingly permitted it to settle on the dark lumps scattered about the plain in numbers too daunting to count: the twisted bodies of lamed or trampled horses; the oxen and sheep viciously slashed in the abdomen or throat for no other reason than to deprive the Greeks of their sustenance and service; and perhaps least unexpected, yet most horrifying, the men.

Thousands of men, or former men, they were, though many were unrecognizable as such. It had been only a day since they fell, yet the furnace-like heat had cooked them where they lay on the hot sand, and many had swollen to twice their size with the gas in their bellies. Most lay deathly still, inert and silent as the rocks and crumpled wagons littering the plain. Others, however, hissed and belched in the heat, their limbs occasionally twitching and jerking. Their repose was further disturbed by the raucous cawing of crows circling and gathering in the sky above, summoning their courage for forays to the ground, aimed precisely at those dead whose inner workings were now most exposed to the heavens. I swallowed my rising disgust and forced myself to absorb the scene, to take in the changing details, noting as I stared that not all the bodies were prone and dead, but that many consisted of the black silhouettes of camp followers or soldiers, wandering aimlessly or kneeling or even sleeping in the fields, shoulder to entrails with the dead. An exhausted Greek follower half rose in sleep to slap at an overeager crow that had tested him with a peck to the eyes, and a bloodied Spartan, still in battle gear, sat up swearing and kicking at a stray pig that had begun rooting at his crotch. A filthy, robed woman rocked back and forth on the ground, her hands clawing at her face and hair as she moaned and keened wordlessly at an unidentifiable loss.

To my right a hundred soldiers and camp followers had organized themselves into funeral brigades, which had started pyres and begun collecting bodies for sorting and burning. Persian soldiers, many of them already half charred from the effects of the Boeotian engines, were stripped of any usable possessions and left naked where they fell, their flesh bled or burnt dry of blood and the skin on their faces a hideous, bluish white mask. A row of cadavers had been collected, fallen camp followers of Cyrus' army, who were being identified as best as possible and laid with a brief ceremony into the crackling bonfires by men robed and hooded in thick blankets to shield them from the intense heat and the stench. To my relief, I saw no armor of Greek soldiers in the rows of the dead.

Wood for the pyres was readily at hand, if only from the thousands of Persian arrows and heavy Egyptian shields lying about the surrounding field, abandoned in their owners' hasty departure. Intact wagons and carts, too, were available, and despite the Persians' attempted slaughter, hundreds of head of cattle and sheep had somehow survived the carnage of their brethren and escaped in the night, and were now wandering in the vicinity of the camp, bawling to be milked and tended. If there were not enough provisions to last the entire return trip home, we were at least sufficiently supplied to tide us over for the next several days.

I wandered the camp, taking stock of our circumstances and searching for Xenophon and Proxenus. A cloud of dust had separated from the main body of enemy troops in the distance, too small to warrant alarm, but meriting my wary attention as it was intercepted by the Spartan scouts Clearchus had remembered to post on the approaches to the camp. I was soon able to make out an incoming rider at the outer periphery of the battlefield, unarmed and bearing a herald's staff. Since I was in the vicinity, I waited for him as he picked his way gingerly around the swelling Persian cadavers, and I then led him to Proxenus' tent, which for want of any better structure had become the informal gathering place of the army's officers.

Clearchus, who alone among the Greeks was in an unaccountably cheerful mood, came to meet him, and found to his surprise that it was Phalinus, an older, morose-looking Spartan who in his younger days had served under him, but had found the experience to be too trying, and had managed to arrange duties elsewhere. Phalinus had always considered himself an expert military strategist, rather than an actual fighter, and several years ago had convinced Tissaphernes to take him on in this capacity. He was said to be held in high regard even by Artaxerxes for his knowledge of Spartan military tactics and ways. Clearchus punched him good-naturedly on the shoulder.

"You old dog!" he said. "So the king hasn't sent you packing by now for your sorry performance yesterday! You must have him by the short hairs with all your stories about your great victories over Athens. Have you told him yet how you used to be my water boy when we were young *hebontes* training in Sparta?" Clearchus guffawed loudly at this, but Phalinus remained dour and stony-faced, his eyes bloodshot and watering from the smoke of the funeral pyres, as he refused to reciprocate his former commander's lighthearted greeting.

Phalinus waited silently for all the Greek captains to arrive, and then coldly called their attention.

"The king," he announced in an authoritative voice, "having killed Cyrus and plundered the Hellene camp, declares a great victory. He orders you to lay down your arms, and to beseech him for what mercy he might deign to offer you."

Utter silence. The Hellenes were speechless, and I saw Clearchus immediately flush, the scar on his cheek turning livid. He paused a few seconds to gain control over his anger.

"It is not for the victors to lay down their arms," he said slowly and coolly, gesturing broadly with his great, hairy arm at the immense field littered with Persian corpses. He then stalked off to complete a sacrifice he had been about to attend, leaving the other officers gathered about Phalinus, muttering to themselves.

Proxenus finally broke the tension. "Phalinus, you yourself are a Greek:

speak to us openly and honestly. Is the king addressing us as a conqueror, or merely asking for our weapons as a gesture of good faith?" At this, all the captains spoke up, either shouting Proxenus down for his candor toward Phalinus, or attempting to ask their own questions. Finally an Athenian captain, Theopompus, a dandy whom I had seen one or two times with Socrates in the agora, managed to gain the others' attention.

"Phalinus," he said. "Put yourself in our place. Now that we have been plundered by the king, we have nothing but our arms and our courage. As long as we keep our weapons, we can still use our courage. But if we give up the weapons, we lose both. Could you blame us if we rejected the king's demand?" He smiled smugly at his compact argument, and waited for Phalinus' reaction. We all watched him.

Phalinus laughed tightly. "Well said, little Socrates! But logic will not advance your cause if the facts are against you. Courage or not, the king still has half a million men in the field, and that many more again in Babylon a few hours' march away. You are foolish to think there is anything you can do to check his power. I am a Greek too. If I thought you had one chance in a thousand to prevail against the king, or even to run from him and return safely back home, I would tell you to do it. By the gods, I've earned my own little stash of gold from the Persians over the years—I would even go with you. The fact that I don't speaks for itself. Ask your great philosopher what he would do in that situation."

By this time, Clearchus had completed the sacrifice and returned, his face black with the fury that had been building up within him. "Take this back to the king," he spat. "If he wishes to be friends with us, we will be more valuable to him with our weapons than without. If he wishes to make war on us, all the more reason for us to keep our weapons. The weapons stay, and will remain sharpened. And you, Phalinus, you ass-kissing son of a bitch: The next time I set eyes on you in my camp I will be carving your balls for my breakfast."

Phalinus smirked. "I am merely the king's representative," he said unctuously. "I can't tell you not to act the fool, Clearchus. But I have one more message from the king. He offers a truce if you stay where you are, but war if you move from this place, either forward or backward. Give me an answer to take back to the king: Will there be a truce, or will there be war?"

"Yes," said Clearchus.

Phalinus looked at him in confusion, then glared. "What am I supposed to tell the king?" he asked in irritation.

"That for once we agree with him. There will be truce if we stay, and war if we move."

But he did not say which he intended.

That evening, Clearchus ordered us to break camp just after dinner. When Xenophon passed the order on to me, I could not believe I had heard him right.

"Do you realize that Clearchus has just signed our death warrant?" I exclaimed. "We are only ten thousand—the king will have his entire army upon us by daybreak!"

Xenophon didn't flinch. "That may be—but Clearchus' hand was forced, by our own troops. Did you know? Three hundred Thracian infantry and forty cavalry deserted to the king this afternoon."

"Three hundred and forty? Couldn't their officers keep them in line until we all came to a decision as a unit?"

Xenophon hesitated, and looked away with an expression of bitterness. "Their own officers led them. And as soon as word of the desertion spreads through the army, there will be others."

I pondered his words. There was no telling how much longer Clearchus would be able to keep the army together in the absence of the common hope of plunder from Cyrus. A frontal attack on Artaxerxes, with badly outnumbered troops, was out of the question. Staying where we were with no provisions, while the king wore us down by delaying, would be to commit passive suicide. Our position simply was not tenable.

"Where does Clearchus intend to march us?" I asked.

Xenophon shrugged. "He sees no choice but to unite with Ariaius and the native troops, and to hope they remain loyal to us rather than to the king."

It remained unspoken, yet implicit, that moving from our present location meant a declaration of war against the entire Persian empire, as surely as our forebears had declared war on the king's own ancestors, Darius and Xerxes.

After a long march in the darkness, we reached Ariaius' camp at midnight. The officers immediately gathered around a council fire, and all of them, Persian and Greek alike, swore to defend each other to the death. At Ariaius' insistence, they sealed the pact by dipping their spears in the blood of a newly sacrificed bull, each man daubing a bit on the breast of his neighbor with his spear point as a sign of mutual trust.

Clearchus then spoke up, impatient.

"Now that we've sworn allegiance to each other with that spear-point bullshit, and recognize that we're both in the same predicament, what do you propose, Ariaius? You know this country. Do we return the way we came?"

Ariaius stared morosely into the fire a few seconds before answering.

"If we return that way, we're sure to starve. On our march here the countryside was a barren desert. For seventeen stages we had to rely on the provisions we brought with us, and now we have none." He paused again for a moment, in thought. "Returning by the northern route is longer, but it at least brings us through fertile country with plenty of villages, where we can take provisions. The key is to move fast, and put as much ground between us and Artaxerxes as possible. He won't dare to attack us with a small force, but if he moves with his entire army he'll be too slow to catch us. I propose we move quickly, while we can."

This set the officers to grumbling, for it looked like the coward's way out—a mere cut and run. No one else had a better idea, however, so by default the officers voted it as their plan, sacrificed to the gods, and each went back to catch what few hours of sleep he could before rousing the exhausted army the next morning and embarking on a forced march.

I lingered for a time in the shadows by the fire, reluctant to return to the tent, my mind whirling and my body tense and restless. Despite the awfulness of that long, bitter day—the burning of the dead, the confrontation with Phalinus, the exhausting march in the dark to Ariaius' camp—I had scarcely been able to think of anything but the event of the night before. My thoughts raced with the vivid dream I had experienced, my near certainty that I was about to die at Asteria's hands from having unknowingly committed some crime of concupiscence, like one of those sticklike male insects I once watched in horror as a child which, even during the very act of mating, is calmly devoured by the female headfirst, right down to his still rutting abdomen. After wandering aimlessly across the camp for some time, I realized with a jolt that my feet had carried me, almost instinctively, to the quarter of the camp followers.

Picking my way through the confused jumble of wagons and tents in the women's section, I sensed the burden of mournful and accusing glances pressing upon me from every shadow and shelter. I wandered blindly and fruitlessly for an hour, uncertain that I would ever be able to find her—when suddenly, seemingly from nowhere, I felt her soft hand slip into mine and tug me gently away. She led me to the edge of the camp, and I tried to pull her close to me, but she stiffened, resisting me, and continued to guide me forward in the dark until the mournful sounds of the camp had been left far behind and we came to a small rock outcropping, sheltered by a forlorn shrub. Here she finally stopped, and without sitting down, turned toward me, her face shadowed in darkness and her body tense.

"Theo, last night was . . . last night I was afraid of everything, and what we did was wrong. I am sorry."

I remained silent, waiting for her to continue, for I had nothing to contribute to a statement such as this.

"You know me but you know nothing about me," she said. "I am a child of the Persian court. I was beholden to the prince, and before that to his family. Yet here in the desert I have nothing. I can bring you only misery."

"Asteria, if you mean a dowry, that is not something I am concerned with. I too have nothing of my own. And a marriage is impossible for the time being anyway, under these circumstances."

She paused for a moment, seemingly puzzled, before I saw a faint, sad smile briefly flit across her face. "That isn't exactly what I meant. It is a question of family honor. My father . . ."

I interrupted her, glowering. "You are concerned about honor and your father—why, because I have no rank? I am a soldier of Athens, a warrior. I have no money, but I have a strong arm, and the vast heritage of my city. Who is your father, what does he have to boast of?"

She sighed. "Theo, you don't understand. If it were merely his disapproval, that I could endure. It is something far more than that, though, something I fear I could not live with. How can I betray my father?"

"Betray him? Where is your father now? Of what possible threat can I be to him, or him to me?"

"I'm not even sure myself . . ."

"Asteria—look at our situation, look at *your* situation. A woman must take protection where she finds it. I am here, and he is not."

She paused for a long time in the darkness, peering into my face, seeming to perceive me as clearly as if it were light, again attempting to divine the response of the gods before acting. After a moment she moved toward me, and I felt her warm, fragile body press against me. I bent down to breathe in her scent, the same powerful perfume of charred wood and crushed flowers that had lingered in my nostrils since her visit the last night. As we settled on the sparse, dusty grass beneath us, I began fumbling clumsily with her tunic, attempting to slip my hand beneath.

"Wait," she said, "we haven't time. The sun is beginning to rise already." The eastern sky had indeed begun to lighten and the camp was beginning to stir with the sounds of morning activity, though hardly anyone had slept more than a few hours.

I relaxed and an almost overwhelming sense of weariness and release washed over me, leaving me grateful for the opportunity merely to lie still with her in my arms. She, too, seemed content, worlds away from the tension and desperation of the night before. Still, the terrible doubts I had harbored earlier continued to nag at me.

"Asteria," I began haltingly, "last night, when you were leaving, I think I had a dream—it was as if you, and your knife . . ." I was at a loss for words, for how do you speak to someone about such an experience? I looked at her face, which was gradually becoming more distinct in the graying sky, her limpid eyes almost glowing in the ethereal gray light, yet still colorless as shadows. Her expression was blank, almost quizzical, as she gazed calmly back at me.

"We don't know from where dreams come," she said, "or why they fade. It's not important. You dream of death but it's only a dream. Our lives move forward."

For the second time in my life I heard four words that struck me, leaving an imprint not to be removed, like a scar, or a family tattoo on the neck of a baby. I held her close and observed the return of Eos, and then for a short time I slept, mercifully free of dreams.

The next day we traveled uneventfully as far as a small cluster of villages without catching sight of any enemy forces, although we were shadowed the entire way by Tissaphernes' cavalry scouts traveling singly or in groups of two or three, keeping well beyond arrow range. That night, the first in over a week that the army had had a chance to rest from sundown to sunup, the men were spooked. Sensing their restlessness, Xenophon asked me to quietly make the rounds among them, to try to identify their fears.

"It's not necessary, Xenophon," I said. "I know what they are feeling. The men have seen too much. They're horrified at losing the prince so far from the sea and home. They fear the Greek gods of their past have left them, and that weighs heavily on their minds."

Xenophon pondered this, but I could see from his expression that he remained skeptical.

"Those are all general concerns," he argued, "but these men are veterans—they have experienced loss as well as victory. Surely the entire camp can't be on the verge of panic because of a vague feeling of abandonment by the gods?"

"There is one thing more," I admitted, as he stared at me expectantly. "The Greek troops, unlike the officers, did not swear an oath of loyalty to Ariaius' men. They don't trust them, particularly given their desertion of the camp followers at Cunaxa. The native troops' camp is only a mile away, and they outnumber us by a factor of ten. Our men can't shake the feeling that a dark shadow has been cast directly over them."

Xenophon gazed out over the camp in understanding, and began walking slowly back to Clearchus' quarters. The sky was dark and glowered with thunderheads, blotting out the moon and stars, and the troops huddled close to their fires and to each other for comfort. Every shout from a neighboring company, every oath from a soldier banging his finger while splitting wood, every whinny of a distant horse made the men jump and peer fearfully into the darkness. Everyone knew, or imagined, that we were surrounded by stealthy Persians, Tissaphernes' assassins or Ariaius' traitors, creeping unseen through the darkness, ready to pick off stragglers with a quick slash across the throat, or whole companies of us by a volley of arrows as we passed in silhouette in front of our bonfires.

Even by the second watch, none of the Greeks had gone to sleep. They began consolidating into larger groups as men sought out those of their own dialect and country for comfort. Twice fearful commotions arose as someone shouted that there was an attack and everyone rushed for their weapons. The army would never survive the night intact—it was on the verge of a riot, and men were ready either to kill their commanders out of fury at the loss of their dreams of wealth, or to break and run wildly into the night, each trying to save his own skin by abandoning what he felt was the certain death of the others.

As the night went on, a third panic fell on the Greeks, this one encompassing the whole camp, and an uproar ensued like one might expect from a surprise enemy attack. Clearchus despaired at the men's fears. He had the trumpets blown, and sent around his veteran herald, Tolmides the Elean, who had a harsh, grating voice that could be heard like a broken bell above the hubbub. At Clearchus' orders Tolmides bellowed for silence, and issued a proclamation from headquarters:

"Let every man know this! Your commander Clearchus beseeches you to return to your individual companies and to remain still, under penalty of death for abandoning the line and rank; and he hereby offers a reward of one talent, or fifteen years' pay, for information leading to the identification of the man who let the wild ass loose in camp and created the unholy commotion that is disturbing the commander's sleep."

To those certain of an enemy attack, the news that the uproar had been caused by a mere runaway donkey brought welcome humorous relief, and reassured them sufficiently that they were able to rest for the remainder of the night. Those who were wiser, who knew the enemy was not present, but who were even more afraid of the army's potential for self-destruction, were calmed at Clearchus' foresight in claiming that he, for one, was sleeping soundly. A few enterprising individuals even spent the night peering into every tent, searching for the rogue donkey.

As for myself, I passed the rest of the evening pondering what the deities could have been thinking, to have blown their poor Greeks, like Odysseus, so far off course.

Proxenus woke us early the next morning, in a cheerful mood.

"Tissaphernes' ambassadors are arriving! Clearchus just received word from our outposts that heralds from the Persians have requested entry to the camp!" I put on a clean tunic, and began sand-polishing Xenophon's armor and mine. Cyrus was dead, yet the king and Tissaphernes appeared to be as wary of the Hellenes as we of them, or they would not have sent a party bearing a flag of truce to parley with us.

In the meantime, Clearchus did not miss the opportunity to make Tissaphernes' ambassadors feel some discomfort. He sent word to the outposts to detain them out of sight of the army until he was ready. Then he called together his commanders to issue orders.

"Form the army into battle array along the top of the ridge," he said. "Place the heavy armor in the center with the targeteers along one side and cavalry on the other. Make sure the ranks are at least three deep, and keep the baggage wagons and camp followers down in the valley. No need for the king to be reminded that he outnumbers us a hundred to one."

When the envoys arrived moments later, he ordered that they be disarmed and dismounted, with even their ceremonial lance bearing Tissaphernes' golden winged-horse pennant taken away. They were escorted by the most hulking and heavily armed Spartans, past a field where six of Proxenus' Boeotian engines were conveniently engaged in horrific practice, to Clearchus' headquarters. This he had arranged something in the manner of a tribal throne, drawing upon the experience of his years spent in Byzantium, inside an enormous tent he had hastily cobbled together from several others. The interior was sumptuous—all armored attendants, veiled harem girls lounging on cushions, priceless carpets and tapestries and worshipful slaves awaiting his slightest order. The whole scene was so foreign to the rest of us who, unlike Clearchus, had no experience with Persian ways, that it was all we could do to keep from laughing, especially at the sight of our austere Spartan leader so surrounded by luxury. He gave us such a black look, however, with his terrible, scarred face and single, bushy eyebrow that ran without pause the entire length of his forehead, that he silenced us dead in our tracks. He then composed his expression into a haughty scowl to receive his guests.

The Persians were impressed with the scene, having at first, outside the tent, mistaken Proxenus for the chief officer because of his commanding appearance. After being suitably berated by a guard for their lack of respect, they were ushered into the dim, smoky coolness of the "throne room." There were three of them—generals, from the looks of their haughty military demeanor, fine silk sashes and robes and carefully oiled and curled beards. As they strode proudly onto the carpets inside the tent, Clearchus reclined sipping a cup of wine, affecting a pose of utter indifference. The envoys launched into the carefully prepared introduction and formulations that precede all Persian court palavers, reciting the litany of honorific titles that garnish the Great King's name like jewels in a crown:

"General Clearchus: On behalf of Lord Tissaphernes, Commander of the King's Cavalry, who speaks for the great King Artaxerxes, King of kings and Judge of men, Ruler of multitudes of lands and peoples, Conqueror of races far and wide across the entire breadth of the earth, Brother of the Sun, Omnipotent among Mortals, Invincible and Exalted, a Persian and son of a Persian . . ." The interpreter raced to keep up.

Clearchus leaned forward and interrupted the florid speech, waving his hand wearily and dismissively.

"I don't have time for your boot-licking introductions," he sneered in his grating voice. "You spew idle flattery like droppings from a fucking she-goat." I prayed that the interpreter was a clever one, or at least not too fluent. "I ran your crack troops into the ground at Cunaxa like a bevy of Chian flute girls. My camp followers ground their bones for meal, and they are eager for more. If your cloven-footed king wishes a truce to arrange matters going forward, he'll have to do better than send dung-eating rump-scratchers like you. Tell Artaxerxes that my army has not yet had breakfast, and that we do not do business on an empty stomach. Greeks don't eat dog turds and thorns, as I'm told Persians do, so if the king is unable to provide some proper provisions willingly, as a sign of good faith, we will have to obtain supplies on our own terms." At that, Clearchus, the ascetic Spartan, leaned back into the darkness with an evil smirk, beckoning one of the trembling girls to refill his glass.

The Persian generals stood frozen in horror, their barely contained rage flushing their cheeks. I had to pinch my arm black and blue to keep from guffawing on the spot, and I could see Proxenus' jaw muscles tensing as he worked to stifle his laughter. The embassy filed out silently, only to see that our men had been arranged into two long files outside the tent entrance, between which the ambassadors had to pass for what seemed an eternity before they finally arrived at their horses and were given back their weapons. As they mounted, on a signal from Proxenus the troops raised a deafening roar and began banging their spears loudly against the bronze rims of their shields. The suddenness of the clamor so frightened the already skittish Persian horses that they bolted, and it was all the enraged generals could do to hang on to the beasts' necks with both arms to keep from falling as they leaped away, back over the ridge to the Persian camp.

Clearchus' ruse succeeded, for the ambassadors were back that afternoon, bearing a considerably humbler and less formal demeanor. This time, he kept them waiting almost two hours before summoning them in to his august presence. Without further introduction, they informed him that Tissaphernes felt his request was more than reasonable, and that as a sign of good faith, he would lead them to a village of suitable size where they could camp comfortably as long as they liked, have ready access to a market for food, and make preparations at their leisure to complete whatever arrangements were agreed to between the king and the Greek leadership.

Clearchus dismissed the ambassadors to a meager supper he had arranged for them (a thorn branch courteously placed on each plate in order, he said, to make them feel more at home), and consulted with his council. It seemed best not to overplay his hand, for sooner or later Tissaphernes would discover the Hellenic forces' true strength, and it would not do to insult him further before a proper truce could be arranged. Clearchus waited an appropriate time, letting the ambassadors become so fearful of the outcome that they hardly touched their food; and when even the Greek officers themselves began questioning whether he might have a change of heart, he finally summoned the ambassadors back and ordered them to return to the king and arrange guides for his army at first light.

II

SUSPECTING THE KING'S potential for treachery, Clearchus marched the army in full battle array. The physical obstacles we encountered, oddly enough, were not of the gods, mountains, or rivers, or even the desert, but rather man-made. The land was riddled with dozens, perhaps hundreds of ditches and irrigation canals that could not be crossed without first building bridges, which we did by cutting down date palms and lashing them together. Clearchus himself set the example in this effort, wading into the mud with the younger men and carrying logs on his shoulders. At one point, spying a shirker resting in the reeds munching on bread he had saved from that morning, he dragged him out by the hair, threw him into the mud at the bank of the canal and beat him brutally with a heavy wooden rod he carried to pry embedded logs. The man was bleeding and unconscious before Clearchus finally laid off the punishment. The troops had gathered around silently and now stood staring, some reproachfully, others in fear and wonder at the harsh treatment.

Clearchus climbed onto the bridge footing and glared at the men. "What the fuck are you all staring at?" He bellowed hoarsely. "Cyrus is dead and you are marching on your own, in enemy territory! By the good grace of the gods, you ass-humpers have been blessed with a Spartan for a general. When I lead men, I expect nothing less of myself than what I order them to do. And I expect nothing less of my men than unquestioning obedience! When a Spartan leads an army, that army is Spartan! And you will work as Spartans and behave as Spartans, or by the gods you will die as Spartans."

The men dispersed sullenly, avoiding Clearchus' harsh gaze, but there was no further shirking as they redoubled their efforts to move the army and its baggage over the rough roads. Xenophon sidled up to me on his horse a few minutes after the incident, his face red with outrage.

"Did you hear him, Theo? The man's a tyrant! 'Work as Spartans or die as Spartans.' That dog-breathed jackass is going to have the men deserting like our Thracians if he doesn't give them a better reason to follow him than the threat of being beaten with a stick in the mud."

"Such as starving in the desert, perhaps?" I suggested evenly. "Or being picked off on the sly by Persian outriders? Those might be good motivations."

He glared at me fiercely, but I held his stare, and he wheeled his horse and galloped off.

When we arrived at the village three days later, we were relieved to see that the conditions were just as the king's ambassadors had promised. There was plenty of wheat, palms, and dates, and the natives had filled cisterns with a kind of date wine, to which the troops immediately took a liking, much to the officers' chagrin. Not only had the men lost their tolerance for drink during the long march from Sardis, but this particular wine had a tendency to immobilize them with a blinding headache. Clearchus banned its consumption, but not until half his army had been knocked supine for a day, during which time Xenophon and I prayed that the king's promise of safe conduct was trustworthy.

Tissaphernes finally arrived with his retinue, which included the queen's brother, the three ambassadors whom we had already met, and a long train of slaves bearing gifts and supplies. Up close he was an older man than I remembered when I saw him in the chaos of the fighting outside Cyrus' tent, much more so than one would have expected for a cavalry commander. He was tall, however, long-limbed and rangy, with leathery skin and a wispy beard, constantly moving about with a kind of nervous energy that belied his age, and with a commanding bearing that indicated he would brook no dissent. His eyes were sharp and pale, a light blue or gray, and after entering the tent with the quick, confident step of a victor, he suddenly stopped short and gazed openly around the space, as if looking for someone in particular. I saw Asteria, standing in attendance behind Clearchus, shrink back behind the slave girl next to her, seeking to avoid his piercing gaze.

Tissaphernes was not so easily cowed as the king's previous representatives. He locked his raptorlike glare on Clearchus, ensuring that he would be received as an equal or a superior, until the Spartan dropped his gaze. Having settled this matter of rank without yet even uttering a word, he further secured his position among the Greek officers by an elaborate distribution of gifts of golden chalices and other luxuries. Xenophon was allotted a beautifully ornate Persian bridle bit crafted of brass and silver, embarrassingly lavish for an officer of his rank, or for any officer serving under Spartan command. He gravely nodded his thanks to Tissaphernes' steward upon receiving this gift, and then handed it off to me, wishing to be rid of it, before returning to his place with the other Greek officers standing along the wall of the tent.

After the ritual opening statements, during which Clearchus ostentatiously yawned, though with no apparent effect on Tissaphernes, the Persian turned and addressed not merely him but all the officers. He used an interpreter, though he was perfectly fluent in Greek.

"Gentlemen," he said, in a surprisingly high-pitched and unctuous voice. "As you may know, my home country is a near neighbor to yours, and I have taken the liberty of proposing to the king that I escort you home personally, on the occasion of a journey I had already previously planned to visit my estates. My hope is that this will earn me the gratitude of you and your country, and would also be to the king's advantage by ridding him of a foreign army occupying his soil.

"The king promised he would consider this plan. But he first told me to ask you why you make war upon his country. Your army is too small and your supply lines too long to establish any permanent presence here; yet you are strong enough to cause considerable damage before you are ultimately defeated. I urge you to forgo your harsh treatment of Persian ambassadors, and to answer my question with all due thoughtfulness, so that I may give a favorable response to the king and thereby assist you in resolving your difficulty."

Clearchus' face softened slightly, as if he were much taken with the general's good sense. Although Tissaphernes was not as humble as might be hoped, at least he was not prone to the idle boasting with which the earlier ambassadors had offended the Greeks. After consulting with Proxenus for a moment, Clearchus replied with an effort at politeness:

"Lord Tissaphernes: We did not originally intend to make war on the king, but rather on the Pisidians. Cyrus convinced us, however, through promises of glory and wealth, to assist him in his true goal, which we did out of loyalty and friendship to him. We have no intention of establishing a presence in your country, nor do we bear you any ill will. Cyrus is dead. We have no further business here, and would like nothing better than to march peacefully home, provided that we are not harassed along the way. Any aggression we will meet with deadly force."

After a few minutes more of ritual chatter, Tissaphernes and his retinue bowed deeply and retired to their carriages, this time surrounded by silent Greeks. He took the message back to the king and returned several days later with a smaller, less ceremonial escort, and most important of all, a positive response. Tissaphernes promised to escort us home with his army, providing markets along the way, if the Greeks agreed to behave as if they were on friendly territory. There was to be no violence by either side. Tissaphernes and Clearchus sealed their agreement with an oath and a handclasp, and the captains and officers on both sides drank to each others' health. Tissaphernes then returned to his troops to make arrangements for the journey, and Proxenus, Xenophon, and I went back to our Boeotians, to announce the plan and to bide our time until departure.

We waited there outside the village, alongside Ariaius' troops, for three weeks, as the men became simultaneously more dissipated from the forced inactivity, and nervous at the lack of progress. The site afforded little in the way of distraction or comfort. The armies were camped near a series of vast grain fields that were now withered and fallow, relentless in their flat, brown monotony. Water we drew from a large, muddy irrigation canal that Tissaphernes had ordered the villagers to open for our use. The water's mineral content stained everything, from our pots to our garments, a kind of dull orange that served as a depressing counterpoint to the unremitting glare of the sun, which was unbroken by the shade of any trees or landscape features. Our hide and canvas tents afforded little respite from the throbbing, airless heat, and in fact were too unbearably close and stifling to sleep in by night. Most of the men simply cut their shelters along the seams and rigged them as awnings propped by spear shafts, to the seething disapproval of Clearchus, who viewed this as one further obstacle to battle readiness. Nevertheless, he ultimately bowed to reason, and complied with Proxenus' suggestion that the men be allowed this small concession to comfort.

Food and supplies were procured by pooling our dwindling funds and sending several squads with pack animals into the wretched, foul-smelling village on market days, to wander among the low-slung mud and thatch huts and attempt to barter better prices in large quantities from the wily locals. Our success was mixed, and the wormy, withered vegetables and rancid horsemeat the marketing squads procured made us long for the hearty, if repetitious fare we had enjoyed during the first months of our march out of Sardis.

During these hot, heavy days of enforced village living, the Greeks and the native troops became increasingly soft, losing all perspective as to their true situation. Ariaius' men were deserting to the enemy in droves, and we feared for Ariaius himself, as he received visitors every day from among his Persian relatives, friends and even former comrades-in-arms from the king's forces. He swore that these were merely messages of reassurance from the king, who had pledged that he bore Ariaius no malice for his campaign with Cyrus, and promised to honor the truce, but Proxenus' suspicions grew daily.

"Why are we dallying?" Proxenus finally exclaimed to me impatiently one day, as we took inventory of our stocks for the thousandth time. "Why are we waiting for the king to collect his troops, or to fortify his position? We are in hostile territory, with no provisions except what the benevolent Tissaphernes has given us, and his strength is increasing daily. Which army has time to bide—ours or theirs? Is the king simply going to let us freely return to Greece to laugh about how we got the better of the massed forces of Persia with our ten thousand men, and had our fill of date wine besides?" He swept his maps off the camp table in disgust and stalked outside the tent to assemble the men for yet another review of arms.

I pondered our position. Was Proxenus advocating retreat without the king's permission? That would be suicide, for if we left Tissaphernes' protection we would have no provisions other than what we could loot from the surrounding countryside—a much less certain method than using the markets the village provided us, notwithstanding our dwindling supply of coin. Pillaging would entail breaking our solemn vow to Tissaphernes to keep the truce. Moreover, we would have no guides to lead us back, although Proxenus had developed severe doubts as to the reliability of the king's guides in any case. And leaving now would severely reduce our forces, for it is certain that Ariaius would not accompany us. Our situation was bleak, although a casual observer would never have concluded this, from the laughter and games of the men outside, as they bided their time in the camp.

If Clearchus was thinking the same thing he gave no indication of it when Proxenus finally decided to approach him with his concerns. Hardly looking up from a procurement report he was reviewing in irritation with a trembling and stammering quartermaster, he dismissively waved off Proxenus' worries.

"If Artaxerxes had wanted to attack us, he would have had no need for the oaths and pledges we swore," he said. "The king and Tissaphernes don't have shit for brains. Let them break their word in front of the whole world. We might all die, but we'll take down five of his for every one of ours, and I'll not add to our disgrace by breaking our word in the bargain."

Proxenus returned to the tent furious at Clearchus' refusal to act, although Xenophon reminded him that one could hardly expect otherwise. We had little time to stew further, however, for the next day Tissaphernes arrived with his forces, who despite our worst fears were not in battle array, and he put Clearchus and Proxenus instantly at ease with his jovial manner. His wife, the king's daughter, was accompanying him, this time with her entire train, and Xenophon and I watched in astonishment and amusement as Clearchus stepped out of the camp to greet them.

"Did you see Tissaphernes' baggage?" I asked, and pointed out to Xenophon the approaching retinue of servants, wagons loaded with gifts, and silk-bedecked slave girls that the general's wife kept in attendance. For sheer opulence, the train rivaled Cyrus' during the march out of Sardis. Xenophon let out a low whistle.

"Looks like Tissaphernes plans to travel home in style," he said.

I peered at the wagons carefully. "Do you think any of them contain weapons? Could he be plotting any treachery?"

Xenophon smiled. "I think just the opposite," he replied. "I don't believe our friend Tissaphernes has any intention of mussing his clothes by getting into a scrap with a few wayward Greeks accompanying him along the way."

The two armies left the next day. Tissaphernes led the way along the Euphrates, gathering retainers as he traveled, and continuing to provide us with supplies by means of a thrice-weekly market, while Ariaius accompanied him leading his own native troops. The Greeks followed behind, still in full battle order, still suspicious of the Persian's intentions, maintaining a wide distance between ourselves and Tissaphernes' forces. Every night we camped several miles behind Tissaphernes' party, which led to grumbling among the men because of the inconvenience this caused them for gaining access to the market and the slave girls, but a fierce harangue by Clearchus about maintaining military discipline quieted their complaints for a time. After several days of this arrangement, however, his paranoia seemed to be having a damaging effect, as unwarranted suspicions gradually increased the level of tension between the two armies. Hostilities even broke out once or twice between companies of Greeks and Persians who ran into each other in the country on routine scouting patrols or while gathering firewood.

It was about this time that the two armies passed over an enormous irrigation canal, as wide and as swiftly flowing as a river, amazing the men with its breadth and depth, and the next day we reached the Tigris, near the city of Sittace, a mile and a half distant on the other side of the river. We camped in an idyllic setting overlooking the river, covered with soft grass and shaded with wide, overhanging trees. Tissaphernes' forces crossed the river first and camped on the other side with Ariaius' men, out of our line of sight, consistent with the custom that had developed over the past several days. That evening, as I strolled around the camp with Proxenus and Xenophon reviewing preparations, a Persian runner approached us, breathless and ruddy-faced, bearing a small pennant identifying him as a member of Tissaphernes' personal escort.

"The gods be with you," he panted. "I seek either Proxenus or Clearchus, with a message from Ariaius."

"I'm your man," Proxenus answered. "Speak your mind." I thought it odd that Ariaius would address a message to Proxenus, rather than to his personal friend Menon, who was a Greek officer of equal rank to Proxenus, but I kept silent and merely edged closer to listen. The runner glanced uncertainly at me, and then continued.

"Ariaius asked me to preface my message with a reminder that although he travels with Tissaphernes in his train, he was true to Cyrus and remains loyal to his Hellenic friends. Ariaius bids me warn you to be on your guard tonight against an attack. Tissaphernes has deployed a large force just on the other side of the bridge, and means to destroy it to prevent you from crossing, trapping you between the river and the canal."

I stared at him in amazement. Proxenus acted swiftly. Seizing the man by the scruff of the neck, he half dragged, half pushed him to Clearchus' headquarters, which stood a few hundred yards away, to make him repeat his story. On the way there I caught sight of Asteria as she staggered up from the river to the camp followers' quarters, a yoke across her frail shoulders, bearing two buckets of water, a task to which she was wholly unsuited. Asteria did not see me at first, for her eyes were fixed on the messenger, focusing on nothing else. I glanced at the messenger's face just as he, in turn, looked at her, and with a hint of recognition his mouth tightened slightly in a grim smile and he nodded almost imperceptibly. Asteria flushed white, not pink as might a woman suddenly confronted by a hidden or past lover, but rather pale in fear, and quickly averted her gaze. The whole episode had taken not more than a few seconds, but it was something that stayed with me for weeks afterwards, though I wondered whether I had merely imagined it.

Clearchus' reaction upon receiving the messenger's news was to let fly a string of oaths that sent every man in the vicinity scurrying for cover, hoping that his wrath was not somehow directed against him. The messenger quaked, for if anything, Clearchus had developed an even more frightening reputation among the Persians than among us, as a result of his execrable treatment of the king's ambassadors. "Let him live," he said grudgingly, for it was apparent from the boy's fear that he was no idle prankster bent on tormenting the Greeks, but rather a genuine messenger from Ariaius, and was telling the truth. Clearchus then sent out Tolmides to summon the officers to his table for a council. The sun was already dropping low in the west, so the matter was urgent.

I attended the meeting with Xenophon, and could see the worry etched on everyone's faces. The men were tired after several days' march, and our position was weak, hemmed in by wide bodies of water passable only by pontoon bridges. Our "island" would be difficult to defend—the terrain was almost perfectly flat, with no natural rises or outcroppings from which we could mount fortifications, and it was ideal for cavalry runs, which the king could send in droves, while we were limited to our forty or so existing horse. Clearchus cursed again and again as he reviewed the situation out loud.

The fact, however, that Ariaius had sent his message not to a friend who knew him intimately, but rather to Proxenus, had raised doubts in Xenophon's mind, and he spoke up for the first time in the presence of the senior officers without first discussing the matter with Proxenus.

"General, with your permission: Ariaius' claim is not logical. Why would the Persians both attack us and eliminate the bridge? If they attack, they will either win or lose. If they win, why destroy such an asset? They will need it afterward to return home, and we would be doomed, bridge or no bridge. If they lose, they will need the bridge all the more, to escape death at our hands, rather than being trapped here on the island."

Clearchus listened to him attentively, with a somewhat surprised look on his face, which I did not know whether to attribute to his having noticed Xenophon in his camp for the first time, or to his actual words. He pondered this for a minute, and then asked the messenger how much country there was between the Tigris and the canal we had passed the morning before.

"A great deal, your lordship, as well as many villages, some cities, and much fruitful land such as that on which you are encamped."

The other officers then saw Xenophon's point, which Clearchus had understood immediately. The Persians had sent this man with a message to be wary of an attack, precisely to dissuade us from cutting the bridge over the Tigris ourselves. This would have afforded us an impregnable position, defended by the river on one side and the canal on the other, with plenty of provisions from the country and villages in between, and able to wring further concessions from Tissaphernes. From our standpoint it was laughable, for since Cyrus' death, there was not a Greek among the entire ten thousand who did not yearn to return home as soon as possible, and be out of this foreign territory with its strange customs and headache-inducing wine. Attempting to hold out against the king's forces, against those odds, was inconceivable. But the Persians remained as fearful of us as we of them, and suspicions of treachery were shared by both sides. Hence the complicated game of cat and mouse Tissaphernes was playing with us, to protect his rear.

Clearchus took no chances, and placed a heavy guard on both ends of the bridge that night, with backup cavalry runners posted to inform him within minutes if an attack had begun. However, he ordered the captains not to breathe a word of the affair to their men; let them get a good night's sleep. Any uproar like the one that had ensued after the battle, which he had quelled with the wild ass story, would this time have much more dire consequences, with the Persians practically within shouting range of us on the other side of the river.

The next morning the army was up before daylight, crossing the thirty-seven vessels that made up the pontoons of the floating bridge before the Persians had even finished their breakfast. Again, Clearchus took every precaution, moving all the heavy troops over first to establish a beachhead and guard against a Persian attack while we were vulnerable on the narrow bridge. Our baggage and camp followers came last, rather than protected in the middle as is usually the case, for our rear was secure, protected by our position on the island. I watched the crossing with Xenophon from a height on the far side. The rising sun reflected red and orange off the glinting river, broken only by the bridge's tenuous line, like a single thread lashing a sleeping Titan to the earth. The bridge bowed outward as the river's current pressed the middle vessels downstream, and it strained in seeming frustration at the restraints holding it fast to the banks at the two ends.

Despite the water's sluggish calm, negotiating a narrow pontoon bridge with wagons and pack animals is tricky business. Like an army or a man, any complex system that appears stable and solid from afar is, from a closer perspective, actually a unit comprising many interconnected components, each engaging in myriad tiny rebellions against the other, constant assertions of independence, and a linked bridge such as this is no exception. The vessels of which it was constructed rocked and tipped, the grass ropes binding them creaked and strained. As each squad of hoplites, each herd of terrified, squealing swine, each tippy cartload of cooking supplies and heavy equipment miraculously made its swaying way across the narrow length, Xenophon let out an audible sigh of relief and offered a small nod of thanks to the gods.

While watching the camp followers I could make out Asteria gamely tramping across with a crowd of other women, bearing a bundle on her shoulders that seemed far larger than she should be required to carry. A feeling of shame that I was unable to do more to help her troubled me greatly during this long phase of marching, tempered only by her smiling dismissals when I asked her about it at night.

"Women are much better marchers than men," she declared, only half-teasingly. "Look at your troops when we make camp. The men sweat and collapse on the ground like pigs, calling for their squires to help them take off their armor. The women don't even pause—we begin immediately to gather firewood and cook. Even I, who had never gathered a piece of firewood in my life!"

I conceded her point, though still sought to assist in any way that would not disrupt my own duties. Her one request was for medical supplies, and here I was able to help, for I had ready access to the officers' kits, and I passed herbs and salves and sutures to her whenever I could, with which she maintained the strength and the health of the group of women she accompanied.

The armies continued their march north along the Tigris for several more weeks, under the same conditions of suspicion, and the constant tension exacted a toll on the men. Marching through foreign terrain with hostile natives on all sides is stressful enough; being dependent upon the mercy of a foreign army ten times your size, which you had fought and humiliated just weeks before, was sufficient to make a Spartan weak in the knees. When we reached the River Zapatas—four hundred feet wide and sufficiently difficult to cross that the armies set up a camp for several days—Clearchus finally decided to take matters into his own hands. He was no diplomat, but the continual stress of the journey and the suspicions between the two armies were moving his men to the flashpoint, and he was concerned that the isolated incidents of patrols coming to blows might ignite into a full-fledged conflagration between the two sides, from which the Greeks would receive the worst. He sent word to Tissaphernes that he wished a private meeting with him, the first since the initial truce had been pledged between them weeks before, and Tissaphernes readily agreed. Surprisingly, Clearchus invited Xenophon to accompany him and his bodyguards, as his official secretary. Proxenus was bemused.

"Looks like your star is rising in Clearchus' eyes," he said. "Is it that Persian fragrance you've taken to wearing lately, or did you slip a potion into his wine? I had better start looking for a new aide-de-camp." But his eyes were laughing. Proxenus had never wished anything but the best for his cousin, and I was hoping this new responsibility fit into his designs. As for Xenophon, although accompanying the general on official business was from any standpoint an honor, I wasn't sure whether he should rejoice or fear for his life—and that, whether at the Persians' hands or Clearchus'.

Xenophon accepted Proxenus' jibes good-naturedly, and offered to leave him his perfume while he was away. "You seem to be doing fine, though, without it, cousin—I've noticed no shortage of sheep around your tent."

Proxenus guffawed. "I'll save one for you!" Then more seriously: "Be on your guard, Xenophon. Clearchus knows what he is about, and has no fear of entering the Persian camp. I trust Tissaphernes and Ariaius to provide him with safekeeping, as we did when Tissaphernes entered our camp. But individual Persian soldiers may hold grudges, and there is nothing Tissaphernes can do if a rogue infantryman determines to avenge the death of a friend by breaking rank and running you through with a spear. Tissaphernes could even 'facilitate' such an event beforehand, and still leave his hands and reputation clean. You and Theo may be targets there. Take heed."

The next day, as our small party rode to the immense Persian camp, Proxenus' warning remained vivid in my mind.

Tissaphernes received us like princes of the realm. The reception was magnificent: rare wines and game birds, golden pitchers and lamps, and a multitude of slave girls and boys, several for each guest in fact, such that not a drop of wine was drunk, not a bit of food eaten, that it was not immediately replaced with another, by a servant standing close, ready to fulfill any whim. Before meeting Cyrus, I had never imagined anyone could travel this way, much less a general on campaign, but Tissaphernes was more than a match for the prince.

Clearchus wasted no time in broaching the reason for our visit. "Lord Tissaphernes," he said gruffly, clearing his throat and belching politely but enthusiastically. "I am grateful for your hospitality. To my mind, that has already answered many of the questions I had when I arrived. I've never doubted your word or your intention to bring us safely back to our homeland. You have entrusted us to your most reliable officers and guides, and I know that no Greek would think to harm even the lowliest baggage carrier in your army."

Tissaphernes gave him a slow, pleased nod at these words, and Clearchus took another swig of the wine from his goblet before continuing.

"Although you and I are confident in our mutual trust, our troops watch each other with suspicion and fear, as if we were still enemies. I know that men often hate each other unnecessarily because of slander. That is why I wished to meet you face to face, to resolve these tensions before they erupt in violence."

He smiled his blackest smile, though the kind words dripped off his tongue like honey.

"You yourself have no reason to mistrust us, if only because of the oath we swore, which to a Greek is sacred. If I broke my oath, where could I run and hide? Not from the gods, who see and know all, and even less from you, dependent as we are. If we were to offend you, we would have to answer to your king on his own territory, or make our way home across a thousand miles of desert without a guide."

Clearchus then leaned in to Tissaphernes, and his voice dropped lower, to a conspiratorial tone. Tissaphernes made no attempt to reciprocate, however, and remained erect in his chair, aloof, though smiling wanly, his fingers tented.

"You, in turn, might also find it in your own interest to keep us safe," Clearchus said quietly. "I know that you face hostilities on your own lands: The Mysians have burned some of your estates, and the Pisidians and Egyptians are making your life miserable. There is not a nation on earth that can stand up to my veterans, and I'd be happy to place my force's strength at your disposal, if this could be of assistance to you."

At this, he reclined back onto his couch, held out his glass for more wine in a confident gesture of familiarity, and hooded his eyes in such a way that he almost appeared to doze. He looked neither at Tissaphernes nor at Xenophon, but seemed satisfied with his statement, and not particularly concerned at any reaction Tissaphernes might have.

Tissaphernes observed him thoughtfully for a few seconds, with an expression almost of amusement, gently twisting the point of his beard and smiling paternalistically. Clearchus' offer of our forces to assist him in his own military campaigns was a brilliant gesture; not only would it ensure our own safe arrival home at Tissaphernes' hands, but would guarantee the troops additional employment for the foreseeable future. A man like Clearchus could want nothing more, and in the best case it would give his men the opportunity to fill their empty purses with some rich Egyptian booty before they returned to their homes.

Tissaphernes then replied, though this time waving away the interpreter. He spoke in fluent Ionian Greek, in language formal and considered.

"My dear Clearchus," he said, assuming a kindly and almost avuncular tone. "I am indeed pleased to hear your words reassuring us of your benign intentions, though I personally would never require such a guarantee from you. Clearly you would have been your own worst enemy had you attempted to do us harm during our travels. For my part, if we had ever felt the need to break our own oath and destroy your army, there would have been no shortage of opportunities to do so. And yet we have never shown you any hostility.

"Though we have so many ways to—dare I say it?—well, *destroy* you, all without harm to ourselves, we would never choose to offend heaven and man by breaking our sacred oath to protect you and accompany you safely homeward. We are not wicked, General, nor are we foolish. Cyrus trusted you and admired your skills, and sought to put them to good use at the head of his conquering army. I see no reason why I should not do the same. What does it matter which Persian you serve, as long as you are treated fairly and receive your share of the rewards? A wise man once said that only the king may wear a crown on his head, but an honest man may wear one on his heart as well, and I intend to do so."

At this Clearchus snorted, but then smiled wickedly. "So, Tissaphernes, we see eye to eye. I am happy to hear confirmation of your peaceful intent, though I never doubted it myself. In order to prevent doubts from arising among the men in the future, however, I see no better way than to punish anyone caught trying to spread lies about us or incite each other's troops. Don't you agree?"

"Indeed," the wily old Persian said, sucking in his breath, after only a moment of hesitation. He remained silent for a moment, as if lost in thought. "If that is our agreed-upon solution, Clearchus, then let us pursue it actively and whole-heartedly, rooting out these sources of tension and destroying them. Come back tomorrow with your captains and officers. I shall do the same, and we shall point out to each other those who have been whispering slander into our men's ears to incite the other side to needless attack."

This was, of course, precisely what Clearchus had sought in his suggestion that slanderers be punished, for he was absolutely confident of the reliability of his own Greek officers, but had begun to suspect the motives of Ariaius and his men, particularly after the Tigris bridge incident several weeks before.

As we rode out of the Persian camp that night, Clearchus was silent, but pleased. He had settled the matter of Tissaphernes' suspicions, and had further consolidated his army's status with the Persians for future campaigns. Further, he looked forward to identifying the traitors among the Persians who had been making so much trouble for the Greeks during the past several weeks' march, putting threatening ideas into their heads and wasting their resources. Xenophon had not spoken a word the entire evening, but did so now, cautiously, reluctant to interrupt Clearchus' thoughts.

"With all due respect, General, are you not concerned that your attempt to draw out accusations might implicate some blameless Greek officer? I would wager that all the plotters in this farce are on the Persian side, but Tissaphernes will hardly be satisfied with our pointing them out to be put to death, without giving him an equal opportunity to see a Hellene or two die."

Clearchus considered this silently for a moment, with a half smile on his face.

"No Greeks will die because of this," he finally said, "and I'd be surprised if any of Tissaphernes' goat-fuckers did either. It's not in either army's interest to lose officers in the middle of a campaign. Watch, though—we'll make Ariaius piss his trousers, and then keep him as useful to us in the future as he has been in the past." He laughed, a short, sterile laugh, and then looked at Xenophon more closely.

"You look familiar," he said. "I'd almost think I'd known you before this whole fucked-up project began, but I couldn't have. You're barely out of your mother's arms. You weren't in Thrace, were you?"

"No, General. I've hardly been out of Athens since I was an ephebe."

Clearchus shrugged, then glanced down at Xenophon's sword. "Looks like a Spartan weapon. You have better taste in arms than your average Athenian," he grunted, and reached across the gap between their horses to pull it out of the scabbard swinging on Xenophon's hip. He inspected the blade and handle in silence for a moment until his glance fell on the deep, crudely engraved Greek letter κ, the first letter of his name, and his eyes bulged.

"Where the fuck did you get this!" he burst, waving the blade dangerously under Xenophon's nose and startling the horses. "This was mine! I exchanged this with that pigheaded Gryllus twenty years ago!" And suddenly an expression of recognition flashed across his face, and he grinned evilly.

"Are you the son of Gryllus the Athenian?" he asked hoarsely, leaning so close that his putrid breath made Xenophon feel nauseous. Clearchus wore the same expression of curled-lip disdain that Gryllus had the day he watched the pancration training. Xenophon stared straight ahead, concentrating on holding his horse's pace even with that of the general's animal.

"Yes, sir, I am," he said evenly. "My father is a great man, or was anyway, for I don't know whether he still lives. Still, he contributed greatly to Athens' glory. I am proud to be the son of Gryllus."

"Proud," Clearchus smirked. "Proud! And how proud would Athens be now, how proud would your father be, to see his spawn marching under a Spartan's command, after fighting for a Persian's family feud? Wasn't your sorry-ass puke-hole of a city exciting enough for you under Spartan control, that you had to come all this way to become a Spartan yourself?"

"He didn't approve at all. I'm sure it killed him when he discovered what I did."

"And the world would be better off for it," Clearchus hissed. "That man, your father, blocked me every time I was ordered to deal with him, stymied me in every treaty I was sent to negotiate with him. I would have cut him down at the knees if I had been allowed, and he knew it. He set my career back ten years."

"I'm not to blame or praise for my father's conduct. He served Athens, and if his actions were to your detriment, they were to Athens' benefit. I am my own man, and I make my own decisions."

"And that, little Xenophon, son of Gryllus, is to *your* detriment. I cursed your father to Hades many times, for he was my enemy. But at least he knew what he was. The only thing worse than an Athenian is a traitor, and even an Athenian traitor is no friend of mine. Get out of my sight. It makes me puke to think of you fighting beside me."

Xenophon spurred his mount forward, his face composed but his eyes stinging in anger and his mind a torrent of emotion. If it wasn't Gryllus tormenting him as a boy, it was Clearchus doing so when he was a man, and both for the same reason: because he was Gryllus' son.

"Wait, Athenian!" Clearchus called just as Xenophon had begun to draw away. He spurred his own mount forward to Xenophon's side. "Take this," and he shoved the sword back into the scabbard. "It'll remind you of your betters."

III

WRATH—THUS SING THE MUSES, for not since the days of Achilles has any man felt such wrath as that which tormented Xenophon. After returning furious from the outing with Clearchus, he refused even to tell Proxenus about it, but rather raged up and down the officers' tent, stirring up dust and breezing past Proxenus' maps and scrolls until Proxenus finally threw him out with orders not to return until he had calmed himself. Xenophon stormed outside, his anger like a great, pustulant boil that refused to burst and settle, and I attached myself to him like a physician's leech, trying to calm him.

Half the night he paced the outskirts of the camp, worrying at the insults he had received, and his silence in the face of Clearchus' vile epithets directed at his father.

"At my own father, Theo! And I did nothing to defend him, nothing to challenge Clearchus!"

"You would have been a fool to try anything," I countered. "You know his temper—he was just waiting for you to lose control. He would have run you through you with your own sword at the slightest pretext, and smiled as he did it."

"Still, I can't ignore his words. If it were my own honor alone at stake I might swallow my pride, but it is my father's!"

"This is not the time for a private quarrel," I counseled. "Settle your squabbles later. Clearchus is baiting you and you'll give him satisfaction if you give in. The army is in peril, and you must focus your energies on that.

Let him act the fool. Call on the gods to give you the wisdom to do what is right."

This seemed to calm him somewhat, and he returned to Proxenus' tent and forced down some cold breakfast. He did not mention the incident again that day, except to inform Proxenus in a matter-of-fact tone that he would not be accompanying him to the peace parley that evening at Tissaphernes' camp. Proxenus raised his eyebrows in surprise, but said nothing.

Just as daylight was fading that evening, Asteria slipped over to the tent where I was tending to Xenophon's kit. I was surprised to see her standing at the door, as in the past we had always made careful plans before meeting after dark, and had not done so now for several days. In fact, her failure to seek me out earlier and now her unexpected arrival by daylight irritated me. I stepped outside the tent and while talking I snapped at her for some trivial remark. She was silent for a moment before turning sadly to leave. I reached for her arm and began to apologize.

"Theo," she said, "It's not important. I came here for just a moment. I can't stay, my friends are expecting me back soon. Please, don't go to Tissaphernes tonight. Don't let your master go either."

I peered into the tent at Xenophon, who was staring absently at the wall. "There doesn't seem to be much chance of that, does there?" I said sarcastically. "The poor brute is in a fury, trying to decide whether to murder Clearchus quickly or devise a more painful method. It doesn't matter. Tonight is just another peace parley, like all the others we've seen."

Asteria looked at me with round eyes, seeming to stare deep into my mind, before shrugging her shoulders and muttering something about lending Xenophon one of her scrolls she had managed to salvage, to improve his mood. Just before turning away a second time, however, she looked at me again, her eyes smoldering in the gathering darkness. "Clearchus is a simple-minded fool, Theo," she whispered, an urgency in her voice. "He is not worthy of Xenophon's anguish. Only an idiot like Clearchus would take Tissaphernes for granted the way he does."

"What are you saying?" I asked skeptically. "He has gotten the better of Tissaphernes every time they've met. What is there to fear?"

Looking around carefully, she dropped her voice until it was barely audible. "Remember who you are, and what Tissaphernes is. He is filled with hate, and treacherous even for a Persian. I know him, Theo, I know him like . . . like my own father. Do not mistake his olive branch for a gesture of peace. The same wood can be used to kindle a funeral pyre. Please—tell Xenophon."

I brushed off her words impatiently as the sentimental drivel of an overwrought woman, and she slipped away. In any case, I would be spending a quiet evening with Xenophon here in the tent, and was relieved not to be returning to the Persian camp again.

Clearchus took Proxenus and four other generals with him to Tissaphernes' camp, along with twenty other officers and some two hundred men to procure supplies at the market being held that evening. Chirisophus was the only senior officer who stayed behind, having been delayed on a journey to scour some distant villages for cheaper provisions. Some of the soldiers protested that no officers, including Clearchus, should entrust themselves to Tissaphernes' camp, but he laughed this off, saying that such fears were merely a sign of how well the conspirators had performed their work among the soldiery. Proxenus reluctantly left Xenophon behind, and said he'd talk with him when he returned that evening. Xenophon was so deeply self-absorbed that he scarcely noticed his cousin's leave-taking.

He retired early that night, exhausted from his ranting of the night before, and soon fell into a deep sleep. As he recounted to me later, his first memory of that evening was of my voice calling to him as if from a tremendous distance—a faint voice, seeking him out, urging him to leave behind the comforting haven of his dreams. I could see him making a conscious effort to block out my words, but I spoke louder, more insistently, as if I were a hunter making my way closer to a stag in the forest, patiently cornering him where he could not escape. I roughly shook him awake, calling him with increasing urgency.

"Xenophon . . . Something terrible has happened. You must get up! Xenophon!"

He sat up groggily, struggling to focus on my face, to grasp the meaning of my disorganized spill of words.

"Come quickly! Nicarchus has returned from the Persian camp, alone. Proxenus and the other officers are still there. Something is wrong."

He stumbled outside as I pointed to where Nicarchus the egg-farmer, one of the lower officers who had accompanied Clearchus to Tissaphernes' camp, was sitting on the ground ashen-faced, surrounded by a growing body of shouting men, a frothing and blood-soaked horse pawing the ground nearby, unattended. As we approached Nicarchus, I saw that a stain of dark blood was spreading blackly in the sand beneath him. He looked at Xenophon with a mixture of horror and unutterable sadness, and when he spread his hands away from his sides in a gesture of resignation and futility, Xenophon nearly choked on his bile, and the fuzziness immediately left his brain. The man's belly had been split open from navel to groin, and what he had been calmly holding in his hands was a glistening, ivory-purplish coil of his own intestines, which had spilled out of his abdomen. Nicarchus tried desperately to hold them in, but shiny, thin loops kept slipping out between his fingers and slithering into the dirt.

Xenophon shouted frantically for someone to fetch a camp surgeon, but with his loss of blood and the corruption of his spilled bowels, it was clear that faithful Nicarchus had but a few minutes of life left to him. I hastily laid a cloak on the ground behind him and helped him to recline in a more comfortable, almost fetal position that would not put too much strain on what must have been an extraordinarily painful wound. How the man bore it as long as he did was beyond my comprehension.

"Nicarchus, by the holy gods, speak! What happened? Where are Clearchus and the other officers?"

By this time, word of Nicarchus' arrival had spread through the neighboring tents, and a growing crowd was pressing in on us, shouting and gesturing.

"Xenophon . . . they're gone! By the gods, they're gone, all of them!" Nicarchus struggled to keep focused, to hold his gaze and stay conscious. "Clearchus and the captains went in the main tent, and the rest of us stayed outside . . . "

He choked on the blood rising up in his throat, spilling out blackly from the corners of his mouth, and gasped for breath again.

"There was a signal, and then the Persians all drew swords and cut us down. I . . . I managed to flop across a horse and ride back here, but the others . . ." Poor Nicarchus by this time was weeping soundlessly, his voice growing fainter. "I should have stayed with them! Maybe I could have helped . . ."

I squeezed the dying man's hand and reassured him that without his brave return, our camp could never have been alerted, and might have been destroyed in its sleep. As grievous as Nicarchus' condition was, we had no time to spare. Xenophon was staggered at the shock of what he had just seen and heard. He shouted to the surrounding men.

"Battle stations! Everyone assume battle stations! Form a box around the baggage and wagons, heavy armor in front, camp followers in the middle. Engine men! Light coals and place the Boeotian engines in the front!" He arranged what few bowmen and targeteers were available at the entrance to the camp to serve as an early warning, and then I helped him to strap on his own cuirass and helmet before clambering up the makeshift lookout tower to see what might be happening at the Persian camp. It had not even occurred to him that he hardly had the rank to be ordering an army of ten thousand men into battle position; but he saw no other superior officers available, and the men, in their shock at the news, were desperately seeking someone to take charge, and to assign them tasks to keep busy.

In the distance, toward the Persian camp, hundreds of torches and fires had been lit. No enemy forces were advancing that I could see, but great numbers of horsemen were galloping about in random patterns, and periodic shouts, cries of jubilation, and screams of agony were faintly carried over by the wind. I saw that most of the activity appeared to be centered near the river, where the nightly market was held, and I feared the worst for the two hundred soldiers who had gone to the Persian camp to procure supplies for the army.

The Hellenes remained at post, terrified of an imminent attack which did not, in fact, materialize. What did arrive was a body of three hundred horsemen, who suddenly broke out of the chaos and fire of the Persian camp, and galloped towards us, heavily armored and in battle formation. Xenophon stalked over to the sentry posts at the front entrance to the camp, and raised a flag of truce to stop them and discover their intent.

As the party of cavalry approached I saw that they were led by Ariaius, Artaozus, and Mithradates, Cyrus' closest friends among the allied army. Xenophon's interpreter, who had arrived breathless behind me, also pointed out Tissaphernes' brother, who kept his face shadowed in a visor and helmet behind Ariaius, but who seemed to be in communication with him and the other two officers. The band drew up their horses in front of Xenophon, looked down disdainfully, and then called for a captain to whom they could deliver the king's message.

Xenophon stared at Ariaius with scorn, that he could have so faithlessly betrayed his Greek comrades, and then sent the interpreter into camp to identify any captains who might have remained behind when Clearchus departed. He came running up a few minutes later with Cleanor and Sophainetos, who had been busy arranging the engines and troops and had not seen the approach of the horsemen. They were the only captains remaining in the camp.

"Hellenes, you dogs!" shouted Ariaius. My neck bristled. "Clearchus broke his oath and the truce, and has now been justly punished with death! But Proxenus and Menon, who faithfully reported his breach and his plot, are even now being honored by the king! The king demands, and Proxenus and Menon support him in this, that you lay down your arms immediately and surrender the camp. All that you have is his, says the king, for it belonged to Cyrus, who was the king's brother and slave."

At this, the Hellenes roared in outrage, the sentries clattering their shields with their spears and raining insults down on the heavily armed Persians. The situation had the potential to evolve for the worst. Finally Cleanor raised his shield and bellowed for silence, as ranking officer present:

"You goat-fucking wretch of a Persian slave, Ariaius! You dare to come riding here with your shit-eating ass-kissers, to the Greeks who saved your hide at Cunaxa, and demand that we surrender to your treachery? Have you no shame before real men? Do you not fear the gods, for having broken a solemn pledge, for having betrayed us to your monkey-faced Tissaphernes and his eunuch of a brother? You murdered the very man to whom you swore allegiance, and joined our enemies! May you die a filthy and god-forsaken death at the hands of those you betrayed!"

Ariaius smiled thinly at Cleanor's threats, and I could see Tissaphernes' brother muttering something to him from behind, his eyes glittering in a cold rage. Xenophon raised his hand for quiet and spoke up in an effort to ward off the imminent riot. "So Clearchus has been punished. If he did betray his word, then he deserved his punishment. But what about Proxenus and Menon, Ariaius? They are our generals. If they are truly safe, send them here—they are friends with both sides, and it is they who should be negotiating any surrender of the Hellenes to your forces."

The Persians discussed this among themselves in their barbarian tongue, in voices so low that our interpreter could not catch their meaning. Then they rode away without saying a word.

Xenophon stared bleary-eyed at the bundle tossed at our tent the next afternoon by a lone Persian rider, who had swiftly turned heel and raced galloping back to his camp. Hellenic informants from the Persian camp had told us that morning that rather than being honored by the king, Proxenus and Menon had, in fact, been hog-tied, dragged by their feet behind horses to the king's tent, flayed alive of what little skin was still left on their bodies, and beheaded. The two hundred soldiers procuring supplies at the market had suffered a somewhat quicker fate, as they had been cut down almost immediately upon a signal, by armed Persian soldiers manning the market stalls.

Half mad with grief, surrounded by confused and terrified men, wondering what would befall us next, Xenophon asked me to slit open the parcel. We found to our horror that it contained Clearchus' head, his long Spartan braids coiled around it, and obvious signs of his having been brutally beaten before his death. After a day in the hot, humid weather, covered only with a thin papyrus wrapping, the head was already badly disfigured, the eyeballs shriveling, the lips bluish, and the skin swollen. The perpetually angry scar on his temple that had so terrified his men was now pure white on the bloodless skin. Flies buzzed about lazily, waiting for me to again leave them to their business. I felt an unutterable loneliness and sadness. The Syracusan chants from my childhood, which had not tormented me for some time, welled up inside; they were threatening and pressing, and it was only with great effort that I was able to push them aside, shunt them off to a corner of my mind, and focus on the terrible business at hand.

After securing the camp the night before, our immediate task had been to put the souls of the murdered men to rest—which would be difficult, as we were unable even to place the customary obols in their mouths to pay the boatman Charon, or to oil their bodies for burial. The Persians kept their remains and no doubt performed atrocities on them, as they had on Clearchus'. We held a hasty ceremony, improvising eulogies, sacrificing a precious ox in their honor, and burying a single effigy in a grave, representing all the men who had died that evening.

Oddly enough, despite my grief at Proxenus' death, I felt my thoughts returning again and again to Clearchus, and to the terrible loss we had suffered by his treacherous assassination. I had not loved the man; he was incapable of giving love, and would have viewed receiving it as the worst of weaknesses. In fact, I hated him for his arrogance, his testiness, his complete inability to accept compromise and any philosophy other than "might makes right." Nevertheless, I had worshiped him in a way, as one does a harsh god, as a small boy does an overly severe father. I had thought the man to be practically immortal or indestructible, and I was unable to reconcile my mind's vision of Clearchus with the bruised, rotting head laying like a discarded cabbage in a sack in the dust.

In any land but Sparta he would have been crowned king, and have been remembered in history as one of the greatest and most brutal. But he was from Sparta, the only land in the world where such men are in surfeit, and he was Clearchus, the only man in the world more Spartan than even the Spartans, and therefore destined, perhaps, to a death more tragic than Sparta's itself. As unlikely as an encomium to such a man may be, Clearchus, no less than any other of the personages populating this halting record, deserves to be remembered for his accomplishments and excused for his shortcomings, even if belatedly by fifty years. His body was dead, but I prayed, for the sake of our very survival, that his spirit would remain with us some while longer, and settle on a man worthy of bearing it.

BOOK SEVEN

DREAMS AND STONES

. . . from deep, chaotic beds of mortal sleep
The gods darkly revealed what erst had been, and what is
Now, and what shall follow yet.

—EURIPIDES

I

WE SLEPT A RESTLESS SLEEP, each dreaming his own dreams, for dreams, like Muses or men, bear a superficial similarity to one another, but are never truly alike. It is as confounding to say, "I dreamed of a man," as to say, "I felt the sun." The first statement tells us nothing useful about the man, nor the second whether the sun was the benign orb that sustains our existence, or the harsh, killing fire that parches our throat and saps our strength if we attempt to defy it. A dream is the dreamer's alone, and no one can know its meaning without knowing the fears and aspirations of the dreamer. We shift from the dreamer to the dream, from the man to the Muses, seeking to reconcile the halves, to make them one, though dreams, by their very nature, are rarely consistent. Nor, for that matter, are men.

Some call dreams the ruminations and calculations of the unconscious mind, as the spirit assumes control over the intellect, unhampered by pain and the pleasure-seeking conceits of the mortal body. Others claim that dreams are direct messages from the gods, capable of being received only when both the body and the mind are lying dormant and vulnerable. A man takes his life into his hands each night in sleep, as he plunges unarmed and naked into a fast-flowing river of changing perspective, where not even the beating of his heart or the rhythm of his breath would be sufficient to sustain him if he were in his wakeful state. In sleep, the dead sometimes venture into his presence, to entice him to cross or to urge him back to his suffering and worldly condition. It is no accident that Hypnos, blessed god of Sleep, is joined by birth to a twin with whom he works in deep collusion—Hades the Winged One, God of Death.

It is strange that we think so little about sleep, even cursing it for diminishing the useful time available to us. Perhaps a certain humility is required to appreciate such a gift, a humbleness not native to the spirits of most men. When asleep, the philosopher and the traitor are scarcely different from each other, a king can hardly be distinguished from the beggar outside his door. Only the gods, who see of what things dreams are made, could tell the difference, if they cared to.

And who knows? To the extent that the deities are too preoccupied with their own petty squabbles to concern themselves with the daily lives of humans, to the extent that a man actually controls his own destiny, a man's mind, particularly his sleeping mind unburdened by physical weakness, *is* his god, and a dream the act and consequence of reasoning unbiased by material concerns. Whether sent from outside by the deities, or created from within by a man's own godlike spirit, a dream is a frightening thing to receive, its mandates not to be taken lightly.

Perhaps most frightening is to be sent a dream such as one has not received in years—since childhood perhaps, when the boundaries between one's physical and spiritual worlds are less solid, and dreams and their recollection more forthcoming—to be sent such a dream, and to not know what its mandate *is*. For such was the dream Xenophon received in his restless sleep the night after Clearchus' death, as he collapsed at my side before the fire. One would think that a dream so portentous and vivid would have been clear in meaning as well, yet to this day I cannot say whether it was an evil omen, or a sign of hope that the gods were watching and would guide us.

"I saw myself standing outside my father's house," he told me, "not at Erchia or Athens, but on a vast, treeless plain—alone—a plain covered in asphodel.

"Huge thunderheads had rolled in," he continued, "but they were not the heavy gray of rain and storms. They were the brightest, most brilliant white, and the warm sun shone down on me, heating my scalp and my aching shoulders with its soothing fingers. I felt surrounded by peace and calm. Looking up, I could see the serene face of Zeus in the thunderheads, a magnificent presence dominating the entire heavens, gazing down on me and smiling gently. I felt overwhelmed by his love and approval.

"But while I stood motionless, watching the god in awe, I saw his huge face suddenly crack into a grimace, with a mouth full of rotten teeth and a livid scar along the temple. Black Spartan braids blew from the back of his head as if in a high wind. As I watched, a thunderbolt shot from the god's eyes, hurtling down to earth with a whine and a hiss like that of a hundred lead missiles hurled from enemy slings. They struck my father's house with a blinding explosion, leveling it in an instant and setting all around me to blazing."

For long minutes afterwards his eyes remained wide, and after taking a long swig from a wineskin to settle his nerves, he stoked the fire, wrapping himself in a cloak against the damp, late-night chill. I repeated his dream silently to myself, searching for an answer as to what it might mean. On the one hand, it seemed a good sign, that despite all the dangers through which we were passing, we were still surrounded by the light and benevolence of the gods, and Zeus was watching us from the heavens; yet the dream was also to be feared, because Xenophon was certain it had been sent by Zeus himself, and portended the destruction and ruin that would result from any attempt to leave this place.

I broke my head with him over this conundrum for an hour, but I am no seer, and have little imagination or skill, much less patience, at divining the meanings of dreams. The thought that kept coming to mind with increasing urgency, however, had little to do with the sorcery of Xenophon's unconscious mind that night, and everything to do with the tactile, fleshy reality of the situation at hand. I found I was becoming disgusted at both myself and the other Hellenes for our lack of discipline, as the night wore on and we did nothing to safeguard against the enemy attack certain to arrive with the morning's light. The troops were scattered randomly about the camp and the adjoining fields wherever they happened to have collapsed from fatigue and despair. Many expected simply to die in their sleep under the sharp hooves of the galloping Persians as they poured into our camp to finish off the destruction they had started. If we fell into the king's hands, we would most surely die, after being subject to terrible torture and cruelty. Hadn't the king cut off the head of his own stepbrother Cyrus, to be mounted on a pole and placed in front of his tent? And hadn't Tissaphernes flayed alive the very Greeks with whom he had feigned friendship just minutes before? No one was preparing for this eventuality. Indeed, there were few officers left in the camp to give orders to the men, and those who had survived were as immobilized by fear and grief as the lowliest squire. I voiced my thoughts on these matters to Xenophon.

Unable to return to sleep, he rose in the moonlight and walked about the vast, chaotic camp, stealthily waking and calling together Proxenus' squad leaders, most of whom were, themselves, resting only fitfully. They emerged filthy and bedraggled from the scattered shrubs and ditches where he found them, sometimes accompanied by a sleepy-eyed camp follower, though most were alone, having lost or given up contact with the troops for which they were responsible. They seemed grateful to have a reason to rise and begin moving about, even if at the request of one with no authority over them. When he finally succeeded in locating and collecting some twenty disheveled men in varying states of numbness and grief, he spoke quietly to them over the blazing fire I had built up.

"It's impossible for me to sleep tonight, and I'm sure it's the same with you, for thinking about the king's forces. Ever since we defeated them at Cunaxa they have held off from attacking us, unless they saw a point of weakness. We allowed them to lead us away from their soft vitals, Babylon—we were only fifty miles away after Cunaxa!—and now we are in the middle of the wilderness, in the country of the Medes no less, and they have killed our leaders. That is the weakness they have been waiting for. They will be watching us from afar in the morning, through their spies and scouts, to see whether the murder of our officers has had the desired effect, and whether now is the time for them to destroy us once and for all.

"Tissaphernes broke a solemn oath to us, sworn before the gods. Yet we are surrounded by a vast country, with endless provisions, flocks of cattle and sheep, untold quantities of plunder. These are prizes to be won by whichever side has the best men, and by whomever the gods support. Our bodies are better trained than theirs to endure hardship, and our souls are hardier. Most importantly, we are free men, while the Persian soldiers are slaves. The gods are the judges in this contest. Whom do you think they will favor, the lying Persians, or us?

"I say we wait no longer. The enemy will be arriving with the dawn. Count on me to follow you without question if you will lead; or if you order me to lead, I will solemnly do so, and make no excuses for my youth or inexperience."

When listening, the officers were silent, staring expressionless into the crackling fire. But when Xenophon finished his short speech, they looked at each other for a long moment, alert, any semblance of sleepiness or grief shaken out of them, considering his words. Finally Hieronymus of Elis, Proxenus' oldest squad leader, a grizzled and sturdy veteran of thirty years of campaigning who was widely respected by the men and general staff alike, slowly stood and walked over to the fire.

"Well spoken, young Xenophon," he said, peering into his eyes. "Your face is that of a boy, but you have voiced tonight what no one else had the heart to do. I, for one, will stand behind you if you will lead."

Several others stood up as well and joined Hieronymus, and then one by one, some eagerly, others rather more grudgingly, all finally agreed to this proposal, by default electing Xenophon as the spokesman for Proxenus' troops.

Xenophon, expressionless, thanked the men for their confidence in him, and then turned again to the matter at hand.

"We have little time to prepare. Split up and go through the camp, finding all surviving officers or squad leaders. Meet here within an hour, and with the help of the gods we will determine our fates."

This we did, while Xenophon withdrew alone to his tent in the darkness. As I wandered through the camp, I could hear it rousing, despite the late hour; men were straggling in, bedraggled and sleepy-eyed, from the fields and the quarters of the camp followers where they had lodged in their despair and lack of discipline. Whispered conferences were held around me, and I heard the name Xenophon muttered in the shadows as men pointed out to each other the location of the fire at which we were to meet shortly.

Returning to Xenophon an hour later, I stooped to make my way through the flaps of the low doorway. Inside I found him sitting cross-legged against the stained canvas wall, his eyes closed, muttering softly under his breath like a naked Indian seer in a trance. The flickering flame from the tiny oil lamp sitting directly on the floor in front of him illuminated a small circle around his body, reflecting the gleaming sheen of perspiration that had beaded on his face and neck. No movement of his body gave the least indication that he had heard me enter.

"Xenophon . . ." I said with some concern, fearing a sudden outbreak of fever. "Xenophon! The men have gathered and are waiting for you. Do you know what you're going say to them?"

He fell silent, and slowly, with a sigh that seemed to issue from deep within his chest, he opened his eyes and looked at me unblinkingly in the dim light.

"No. I am praying."

I paused in surprise, and stared into his eyes a long moment.

"Alone? Without sacrifice or libation?" When praying for something as precious as survival, one should at least take the trouble to acquire a kid goat and assign a priest, and perform a proper sacrifice in front of the men.

Xenophon shook his head. "There's no time for that. The gods saw within my heart at Delphi, and they see within it now. They know the sacrifice I've made goes beyond a kid goat on an altar. And no, I do not pray for survival."

"Then surely you pray for the enemy's hand to be stayed from us . . . ?"

"Nor that. We will all die, in five hours or fifty years, and in all truth, I don't believe it proper to beg the gods to extend my allotted time. My soul is burdened, Theo; I feel I have been assigned a duty of great weight. I pray merely that whatever time remains to me, the gods may give me the strength to live it as honorably as I can." He looked at me and opened his lips as if about to say more, then fell silent. I motioned with my head in the direction of the men waiting outside. He nodded and stood up, and we stepped out of the tent and toward the light.

As we arrived at the meeting site, I saw that an enormous bonfire had been built, a huge flame that drove away the darkness for fifty feet or more in all directions. It illuminated the expectant and alert faces of a hundred men, most of whom I had seen or had dealings with during our march thus far, but whose names I did not know. Word had spread throughout the camp that a meeting was being held to decide the army's fate. Some of the common troops, too, in their curiosity and fear, had crowded up behind the circle of junior officers around the campfire, waiting to hear what might happen and spread the word among their fellows. The fire crackled and spit, and as the whole logs that had been heaved onto the top gradually caught flame, the blaze began roaring like a river or the crashing sea, sending tongues of flame and sparks licking upward to blend with the stars, an enormous signal beacon flaring defiance to the enemy, beaming out our location, fairly daring them to attack, its warmth beckoning and yet at the same time its fierce, urgent roar dissuading and threatening. The men stared hypnotically into its sun-bright center, their faces, like Xenophon's, gleaming with a sheen of sweat, some of them mumbling as well. I wondered if the men, in losing their hope, were losing their minds also, and whether Xenophon, in bringing them here, was leading them into madness.

Hieronymus approached the fire, the flickering shadows exaggerating the already deep furrows in the skin of his weather-beaten, leathery face, and spoke tersely, in his gruff voice.

"Officers of the Greek army: We meet together this night to devise a common strategy. One among us, young Xenophon, has taken the initiative in this, and I call upon him to speak as he did to Proxenus' officers earlier this evening."

Xenophon got up, and covered the same matters as he had earlier, though more slowly and at greater length. But before he concluded his speech, I looked past the immediate light of the fire and was astonished to see not merely the hundred officers and the straggling companies of curious soldiers; but rather the entire camp, ten thousand men and half again as many camp followers, gathered for hundreds of feet around our meeting place, far beyond the reach of the firelight. Soldiers stood in rank, laundry women lifted each other onto their shoulders to see more clearly, vendors straggled in from the countryside—yet the enormous crowd was silent. All eyes were upon Xenophon, waiting for the words that would decide whether they were to be surrendered up to the enemy for slavery and death, or whether they had reason to hope they might return to their homeland. He concluded his plea to the officers:

"We have an opportunity before us. Ten thousand soldiers have their eyes upon you. For two days they have been despondent, almost without will to live. Yet here they are now, summoning up the little hope still left to them. If they see you are discouraged and afraid, they will be cowards. If they are left wondering what will happen to them, and believe they are helpless, they will remain passive. But if they see you taking control of your fate, preparing against the enemy, and calling them to help you in this task, you can be sure they will follow you and imitate you, and do so cheerfully. In the army, you men are the privileged ones. You carry no packs, you receive higher pay, you direct battles from behind the lines. It is only fair that you should shoulder an extra burden now.

"We know that Tissaphernes has seized from us everything he could until now. He believes we are beaten, and plans to destroy us and rid the country of us. But he is a barbarian! We must turn the tables on him, do what we can to resist him. We have the more powerful weapon—ten thousand strong, skilled, cohesive fighting men. And you know it is not numbers or strength that bring victory in war, but rather fortitude and willingness of soul. Whichever army is more determined, that is the one that will prevail. Learn this lesson, and apply it. Be men! And you can be sure the others will follow."

The sigh of relief and approval from the hundred men around the campfire was almost palpable. The enthusiasm spread back beyond the fire's light in waves, gaining momentum as it swept away and then bounced back, increasing in strength like ocean tides reflecting off the beach and adding to the cresting force of the incoming waves. The men began talking among themselves, first in a hush, and then in increasing volume, until an isolated voice began chanting "Xen-o-phon! Xen-o-phon!" and was immediately joined by a dozen more, then a hundred, until the entire army was standing, radiating out from the blinding fire and roaring his name. I stood transfixed and disturbed, at the impulse that had been created from just a few short hours before as the result of a troublesome dream. For the second time that night I saw the clarifying and simultaneously destructive force of fire on the fates of men, but I followed Xenophon's advice by placing a confident expression on my face and smilingly chatting with some of the troops while the shouts rained down upon us.

"Do you truly believe he can do this?" Asteria looked up at me skeptically as we sat against a large stone, watching the bonfire die to coals. The last of the soldiers and camp followers had drifted off to their blankets.

I shrugged. "What is there not to believe? He had a dream—a powerful dream, and he feels he has been ordained by the gods."

"Ordained by the gods! Theo, these people are rabble! To the camp followers at least, Clearchus was just a name—they had no knowledge of his history, his skills, his qualifications, they followed him merely because he called himself the army's leader. You mustn't assume they will have any more personal loyalty to Xenophon than they had for him. Cyrus' jester could have stood up and declared himself general, and they would have hailed him just as loudly."

I winced at the mention of Cyrus' name.

"Asteria, Xenophon wasn't acclaimed by the camp followers alone—it was the Greek troops themselves who first supported him this evening."

She looked at me in dismay. "If that gives you comfort, then you are as much a part of the rabble as they are."

I tensed at her words, and noticing this she put her hand lightly on my arm.

"Theo, you are a freedman, not a slave, and even if you were bound to him, these are extraordinary circumstances, when the distinctions between slave and master do not always apply. You need not be beholden to mob rule. You are educated, strong, able to think—why be subject to the passing whims of Clearchus' bullying Spartans?"

I glanced at her dismissively. "I reject your point. It's useless to even entertain such thinking. What am I to do—stand up and count myself as an army of one, protest that Xenophon's credentials as a general are not quite as impressive as I would hope, threaten to withhold my approval? I will take my chances with the rabble, thank you."

Asteria pursed her lips tightly and stared down at the ground in silence, absent-mindedly massaging the fingers of her hands, stiff from hours of carrying water gourds and bundles suspended from thin leather thongs.

"That is not what I meant, and you know it," she muttered softly. "Sometimes I think you purposely act dense."

"You flatter me," I retorted dryly, "by suggesting it is only an act."

"Theo, it doesn't have to be this way. We don't have to live in filth, fearing every day for our lives, wondering where our next meal will come from."

"What are you saying?"

"I have . . . people over there. We would be welcomed, and for life. You would owe nothing to anyone, in fact you would be honored, and I could . . ."

Her words began tripping over each other in her excitement, her hands fluttering in an attempt to prop her racing syntax. I seized her shoulders, hard, and turned her to squarely face me as I forced her gaze to mine.

"Are you saying we should *defect?* Have all these Greek deaths, has *Cyrus'* death meant so little to you that it comes down to this? Defect to the enemy?"

She licked her lips and weighed her words carefully before answering.

"Theo, you see everything in such black and white. Not all Persians are your enemy, nor all Greeks your friend. Even a single man may simultaneously be both, be of mixed mind and intent, even act at times as if he were two different individuals. Cyrus was a Persian, yet you fought for him. My own father is a Persian, yet . . . here I am. I was raised among Persians. Artaxerxes always treated me kindly, like a beloved niece, and he would accept you as a . . . as a nephew."

"What about your father, Asteria? You were concerned he would view me as a betrayal of his honor."

"I have thought about this. Measures could be taken before we departed that would soften his heart . . . if you were willing . . ."

I stared into her pleading eyes, losing myself in them for a moment as I vaguely considered her extraordinary suggestion; as I came back to myself, however, I shook my head in wonder that I could ever entertain such a notion.

"It's out of the question. I know you mean well, but I could never leave the Greeks, never betray Xenophon."

She bit her lip and stared at the ground in silent disappointment.

"I won't mention it again, Theo."

I nodded at her silently, a wave of gratefulness and relief washing over me. A disturbing thought, however, suddenly crossed my mind.

"Asteria—at Cunaxa, when you were being dragged out of Cyrus' tent, why did Tissaphernes kill his own guard, instead of you?"

She looked at me evenly, and gently eased my heavy hands from her shoulders.

"It's as I said before—not all Persians are your enemy. And, Theo—"

I remained staring at her silently, waiting for her to finish.

"Not all Greeks are your friends."

II

THE NEXT MORNING DAWNED chilly and cold, with a heavy drizzle that belied our position on a vast, desertlike plain. The clouds hung low over our heads and the hard-baked ground had long since absorbed what little moisture it was able to hold, and now refused to accept any more. The water simply lay on the surface, like an enormous, shallow, muddy pond, reflecting our misery and rejecting our every wretched attempt to find a dry place to sit or stand, or to build a fire.

The men were tired and restless, and there was no breakfast to be had. The soldiers milled about aimlessly, performing their tasks only desultorily, falling back into the habits of despair that had been burdening them since the slaughter of Clearchus and the other officers. Up on the ridge was a growing body of enemy cavalry aligned and facing us, lances poised and pennants fluttering, seemingly preparing a charge, much to the dismay of our own troops, whose entire body of horses numbered no more than forty.

Xenophon approached Chirisophus, the ranking Spartan remaining in the army and a fine old soldier, greatly respected by the men. An initial glance at the veteran's weathered skin and flowing, steel-gray hair and beard would cause one to wonder how a man of such years could have survived the difficult march thus far. Indeed he often sat silent and apart from the troops, seeming to doze, like an elderly servant fading quietly into retirement. His appearance was deceptive, however, for Chirisophus was merely a master at conserving his strength. When called upon to act, he was as vigorous as a twenty-year-old ephebe, and if crossed, would erupt in a deafening string of oaths that would curl the beard of the most blasphemous Spartan in the vicinity. Chirisophus had fought at Clearchus' side for twenty years, and was the only man able to stand up to the brutal general's threats and bluster without fear of punishment, possibly the only other soldier Clearchus had truly respected. It was this man whom Xenophon approached.

"Chirisophus, I need your counsel. Your Spartans are breaking camp and maintaining order like soldiers on a parade ground, but the rest of the troops look like old women."

"So I noticed," Chirisophus said dryly, chewing on a blade of grass and observing the sloppy preparations of the other troops and the barely organized chaos of the camp followers. The deep creases at the corners of his eye were not cheerful, as they are in some older men, but rather betokened long hours of staring into the glaring sun, and ultimately a sort of weariness or boredom with the world. "And I believe some of them camp followers ought to be put out of our misery."

Xenophon ignored the cruel remark. "Look—last night you voted for me to lead the troops—I saw you. But I am an unknown quantity. The men look up to you. Take a few of your colleagues and fan out among the troops. Talk to them and raise their spirits if you can, speak to them as a fellow soldier. I have no ulterior motives for leading the men, but they may not believe this. Convince them that we need to move on."

Chirisophus looked at him a long moment, as if sizing him up. I wondered whether the old soldier might not choose to simply strike off for home on his own, accompanied only by his Spartan troops, rather than encumbered by a massive crew of inferior soldiers from the other Greek states and a veritable second army of motley camp followers. He apparently decided in Xenophon's favor, however, for shifting the grass blade noncommittally to the other corner of his mouth, he glanced toward his troops and called for three or four of his squad leaders.

While Chirisophus walked about and talked quietly to the men in small groups, Xenophon himself arranged to happen upon their conversation as if by accident, and asked the men to tell him their concerns.

"The cavalry!" One of the men shouted. "How do you expect us to fight our way up the Tigris against ten thousand cavalry, when we have none?"

Xenophon looked pensively up the ridge where the king's cavalry brigade was continuing to grow in strength, and was now hovering over us like an evil black thunderhead ready to explode. He forced himself to gaze back down to the troops, who had locked their eyes on him in silent expectation. I saw their scars, their knotted, muscled shoulders, their long Spartan braids that never failed to strike fear into the enemy. I saw their massive, thirty-pound oak and bronze shields that they swung about as if made of papyrus, and their short but deadly swords, each of which had killed a dozen men in battle, or more. And I knew beyond a doubt that the Persian cavalry, though they were the best horsemen in the world, on the finest mounts, were men like us, but not like us. For they were Persians, and we were Greeks.

"You're discouraged because the enemy has cavalry and we do not?" Xenophon asked, assuming an incredulous expression. "But cavalry are only men on horseback! I would pit their ten thousand men on parade horses against our ten thousand men on the safe and solid ground any day. No man has ever died in battle from the kick of a horse, only from a sword or spear; and your own blades have spent more time in Persian bellies than ever a weapon was meant to. The Persians are up on the ridge, trying to screw up their courage to attack us, and fearing a fall off their horses as much as they fear Greek iron in their bowels. I'm a trained cavalry man, believe me; horses are frightening because of their size and speed, but they are no advantage against a phalanx of Greek hoplites—except that a coward can retreat more easily on a horse!"

At this, the men laughed and visibly revived, and there was some scattered clanking of swords against shields in approval. I could see Tissaphernes' cavalry standing still in silhouette on the ridge, watching the matter with interest, even if unable to hear the words.

"I'll cut my words short. The enemy thought that by destroying our commanders, we would fall into chaos and could be eliminated. But they were wrong. The Persians' troops are foreigners, forced to fight under threat of flogging and execution. They think that because their own army would disintegrate without their officers' whips, all armies are that way. But we are Greeks! By killing Clearchus they will see ten thousand new Clearchuses spring up to take his place. You are all Clearchuses now!"

The men cheered lustily, and as the sound rolled across the empty plain with the blustery wind I saw scattered Persian horses rear in alarm.

"If you wish to see your loved ones again, keep your eyes on the road north to the Black Sea. That is the only way we can go. Burn the excess wagons, so we don't travel as slaves to our baggage train. Burn the tents too, sleep like the Spartans. Possessions are a burden, and don't contribute to our fighting. The more men under arms, and the fewer pushing baggage wagons, the better off we'll be. If we lose, all that we carry will belong to the enemy in any case; and if we win, we'll take plunder and use the enemy as our porters."

Clanging their weapons, the men burst out in a great cheer, and ran off to gather the tents and superfluous supplies for the great fire to be set. The camp followers wept and wrung their hands, but the men ignored them, or brutally wrenched goods from their grasp. They knew that every pound of useless gear eliminated now would allow an extra brace of arrows to be carried, and possibly save the life of the wretch whose goods were being cruelly set aflame. A great cloud of greasy black smoke rose into the air, but lifted only a few feet, for the drizzle had increased to a steady downpour and seemed to press and weigh down on the smoke itself as it drifted across the plain, obscuring the watching Persian cavalry from our view. Xenophon sent riders galloping out on the remaining ponies to keep an eye on Tissaphernes' troops while we broke camp. With the little baggage we had left, this task did not take long.

I cornered him during a brief moment of quiet. "The Black Sea, Xenophon? It's a thousand miles from here, through Media and the land of the Kurds and across the mountains of Armenia. Winter is coming on. Do you realize what you are demanding?"

He avoided my gaze as he laced his sandals. "It's the only route we have," he muttered, for the first time allowing an expression of discouragement to cross his face. "You know we can't go back the way we came, over the desert, and there are no passable roads west, across Asia Minor. Our only hope is to strike north, across the mountain passes to the Black Sea. There are little Greek trading cities clinging to the southern shore like a string of pearls—Sinope, Cotyora, Trapezus. We could raise a fleet in one of them and return through the Hellespont to Ionia and the mainland."

I snorted. "And how do you think to buy a fleet? You expect to extract gold and booty from the mountain tribes we conquer along the way? My recollection from Herodotus is that they're scarcely more than savages."

He stopped fiddling and finally looked straight up at me, almost angrily. "Who said anything about *buying* a fleet? Don't you sell me short, Theo.

This was not an impulsive decision. Of course we won't buy a fleet. We'll extort one."

I looked at him quizzically.

"There are Greeks along that string of trading posts, Theo," he continued, "but does that mean they're our brothers? Hardly. They'll be as dismayed as Artaxerxes was to see us arrive, and as delighted when we leave. They'll trip all over themselves to give us ships. If you were a citizen of muddy little Trapezus, how would you like to see ten thousand ugly, hungry mercenaries camped outside your city walls?"

I conceded his point, but was still doubtful that this was sufficient basis to drag ten thousand men through the mountains in the middle of winter.

Xenophon conferred again with Chirisophus as we arranged our battle lines, and they decided to form the troops into a hollow square, with the remaining baggage and mob of camp followers in the middle for protection. Chirisophus and his Spartans would lead and break through any Persian troops attacking us head on, while Xenophon would command the rear guard, fending off any nipping from Tissaphernes' cavalry in its attempts to break through the ranks into our supply train.

Just before leaving, we were informed by our scouts that a Persian embassy was arriving and Xenophon and I went reluctantly to meet them, wondering what good news they could possibly have for us, and whether any they did bring could ever be trusted. To my surprise Mithradates, a Hellene who had served under Ariaius and had recently deserted to Tissaphernes, came galloping up with thirty horsemen. He affected a warm greeting for his fellow Greeks, but Xenophon remained distant.

"Be quick about your business, Mithradates, or I'll make your safe-conduct as worthless as the one your Persian puppet masters offered Clearchus. You'll be yapping back to your own lines with your tail between your legs."

Mithradates set his mouth in a tight expression and dismounted. At a nod from Xenophon, a squad of burly hoplites seized his horse and led it away. They forced his Persian colleagues off their mounts too, and took those horses to the baggage train. Mithradates protested at this treatment, but Xenophon explained. "The gods forbid us from violating a sacred oath of safe conduct for heralds and ambassadors," he said with a bitter laugh, "but to my knowledge they say nothing of our treatment of livestock."

A crowd started to gather to listen to the parley, and I saw Asteria standing with a group of camp followers, craning her neck to see above the men in front of her. I caught her eye, and she gave me a tight-lipped nod of acknowledgment, barely perceptible, a grim expression in her eyes.

Mithradates collected his composure, and began. "You know I was faithful to Cyrus while he was alive, and I remain a Greek," he said after a pause, wistfully watching the rich trappings being removed from his animal. "Tell me what you propose, and if I believe you have any chance at all, I will gladly join you, with all the men at my disposal. Think of me as a friend and advisor."

Chirisophus, who had joined me by that time, scoffed. "We're going home. You can tell your masters we'll be moving fast through the country, taking only what we need and doing as little damage as possible, if we're let alone; but if anyone tries to hinder us they'll be sent back squealing like a pig, whether they be Persian or otherwise." He glowered at Mithradates.

Mithradates held his gaze evenly, then turned away dismissively and addressed Xenophon again. "It's impossible for you to move through this country without the king's consent. You have no provisions and I see now that you have burnt your supplies. Is the king to provide tents for you now, as well as a safe conduct? Are you going to start complaining about the quality of the wine he sends to quench your thirst?"

Chirisophus roared in a rage and lunged at Mithradates, his dagger aimed at his throat. I and some others held him back, but Mithradates barely flinched.

"Mithradates, you're under a safe-conduct, and I'd advise you to leave now while you still can," said Xenophon quietly. "The troops are under control, we have a new command. Remind Tissaphernes of his men's cowardly performance at Cunaxa. We will be marching through the king's country today, consent or no consent."

Mithradates glared at him for an instant in a cold fury, then recovered his poise. Taking a deep breath to collect himself, he again pointedly ignored Chirisophus and addressed Xenophon directly.

"Tissaphernes has one more request," he said. "Release all Persians you are holding as hostages, and he will then consider giving you safe passage out of the king's lands."

At this, the Greek officers fell silent, looking to one another in bewilderment. My conversation with Asteria the night before came back to me, and as I glanced at her now she avoided my gaze, fixing her eyes on Mithradates alone. Xenophon stepped forward, to the front of the Greeks, and turned to face us.

"Fellow Greeks!" he shouted in a clear, commanding voice, and all went silent. "Anyone who feels they are traveling under coercion, or who believes it to their advantage to join the Persians, may do so now, unimpeded. I stand here prepared, this very minute, to grant safe conduct to the Persian lines to all who desire." He then stood still and silent, searching the crowd of muttering soldiers from face to face, fiercely holding their stares for a long moment. My eyes locked on Asteria's, and hers, wide and unblinking, focused fixedly on Xenophon, her face bloodless and her lips slightly parted and trembling. I held my breath as I waited for her to react. She stood distraught and tense, poised as if to walk forward at any moment, yet she remained still.

Xenophon finally dropped his gaze and turned back to Mithradates. "We have no Persian hostages," he said evenly, "and Tissaphernes knows that. Everyone traveling with us does so voluntarily. If Tissaphernes is trying to create a pretext for moving against us, then he needn't go to the trouble. Tell him to simply attack, openly and like a man, and then he'll see what it's like to taste Greek iron, rather than holding back in cowardice as he did at Cunaxa."

Mithradates stared at Xenophon wrathfully, then turned on his heels and stalked back out of the camp in the direction from which he had come. His Persian assistants followed, wrapping themselves in as much dignity as they could muster, tramping through the mud and horseshit in their thin pointed slippers. Their stallions had already been disposed of. Chirisophus was still breathing hard, but had calmed down sufficiently to stalk back to his own troops, and had them arranged in marching formation in a trice. The camp followers and rear guard took somewhat longer, but by midmorning the army was ready, and we moved slowly across the plain, leaving nothing behind but a pile of charred remains emitting putrid black smoke, and the last of our dreams of a triumphant return to Greece through the front door.

III

MITHRADATES GOT HIS REVENGE for the disgrace he suffered at Xenophon's hands. We had hardly started off that day when he appeared again at our rear, this time accompanied by two hundred cavalry and four hundred light infantry. His herald bore a flag of truce, and although we did not halt our march to receive him, Xenophon and several junior officers held back and waited for him to approach, neglecting to call any supporting infantry for protection.

This was a mistake, for as soon as a sufficient gap had opened up between Xenophon's group and the army, Mithradates' cavalry whipped their horses along our flanks, seeking to drive a wedge between us and the main body of our troops and cut us down. We galloped frantically back to the safety of our troops, narrowly avoiding being encircled, but Mithradates' near approach nevertheless caught the army unprepared. Both the arrows from the Persian cavalry and the missiles from their well-trained slingers caused a number of casualties among our rearguard before we were finally able to drive them away by sheer force of numbers. We were accustomed to the powerful, body-length bows the Persians used in warfare, which although difficult to handle gave them a range beyond that of our own Cretan bowmen; but we had not counted on the deadly force of the Persian slingers, whose large stones, though not actually killing any of our men, kept them cowering under their shields and exposed to Persian cavalry charges.

Xenophon ordered pursuit, but without sufficient horsemen we could catch none of the Persian cavalry, and even our fleetest footmen could not gain ground against their slingers and bowmen with such a long head start. By the end of the day the army had covered no more than three miles, and the rearguard troops straggled in from all directions over a period of two hours or more, in complete disarray. Our first day on the march without senior officers had been disastrous, and Chirisophus and the older captains made it clear that there was no one to blame for the debacle but Xenophon. He had allowed himself to be drawn out by the Persians to an exposed position, and then risked his own neck to pursue their retreating troops.

He listened to their criticisms silently, a blank expression on his face, and acknowledged his blame, speaking only to humbly thank the gods that his first trial by fire had involved only a small Persian skirmishing force, rather than the full strength of Tissaphernes' army. As we were walking back to our tent, I could see that, rather than looking discouraged, he was busily puzzling something over in his mind.

"The Spartans disdain slingers," he said. "They call their weapons children's toys, unfit to be used by real men with swords and lances. But did you notice how the enemy slingers cowed our troops today, even the Spartans? The Persians were able to stand far beyond our own range, and yet kept us squatting under our shields like turtles. Do we have any slingers in the army to use in the same way?"

I thought for a moment. "The Rhodians are the most famous among the Greeks for their slinging," I answered. "But no, we have no company of slingers. Our Rhodians are distributed among the other companies according to their various skills—a few are hoplites, most are peltasts and bowmen. I know one—I'll ask him if there are any slingers here among his countrymen."

I sought out an acquaintance I had made during the march across the desert, a young scout named Nicolaus of Rhodes, and asked him whether any of his compatriots knew how to use a sling. Nicolaus was a dark, slightly built youth, with delicate, almost feminine features and short-cropped hair, as was the custom on his island. He seemed barely strong enough to draw a bowstring. Political events on his island had conspired to drive him and many others like him into exile at a very young age, but the Rhodians' reputation as effective mountain scouts and crack marksmen had enabled them to easily gain employment with mercenary armies around the Mediterranean. The Rhodians were known for their good cheer and relentless endurance under conditions of hardship. Nicolaus was delighted that I had taken the trouble to seek him out, and he smiled wryly at my question.

"Take me to Xenophon," he said, fishing out a long, tangled sling from deep within his pack, and seizing a walking stick, "and round up a half dozen sheep to be butchered tonight for the troops." As we trotted back, he whistled to several of his friends billeted in the units through which we passed, all as boyish-looking as himself, and shouted to them in his guttural Rhodian dialect to follow along and bring their slings and sticks.

Arriving at Xenophon's tent, I staked the sheep to the ground in the adjoining field, and while Xenophon and I watched, the Rhodians measured off a distance of one hundred paces from the sheep and stood waiting for us. We looked at the distance skeptically.

"You think you can hit a sheep from this distance?" Xenophon asked doubtfully.

Nicolaus smiled. "One hundred paces," he said, "is the distance from which Tissaphernes' Persian slingers can hit a sheep with those fist-sized rocks they use."

I was astounded. Rocks that size were big enough to knock a shield out of a hoplite's hand, and they could easily dent a man's bronze helmet into his skull. No wonder our men were being pounded by the Persian light infantry. The Rhodians stepped off another hundred paces, while we followed in even more doubt.

"Two hundred paces," said Nicolaus, "is the distance at which a Rhodian slinger can hit a sheep using a small river stone found on the ground."

I looked at Xenophon, who was beginning to think this show of bluster a waste of time. Nicolaus stepped off an additional hundred paces, a total of three hundred yards. By now the sheep were at a ludicrous distance, beyond the range even of our archers, and the Rhodians were laughing and elbowing each other as if this were a joke.

"And this is the distance from which I can hit a sheep using a lead bullet and my 'walking stick.' "

Nicolaus produced from a small bag around his waist a collection of what he called lead bullets, each perhaps the length of a man's thumb and twice the thickness, formed in the shape of an acorn, tapering to a point on one end and blunt on the other. He explained that they were called *balanoi* in his dialect and he kept them for hunting, a practice he had indulged in since boyhood, but he had very few such pellets left. I began to see now why the Spartans disdained such a weapon as these insignificant, soft metal pellets. At the same time, I recalled that it was Nicolaus who had bagged the army's only ostrich during our march across the Syrian desert months earlier. At the time I had not even wondered how; now I was beginning to become interested.

Xenophon shrugged in resignation. "Well," he said, "you've dragged us out this far. Show us your target practice." Nicolaus deftly slipped one knotted end of his sling into a notch on the tip of his walking stick, which he called a "sling-staff." He chose a bullet, placed it into the leather pocket of his four-foot sling, then looped the other end of the sling, which was considerably longer, around a small burr on the end of the staff and down the shaft to his hand. Whipping the entire contraption around his head two or three times, he let fly the bullet.

None of us could see it after it left his weapon, but we could hear the device humming evilly through the air for a moment like an angry bee. The sheep scarcely had time to look up in question at the odd sound before we saw the eye of one of them explode in a burst of blood and brains and the animal drop in its tracks without so much as a twitch. The remaining sheep stared dumbly at their fellow, but did not have long to wonder at his fate, for the other Rhodians had limbered up their slings and sticks and sent their own pellets whizzing, straight and true, at their heads. All the sheep dropped as if struck by lightning, in a small puff of blood and fleece, except one that had been hit on the upper neck rather than the head. That one struggled gamely back to its feet and began hopping and bucking about in pain like an untrained horse, as the blood from the deep hole spurted over its dirty white fleece. The Rhodian that had fired that pellet apologized for his clumsiness, calmly loaded another bullet and let fly again at the madly prancing animal, this time striking it square in the face, despite its frantic movements, and dropping it as dead as the others.

Xenophon's jaw dropped. "By Zeus!" he said at last, "How many Rhodians are you in the army?"

"No more than two hundred, sir, but all of us can fire a sling."

"Gather them all here in a quarter hour. I have a proposal."

Nicolaus looked at me, his eyes sparkling gratefully. "I'm in your debt," he said.

"Nonsense. It's proper recognition for the only man in the army able to kill an ostrich."

He grinned happily, and ran off to search for his countrymen.

That evening Xenophon organized the army's company of slingers, promoting Nicolaus to captain them and promising to pay them double wages for their services after we had returned home safely. In return for this, he gained their permanent gratitude and unquestioning loyalty. That night also, a cartload of axes and tools were confiscated from the camp followers for their lead cores to be melted down into uniform bullets for the slingers. The camp's blacksmiths were ordered to stay up all night if necessary, to produce sixty balanoi for every man. Nicolaus himself taught the blacksmiths how to cast them, and added the further innovation of having them carve a shallow spiral groove around each bullet, running from the tip to the back and around the pellet five or six times. Such a groove was chiseled into the soft metal after the cast bullets had cooled, and left rough-edged burrs that could cut one's hand if they were not handled carefully. When I complained to Nicolaus about the considerable additional effort it took to perform this step, he grinned and added mysteriously, "It makes them sing." The Rhodians themselves, when they each received their allotment of bullets, joyously took out their knives and began personalizing the missiles with small marks or carvings, the better, they said, to be able to reclaim them after target practice. Some of those who could write even carved taunting inscriptions—*Die, dog* or *Eat this*—the impact of which would certainly be lost on any enemy soldier in whose throat such a bullet might be buried.

Meanwhile, twenty horses were scavenged from among the pack animals, and additional baggage was eliminated to make up for the loss of their carrying capacity. Cavalry fittings were improvised from various leather scraps and blankets. When combined with the thirty horses that had been confiscated from Mithradates and his men the day before, as well as a few strays remaining from Cyrus' household guard, Xenophon found that he now had a squad of almost a hundred cavalry at his disposal, over which he appointed a young friend of his, Lycius the Athenian, as commander. A hundred cavalry, almost half of which were swaybacked pack animals, was ludicrous in comparison to Tissaphernes' ten thousand, but it would have to do.

We did not have to wait long to test the mettle of our newly appointed slingers and horse troops. The next morning the army departed at daybreak, forgoing breakfast. We had to pass through a narrow ravine during the day, and hoped to arrive before the Persians. Mithradates, meanwhile, had been encouraged by his success against our troops the day before with such a small number of men. He convinced Tissaphernes to give him a thousand cavalry and four thousand light troops, promising the surrender of the entire Greek army and the delivery of Xenophon's head by nightfall. At least, so said Mithradates' herald later that afternoon, when insolently demanding our surrender.

This time Xenophon had spent a great deal of time discussing with Chirisophus and the other older officers exactly which troops would be allowed to range out, which would be required to stay with the rear guard, and the precise role of our slingers. The Spartan hoplites were not informed of our experimental tactics until just before Mithradates' approach. When they saw the young, delicate-featured Rhodians, with their boyish physiques and "children's weapons," move into position, the scarred, muscular Spartans hooted in derision, some even turning away in disgust that Xenophon would risk the army's safety by assigning these hairless Ganymedes twirling overgrown sandal-laces to the front lines.

Mithradates did not bother with a complicated plan of action, as successful as his method had been the day before. When his troops caught up with our rear guard, we let their cavalry and slingers approach in a mass within the confines of the ravine, until their missiles began to inflict damage. At a signal from Xenophon, our heavy troops parted, and the two hundred Rhodians stepped through the front lines, wearing light armor and helmets but carrying no shields, and oblivious to the Persian arrows darting past them. At that close range the Persians were practically point-blank targets for the skilled Rhodians, and as planned, the Rhodians did not even attempt to fire through the enemy's heavy bronze breastplates or helmets. Instead, they aimed their deadly lead "bees" directly at the unprotected necks and flanks of the horses, and we watched with a mixture of admiration and horror as the rough-edged pellets drilled deep holes into the horses' neck muscles and windpipes. The spiral grooves on the balanoi had the "singing" effect Nicolaus had intended—a terrifying, high-pitched scream as the burrs on the missiles spun rapidly through the air. The combined effect of a hundred of these eerily whining bullets at a time, and the moist, thwacking sounds they made as they slammed into their fleshy targets, drove the enemy horses into a frenzy. Within seconds the Persian lines had reverted from the confident march of cavalry and infantry bent on destroying the foe and returning home in time for supper, to utter chaos and devastation. Horses reared and fell, toppling and trampling their riders, and the Persian bowmen and slingers were unable to maneuver their large and ungainly weapons in the close quarters and crush of men.

The Spartan hoplites shook their heads in wonder. As the enemy finally managed to flee back into the ravine, our new cavalry troops doubled out in pursuit, followed by the Spartans, trampling and slashing at the terrified Persians they encountered along the way. Xenophon and I watched the rout in admiration and delight.

"By the gods," he said in amazement, "if only I had an entire army of these boys. Each of them is worth five Spartans, and they sure as hell eat less!"

I laughed, but immediately became serious. "They're grateful to you, Xenophon, for uniting them and recognizing their skills. They're the most loyal troops you have in the army."

Xenophon gazed thoughtfully at the pursuing Greek cavalry, which had now receded far into the distance in their chase. "And that loyalty must not be taken for granted," he said. "There may come a time when we'll need it. We must take good care of our Rhodians—especially Nicolaus," and he trotted back to the lines to confer with the officers.

Eighteen fine Persian horses were captured unharmed during the pursuit, which made a useful addition to our cavalry, and fine meals in the months to follow. As for the Persian dead, after much discussion with Chirisophus, Xenophon reluctantly ordered them mutilated and dishonored, Persian-style, to strike terror into the enemy. The Spartans praised what they called Xenophon's "beekeepers" as only Spartans could, solemnly chanting the victory hymn to Ares, the god of war, and awarding simple myrtle crowns, the Spartans' highest military honor, to the beaming young Rhodians.

Tissaphernes continued to dog our steps, but now kept a prudent distance. Thus we marched for three hundred miles, moving north along the left bank of the Tigris to the ancient cities of Nimrud and Nineveh, which had once been inhabited by the fearsome Medes but had been conquered by the Great King one hundred and fifty years earlier. To think that any Persian army such as the one tormenting us now had once been able to overcome such fearsome fortifications as these was staggering. The walls of these cities were twenty-five feet thick and a hundred feet high, their positions seemingly impregnable. But the Great King was much more of a man than was his unfortunate descendant Artaxerxes—unfortunate, I say, because King Artaxerxes' inferiority was acknowledged not only by the peoples and troops of both sides, but also by himself. It is a sad thing for one to have to submit so humbly to the obvious excellence of one's ancestor. It is as if one has become a disappointment to the procreation of the generations, an offspring as sterile as a mule, not in terms of fecundity but of strength and honor. It is terrible to look back on the glorious history of one's family, and to see its many and famous branches converge to an insignificant point, like the drooping and wilted tip of an immense hemlock tree, and to realize that such a laughable, incongruous apex of the generations, such a shadow of a great name, is oneself.

We gazed in wonder at the ruins of these mighty cities, now half filled with sand and dust, their baked clay walls crumbling to rubble. The only inhabitants were hyenas slinking through the alleys, howling at their own shadows, and vultures perched on the ancient battlements, their pink heads raw and boiled-looking, their brains ingrained with ancestral memories of rotting cadavers piled against the city walls, which had not furnished sustenance for them for five generations or more. Only the occasional trading caravan or band of Bedouins passed through, rarely staying more than a night.

For three days we camped inside the walls, most of the troops fearing the spirits and arraying themselves by unit in the open squares. Only a few dared to venture into the courtyards of the ruined palaces, or to enter the abandoned shells of the houses or apartment blocks, and to wander through the silent, deserted rooms. What manner of men had inhabited these dwellings, I wondered. How can a hundred years or five hundred years of men's lives spent in these rooms—centuries of laughter, plotting, lovemaking, eating and pissing, experiences so vivid and intense to the participants at the time—be so completely effaced from the earth and from memory that not even ghosts remain to tell us of them, having disappeared in frustration at the dearth of living visitors to torment in their hauntings? In vain I combed through the ancient rooms and hearths, seeking—I am not sure what—some evidence of a man's ability to make his existence felt, some small dropping or sign, some token, a toy or a tool, that here lived an individual, a man like me, that despite the horror of his city's destruction, some small proof of his one-time presence lives on; but all I found, until the final night, were ashes.

On that night, at the intersection of two massive, perpendicular walls, a deserted place where Asteria and I found ourselves in one of our aimless nocturnal wanderings, I kicked aside some pieces of rubble to clear a place to sit, and was startled to discover a neatly preserved human hand emerging from the earth. The smooth, oversized member gleamed a malignant gray, one of its marble fingers chipped off, the rough stone inside the break sparkling in reflection of the starry, moonless sky above. The ghostly limb seemed almost to tremble in the flickering light of my tiny lamp, and for a moment I thought I saw it move, admonishing us for disturbing its owner's rest, or beckoning us closer with its remaining fingers. We recoiled from the site in terror and awe, and returned to camp glancing anxiously over our shoulders, fearing lest the shades of ancient kings be stalking us through the city's crumbling courtyards and streets. For long hours that night I lay sleepless, staring at the ceiling and listening to the soft rustling and random growling of the feral curs skulking outside the tent, sniffing for stale crusts of bread or untended flesh.

The next afternoon we made camp a day's march from the abandoned city walls, under storm-whipped and chilling skies with black thunderheads glowering threateningly at the massed armies below. Tissaphernes himself appeared on the plain in clear view at the head of his troops, his black and gold winged-horse banners slapping in the wind. Over the weeks spent pursuing us thus far, he had combined his forces with those of Orontas, another son-in-law of the king's, and Ariaius' hundred thousand native forces that had traveled up country as our friends, and who were now arrayed against us as enemies. The combined forces were enormous and seemed to cover the plain. I climbed gingerly to the peak of a crumbling battlement and surveyed the Persians' huge army. When I compared it to our insignificant band of tattered Greeks, hundreds of them wounded and many others burdened with the supply wagons, our resources seemed pathetically feeble, and I feared what the gods had in store for us.

BOOK EIGHT

BARBARIANS

. . . The glowering Fates gnashed their white fangs,
Descending grimly, blood-spattered and terrifying,
Seeking out the fallen and longing to gorge on dark
Blood. Upon catching a man thrown down or wounded,
One of them would grasp him in her great claws, and
His soul would descend screaming to Hades and cold Tartarus. After
Satisfying her taste for human blood, she would hurl his body behind
And rush back again into the clamor and fray . . .

—HESIOD

I

EARLY ON, WE HAD FOUND that trying to march while simultaneously fending off Tissaphernes' harassing forces was impossible; so in each village through which we passed, we lingered long, caring for our wounded, burying our dead and scouring the countryside for provisions. When the enemy appeared to have lost its alertness, usually at night, we would stealthily break camp and steal quickly across the countryside under cover of darkness to the next village, where we would wait for another opportunity to make a break. We skipped thus from haven to haven as if in a child's game, one in which the loser suffered the ultimate, permanent penalty. The Persian forces were useless at night—they kept their horses tied up, hobbled and unsaddled, and in the event of a night attack they were unable to quickly prepare their mounts, armor and weaponry. To guard against our hoplites' surprising them in the darkness they customarily camped seven or eight miles away from our position. In the evening, as soon as we saw them blowing their trumpets to retreat for the night, we would prepare our baggage, and when the Persians had moved out of sight, we would force a march, putting a wide distance between the two armies and forcing the Persians to travel double the distance the next day.

One night, however, the Persians reversed their custom. They feigned departure in the evening and instead sent a large detachment ahead of us behind a range of hills, seizing a high position over the road along which we would have to pass.

On the next day's march, when Chirisophus in the vanguard noticed that the hill ahead of us had already been taken, he sent riders back to Xenophon in the rear, asking him to advance with his slingers. We were tied down, however, because the remainder of Tissaphernes' army was following us close behind, engaging our slingers and bowmen at every opportunity. Exasperated at Chirisophus' increasing demands and at Tissaphernes' relentless harrying, Xenophon finally left Lycius temporarily in charge of the rear, and rode to the front himself, accompanied by Nicolaus and me.

"Where the fuck have you been?" Chirisophus snapped, furious at the time we had taken to arrive. "Where are the rest of your string-twirlers? Cowering with the baggage train?"

Nicolaus flushed crimson and glared at him, but Xenophon ignored the Spartan's rudeness and coolly stared him down. "If I had brought my slingers, Tissaphernes would have been running his pennant up your ass before sundown. The slingers stay at the rear as long as the Persian army is still there."

Chirisophus swore under his breath. "The hill above us has been taken and we're stuck here like turds in a bucket until we get rid of those fucking Persian sharpshooters. They're eating my men alive."

Xenophon looked up pensively. When fighting on a steeply sloping plain, defensive forces at the top are able to aim their weapons at the entire body of downhill attackers, from front line to rear; shields are useless to the attackers, unless held straight up and horizontal, like turtle shells, an awkward position in which to climb and fight. Even worse, the downhill attackers, if they are able to throw or shoot at all, can target only the front lines of the forces at the top, and if the defenders are well entrenched, even that is impossible.

Trotting several hundred yards along the road to a better vantage point, Xenophon noticed another steep hill behind the one occupied by the enemy. It had not yet been taken by the Persians and was substantially higher, with a narrow, rocky approach separating them. He returned to Chirisophus, slightly breathless.

"We have to seize that height now," he said, "before the Persians figure out what's going on. My troops are tied down by Tissaphernes three miles back. Either you send your Spartans up to take that hill, or stay here and command the army while I take up a detachment of your men. Either way, make yourself useful."

Chirisophus glared at him. "Your choice, General," he said sarcastically, emphasizing the last word for effect. "It is for me to follow your orders."

I took a deep breath as I saw Xenophon pause for a moment, deliberately sizing the Spartan up before finally deciding, yet again, to ignore his insulting tone of voice. I could only attribute Xenophon's restraint to his overriding desire to maintain the army's unity at all costs, even in the face of personal insult. Gryllus had long ago warned that Spartans were not to be trusted. Thank the gods, I thought, for the Rhodians' unquestioning loyalty, for this was a great source of comfort, as well as a considerable defensive advantage.

Xenophon shielded his eyes against the sun and peered back up at the hill. "I'll need three hundred men," he said. "You'll know in an hour whether or not we are successful." Chirisophus nodded and began selecting men, and I will give him credit, he picked three hundred of the biggest, meanest, ugliest sons of Orcus he had, and assigned them to Xenophon for the rush up the hill. We set off immediately, but Xenophon stopped Nicolaus and pulled him aside. "You wait here."

The Rhodian looked at him quizzically, then his eyes narrowed in resentment. Like all his countrymen, he was sensitive about his youth and small stature, and resisted every attempt to favor him with lighter duties.

"Why, Xenophon? I'll take down three Persians with my sling for every one your Spartans trample."

Xenophon grinned at the boy's spirit. "It's not that—I need someone I trust to wait here for Lycius and explain the situation to him. I don't want him to receive all his news from Chirisophus."

Nicolaus nodded warily at this, and Xenophon wheeled his horse to gallop off after the troops, who by now had already started their ascent.

As soon as the Persians on the lower hill noticed the squad circling behind them and aiming for the unoccupied heights, they too detached a squad of several hundred men, who began racing for the same position. A silence fell over both armies. Although neither of the attacking squads could see the other one climbing the opposite side of the hill, both armies down on the plain could see the entire race. A cheer was suddenly loosed from the Greeks down below, followed a second later by an echoing cheer from the Persian camp, as the Greeks lapsed back into silence. Like a race in the Olympic games with every spectator in the stadium urging on his own countrymen, the troops roared their encouragement to their fellows on the hill.

Xenophon rode back and forth on his struggling horse among the panting Hellenes in the climbing squad, waving his sword and shouting until his voice was raw. "Move, you bastards, move! The Persians are attacking on the other side! This is a race for Greece!"

The men sweated and panted, pushing themselves to exhaustion, their eyes fixed only on the summit. One strapping fellow, his chest barrel-thick and his thighs as sturdy as stone pillars, began complaining in a voice that could be heard even over the grunting and swearing of his comrades. I looked closely at the soldier—he was clearly an athlete, or a former one, a man who should have been leading the charge rather than tailing behind and moaning. I was certain I had seen him before, but was unable to recognize him, with his face obscured behind the nasal and cheekplates of his battle helmet. I pointed the man out to Xenophon, and as we watched, he pulled up short and straightened his back, panting, his hand groping behind him in a frantic attempt to scratch his shoulder where the straps to his breast and back plates must have been rubbing him raw.

"Fucking officers!" he burst out in a fury to the men around him. "They ride their stinking horses, while we slog up this mountain in the dirt, lugging our gear like fucking slaves in the salt mines!"

The man continued to rant, but it was this insult that hit Xenophon like a slap in the face, and he turned beet red in fury—it was a look I had seen many times in the past, but mostly adorning the expressions of Spartan drill sergeants, and I had usually managed to avoid its being directed my way. He leaped off his horse without a word, tossing me the reins, raced over to the laggard and placed his face within inches of the enormous, raving brute.

"Get your ass back to camp and help out the laundry girls!" he shouted. He then grabbed the dumbfounded man's shield and began racing up the hill with it himself, no mean feat while wearing his stiff cavalry armor and continuing to bellow at the troops to urge them on. The other men whacked the soldier on the head and back with the flats of their swords as they passed, jeering and insulting him as he stood motionless and dumb. Finally, out of sheer shame, he put his head down and again charged up the hill, bellowing the paean to mighty Apollo, which was soon taken up by the rest of the climbers and the army on the plain below. Catching up, he swiped his shield back with a glare, and Xenophon, exhausted, caught the reins of his horse I threw him and struggled to remount in his armor.

The roaring of both armies below indicated it was a close race. Xenophon was forced back off his horse by the steepness of the pitch, and he struggled to tear off his unwieldy armor to continue the assault on foot. The men were climbing now hand over hand, loose rocks and gravel rolling down on the climbers below as they scrambled furiously upwards, sweating, swearing, struggling to hold onto their shields and swords. The lead climbers were only twenty-five feet from the summit, then ten feet, when I saw to my horror the flat-ridged crest of a bronze Persian helmet appear on the summit from the other side, and then another. The leading Greeks, engrossed in the effort of the climb, did not themselves notice this until the first half dozen of them had flopped in exhaustion on the topmost boulders—and there was a moment of pause as the exhausted climbers from both sides opened their eyes and noticed their mortal enemies facing them not six feet away.

Greeks and Persians struggled to their feet, uncertain whether to come to blows with each other or to peer down the opposite sides of the peak to see how many more of the enemy might be close at hand. The two Persian climbers had far outstripped their fellows in their race for the summit, while practically the entire body of Greeks, at Xenophon's desperate urging, had remained close together during the climb and were now poised to arrive at the summit as a body. As a result, the lead Greeks and Persians did not come to blows at all; for as soon as the Persians looked down both sides and compared the relative distances of the two attacking squads, they decided their best chance for safety was in yielding the summit to the Greeks. With a shout they leaped off their side onto the heads of their fellows below, who quickly turned and half ran, half slid down the steep incline. The cheers on the Persian side of the plain fell silent, while those on the Greek side rose to a deafening thunder. We took the summit without a single loss, and as Xenophon and the remaining hoplites struggled gasping to the top, we peered down on the Persian troops occupying the neighboring height overlooking the road to the north. They, in turn, had ceased their jeering and shooting at Chirisophus' forces below them, and were now standing still, staring up at us in consternation.

"Watch this," Xenophon said to the men with a grim smile. "Theo, wave the attack to Chirisophus."

I tore off my helmet and mounted it on the point of an eight-foot spear I seized from a hoplite standing nearby, and raising it high, pumped it up and down three times in the prearranged signal. A moment later, a tremendous roar lifted up from Chirisophus' troops far below, as they rushed to the foot of the slope and began climbing hand over hand toward the top of the near height; the Persians between our two bodies of men whirled back, startled, to face the onslaught.

Xenophon then bawled, "Attack!" and our hoplites, their eyes gleaming fiercely through the helmet slits and their teeth flashing wolfishly behind their visors, fairly leaped in their rush to descend upon the outnumbered mob of Persian forces below.

The Persians did not wait to see a preordained outcome fulfilled. Dropping their weapons and flailing their arms in terror, they practically rolled down the side of their now indefensible stronghold, in a panic to escape the murderously bellowing hoplites storming them from above and below. After a moment, Xenophon unexpectedly raised his hand in the signal to halt, and it was only with great difficulty that he was able to restrain the fired-up men.

"Let them go!" he shouted, laughing, as the terror-stricken Persians tumbled and fell over each other in the loose gravel of the mountainside in their haste to escape. "Even one broken ankle among us is not worth the sorry booty we might capture from them." The men grudgingly assented and clambered back down to Chirisophus' troops in a jubilant mood.

From that time on, we had no further engagement with Tissaphernes' main forces, although small Persian raiding parties occasionally cut down Hellenes if they strayed too far from the army in their plundering. The Persians sent outriders ahead to burn the rich Tigris villages and crops along our projected path, which we interpreted as a last-ditch sign of desperation on their part. Although it posed considerable hardship for our troops in finding sufficient provisions, we knew this would be only temporary—a native army cannot continue to burn its own country without soon meeting resistance from the people.

And of course we were right, for a few days later Tissaphernes gave up the attack completely, limiting his presence merely to a few isolated scouts who continued to dog us from a distance for a few weeks more as we moved beyond the king's sphere of control. When talking with Asteria that night, as I helped her draw water for the camp followers from a nearby stream, a look of shock passed across her face when I mentioned that we were unlikely to see Tissaphernes again. She stared at me questioningly for a moment, silently asking me once more if I would accept the proposition she had put to me earlier, and I slowly, but emphatically, shook my head no. She sighed, hoisted the heavy leather buckets up to her shoulders with the yoke, and trudged silently up to her camp, where I left her to return to my duties with Xenophon.

II

SEVERAL DAYS LATER, just at sunset, as the army's scouts were returning to camp for the evening, I was startled to see Nicolaus emerge from the trees limping painfully, a grimace on his face. His arm was draped over the shoulders of another Rhodian who supported him in his painstaking walk out of the forest, and his right foot was tightly wrapped in a filthy rag torn from his tattered tunic. Despite the swaddling, he left a trail of blood on the earth behind him as he moved.

"Nicolaus, what happened?" I exclaimed, sprinting up and relieving his exhausted comrade of the burden. The loss of any of the Rhodians, whether to death or injury, would be a considerable blow to the army, but Nicolaus in particular, who was developing into a tactician of no mean skill and a valuable advisor to Xenophon, was to be protected at all costs. "Has there been an attack?"

Nicolaus grimaced again and rolled his eyes. "Only on me, for my own stupidity. I walked too close to a badger hole, and the fucker must have been waiting for me. He tore into my foot like a slab of raw meat, and locked his jaws on me. I had to club him to death with a stick, and then use another stick to pry his jaws. He took a chunk off my foot." Nicolaus' comrade proudly pulled the dead creature from a cloth bag slung over his shoulder, its head flattened and pulpy. It was the largest I had ever seen, the weight of a kid goat, with a row of evil, pointed teeth on its lower jaw that protruded around the bared lip in a hideous grin, still stained with Nicolaus' blood. "Can you help me into camp?" Nicolaus asked.

I could not yet tell how serious the injury might be, but any animal bite was notoriously prone to life-threatening fever, and if the badger had been rabid as well—best not to think about the consequences for now.

After draping his thin body carefully over my shoulders and carrying him to the Rhodians' campsite, I raced off to fetch Asteria, who had accumulated a large stash of medical supplies. I found her outside her tent, on her elbows and knees, her face almost touching the ground. She was struggling with the unaccustomed task of blowing on glowing embers to ignite a clumsily stacked pile of unseasoned branches she had gathered. I squatted beside her and spoke her name, startling her. She jumped and looked up, and then with a sheepish expression pushed herself up to a more dignified kneeling position, wiping stray strands of hair from her perspiring face. As she did so, she left a long, sooty finger-smudge across one cheek.

"Asteria, I need help with an injured man," I said. "Bring your medical supplies."

Returning with her to the Rhodians' camp a few minutes later, I pointed out the injured boy, while Nicolaus' comrades stood in awkward and deferential silence, unaccustomed to the presence of a woman in their midst.

Asteria did not shrink from the blood-soaked wrapping, but quickly and efficiently exposed the foot, calling for more light as she did so. As someone trained the glare from a torch directly on it, she muttered softly under her breath.

"This is beyond my experience," she finally said. "Clean arrow wounds, broken bones, fevers I have handled, but this—" and she looked almost sadly down at Nicolaus' foot. I bent down myself to have a closer view, and sucked in my breath in dismay.

The limb had already swelled to twice its normal size, engulfing the toes, which emerged from the bulbous foot like tiny, newly sprouted buds on a tuber. Much of the skin had been torn off or hung in shreds, as if flayed with a dull knife, and a large piece of the inner heel was missing, just below the ankle, where I guessed the furious creature had clamped down in his final death throes. The foot was riddled with deep puncture marks where the beast had chewed and gnawed, seeking purchase—some had penetrated down to the bone.

Asteria gently palpated the instep, toes and ankle while Nicolaus writhed and moaned in pain, two of his colleagues pressing his shoulders flat to the ground and muttering reassurance to him.

"I don't think anything is broken," she said finally. "That is fortunate. The foot is a complicated limb and rarely heals properly after being set. I'm worried about this bite, though, and the punctures. This type of injury is ripe for gangrene. Once that sets in, the whole foot is lost—possibly even more."

Of this I was only too aware, for the sickly-sweet smell of rotting flesh which is symptomatic of this disease was a familiar one in the Greek camp.

Asteria hesitated, staring at the foot, before getting up and strolling impassively over to the nearest campfire, deep in thought. She knelt beside it, poking gently in the embers, pondering her next course of action. After a moment she stood up again, having apparently made a decision, and returned, her eyes avoiding Nicolaus' sweating, inquiring face.

"Sit on his knee, Theo," she commanded in a low voice, "and hold his shin tight. Don't let his foot move." I jumped to the task, eager for something useful to do, and no sooner had I seized the bony shin and calf than she withdrew from behind her back the knife she was holding, which she had brought to a pulsing, red-hot glow in the coals. Kneeling quickly, she pressed the flat of the glowing blade hard against the enormous bite in the flesh of the foot, eliciting a loud sizzling sound from the steaming wound, as of fat dripping from a roasting flank into the fire. The sharp, acrid stench of burning flesh assaulted my nostrils as fiercely as it had when the flaming naphtha had seared the attacking Persians at Cunaxa.

For a moment Nicolaus was silent, perhaps in shock, or during that brief, merciful delay between the touch of burning metal to one's skin and the blinding white explosion of pain that bursts in one's head. Then he erupted into a desperate, sustained howl, a cry of rage and pain that shocked and silenced the rest of the camp, as men for hundreds of yards around stopped what they were doing to listen. His scream died down to a gasping choke as his lungs became depleted, but resumed again as Asteria turned the blade over to the other, still red-hot side and again pressed its sizzling flatness into the now crispened wound. The bleeding ceased almost immediately, and was now reduced to a quiet, insignificant oozing. She gazed at her handiwork in satisfaction. "Almost done, now," she whispered to Nicolaus soothingly, though whatever comfort he may have derived from these words was blotted out when he saw her step back to the fire to plunge her blade again into the coals.

Returning a moment later, she this time gently inserted the red-hot tip into each puncture wound, rotating the searing blade slowly to cauterize all sides of the holes. Nicolaus was passing in and out of consciousness from the excruciating pain, and when lucid, he was reduced to a despairing, breathless whimper.

The ghastly treatment was over as quickly as it had begun, though not soon enough for those of us watching in horrified fascination. Removing a long needle and a length of gut from her kit, she quickly and efficiently sutured the flaps of skin she found hanging freely from around the ankle and instep, and then rummaging again through her bag, found a small ceramic jar sealed with a piece of oiled fabric tied tightly around the top. Opening this up, she dipped in her fingers and swabbed Nicolaus' entire foot, both inside the wounds and out, with a greasy, foul-smelling balm that appeared to give the ashen-faced boy some relief. She then wrapped the entire limb in clean gauze up to the knee, tied it off tightly, and stood up, wiping her hands dry on her hips.

"Theo," she said, in a low voice of authority, "find him some uncut wine to help him sleep. I'll check on him in the morning and change the dressing. If we can stave off fever for three days he'll recover without loss."

I rushed off to take some wine from Xenophon's private store, which he used for libations during the sacrifices, and returned to find Asteria chatting quietly with several of the Rhodian boys, each of whom was asking her about their own wounds and ailments. Asteria patiently answered their queries as best she could, but I could see from her face that she was drained and exhausted, and I gently led her away from the grateful slingers, and sleeping Nicolaus.

Walking quietly back to the camp followers' quarters, we paused near a high hedge to rest. I was deeply impressed with her work on Nicolaus, and told her as much, but she wearily waved off my compliments.

"I learned about treating foot injuries from some notes left at the palace years ago by Democedes of Croton," she said, "but it was your countryman Hippocrates who perfected the cauterizing technique. I never had the courage to try it, until now. The pain is terrible, but short-lived. Thank the gods it was only his foot. It could have been much worse."

"Worse? His foot was in shreds!"

"True, but Hippocrates recommends the technique for treating hemorrhoids."

I recoiled, and she rolled her eyes at my squeamishness. "Theo, please, let us talk of something else. My spirit needs distracting."

I was not sure what she wished to discuss, but my mind immediately ventured to a question that had been gnawing at me for weeks, afraid to hear the answer from her for fear it might cause her to reconsider her own motives.

"Asteria, you had hardly even spoken to me before. What possessed you to steal into my tent in Cunaxa?"

She looked at me in surprise. "Because I am Lydian, of course," she said.

This response failed to penetrate, which she gathered from my silence.

"Of course, I was born in Miletus," she explained, which only confused me further. "Miletus has been under Lydian rule for centuries, but my mother traces her lineage directly from King Croesus, so I consider myself Lydian, even though the Persians insisted on calling me 'the Milesian.' "

I was thoroughly baffled by now, which seemed to flummox her.

"I'm surprised at you," she said, in exasperation.

"Then we're even," I answered. "I've known Lydians all my life—Athens is full of them—but I've never known one to grant me the favors you did, simply because you were born a Lydian!" I winked, but she ignored, or failed to notice, the jesting tone in my voice.

"Have you ever read Archilochus of Paros?" she asked, her eyebrows raised.

Naturally I had read the old Parian, back when Xenophon and I were schoolboys, but I had retained precious little, and indeed I had to confess that I had understood even less at the time I had read him. To me, his lyric poetry was of the densest sort.

"And you call us barbarians," she said dismissively. "Athenians seem to think that unless their history comes spoon-fed in simple prose straight from Herodotus, it can't be worth listening to."

The conversation had now shifted to a topic with which I was familiar. "Herodotus was a great man," I asserted, straightening my back and raising my chin at this rare chance to demonstrate my superior knowledge. "I once even met the master personally, when I was a young boy and he a very old man—though you can't imagine a crustier old gaffer than he was, and one less likely to attract the favors of a Lydian wench." I pinched her playfully on the haunches but she swatted my hand away.

"Well, since you are such a *cultured* Athenian," she retorted sarcastically, "you certainly know Herodotus' chronicle of King Candaules of Lydia."

"Of course, but I still dispute your characterization of Herodotus . . ."

"Would you care for me to recite Archilochus' verse form of the tale? Then you may be better capable of judging the prose of your own leaden-tongued hero."

Ignoring her dismissal of the education and culture I had struggled so hard to acquire at Xenophon's side, I took the bait and happily agreed to the recitation. She launched effortlessly into the polished iambic trimeter that Archilocus employed only for his most salacious verse, though from her lips it sounded as pure as a prayer. I would be wholly incapable of transcribing here her perfectly modulated pitch and crystalline vocalizing—it is impossible for a mediocre intellect to accurately render the speech of a superior one, especially fifty years into one's dotage. I will therefore limit myself to recalling it to the best of my ability in the thick Attic prose Asteria so disdained, but with which my pedestrian Muses have cursed me.

"You know, of course, that Candaules was madly, passionately in love with his wife," she began. "He was a very fortunate man, for if the gods ordain both that a man fall in love, which happens often, and that he love the very person with whom they ordain he is to spend the rest of his life, which happens only rarely, then that man is indeed blessed. And Candaules was thrice blessed, in that he also believed that his wife was the most beautiful woman in the world. It is just such an overabundance of fortune that leads the gods to take notice, and to pound in the nail whose head extends higher than the rest."

She paused to look at me, confirming that I was paying close attention, then continued.

"Candaules had one bodyguard, Gyges, whom he favored above all others, and to whom he confided all his affairs, even his most intimate thoughts; and Gyges never once betrayed his master's confidence. He was loyal to a fault. Candaules often rapturously described his wife's beauty and voluptuousness to Gyges," and breaking out of character and rhythm, Asteria added, "though you know better than I do what men talk about to each other when alone."

I felt the blood rising to my face and began heatedly denying that men discuss any such things with each other, but she rolled her eyes dismissively at me and continued.

"One day, while they were discussing Candaules' favorite topic, he remarked that Gyges did not seem to believe the claims he made of his wife's physical perfection. 'Since the truth is more persuasive to men's eyes than to their ears,' he said, 'I will find a way for you to see her naked, and then you will be convinced of what I say, not only with regard to her beauty, but to her other talents as well.'

"Naturally, Gyges was appalled at this suggestion, as any honorable man would be. 'What are you saying, master?' he said. 'You wish me to see your wife naked? Believe me, I know you are telling the truth when you say there is no woman on earth with a body like hers. But I was taught by my father to distinguish between right and wrong. Don't ask me to do evil merely to confirm what I already know is true. I would rather you blinded me.'

"But the king would have none of this. 'Courage, Gyges,' he chided. 'Do not take me the wrong way. I only wish to dispel any doubts you might have in your mind. Believe me, perfect white buttocks like hers are not seen every day, at least not by mortal men. I will manage it so that you will be able to inspect her beauty at your leisure, while she remains completely unaware that you are watching. Evil unnoticed by the victim is not evil at all, but merely a benefit to the perpetrator, and no one will be the worse for it.

" 'Tonight, stand behind the open door of our bedchamber. When I go there to sleep, she will follow me. There is a chair close to the entrance, on which she will drape her garments one by one as she takes them off. She sleeps naked, and you, standing in the shadows behind the door, will be able to see her illuminated in the light of the lamp as if it were your own bed for which she was preparing. After she has finished undressing and turned her back on you to go to bed, you may stay and watch further, or slip quietly out the door without her seeing.'

"Gyges tried repeatedly to escape his master's request, but to no avail. That night, Candaules led Gyges to the hiding place, and a moment later the queen followed, carefully laying out each garment on the chair just as the king had predicted. Gyges watched in awe, his heart in his throat at the queen's beauty, which was more wondrous than he had ever imagined or that the king had described. He could scarcely breathe in his passion and fear, and his knees were so weak from trembling that he was afraid they would buckle beneath him and drop him gasping to the floor at the feet of the surprised queen.

"Shortly afterwards she moved toward the bed, and when he saw her smooth, white buttocks moving away from him, he cautiously slipped out of the room, in utter stealth and silence. Just as he disappeared through the doorway, however, the clever queen happened to glance back and see his shadow, and although she instantly guessed what had happened, she neither screamed nor gave any other sign that she was aware of her husband's and Gyges' terrible offense."

Again breaking out of character, Asteria explained to me slowly and carefully, as if speaking to a dense child, "Among Lydians, even men, it is considered to be a deep disgrace to be seen unclothed."

I felt my face heating up, as she paused and stared at me pointedly. All this time I had never been sure whether or not she had recognized me at Cunaxa as I watched her struggle out of her robe and escape naked behind the Greek lines.

"The queen mentioned nothing to her husband," Asteria continued, "but at daybreak, she summoned Gyges. She had often in the past spoken with him alone on official matters, and he was accustomed to responding to her call, thinking nothing of it. So this time as well, he obeyed her summons, not suspecting that she knew of his indiscretion the night before. Arriving in her presence, he knelt down before her with his head bowed, as was the custom in the Lydian court.

" 'You have committed a foul deed, Gyges,' she said sternly, casting a baleful eye at the terrified soldier and holding the point of a large dagger to the back of his neck, 'for you have seen me naked, thus breaking the sacred mystery that holds between man and wife. You now have a choice. Kill the king, thereby assuming the Lydian throne and becoming my lord; or die now at my hands. In either case, you will never again obey my husband's unlawful orders.'

"Poor Gyges remained motionless, in shock. Quickly recovering, however, he begged the queen not to force him to choose such a thing. But the queen had set her heart, and the more he pleaded not to kill or be killed, the harder she pressed the dagger to his neck. Finally, seeing no alternative, he gave in. 'If I must be forced to commit a foul deed for the second time in two days, then I choose to save my own life over my master's. Tell me how you wish me to kill him.'

" 'You must attack him,' she answered, 'on the very spot where he showed me naked to your prying eyes, and you must wait till he is asleep, to ensure your success.'

"When night fell Gyges, seeing he had no alternative but to slay his master, hid behind the same door as he had the night before, this time with the queen's own dagger in his hand. The king entered first, as was his custom, and then the queen, who again, slowly and deliberately, took off each garment in the full light of the lamp, laying them on the chair as Gyges watched. After undressing completely she paused for a long moment, motionless, her full body visible to the watching soldier. He again could hardly contain his trembling from the combination of fear and lust, the two most violent urges that possess a man, both of them rising from the loins and up through the belly, feeding on and gathering strength from each other, constricting the chest, stopping the breathing, closing the throat, drying the lips and making the head swoon. The queen stood there in the light, as if giving him the opportunity to gaze upon her, and to strengthen his heart for the task, as he contemplated the reward that would be his after successfully completing his mission."

Again Asteria paused, staring hard at me with what seemed to be a mixture of desire and reproach. I reached my hand toward her face, but she shook her head distractedly, as if breaking a spell, and with a shrug indicated a note of finality.

"Of course you know the rest," she concluded with a wry smile. "Gyges stabbed the king to death in his sleep. Candaules' pale, plump wife passed into Gyges' happy hands, as did the kingdom, which was later approved by the Pythia at Delphi. Generations later, Gyges' descendant, King Croesus, brought on Lydia's war with the Persians and eventually its downfall."

This latter event was, of course, precisely the story that Xenophon had recounted to Aglaia on the road to Delphi so long ago. The chiastic structure of the sequences and genders amused me, but after a moment another thought occurred to me, clouding my spirits, and I brought it up to her only half in jest.

"Do you mean to say then, that since I saw you naked, I would have either had to have killed Cyrus myself and taken you as my wife, or you would have killed me?"

She smiled serenely. "You were ignorant of Archilochus; perhaps you know your Homer?

> *" 'Truly you are a wicked man, but not short on brains.*
> *How could you say such a thing, how could you even imagine it?*
> *As heaven and earth are my witness—I swear*
> *I would never plot any harm to you. Trust me when I say*
> *My heart is not iron. I have only compassion.' "*

"You know too much," I muttered. "And it is you who are wicked. I refuse to play dueling quotations with a woman."

"That was Calypso, comforting Odysseus, in case you were unsure," she cooed sweetly, patting my hand, "and I would venture to say that it is not I who know too much, but you who know too little."

"Calypso was a nymph who nearly drove Odysseus mad," I said peevishly, "and I sympathize with him deeply. I asked a simple question. It is a mark of intelligence, not to mention good breeding, to say no more than is necessary but to tell at least what is required. You skirt the issue. Would I have had to kill Cyrus, to prevent you from killing me, my good queen?"

"Perhaps it is fortunate, dear Gyges," she said, "that Cyrus died the way he did, saving you the trouble. After all, I am Lydian."

At this she mashed her lips against mine in a clear sign that our verbal jousting had come to an end, for which I was grateful. As I ran my hands down her sides and waist, however, I was given pause when I again felt the large dagger in its sheath at her belt, which since her first night with me at Cunaxa she had never been without.

The next morning we felt the first frost of winter's approach, and as the pale sun rose we could make out a broad, open plain ahead of us, through the northern mountains to the country of the Kurds, and beyond that Armenia, a large and rich territory bordering the Black Sea where supplies would be plentiful. The Kurds, however, were a force terrifying to the troops. Word had spread among the men that several years earlier a Persian invading force of a hundred and twenty thousand men had entered the mountains to subjugate them, and not single man had returned alive. The only clue as to their fate was a donkey that had been set loose to wander from the Kurdish border back into Persian territory bearing an enormous sack on its back. When the animal was found by Persian scouts and the sack cut open they were horrified to find one hundred and twenty thousand human prepuces, dried and strung from a long wrought chain like those worn by Kurdish slaves. We hoped the story was an exaggeration, but it was impossible to say.

Xenophon offered sacrifice to the gods, for we feared that the mountain passes across the plain might already be occupied by Kurdish forces anticipating our arrival. The gods sent us an eagle, which circled the camp once and slowly drifted away over the northern peaks.

The army left at midnight.

III

THROUGH THE COLD CLEAR NIGHT we marched in silence, each man keeping his own thoughts, each enveloped in his own fears. Terrified of hearing at any moment the thundering hoofbeats of crazed, fur-clad barbarians descending upon us in the darkness with torches and razor lances, we churned across the unprotected plain, and by sunrise we had reached the cover of the mountains. Even this shelter was deceiving, however, as we found in the days after. While traveling through the canyons and steep mountain passes, the army was forced to string out in an exposed line miles long, leaving us open to lightning attacks by small bands of Kurds, who would melt back into the rocks after their murderous raids, to the fury of our frustrated hoplites.

In an effort to reduce our vulnerability, Chirisophus cautiously sent squads of Spartan rangers and other light-armed peltasts ahead to determine the location of any barbarian raiding parties, and to assay the route for ease of passage. More than once, an unfortunate scout would return to camp a day late and half mad, holding his tongue or other body part in his hands, as a warning from a hostile band of Kurds he had stumbled across. The rest of the army fearfully followed behind this vanguard, picking its way up each series of hills, pausing to examine the countryside for potential pockets of danger and to allow the slower trailing units to catch up; then the entire force would seize momentum and roll quickly down the other side. Xenophon, as was customary, brought up the rear, commanding the hoplites and protecting the baggage, camp followers and the increasing numbers of sick and wounded, victims of the journey's hardship and disease, and of the Kurdish raids on stragglers.

When the gods favored us, our scouts were able to eliminate the Kurdish outriders before they could warn the villages of our approach and raise a general alarm. In these cases, the local inhabitants, caught unawares by the sudden presence of a foreign army in their midst, fled their villages into the hills with their wives and children, leaving soup boiling on the fires and goats wandering in the squalid streets, pleading to be milked as their tethers caught in branches and stones behind them. Provisions were available to us in quantity—cisterns of wine, huge brass pots in every household, livestock that far exceeded the numbers available to us in our own stores; but Xenophon gave strict orders against looting, killing or taking prisoners, except in self-defense. We spared the country in the fruitless hope that the Kurds might let us pass safely, if not as allies then at least as enemies of their enemy the king. We took only such provisions as we could eat in a single day, so we would not starve. We sent heralds up into the hills, crying out in eight tongues that we were not invaders and meant no harm; but either for want of fluency in the local barbarian dialect, or because of sheer hardheadedness and suspicion on their part, we could elicit no response from the Kurds, nor gain any assistance from them.

At night, whenever possible we camped within the confines of abandoned villages to take advantage of their fortifications, and we maintained a heavy guard. The displaced Kurds and their allies and relatives from miles around, who were clearly gathering into a larger, more cohesive force, lit hundreds of campfires in the hills above us. These looked like pinpoints of light covering the slopes of the mountains and receding in the distance until they blended seamlessly, but for their yellow tint, with the starry, sparkling skies around us, skies that were the same as those I had worshiped in my days of innocence in Athens. I do not know whether the Kurds were attempting to intimidate us by exaggerating their presence through so many fires, or whether they really did have so many thousands of men surveying us from the mountains, for by the time the sun rose, they had all disappeared, like so many shades summoned back to the underworld at daybreak, leaving nothing behind but faint wisps of smoke.

After spending one of many nights like this, during which not a single man got a wink of sleep except for possibly the most battle-hardened or brain-damaged Spartans, Xenophon summoned all the officers to his quarters. The expression on his face indicated that the news he was about to give would not be easy for him to impart.

"Gentlemen," he said grimly, scratching the lice-ridden beard he had recently grown to avoid the needless difficulty of daily shaving, "the Kurds are building up their forces and readying an attack. The scouts report signs of large bodies of men now moving as a single unit. We are ten thousand, but already a third of our troops are sick or wounded, and another third are occupied driving animals or forcing the supplies through. That leaves only one-third of the army as able-bodied fighters. The animals, baggage and camp followers are slowing us down, occupying men who could be defending our route. For the love of the gods, the camp followers number over five thousand, many of them women! They are dragging us to our deaths."

He paused to let this sink in, and to let us draw our conclusions. This we did, with heavy hearts, for without his explicitly saying so, it had become clear to us all since we had first entered the mountains that every extraneous ounce, every cooking pot, every crumb, every person that could not be counted upon to somehow further our progress, would eventually have to be eliminated. Even Proxenus' Boeotian engines, which Xenophon had faithfully dragged this entire distance over Chirisophus' strident protests, were ordered left behind, as being inappropriate for defending the army against the kind of warfare we were facing. The only exception to nonuseful burdens was the wounded or sick soldiers, whom we would rather die defending than abandon. Many of the men had accumulated large quantities of plunder from the towns and cities through which we had passed since Cilicia, and since they had not had the opportunity to convert it to specie, it was still in its bulk form: cups and plates, decorative armor, slaves, rolls of silk and other precious fabrics; all would have to be discarded. And many, too, had developed intimate friendships among the camp followers, boys, women, and men. These were ordered left behind.

Heralds were sent through the camp to cry the orders, and the men and camp followers listened in stunned silence. One of the officers mentioned to Xenophon that he was afraid it might give rise to a mutiny or to desertions, but Chirisophus, overhearing, scoffed at this. "What option do they have?" he burst out angrily. "If those dickheads prefer to stay with their trollops and pretty boys, they'll see how far they'll get through those mountains alone. Let 'em desert. If they're so keen on fucking, they'll certainly be fucked when we leave them to the Kurds."

Orders were given to march after breakfast, and camp was breaking already, amidst the wails and protests of those being forced to be left behind. Even the Persians we had captured from Tissaphernes weeks before begged to be driven along with the army among the goats rather than released to the Kurds' devices. Women clutched desperately at the soldiers, some their husbands and others complete strangers, offering all their possessions, their very bodies, for a chance to continue trailing the army. Merchants and smiths pleaded frantically with Xenophon and stony-faced Spartans, arguing the army's need for their skills, their own willingness to take up arms or to care for the dead if allowed to accompany the troops. Livestock, sensing the rising panic and chaos among their tenders, ran untethered and unfed through the milling crowds, rooting through the forlorn piles of personal possessions being heaped for burning. I raced through the quarters of the camp followers peering into wagons, looking behind stacks of weapons and provisions, searching for Asteria. I was certain she must already be in hiding, perhaps pretending to be a sick or wounded soldier and wrapped in a blanket on one of the hospital carts. I tore through the carts bearing the injured soldiers, examining each suspicious lump under the blankets and finding no sign of her. I had no idea what I would do once I found her—and the situation was becoming more critical, as another set of heralds were already marching through the camp, announcing that an inspection would be held as the army passed a narrow spot in the road two miles down, to ensure that no unwarranted baggage was being smuggled through.

Asteria was nowhere to be found, either among her friends or in any hiding place I could think of, and my duties could not allow me to continue searching any longer. Returning through the Rhodians' camp, I spotted Nicolaus, his foot now healing cleanly, and quickly pulled him off to the side.

"Nicolaus, you heard Xenophon's orders," I whispered huskily, out of breath. "All useless plunder and camp followers are to be left behind."

He shrugged his shoulders and stared at me in puzzlement. It occurred to me that the Rhodian boys were perhaps the only soldiers in the entire army completely unaffected by Xenophon's measure, being too young to have wives among the camp followers, and too new in their battle positions to have earned any plunder. I grasped him by the upper arm to prevent him from leaving.

"Have you seen Asteria?" I asked.

A shadow of concern flickered across his face as he shook his head no.

The fear I had felt when Asteria first suggested defecting to the Persians weeks before rose up again in my throat.

"Have you seen any of Tissaphernes' scouts still tailing us?" I pressed.

Puzzled now, Nicolaus considered the question carefully. "Occasionally, yes, but only from a great distance. They are few in number, and prefer to remain out of sight, for fear of our slings."

"Nicolaus: In the name of all that Xenophon has done for you, in the name of everything you believe in—if you see Asteria, find me."

Nicolaus stood rooted to his spot, astonished at my intensity. I realized the grip I had on his thin arm must have been hurting him terribly, yet he said nothing as he looked at me.

I persisted. "Will you swear it?"

"Yes."

"By all you hold sacred?"

Nicolaus hesitated, and I realized what I had asked of this orphaned boy, exiled from his country, lamed by a wild animal, without an obol to his name. He smiled bitterly.

"Theo, go back to your duties. I'll let you know if I see her."

I trotted back to Xenophon's camp to find him saddling up his own horse in irritation. He threw me a tight-lipped glance and I could tell by his expression that he was aware of my loss—but he methodically continued his cinching and preparations, and when finished, climbed up on his mount and trotted off wordlessly to confer again with Chirisophus. His silence to me spoke volumes. I knew he had been voted general by popular acclaim, rather than appointed. He was utterly trusted by the men; he could speak to them and carry a sword like them. I also knew that he bore the burden of his duty to them like a permanent weight, like a battle scar or a trophy shield which to him represented a sense of honor more precious than life or love or his very happiness. An inviolable confidence would be shattered if he were to ever betray the men by breaking one of the rules he himself had laid down, or if he willingly allowed another to do so. I was his friend, his lifelong servant, his brother; my entire life I had forsaken my personal desires in order to serve and follow him, and he knew this, and I believe was grateful for it—but he would not, could not, make an exception for me. His duty was clear, and I would have rather driven my own sword into my belly than ask him to violate it. Yet even that might have been preferable to his silence.

The army passed through the inspection that Chirisophus and Xenophon had set up at the road narrows, and hundreds of pounds of surplus supplies, lame livestock, unneeded wagons and heavy baggage, and dozens more camp followers, slaves and captives were caught attempting to be smuggled past and were left behind, forbidden on pain of death from following the army. Soldiers involved in the smuggling were flogged, and the troops passing by averted their eyes from the scene, either in shame at their comrades' disobedience of orders, or so as not to attract attention to their own violations, large and small. The occasional good-looking boy or woman might get through, I was sure, in exchange for favors, and all I could do was pray that Asteria, in her cleverness, would herself find a way to do so unscathed and to somehow remain with the army; but I had no such hope.

The entire day and half the night we marched, twenty-five miles, as the enemy continued to slow our progress, skirmishing with us, rolling logs and boulders into our path to obstruct the wagons, throwing rocks from the steep cliffs overhead, pelting us with stones and arrows from behind trees. The men collapsed in exhaustion when Xenophon finally called a halt, most without even bothering to start fires or cook supper. The emotional pain of the morning, and the physical exhaustion of the day's events had done us in. He had still not said a word to me, but watched me carefully from under his brows. I, in turn, could not find it in my heart to say anything to him, in his unrelenting movement and action and confounded busyness. There was neither the time nor the occasion for any words that might lift the weight pressing on my soul.

The next day dawned stormy, with heavy winds and sleet; the men were exhausted, yet we could not remain where we were, without the shelter of a village and with no provisions at hand, so the officers made the decision to press on, hoping to find respite within a day's march. Chirisophus, as usual, led the van, with Xenophon guarding the rear, and enemy skirmishers attacked vigorously and from close range, not only with their usual slings, stones and rolled boulders, but with bows the likes of which we had never seen before, which threw even the Spartan men-at-arms into consternation. Composite bows they were, with the main shaft made of fine, stiff ash, while on the "belly" of the bow, by which I mean the inner surface facing the archer as he shoots, a thin layer of horn had been glued for further stiffening and resistance. More important, however, was the thick layer of sinew taken from the neck tendon of an ox or stag, which was glued to the outside of the bow, and which, when stretched as the bow was drawn, provided for considerably greater springiness and a much more powerful snap as the sinew returned to its original shape, than did a bow made of wood only.

The bows were not only powerful, but enormous: as tall as a man, and when fired, they required that the bowman brace his foot against the lower end while drawing the string almost the length of his arm stretched out behind him. The arrows were as long as the peltasts' javelins, and in fact the Cretans, who were the finest javelin men in the Hellenic army, made a point of saving every such arrow they found and using them for just that purpose, after adding a small finger loop to each one for better throwing. We lost two very good men before we even realized the power of these formidable weapons: Leonymus, a Spartan, was shot by such an arrow, which penetrated right through his solid oak and bronze shield, his corselet and his ribs; and the Arcadian Basias, who to the amazement and dismay of all was shot square through the skull, the arrow emerging to half its length on the other side of his head, despite the fact that he was wearing a heavy bronze war helmet.

At one point, when the rear was being particularly heavily besieged, Xenophon sent word up to Chirisophus at the front to call a halt and send back reinforcements. The army's vanguard was several miles ahead along the road, and it took some time for messages to flow back and forth; yet when the runner returned he reported that not only had Chirisophus refused to send reinforcements, he had picked up his pace, spurring his peltasts and Spartan rangers on to a trot.

Xenophon was furious, though I tried to point out to him that Chirisophus was an experienced officer, and most likely had good reason to have advanced so rapidly. That afternoon, when we finally caught up with the vanguard below a summit where they had halted, he galloped straight up to Chirisophus, his face black with anger.

"Why the hell didn't you halt?" Xenophon spat. I rarely heard him speak coarsely, though it was a technique at which he was gaining more skill over time, as Chirisophus seemed to understand no other language. "My men-at-arms were getting torn to shreds back there by the Kurds' longbows and we had no shelter—we had to march and fight at the same time! By the twelve gods, Chirisophus, are we two armies or one? I lost two good men, one of them a Spartan, and we couldn't even make the fucking Kurds hold fire long enough for us to collect the bodies—they used them for target practice and laughed at us from the distance!"

Leaving the body of a fallen comrade on the field of battle is a grievous sin. Chirisophus, who was in as vile a mood as Xenophon and prepared to give as much he had taken, suddenly became very sober. "Look at the mountains there, General," he said to Xenophon with a sweep of his hand, only a slight note of sarcasm tingeing his voice. "They're impassable. The Kurds have blocked up the routes tighter than a Scythian's asshole. There's only one way up, the steep trail you see ahead of you, and I was trying to occupy the pass before that mob up there seized it. The guides I've captured say there's no other way through."

Xenophon gazed thoughtfully up the mountain where several hundred Kurds were visible, busily rolling boulders and logs to the edge of the path, preparing to defend the route. They were undisciplined, lacking in order and coordination, and even their hastily arranged boulder defenses were scattered and slipshod. Still—there were so many, and their position was very strong. There was no doubt that we could take them and force our way through the pass—but at what cost, and to what end? How many more identical passes with identical defenses would we have to force our way through? Every man lost here would make it that much more difficult to break through the next roadblock, and the next, until the Kurds finally wore us out or starved us by sheer, mule-headed persistence.

The troops were becoming impatient, to either halt for the day or resume the march to a safer location. A blackness almost of night had descended, though it was only mid-afternoon, and the freezing rain had begun to fall in torrents, churning the road into a slurry of mud, chilling us to the bone. Xenophon turned to me.

"Theo, bring up the two prisoners we captured today and tie them to stakes for interrogation."

I did not like the expression in his eye or the tone in his voice, and I balked at fulfilling his request.

"Xenophon, this isn't necessary. Chirisophus' guides have already give us the information you need . . ."

He cut me off. "I believe I gave you an order," he said, his voice low and menacing, his eyes glaring at me, bloodshot from lack of sleep.

I stared at him in surprise, then hastened to comply and bound the prisoners securely to two adjacent stakes. The first of the men, a small, wiry, wizened fellow with a hard look about his eyes, confirmed the earlier account, swearing that there was no route other than the one before us. His half smile showed that he relished our army's making the attempt to assault the pass, and this infuriated Xenophon.

Infuriated—perhaps this is not the best choice of words. The effect on him was more of a transformation, even an aging, as a hard look came into his eyes which I had never before seen on him, a look that bespoke his father, perhaps, or one of the Spartan infantrymen surrounding him, but not Xenophon. Xenophon, taught by Socrates to revere the sanctity of human life, and who, unlike the Spartans, loved war for its intellectual challenge, for its pitting of opposing minds, for the development of strategy; Xenophon, who though never shirking his duty, though unexcelled in wielding a spear and a shield, would never willingly seek out bloodshed for the pleasure of it—this Xenophon was changing before my eyes, becoming someone I had not known before, yet whom I always had. Of course he was changing—the transformation had occurred long before now, the night of his dream, the night he was acclaimed general. Qualities that had lain dormant in him, inherited qualities of leadership and command, coursing quietly through his blood, had risen to the surface that night, qualities of which I had always seen glimmers, tiny, latent specks of genius glowing like flakes of gold in a pan among the mud and gravel. I watched in wonder as they emerged and developed, creating a purposeful man, one who was hard and even godlike, from a man-boy who until now had been wandering vaguely through life.

But such qualities had a darker, more sinister side of which I was not aware, a ruthless side, a desperation that caught me off guard. I had seen it rise to the surface with increasing frequency—in his reaction to my questioning glance after losing Asteria the day before, in the fury on his face when he confronted Chirisophus about not halting to assist the rearguard. Now I saw his rage explode into a physical brutality that astounded me and left me more doubtful of his sanity, and of the fate of the army, than I had ever been before.

He inquired of the prisoner again where there might be alternate roads that could take us around or behind the pass, and this time the prisoner merely jeered at him, jabbering rapid-fire words in his barbarian tongue and broken Persian, which our interpreter refused to even render into Greek for fear of offending Xenophon further.

Trembling with rage, Xenophon placed his face directly into that of the prisoner, screaming at him to tell us the route, losing control of his emotions and his body. The troops nearby fell silent, embarrassed at their commander's loss of discretion, pretending to look the other way. The prisoner smiled coolly and tossed off a wisecrack to his compatriot tied to the stake nearby. Xenophon was rabid. Reaching out and seizing a shield from the nearest soldier, he brutally slammed the rolled bronze edge of the disk hard into the side of the man's face, knocking his head back into the post behind him. The man's smirk was instantly replaced by a mass of blood, his nose flattened against one cheek, and he howled in rage and pain, spitting bits of tongue flesh and shattered teeth out of his mouth until he could scarcely breathe, while Xenophon stepped back a pace and coolly watched the gore sheeting the man's face and dripping into a pool of black mud on the ground. Chirisophus stood nearby, gazing impassively and expressionless as the prisoner vented his rage.

After a moment, Xenophon shoved the interpreter away and then thrust his face back into the prisoner's, wordlessly, simply staring at him. I realized then that the man had become stone quiet, staring straight back into Xenophon's eyes, this time with all trace of contempt erased from his expression, his gaze filled only with malice and fear. The rain poured down on us, on those who were bloodied and those who were sound, making no distinction as to whom it might wash clean and whom it might bespatter with filth, and as I looked down Xenophon's cloak, I saw that he had drawn his short xiphos sword, and that the tip was resting lightly against the man's belly just below his naval. I tried to call out but I was frozen, unable to move, the words sticking immutably to my tongue like a wad of flax to pine-pitch. I felt a thundering in my ears, the deafening chorus of Syracusan chanting I had so often dreaded, drowning out even the roaring of the torrential rain, and the outside world seemed to become silent and to move unutterably slowly.

Xenophon—you asked the prisoner your question one more time, slowly and deliberately, so quietly that only he could hear your words, though your language was unknown to him. To me all was silence, overpowered by the hellish roaring in my ears. I saw the man stare at you in complete understanding, despite the interpreter's absence, for this struggle of wills was no longer slave to the use of mere speech as a medium but had reverted to something much more primitive, more reptilian in nature, something more base and primeval than I had ever thought you capable of. The medium of communication between you and the man was fear and pain and hate, and in that language you understood each other perfectly. For after considering his options and the fate awaiting him, the man gave you another half smile, as best as he could through his split and bleeding lips, and then closing his eyes he slowly, barely perceptibly, shook his head no, and your fiendish knife did the work for which it had been created, for which it had been manufactured years before by the hairy, burn-scarred hands of a helot blacksmith in a sweltering Spartan foundry. The man's face wrenched in pain and he writhed like a live fish on a skewer, and as I watched, his eyes clouded over and he slumped against his ropes, his vacant orbs still staring at your feet.

Did you have any thoughts for Athens when you murdered a helpless, fettered man, Xenophon? Did you give any consideration to all you had been taught, to the ideals you had learned at the knees of Socrates, to the benevolence of the gods upon whose belief you sacrifice daily? Perhaps not, and in hindsight it was for the best, since your actions, both then and in the days to follow, successfully brought the army closer to its final destination. Men are needed in this world who are able to block out the fear and consequences of their immediate actions, to look beyond the sordidness of day-to-day suffering, warfare and squalor, to commit base deeds for a greater good. Men are needed like Gryllus and Clearchus, for it is by such men that civilization is advanced and the inferior is eliminated, or made beholden to the superior. Such brutal, unthinking men are needed; our most sublime institutions could never have been created without them, at least in some misty past that may be best left forgotten. This is one of the world's darkest, most unspoken secrets, for such is the evil—such the beauty—of war. The Spartans are trained their entire lives to close their eyes and their minds to physical fear and suffering and to seek victory at all costs for the common good. But they are Spartan, and you Athenian, or at least you had been until now; and I suddenly remembered the fervent wish I had expressed to the gods the night after Clearchus' head had been thrown into our camp, and I realized that it had been fulfilled in you.

IV

XENOPHON DREW A DEEP BREATH, holding the air in his chest for a moment with his eyes half shut, and summoned every depleted reserve of self-control to regain his rigor as an Athenian noble and an officer. He then turned his attention slowly and deliberately to the second prisoner, who had watched the entire proceeding with eyes wide in terror. He was shivering violently, his teeth chattering and his knees barely able to support him, both from having stood cloakless for hours under the freezing rain, and from fear; and Xenophon had barely approached him before he began singing like a bird. The man said he would guide the army to an alternate road along which even the animals could travel, which would lead us behind the heavily guarded pass. A separate detachment must precede the main force, however, because the new route also passed under a height that must be occupied first, or nothing else could get by. He also confessed that the first prisoner had denied knowledge of that other route because his daughter lived there with her husband and family.

Xenophon turned away in exhaustion and nodded to Chirisophus, who called over the senior captains of both the heavy and light infantry to determine whether any of them would volunteer their units to follow the guide and seize the heights. Two Arcadian officers stepped forward to volunteer their two thousand heavy and light troops, and since by now it was late afternoon, they wolfed an early supper and slipped away into the blinding torrents of rain before darkness overwhelmed them completely. The surviving prisoner was bound and gagged and sent with them, while Xenophon and Chirisophus led the heavy infantry of the rear guard forward to the guarded pass we were facing, to draw the enemy's attention away from the Arcadians slipping behind and above them.

The Kurds had placed huge boulders in our path, and whenever a knot of our men gathered to try to lever the stones out of the way, they became targets for missiles and more boulders, some as large as wagons, hurled down on them from above. Xenophon finally ordered us to pitch camp when it became too dark to shoot our arrows, and he forbade all fires, for that would give the enemy too easy a target for their missiles. We spent a miserable night huddled in the cold, pouring rain with the warm campfires of the enemy clearly visible on the heights above us. All night the Kurds rolled their infernal boulders down among us, adding to the hellish atmosphere.

Meanwhile, the detachment with the prisoner tramped through the rain and dark and caught the enemy outposts unawares, destroying them utterly and seizing their camp. In the morning, the Arcadians blew a trumpet as a signal that they had taken the hill, and Chirisophus then charged straight up the main road with the bulk of the army, his scouts climbing the cliffs to attack the enemy defenders above, hoisting each other up the sides of boulders with their spears, to unite with the Arcadians on the heights.

Xenophon and his rearguard backtracked to join the baggage train laboring up the path the Arcadians had supposedly secured the night before. Alarmingly, however, every hill we climbed was occupied anew with enraged Kurds, and we would no sooner chase them off one than more would appear on the next, or on the one we had just left, flowing like water over and around the boulders and rocks, giving us no respite. On our own we could have easily climbed off the path and run the Kurds off the ridges above; but the path was the only means by which we could force the terrified pack animals and baggage through, and so we had a long and bitter struggle that day before the three dispersed units of the Hellenic army were finally united.

Though this battle was like so many others we fought on the march, I risk the reader's impatience by recounting it, because of a singular event that befell me. Xenophon was leading a charge up a rocky incline while I carried his shield. I tripped over a root, however, and rolled down a steep ravine, twisting my ankle and hitting my head so hard against a rock it cracked my helmet and knocked me momentarily senseless. Xenophon had been looking the other way and had not seen me fall, and when he turned and saw I was not there he became furious, thinking I had deserted him in fear of the rocks rolling down on us from the barbarians above. In part he was right, for I was terrified, as was every man among us that day having to fight boulders rather than flesh and blood warriors we could defeat. But as for deserting him—I was infuriated by his accusation, for in all the battles we had fought together, never once had I left his side, never had I failed to shelter him faithfully behind the shadow of my shield, even at the risk of exposing myself to the enemy. Another hoplite, Eurylochus, saw him standing in the field alone, and bravely ran up to cover him with his own shield.

When Xenophon later saw my swollen ankle and bloody head as I limped into camp, he understood and promptly apologized; I am not sure that I, however, have ever forgiven him his unfounded suspicion, which drove another thorn into my heart, contributing to the widening gulf being created between us.

BOOK NINE

THE RHODIAN SCOUT

Listen closely to me. Heed what I say.
Of all the creatures that move and breathe in this world,
Mother Earth breeds nothing more feeble than man.
As long as he prospers, has strength in his knees,
He believes no thing can harm him, nor evil befall him.
But when the same blessed gods bring him sorrow,
Man must endure it, come what may, and harden his very heart.

—HOMER

I

THAT NIGHT I LAY ALONE on a coarse, moss-filled mattress in the stone hut I had commandeered for Xenophon and myself, unable to sleep, my mind troubled. At about midnight he walked quietly into the room, pausing to let his eyes adjust to the lamp's low light and glancing at me to see if I was awake. From the lateness of the hour and the sounds of soldiers carousing in the village, I would have expected him to be smelling of wine and feeling in high spirits. He was completely sober, however, and stood motionless, gazing out the tiny, plaster-edged window punched through the thick stone walls, while the drizzle fell softly outside.

Moisture seemed to hang in the very air, drops accumulating and falling lazily from every surface as if counting the slow passage of time. I thought of the rain falling on the white, sightless eyes of the fallen soldiers we had been forced to leave behind, washing the blood and grime from their faces and hands, like weeping Niobe grieving over the stone-dead bodies of her children. I envisioned her tears gently caressing their lifeless faces, as white and cold as the marble in the Parthenon, as expressive in their final agonies as plaster masks hung in the theater. Though the bodies were abandoned by the living, unable to be prepared for Charon's crossing of the river, no mere army priest, no crone in black bearing myrrh and incense, no trained undertaker could have washed and caressed and blessed the remains of the fallen Greeks more carefully than did Nature herself. Even if a soldier is returned home, his most likely resting place is merely an abandoned cemetery, where after a few years he lies unsung and unhonored by those who have forgotten to cherish their dead. Perhaps in the absence of a mother's tears or a wife's embrace, a sodden field in a hostile land is the most appropriate monument to the fallen, for the rain conveys just as sacred a blessing on the brow of a dead son. Even more so, for the caress of the rain, with its qualities both destructive and life-giving, derives from the very gods themselves, a fact that has both comforted and terrified men since the beginning of time.

Xenophon stared out the window for a long time, knowing I was awake and watching him, yet saying nothing. Nor did I break the silence, for I had no desire or willingness to talk. Finally he turned and faced me, peering at me, though unable to see my face hidden in the shadows. Giving up, after a moment, his attempt to read my eyes, he slumped back against his wall and began to talk, to muse really, in a voice that was barely audible.

"Sometimes, what you most want in the world is within your grasp, there for the taking, like a peach hanging on its twig so ripe it is ready to drop," he said. "You pause a moment to savor not its taste, but rather its *potential* taste, the anticipation of possessing it and making it your own and consuming it, because anticipating a pleasure is the better part of pleasure itself. But then some unforeseen event—a sharp wind, a clever thief, a destructive worm, a more worthy friend—slips in front of your hand and steals away the object of pleasure before you are even able to realize the anticipation. You are left worse off than before, for knowing what might have been."

He stared at me, but I remained silent. After what I had seen today, words, Xenophon's words in particular, had little meaning; his sentiments were shallow. If he were trying to console me with cheap philosophy, I was not about to be bought so easily.

He sighed and paced across the small room several times before finally settling down on his own cot to prepare for sleep. His face had hardened again.

"I almost forgot to tell you. Nicolaus the Rhodian wanted to see you." He stared at me with a strange expression.

Despite my weariness I was relieved at having the opportunity to occupy my mind again with other thoughts and to escape his presence. I buckled my sandals and threw a cloak over my shoulders as he quickly explained the location of the cluster of buildings in which the Rhodian slingers were billeted. Seizing the single oil lamp, I stalked out the door in silence, rudely leaving him in darkness. He didn't say a word.

The muddy streets of the little town were deserted and the soldiers' laughter and merrymaking had by now died down to silence, with only an isolated guffaw floating out of the tiny windows here and there. The steady rain and the sagging, soggy vegetation lent a dismal, funereal aspect to the village, and to nature itself. I limped down the road, my ankle stiff after my hours of inactivity, and the route led me out of the main concentration of buildings to another collection of low-roofed peasant huts hard by the river, two or three hundred yards away. This secondary hamlet consisted of several tiny huts for the farmers or fieldworkers, a half dozen small, beehive-shaped stone shelters for poultry and other animals, most of which had already been slaughtered and eaten by the hungry Rhodian boys, and a large granary, where the bulk of the slingers were lodged. I knocked on the door of the hut that Xenophon had told me housed Nicolaus, and entered.

The single room was smoky and dark, with a small peat fire burning in the corner, billowing acrid smoke into the room with every gust of wind from outside. My eyes required no adjustment, as I had already been walking with only the dim light of my tiny oil lamp to guide me. I immediately picked out Nicolaus from among the half dozen young squad leaders reclining on the floor in front of the fire, chatting quietly over a small scrap of a map they were examining. Nicolaus stood up solemnly, slightly favoring his uninjured foot, the flickering light of the fire on his smooth, olive skin making him seem even more the adolescent boy than he actually was. I wanted nothing more than to be away from their company, and with an irritated grunt I told him that Xenophon had sent me.

Nicolaus glanced warily at my eyes, as if trying to guess my mood before speaking to me. I stared back at him unblinking, giving him no satisfaction on that score, and he slowly squatted back down close to the fire, squinting through the light at his comrades as he hastily finished off the conversation he had been having with them. His words died off, and he tossed the scrap of papyrus onto the coals, where the edges caught fire, turning black and curling, creating a small bluish tongue of flame that grew and intensified the flickering shadows in the room, emphasizing the deep silence that had enveloped the boys. Nicolaus again thoughtfully stared at me.

"Come," he said, nodding in my direction and slipping out the low door, which caused even him to stoop as he passed into the freezing rain. I seethed at this unforeseen delay, for I had not anticipated that Nicolaus' message would require me to wait for him, or to perform a task before I would be able to depart. He led me around the large granary, from which I could hear muffled snores and low voices, to the small collection of coops and outbuildings. Taking me to the smallest and farthest one, apparently a chicken coop for its tiny entrance that stood no higher than the middle of my thighs, he pointed to the door and said simply, "In there."

I stared at him uncomprehendingly as his gaze flitted back and forth between the entrance and my face; then he gave me a wry smile, turned and splashed through the mud back to his hut.

I had no idea what I was supposed to do. Was this some kind of a prank? I smoldered at Nicolaus' growing impertinence and lack of respect, and at my own foolish indiscretion in having confided my fears to him the other day. I was no doubt the butt of every joke among the Rhodian camp. Finally, however, my curiosity got the better of me, and dropping to my hands and knees in the mud and pushing my lamp along the ground ahead of me, I crawled carefully through the hole in the tiny stone structure. The Fates, in their exaggerated zeal to bring me to this spot, roughly shouldered past me, becoming over-cooperative emissaries and leaving me completely unprepared for what I was to find inside.

Because of its domed shape, there was room to stand in the tiny structure, though scarcely sufficient horizontal space to lie down, and the room was completely empty save for a narrow stone shelf built into the far wall about two feet off the packed earth floor. It was dry inside, though the cobwebs brushing my skin from every side at first gave the sensation of mist or tiny streams of water trickling down on me from the porous stone above. I stood up before even taking the time to look around, and after carefully clearing away the cobwebs from the ceiling in the middle of the room, the only spot high enough for me to stand erect, I extended my arm with the dim light, to shine it on the dark shadows occupying the low stone shelf.

In a flash of understanding I realized why Nicolaus had brought me here, for it was as if the gods themselves had descended in all their radiance and glory and possessed this crumbling, miserable hut. My knees buckled and I knelt down, the lamp dropping from my hand into the dirt, extinguishing itself and leaving the small, close room in darkness. I stretched my hands out in front of me, hardly daring to credit my own senses, and clutched Asteria's yielding body tight against my chest.

"How . . . ?" I blurted, trying to speak, but she stifled my words, pressing my face tightly to her warm breasts, cloaked in the rough fabric she was wearing. Her grimy Rhodian tunic enhanced the pleasure of the anticipation, like Xenophon's peach, and it was only after many moments that I was finally able to lessen my grip. I nuzzled her smooth throat as she clasped her hands behind my neck, murmuring wordlessly, and the rain outside continued to fall silently on the rough stones as the feathery cobwebs lazily brushed our skin.

II

AFTERWARDS, AS THERE WAS no room to lie down on the stone bench, I remained simply as I was, leaning back against the rough masonry as she straddled my thighs, gathering my cloak around us both, to keep out the night chill. Aphrodite and Hephaestus, Hephaestus and Aphrodite. There is no more doomed and mismatched a pair of lovers in history, the exquisite goddess of beauty and the irascible god of fire. My indulgent reader must forgive the heavy-handed reference to the old myths. The allusion is excusable, however, for who could overlook the true divinity of Asteria's body beneath her coarse tunic? Or the fact that I myself was as filthy and smoke-begrimed as the blacksmith, not to mention lamed like him by my earlier fall? Every chorus in Athens would lift its song to Aphrodite were that goddess half as beautiful as Asteria, and that is as it should be, though the jealous deity suffers rivals impatiently. Even mere mortals, however, must occasionally glimpse heaven's threshold, and in this stone hut I drew near it, for though unfortunate Hephaestus lost his beloved to War, I would not so lose my Asteria.

Complete darkness enveloped us like a shroud, the only sound being the soft trickle of water from a tiny rivulet flowing from the base of the far wall and meandering lazily out the low door. Asteria's breathing was slow and even against my neck. At length she spoke.

"He saved me because you told him to. He knew that was what you wanted."

For a moment I didn't speak as I digested her words. She sat motionless on my legs, even her fingers now having stopped their caresses as she waited for my reaction before she continued. I remained frozen, collecting my racing thoughts.

"I told him to?" I asked cautiously, keeping my voice even. "Who was it that saved you?" I thanked the gods for the all-enveloping darkness that hid my face from her view.

Asteria stiffened for an instant and then slowly straightened her back, and despite the darkness I could feel her peering at me, trying to discern my expression, the reasoning behind what I now realized was to her an astonishing question.

"You don't know?" she exclaimed. "By the gods, he didn't tell you? Where did you think I'd been these past days?" She burst into tears, clutching me tightly as my hands rested stiffly on her back. I remained frozen, my thoughts churning as I struggled to imagine who it was that had been keeping her for three days, at my alleged orders. I strained to remain still, to keep from standing and dropping her to the ground, torn between comforting her and storming out with my dignity intact. I am ashamed now, truly ashamed to say that the one thing that kept me from leaving forever—and this thought I remember as clearly as if it had happened yesterday—was the recollection that the door to the coop was scarcely higher than my knees and that finding my way through it in the pitch dark and mud while maintaining any level of decorum would not be an easy thing to accomplish.

I waited for what I am sure were many fewer minutes than it actually seemed, until she was able to regain her breath and resume talking. I didn't utter a sound. All I could think was that it seemed as though over the past few days I had been waiting interminably for other people to say the right words, and they never came. Finally she spoke.

"Nicolaus came to me three days ago," she said in her softly accented Greek, "the day Xenophon gave the order to leave the camp followers. One of his scouts saw me climbing into the hills, looking for a hiding place where I could survive without the army. I had never spoken to Nicolaus in my life, I swear, except when changing the dressings on his foot. He came running on my trail—I hadn't gone very far, and he dragged me back down, making me walk casually as we entered the camp. I was terrified—I had no idea what this boy would do to me."

I remained still. Nicolaus. My mind was already preparing for vengeance.

"He told me you couldn't bear the thought of my falling into the barbarians' hands, and had ordered him to smuggle me. He said it was my decision, to be smuggled, or to risk my fate with the Kurds, but that if I went with him, I would have to keep silent. He said he owed everything to you and Xenophon, and that if anyone found out about me, it would be death for us both and a terrible disgrace to you.

"Nicolaus didn't even let me tell my friends, or return to gather my things. He said it was too dangerous, that it had to look as if I had simply disappeared, like so many other camp followers. He found a Rhodian slinger's tunic and cape for me to wear. I was skeptical at first, but I looked around and saw that everyone in his company were only thin boys, hardly bigger than me. I could easily look like one of them if I bound myself properly and carried myself right. I laughed when I saw my reflection in the shield they held up for me, but not when I saw what was behind me—Nicolaus was standing there with his blade, preparing to cut my hair! Of course I knew my hair had to go, all the Rhodians have cropped hair, but still I wept—my hair had never been cut."

At this I was astonished, for in the darkness I had not even noticed that the thing that had most attracted me to her at first, the beautiful hair that fell to her nates and which she kept lovingly combed and dressed, had been cut as short as a galley slave's. I lightly brushed my hand over her stubbly head, and could feel her involuntarily shudder.

"Since then I've traveled with the Rhodians, in scouting parties along the army's flanks so that no one would look at me closely. My feet and legs are in agony, Theo, and the sandals they gave me don't fit. I keep my face grimy, which isn't hard, and I'm not permitted to talk. Once Nicolaus caught me humming and he slapped me hard in the face. He's terrified as much for himself as for me if I were to be caught. I still have the black eye—it's the make-up that best goes with the costume, is it not?" She gave a short, bitter laugh.

We talked more that night, much more. Asteria said that the Rhodian boys treated her like one of them, though they managed to make special efforts for her personal needs and privacy. She trusted them implicitly, as a sister her brothers, and what choice did she have? Or did I have, for that matter, for she was now completely beyond my assistance and protection, and at the mercy of these rough country boys, and whatever extra prayers I might be able to offer on their behalf for their troubles.

Dawn with her pink-tipped fingers might have shone all too early that morning had the gods not thought, in their benevolence, to slow the passing night, reining in Blaze and Aurora, the frisking colts that usher in the morning. Finally, however, the doorway began to grow visible as the darkness gave way to a gray mist. Tiny chinks in the stonework above us let shine narrow beams of light, which pierced and illuminated the feathery cobwebs, still waving vaguely in the invisible breezes caused by our rustling or our breath, or perhaps by even smaller movements, the blinking of eyelashes, the parting of lips. I stood to go, reluctant though at the same time eager to depart before Nicolaus and his comrades emerged from their huts and shot me their sly, questioning glances as I crawled awkwardly from the coop. There was much to be done, and Xenophon would be waiting.

III

RIVERS.

Never in my life had I seen so many rivers.

Greece is a parched and rocky land, with sufficient water, to be sure, to irrigate the crops and raise the livestock we require, but our water of life usually flows in the form of seasonal rivulets, small streams or wells. Large, wide-flowing, navigable rivers are a rarity.

When we crossed the Syrian desert, what seemed like a lifetime ago, even we river-starved Greeks were struck by the paucity of water, the fact that one could travel days or even weeks without catching so much as a glint of dew in the sun, the only water being that which had lain lukewarm and festering in the goatskin bags we carried in full sun on the backs of mules, water that made one gag with its slimy texture and long for the cool, clear, mountain-fed creeks of our native land.

But unlike Socrates, the gods know nothing of moderation, nor seek it in anything; in fact they spurn it as unworthy of themselves, and search always for the extreme, as being more godlike in essence and glorifying to them, irrespective of its positive or negative quality. Crossing through the country of the Kurds we could measure our days by the number of rivers we crossed—not the passive and refreshing little streams of Greece, along which nymphs and naiads are said to frolic, but rather large, deadly, rushing waters, devoid of plant life along their rocky, gravelly banks, crashing thunderously through steep-walled canyons, defying mortals to peer into the brownish, slit-laden waters originating from the mountains of some distant and barbaric fastness, challenging us at every step to find a route to circumvent their rushing, death-dealing flows. Fords we would sometimes find after exploring for miles in either direction. At other times we would be reduced to improvising rafts or even floats from inflated goatskins. Occasionally—only very occasionally—we would be fortunate enough to find an intact log or stone bridge that the hostile inhabitants had not destroyed ahead of us to hinder our passage.

Always we found a way, always we crossed to the other side, though this was not without hardship. On every occasion a wagon would be lost, or one or two of our precious horses would trip and become lame or worse, or a man would lose his footing on the slippery river bed and sink beneath the torrent, dragged by armor or injury, and would not rise again. Were this to happen once or twice the harm would be regrettable, though not serious, and the army would shrug its collective shoulders and move on as it was trained to do. But the rivers were many, unending in number, and the accumulating impact of all these small losses was taking a toll on our provisions, our manpower, and our morale. What is more, the season was advancing, and as we moved higher into the mountains the water became colder, sometimes mixed with ice or snow. It was becoming increasingly difficult to wade into the freezing current for the second or the eighth time in a single day, and harder to dry out our tattered clothing and hides at night before undertaking the next day's trudge. And what had we to look forward to, upon successfully completing the crossing of the day's last river? What had we to anticipate when trying to determine by calculation or by guess how far we had come, what distance we still had before us? What had we to expect the next day?

Another fucking river.

And so it was this day as well, seven days after recovering Asteria, a hundred miles of marching through hell, fighting the Kurds at every step, seeing them inflict more damage through their daily, deadly raids than Tissaphernes' troops had caused during the entire battle at Cunaxa and their subsequent pursuit.

As Eos dawned cold and gray that morning, we had been cheered by a vision we had not seen in some weeks—a plain, or rather a broad valley, which promised flat walking and unrestricted visibility for as long as we were able follow it. The only feature marring our view was a broad river winding through the middle, which we later learned was the eastern branch of the Tigris, and which at this point was some two hundred feet across. The prisoners had told us that this river marked the boundary between the country of the Kurds and Armenia, and this was further cause for rejoicing, that we would at last be leaving the murderous Kurds behind us. They had been like death to us, death by a thousand small mosquitoes.

As the morning mist lifted, however, and we were able to better view our route for the day, Xenophon's scouts reported to our dismay that horsemen were massing along the far bank, prepared to hinder our crossing into Armenia with arrows and slings, and a large quantity of foot soldiers were marshaling above them, to further assist in preventing our landing. They were mercenaries like ourselves, Armenians and Mardians and Chaldeans in the pay of Orontas—the long arm of Tissaphernes reaching out and tapping our shoulders in lands even as distant as this. The Chaldeans had an evil reputation, and were as feared as the Scythians—for like the Greeks, they were free men, and warlike. They carried body-length wicker shields against which our pikes and swords were useless, becoming hopelessly entangled in the weaving; and their soldiers were large, muscular and well trained. They were prepared to present a vigorous defense to our phalanx, the only technique effective against their light shields—simply running them over, like a runaway horse trapped in a chicken coop.

The army marched quickly to the river, hoping to ford it without delay if it were shallow, and engage the enemy troops on the other side. We found to our dismay, however, upon wading in, that the icy water rose to our necks well before we even reached the halfway point, and the current was swift. We could not wade through it in armor, or the flow would sweep us off our feet and carry us down; nor could we walk across carrying our arms on our heads, for then we would be unprotected, when we clambered up the far side, from the missiles and arrows that would rain down on us from the defenders. The troops gathered at the near bank, milling about aimlessly while the captains discussed the situation. Our prospects worsened when we saw to our dismay that the Kurds now occupied the heights behind us on our side of the river, preventing any possibility of retreat and penning us in between two hostile armies.

We sat there on the broad, frozen gravel bank an entire day and night, with little food and smoldering campfires, for what little driftwood we were able to gather from the river bank was hopelessly sodden. The army was despondent, though Xenophon, putting on a bold front, walking ceaselessly from squad to squad, dispensing cheery advice and lascivious jokes to keep the men's spirits up, despite his own emotional and physical exhaustion. I was not sure how long he would be able to continue pushing himself at this pace, and was relieved when he decided to go to bed shortly after sundown.

Of bones and dreams are men made, say the ancients, and Xenophon more the latter than the former, for lately his dreams had been coming with increasing frequency. Most of the army's seers had been killed or left behind, so he forswore seeking the advice of the remaining one or two except in the event of an emergency. He said they were already busy enough preparing and performing the thrice-daily sacrifice, a task that our army, fragile as it was, could not afford to neglect. Tonight was no different, and his dream was so vivid and intense that he woke with a start, shortly after midnight, and began recounting it to me before he was even fully lucid. Numb with the cold and the damp cloak I had wrapped around myself for a blanket, I welcomed the opportunity to set down the blades and whetstones with which I had been working, and begin kneading some life into my aching limbs as I listened intently to Xenophon's omen.

"Theo, I dreamed I was chained, fettered in thick iron rings and staked to the ground, exposed to the elements, while the gods above laughed at their tricks and ignored my pleas. I was hoping to die, I was so miserable from the vultures pecking at my face and the cold wind scarring my skin. Suddenly, with no warning, the chains dropped off by themselves, and I was free, able to walk, to bring my hands together again! I leaped up and ran, and that's when I awoke."

I drew my wet cloak more tightly over my shoulders and peered at him skeptically in the dim starlight, his hair matted and greasy, his eyes wild, his face hard and gaunt. A man dreams of freedom and a miracle, yet wakes to a stale crust of bread. Still, under such circumstances, even a crust can be a feast, and he was so heartened by his vision that he decided to tell Chirisophus, thinking it might be an omen that would comfort him as well. I accompanied him as he trotted across camp. All around us men slept fitfully in the open, singly or in pairs, huddled against each other, not, as the Persians might have mockingly described, in the habit of Greek soldiers on the march who had for too long been separated from their women, but rather in a desperate effort to keep warm by sharing precious body heat.

The troops were silent and miserable, simply trying to survive another night. It had been weeks since I had been kept awake by the raucous laughter and joking typical of an army of confident warriors on the march, and it was not until now that I realized how much I missed the comforting buzz of an insomniac army.

We passed several hundred yards through the gravel to the far side of the camp, where Chirisophus and his staff had set up their headquarters, and were not at all surprised to see that they were still awake, interrogating prisoners, updating maps, attempting to plot a plan of attack for tomorrow to let us cross the river as safely as possible, even cleaning and burnishing weapons—do Spartans never sleep?

Xenophon's recounting of his dream was cause for cautious optimism, and the two generals and a gathering cluster of squad leaders spent hours in the dark discussing their next steps. At the light of dawn, with all the army's officers present, a special sacrifice was offered, the largest we had dared make in weeks given the force's rapidly dwindling supply of livestock; the omens were favorable on the very first victim. Leaving the sacrifice in high spirits, the officers sent word round to the troops to eat their breakfast and pack.

Xenophon forced down his meager breakfast of curdled goat's milk and was sitting by the comfortless fire, staring moodily into the coals, when two Rhodian slingers from Nicolaus' squadron trotted up out of the frigid mist naked and breathless, as if having just completed their *gymnastica.* All the troops knew that Xenophon permitted anyone to approach him at any time, without protocol, whether at breakfast or supper, or even while he was sleeping, and tell him anything that might be in the army's interest. Still, it was unusual for the shy Rhodian boys to be so bold as to approach him directly. They usually preferred the intermediation of Nicolaus or myself.

"With reverence, my general," the first said, bowing his head in respect.

Xenophon had been absentmindedly rooting under his arm for small life and now he held up his quarry to the light for brief inspection before cracking it between the split, dirty nails of his thumb and forefinger and flicking it into the fire. He glanced down in bemusement at his own filthy and threadbare tunic, and then looked up at the boys with a resigned smile.

"At ease," he said. "By the gods, I'm scarcely older than you, and twice as ugly. No need to stand on ceremony. And put some clothes on yourselves—you make me cold just looking at you. Your skin is blue, and those pigs of yours have shriveled up smaller than a Rhodian's. Oh, pardon me, I see that you are Rhodian . . ."

The boys grinned, and sheepishly threw over their shoulders a couple of tattered blankets I produced for them. Their teeth still chattering from the cold and the excitement of their recent adventure, they narrated in turns what had happened, tripping over their words in their impatience to relate their finding.

"We were collecting firewood for breakfast around the bend of the river, when we saw a family on the opposite bank laying some sacks in a little cave in the rock. We thought it might be wealth being hidden from plundering, so we stayed out of sight until they were gone. Then we stripped and dove into the water with only our knives, to swim over and steal it. We almost broke our necks, though—the water was only knee deep there, so we started wading. We crossed all the way to the other side without even wetting ourselves above the waist! The bags were nothing—just old clothes—but the crossing point is good. There are steep banks and loose sand along both sides, enemy horsemen can't come near it. So we came straight to you, and forgot our clothes . . ."

Xenophon poured a libation at once from the precious store he and Chirisophus kept for the sacrifices, and told the boys to drink up, because they were the gods' fulfillment of his dream. We took the lads to Chirisophus, to whom they related the same story, and with much rejoicing and further libations the decision was quickly made that the Rhodians would lead the army to the crossing point a mile upstream.

The men kept magnificent order, remaining in a single compact unit with the baggage train in the middle of the hollow square. The troops' armor and weapons shone in the weak sun that was just beginning to burn off the mist, through which they emerged, rank by rank, into the view of the Armenians glaring at us in hostile formation on the other side of the river. Chirisophus positioned himself on a small hillock facing the enemy troops on the far bank. Throwing off his scarlet cloak with a broad, dramatic flourish that they could not help but notice, he disdainfully placed a wreath on his head, as if already crowning himself for a great victory. The Spartans around him hooted at Chirisophus' mocking gesture, but as I looked across at the Armenians I saw no reaction among their troops. The fore ranks of their archers and men-at-arms stood motionless, in an attitude more of puzzlement, I thought, than of contempt, while the enormous band of undisciplined, skittish mountain ponies ridden by their cavalry troops stamped impatiently, snorting puffs of vapor into the crisp air as their riders struggled to hold them to alignment.

Xenophon's soothsayer advanced to the water's edge, and the troops on both sides of the river fell silent, anticipating the outcome of the sacrifice. In full view of all three armies he seized the freshly washed and bawling he-goat from the waiting herdboy, and straddling it from behind he paused deliberately, as if to ensure that all eyes were properly trained on the victim. Not a sound could be heard but the dull rushing of the river behind him as he pulled back the flowing sleeve of his knife arm and held the instrument high into the air, allowing the sun's rays to catch and bless the flashing blade, and then slowly lowered it to the quivering creature's throat.

Drawing the blade quickly across the animal's neck, the seer grasped the horns more tightly with his free hand as the beast's head jerked once in shock and pain, and then he let it collapse limply, as the blood spurted and sprayed into the water, spattering the hems of the priest's white vestments a bright crimson. We craned our necks, peering intently at the scene, as the priest straightened up slowly from his bloody task, and with a triumphant shout that carried bell-like across the din of the water, he proclaimed, "Zeus Savior, Lord and Protector: Victory!" We lifted our weapons and shields and erupted in a great cry that resounded between the steep sides of the riverbank. The massed enemy troops on the other side, both cavalry and footmen, stood watching in silence, unmoving and expressionless, their own weapons and armor glinting fiercely in the sun.

Chirisophus gave a shout, and then plunged into the water with his division, half the army, wading in near perfect formation across the deepening river. They were led by Lycius and his ragtag band of cavalry, and as the men marched into the steadily deepening flow they trusted implicitly in the Rhodians' account that the water would not rise above their waists. In reality, the crossing was even easier than expected, for Rhodian boys are short, and the water scarcely rose to the middle of a full-grown man's thighs. The Armenian troops on the far side let loose a barrage of arrow and sling fire, but since they dared not approach closer to the Greeks, most of their missiles fell short, to the chagrin of their officers whom we could see exhorting and even beating their targeteers to advance within shooting range.

Xenophon, meanwhile, had split his half of the army again into two parts, his hoplites remaining at the river bank to guard the provisions and cover Chirisophus' crossing, while the Rhodian slingers and other light troops doubled back downstream toward our previous night's camp. As they progressed in a quick trot, they loudly sounded the horns and reeds, purposely warning the enemy of their march and leading the Armenians to assume that Xenophon wished to cross at a point downstream, thus trapping the enemy in a pincer maneuver between his and Chirisophus' troops. Taking the bait, the overeager Armenian cavalry leaped into action, falling out of their tenuous formation, and galloped madly downstream in a disorganized mob to defend against Xenophon's audacious assault on their flank.

Seeing this, Lycius whipped his horse in the middle of his crossing, and in an inspired display of sheer nerve, raced his band of cavalry straight across at the larger, but unorganized, mass of enemy riders, to the accompanying roar of Chirisophus' marching infantry. The astonished Armenian cavalry skidded to a halt in confusion as to which of the two attacks, Xenophon's or Lycius', most required their attention. They stood dumbly for a moment, their horses milling and rearing in growing alarm at Lycius' fast-approaching and frenetically screaming riders. Suddenly, the Armenian cavalry wheeled as one, like a flock of starlings startled by a loud noise from below, and scattered in panic into the hills, to the deafening shouts of Xenophon's light troops who had been watching the scene unfold from the near side of the river.

Chirisophus, meanwhile, who was steadily completing his own crossing, kept his men in formation and pressed straight toward the wonder-struck Armenian foot soldiers. The Armenians, seeing their cavalry fleeing like rabbits and the strangely armored, hypnotically chanting Greek warriors advancing relentlessly toward them out of the misty depths of the river, themselves panicked and quickly retreated off the high banks.

Chirisophus captured the heights without a struggle and pumped his fist in triumph, and Xenophon, seeing that all had gone well with the initial crossing, now doubled back toward the pack animals and hoplites. By the time he returned with his winded troops, the last of the Hellenic baggage train had crossed and was now safely in Chirisophus' protection. Xenophon then lined up his hoplites with their backs to the river, facing the gathering Kurd forces, and prayed for the strength and time to cover the Rhodians' crossing before the Kurds charged and overwhelmed our now vastly diminished and outnumbered troops. As his men stood nervously in array, facing the approaching Kurdish army, he paced in front of them, his mind racing to improvise a strategy.

"Hold your weapons!" he shouted finally, "until the first Kurdish sling-stone hits a shield. When you hear the rattle of that stone, chant the battle hymn, sound the salpinx and go at the enemy for all you're worth. We have only one chance—terrify them!"

At the first sling-shot from the now-charging Kurds, the men erupted in a massive roar, echoed by the Rhodians picking their way gingerly behind us through the water, and the Hellenic troops eagerly watching the action on the heights above the far bank. The deafening bellow hit the startled Kurds like a blast from an open furnace, and they falteringly careened to a halt and stared. As the Greek salpinx blared, the hoplites sprinted through the gravel straight at the enemy lines in a massed charge worthy of Plataea. The lightly armored Kurds did not wait to test our mettle in hand-to-hand fighting. Spinning in terror, they dropped their weapons where they stood and began clambering hand over hand back up the steep banks which they had just charged down only moments before. As soon as Xenophon saw that the Kurds had turned, he ordered the salpinx to sound a general retreat, and the Greeks, needing no further encouragement, themselves skidded to a halt, and again in a frenzied sprint, went tearing in the opposite direction back toward the river, leaping into the water and wading frantically for the other side.

For a moment Chirisophus' troops on the far heights had an unprecedented view of the two armies, thousands of men, their front lines barely yards apart, both simultaneously fleeing each other in terror, and they roared out their laughter and encouragement to the splashing hoplites. The Kurds finally realized they had been tricked, and it was with no small effort that the Kurdish officers succeeded in reversing their men's course to give chase to the fleeing Greeks.

At this point, however, Chirisophus' peltasts, who had been waiting on the far bank for just such an emergency, themselves charged into the water, javelins at the thong and arrows at the string. They met Xenophon's troops midstream and covered their retreat with a withering fire straight into the faces of the baffled Kurds, who again were forced to halt their charge and retreat in chaos. To cheers from the spectators above, the entire army was able to complete the terrible crossing with scarcely a single casualty, except for a few overeager peltasts who gave chase to the Kurds beyond the midpoint of the river and were cut down upon their arrival at the other side.

For once, the gods had been with us.

BOOK TEN

WINTER

In vain, man's expectations, in vain, his boastful words.
God brings the unthought to be,
As here we see.

—EURIPIDES

THE AGONY OF HATRED, the ecstasy of love. Trite notions, easily separable into their distinct, almost opposite component parts, sung of by poets and wept at by lovers from time immemorial and undoubtedly for a hundred generations to come. The ecstasy of hatred, the agony of love. A no-less-common state of affairs, though comprehended by fewer numbers, perhaps only the Clearchuses among us: the impetus behind the movers of the world, the creators and killers and bestirrers of humanity. Again, they are sentiments easily divided into their identifiable and perfectly contrasting elements, like gold so assayed by fire as to congeal into pure, glistening droplets, distinguishing itself from the surrounding slag.

Pain, denial, triumph, tears, passion, revenge, betrayal, rapture. To which condition do we ascribe these emotions and motivations, to hatred, or to love? The admixture becomes more dense, more difficult to define, and the two seem to meld seamlessly into each other. Although the two perfect, unalloyed extremes may be easily distinguished, and unskilled poets and petty philosophers will make much of their facile ability to do so, the twilight region between the two, that murky area that incorporates irreducible elements of both, or perhaps of a third component newly created by the commingling of the others, is much less easily described. War and hatred are evil, love sublime. And yet: there are good men who could, if they wished, live in peace but who choose instead to fight; who could live a life of ease, but instead enjoy hardship; who could derive joy from lavishing riches on their beloved, but instead spend their wealth on warfare, toiling under the command of Ares rather than of Aphrodite, and even putting the former in the service of the latter.

Such is the complexity of humanity, which at times confounds even the gods, and ultimately prevents them from being mere celestial puppeteers, from representing the earth as a malleable stage set. The world in which men live and act, although not totally inexplicable, is not completely rational either. Reason and folly, the foreseen and the unexpected, madness and calm exist side by side, not only between two individuals but within the same person as well, all to different degrees. The contradictions of life, the simultaneous sorrow and relief at parting, the destruction inherent in creation itself, all these befuddle the mind, as well as illumine it. In my memoir thus far I have written of war and love as two separate entities, unrelated to each other, perhaps even in direct defiance of each other, one the sickness and the other the cure, each pushing and struggling like wrestlers for whom the dusty ring holds room for only one champion. It is time to move beyond such shallow poesy, for this is not life, nor is it my story.

I

THE WINTER, WHICH HAD long been threatening the army with graying skies and freezing temperatures, finally descended in all its fury. Just as a long-awaited battle, when it finally arrives, is more a source of relief than a cause for fear, so too, at least at first, was the vicious cold of the winter we had so long dreaded. When it arrived the army was actually billeted under shelter, in comfortable barracks and huts surrounding the palace of Tiribazus, King Artaxerxes' satrap and governor of southern Armenia, who had grudgingly agreed to a truce provided that we not burn his villages and that we take only the supplies we needed. We had secured food and comfortably settled in for a few days to tend to the sick and injured, which in truth included all of us, and to reorganize our supplies. The first night we were there Zeus dropped two feet of snow on our roofs, and over the next few days several feet more, raising the level of the drifts up to the eaves of our low huts and keeping the men and animals practically immobilized in the cluster of villages into which we had moved. Not a word of complaint was heard, however. In fact, the silent snow muffled all words completely, and as I trudged out on my rounds, bearing messages between Xenophon and the captains and beating a path to the tiny woodshed occupied by Asteria, the only other humans I saw were Chirisophus' and the captains' own couriers, bundled, like me, in skins in a fruitless attempt to ward off the bitter cold. Rumors flew among the men that the army would remain here for the winter, that further travel in the snow beyond this point would be suicidal. Xenophon and Chirisophus, despite their reluctance to delay their stay among the enemy for any longer than necessary, were seriously discussing this option.

Trudging through the snow to Asteria's hut to discuss this news with her, and wondering why she had not sought me out as often lately as before, I was surprised at the number of tracks I found in the snow leading to her entrance. Normally Asteria picked the most secluded shelter possible in which to make her bed, an isolated pigsty or chicken coop known only to me and a few of the Rhodians. This time, however, the path to her coop was as heavily traveled as the road to Delphi. Turning the corner around a rocky outcropping behind which her little stone hut was hidden, I was taken aback to find at least thirty Rhodians milling about outside the shelter in various states of limping dishevelment, attempting to keep warm by standing around several campfires that had been built. Other boys were passing in and out of the hut, lifting the stiff, heavy hide she had hung for a door, which had now frozen to the thickness and consistency of a board.

I stood briefly in the snow, amazed at the sight, a growing anger welling within me, as the Rhodian boys looked up briefly and then returned to their own conversations. Shouldering roughly past those standing closest to the doorway, I bent down to a squat to make my way in, and slammed my head painfully against that of a boy attempting to exit at the same time, sending us both sprawling backwards. Seething, I got up and again duck-walked into the hut, this time with my hands extended in front of me to seize the idiot who had run into me. Before I was able to, however, he slipped past me in the darkness and pushed his way out the low door, and I forgot about him almost immediately as I concentrated on regaining my bearings in the stone structure. Having entered from the snowy glare outside, my eyes took several seconds to adjust to the darkness, and when they did I found Asteria sitting cross-legged in a corner, a Rhodian sprawled on his back in front of her with his foot in her lap, both of them staring at me in surprise.

"In the name of the twelve gods, Asteria," I hissed, unwilling to let my voice resound too loudly. "What are you doing? Do you know how many Rhodians are lined up outside your door?"

Asteria and the boy continued to stare at me in astonishment, and then Asteria, her lips a thin, hard line and her eyes narrowed in anger, bent her head back to the boy's foot in silence, and began applying a salve to the deep, raw grooves where the untanned leather of the sandal thongs had shrunk and cut into the boy's skin. She moved quickly and, I fear, somewhat roughly on account of my having startled her, and the boy winced and grunted several times in pain as she worked her greasy finger deep into the bloody score marks. Finally, she reached behind her and seized a tattered piece of fabric, which I saw with some surprise was the remnant of a gown she had once worn herself in better days and had somehow managed to smuggle this far. She carefully tore a strip along the hem, and wrapped it sparingly around the boy's treated foot in the same pattern as the sandal straps, wasting not an inch of the precious fabric. "Keep your sandal straps over the cloth, not against your skin," she counseled, "and if the cloth slips off or wears through, come to me for more, or use grass or leaves for padding. Whatever you do, don't use untanned hide directly on the skin."

The boy nodded and rose to leave, but as he bent to make his way through the flap, Asteria called him back. "Peleus—ask the next one to wait a moment before coming in." The boy nodded again, silently, and slipped out the door.

As the flap fell back over the entrance and the hut descended again into its semidarkness, Asteria turned on me in a fury.

"By what right do you humiliate me, breaking in on me like this to question what I do?"

"You complain of me?" I said in amazement, no longer even bothering to keep my voice down. "I . . . we have taken great risks to shield your identity. Do you realize the trouble I endure to steal away at night to see you? And then when I arrive I find a small village camped around your hut, like Penelope's hundred and thirty-six suitors. Truly, you are the army's worst-kept secret."

Asteria stared at me, her eyes wide in astonishment, her mouth working soundlessly as she struggled for words. Finally, she found her voice.

"Are you a prince?" she spat, her words stinging. "Did you inherit me from the Persian royal family? By what law, by whose *commandment*, do you possess me?!" Her voice was a barely controlled hiss, and in her tense rage I felt as though I were trapped in the close room with a coiled serpent.

"It was these boys who saved me and continued to protect me—" she continued, trembling in her fury, "and for what? What have you done for them? What gold do you have to give them for me? Perhaps I should pay them with this currency?" and she tore open the front of her tunic, exposing her delicate breasts, her slender chest heaving from the exertion of her pent-up fury, her fragile ribs protruding sharply beneath and emphasizing the flat hollow of her stomach. I stared at her in horror.

"Asteria," I said calmly, reaching my hand out to her as I struggled to regain my composure, "for the love of the gods! It was I who asked them to watch over you. You know my situation—I can't be caring for you every minute of the day as we march . . ."

She shook my hand off her shoulder roughly, glaring like a Fury.

"Did I ever ask you to? Have I ever asked you for a single thing, other than salves and medical supplies? Did you think those were all for me?"

"Asteria, please," I said placatingly, "your tunic. You know what I meant . . ."

"I know precisely what you meant, and I reject it absolutely. I refuse to be a comfort for you by night and a burden to these boys by day. The only thing I have to give them in return for their protection is myself, and I alone will be the judge of how I do that. I have chosen to be their physician. But if I had decided otherwise, you would have no right to complain."

I glared at her as she slowly, deliberately fastened the hook and loop at the neck of her tunic, and threw a tattered blanket over her shoulders for warmth, holding my stare with her own determined gaze. Finally she looked down and sighed loudly in exasperation.

"Perhaps I should have told you earlier that I was treating their ailments. I distrusted your reaction, and now I see, with good reason. When word spread how I had helped Nicolaus, dozens of the other Rhodians came seeking treatment as well. How am I to turn them away?—I am dependent upon them. They are merely boys, though Xenophon has turned them into killers, and they themselves are now dying like men—but they are still only boys."

"They're doing their duty," I said coldly, "as Xenophon has led them to do, no more nor less than the rest of us. The only breach of this pact binding us all to each other is you. This is a dangerous thing we have done. You are being smuggled. And if word of this violation were to become known throughout the army, the whole thread could unravel, and . . ."

She cut me off dismissively, tossing her shorn head in anger as she flopped back down in the corner among her supplies.

"So now my existence has been reduced to someone's breach of duty? I have my own betrayal burdening my soul."

"You bring up your father again, your invisible father? I see no betrayal—he's not here to help you, nor to suffer any disloyalty. Betrayal of a phantom is a phantom betrayal. I am speaking of something real, of my duty and honor to the army . . ."

"Men's honor, *your* precious honor, is the least of my worries. I am more concerned with the Rhodians' infected toes. I trust these boys with my life. There is no love lost between them and the rest of your thugs. The Rhodians have been made to feel like outsiders, like inferiors, for so long that you may rest assured they will not be doing any favors for anyone outside their little group—except perhaps Xenophon, who brought them together. I think they would die for him—or at least smuggle."

I stood fuming silently at this, at a loss for words, while she rearranged her tinctures and ointments in silence, as if she had forgotten I was even there. Finally, she looked up at me, a cold and impatient expression on her face.

"Would you please send in the next boy as you leave?"

The fourth night we spent in our lodgings, three Hellenic scouts who had become separated from the main body of troops after the previous river crossing finally straggled into camp, starving and nearly frozen to death, ill-prepared in their short tunics and oxhide sandals for the bitter conditions they had faced. The army surgeons were forced to remove the men's feet, ears and fingers, which had frozen under the influence of what the locals termed "frostbite." They were showing signs of gangrene, the flesh-rotting disease which, if not immediately cut from the body, would be sure to send its fatal poison throughout the entire organism. Before they died of sheer pain the next day, the hapless soldiers called for Xenophon, who came to their cots immediately, showering them with praise for their valor and promising them ample rewards upon their recovery and return to Greece. This the men shrugged off miserably, knowing perhaps that they were merely empty words of comfort. But the eldest among them, a veteran Cretan named Syphion, gestured to Xenophon to bend closer, to hear his final words.

"The fires, General," he croaked. Xenophon looked at the man, puzzled. "One day out, no more, for a man with healthy legs—thousands of fires in the hills. The Armenians—they're massing."

The other two men nodded in silence, and I shuddered. The wretched creatures had been staggering through the snow lame and frozen for days, surrounded by the sight of thousands of comforting campfires built to warm the asses of the enemy troops forming up in the hills, while unable to build their own tiny flame for fear of giving away their position. Xenophon helped the men drink a cup of wine, to warm their hearts and deaden their pain and fear of death, then wandered away thoughtfully.

"We can't stay here, Theo," he finally said in dismay. "Tiribazus has taken a lesson from Tissaphernes—he's breaking his truce and hoping to kill us in our beds. It's not safe for the army to be dispersed among the villages while the enemy masses on the heights."

I looked at the snow-covered hills, forage for the animals buried under two yards of white stuff, the troops ill-prepared to travel through the bitter cold. "How can you even think of marching the men under these conditions?" I asked. "Can't you see us, days hence? An army of ten thousand, crawling through the snow like poor Syphion, but without a warm village ahead of us at which we could hope to receive shelter."

He refused to meet my gaze. "We are divided among five villages, miles apart. We could never defend ourselves under these conditions. Better a chance of escape into the mountains, than certain death here in our beds."

He ordered the men to pack that very day and the army left the next morning, two hours before dawn, before the Armenians, whose campfires in the hills even our local scouts could now see on their nightly rounds, realized that we were departing. Some of the men, out of sheer malice and disregard for orders, burnt the huts they were leaving behind, and Xenophon ordered the scoundrels to be committed to baggage detail for an entire month as punishment. The skies cleared during the day and the men's hopes rose that the winter cold might lift for a time, and afford us proper traveling weather. This was in vain, however, for during the entire day we were scarcely able to lurch six miles through the deep drifts. That night, as we huddled under our blankets and improvised shelters of branches and wagons, a driving snow fell upon us, a snow that rose to the tops of the cart wheels, dousing our fires, collapsing our tents and covering the weapons and the men lying near them.

In the freezing, blinding storm, I picked my way carefully through the drifts to the Rhodian camp, or what I could find of it. Through a series of grunted questions and answers, I was able to make out Asteria's lodging—a shallow hollow against a large, rotten stump, not apart from the other troops this time, but rather shared with three or four exhausted, shivering boys. I wordlessly squeezed in beside her, surprised to hear no complaint from the Rhodian next to her about my clumsy jostling, until on a sudden impulse I touched his face and found he was dead. Horrified, I dragged the stiffened body a few feet away and lay it for protection in a deep drift. I then returned and mounded a low wall of snow around us all, as a desperate shelter from the roaring wind, checked the faces of the other Rhodians to be sure they were only sleeping and not expired as well, and nestled Asteria's shivering body against mine under the thin blanket. Though she made no effort to assist me, possibly still angry at my harsh words of several days earlier, neither did she protest. I pulled the blanker tighter, and watched the snow fall around and over us, and set myself to survive the endless night.

Even with the dim light of morning, the soldiers were too numb to rouse themselves to remove the snow's weight, having only enough energy left to clear out a pocket of air in front of their faces so as not to suffocate. They became somnolent in their cold cocoons. In their bleary-eyed moments of wakefulness they had no idea how much time had passed since they were last awake—whether an hour, a night or the entire past day. The water in their leather canteens was frozen as solid as their minds, and the silence, both without and within, was at the same time comforting and deadly. We began to think that it had always been winter and that we could feel nothing else, just a vague awareness of the passage of time, like a lost childhood phrase that surfaces occasionally in one's speech, or the indistinct tingling of a limb long removed. The entire universe had collapsed in on itself to this tiny, white, dreary place, asleep, infinitely cold, unspeakably far from home.

Many of the pack animals, weakened already from lack of food and water, simply lay down and died, where they were found later frozen solid as stones, their eyes open and sightless, their hides too hard even to be flayed for the leather. The men found that as long as they remained still beneath their burden of snow and did not try to shake it off, they could retain enough body heat to survive for a time, the entire night if necessary. Xenophon could not give in to this luxury, however, and finally, just after the gray dawn the next morning, he stood up and shook off the snow. I had already crawled out of my own burrow and was waiting for him, shivering in the semi-shelter of the overhanging bows of a large fir tree. As I stepped forward, he greeted me with a grim, silent nod, and then we walked around camp to view the remains of our army.

The sight was eerie, and frightening. "This doesn't even look like the same country we saw last night, Xenophon," I whispered in awe. "Have the gods carried us away?"

He, too, looked about him with eyes wide in amazement, then swallowed and licked his cracked lips. "Don't think such things, Theo," he said. "Or if you do, don't speak them."

The entire landscape had changed under the effect of the snow, which was still falling heavily, obscuring all but the hundred feet or so we could see around us. Not a sign of life was visible; not the slightest curl of smoke from an untended fire, not a single snuffle from a horse, not a whisper from the usually profanely joking and singing soldiers. Just the smooth flatness of the frozen riverbed on which we were camped, with soft mounds of boulders under the snow scattered randomly about the gravel flats. All was utterly silent and still, save for the soft plopping sound made by an occasional handful of snow sliding off the branches above. The thought occurred to me that the army had left in the night, forgetting to wake us, or that the enemy had attacked after all, killing all but us fortunate or wretched few who had lain unawares beneath the silent blanket of snow. My spirit said that this could not possibly be true, but no other explanation for the deathly silence and stillness presented itself.

Xenophon, however, shuddering with cold, used his arms to sweep away a mound of snow from the bed of a cart almost invisible under its deep blanket. Then clambering onto it, he took a deep breath, and to my amazement began bellowing into the frozen air, sending a flock of crows frantically flapping and cackling into the sky from the trees where they had been silently observing us. He shouted curses into the stillness, commanding the forest to awaken, ordering the nymphs and the naiads to dress themselves and split him some firewood, calling, as if he had taken leave of his senses, invoking I know not whom—Pan and the satyrs and the other forest gods perhaps—to stand up and praise their Maker for their continued existence, offering a goat for breakfast to anyone who could find one still living under the snow. I watched in wonder as he declaimed to the stillness, exhorting the rocks and the hills, and then I watched in even greater amazement as the rocks and hills answered him in reply.

The mounds and boulders scattered about the riverbed shivered and quaked, cracks appearing in the layer of snow covering them, and then they slowly rose as if being pushed out of the earth from the depths of hell, emerging unsteadily like enormous mushrooms, the snow sliding off into crumpled mounds on the side. Sharp, piercing eyes appeared from beneath, beastlike men with bushy, unkempt beards stood straight up out of the snow, raising their cloaks over their heads and shoulders and shaking the powder off, stamping their feet to bring feeling back to their frozen members, blowing puffs of vapor on their hands and rubbing their dry, cracked palms together. Xenophon stepped up the pace of his harangue, calling upon the men to seek out their brothers who might be too weak or demoralized to emerge from the snow, pleading with them to build their fires high and warm themselves. He denied the bitter cold and threw off his cloak, stripping himself naked in the biting air as if for his morning exercises, insisting that he felt no discomfort. He seized an axe that had been stuck into a tree for safekeeping and began to noisily hack at a rotten stump, until before my very eyes hundreds, thousands of men and surviving animals emerged from their frozen hell and began reentering the land of the living. Someone took Xenophon's axe from his hands and started to split the wood, someone else kindled a fire, and soon the air was redolent again of the fragrance of smoke and oil and roasted mule, the sounds of men groaning and complaining, belching and bitching and farting and scratching, the sounds of ten thousand men, starving and frozen and aching for women, the sounds of an army that has survived its most difficult battle yet, the sweetest sounds on earth.

Taking a head count, we discovered we had lost dozens of men that night to death and frostbite, and uncounted head of pack animals and other livestock. The short journey into the mountains had been disastrous. Conferring with each other, Xenophon and Chirisophus decided that despite the approach of Tiribazus' hordes at the rear, it would be foolhardy to continue on into the mountains under these conditions. The decision was made to billet again under shelter, in the same villages we had departed, if the enemy had not already taken over the hearths we had vacated. The men cheered when it was announced we would be returning—and in their enthusiasm to be again under a warm roof, they made the return trip in half the time as the outgoing one, sliding down the hills on frozen hides or their own backs, whooping like small boys and ignoring the freezing of their outer extremities, which was taking a terrible toll. We arrived at the villages before the enemy had taken them over, though our vanguard had not a little trouble ousting the enemy scouts who had arrived just a few hours before and were beginning to settle in. Those of the Hellenes who had burnt their quarters upon their departure now had their comeuppance, and were forced to beg or bribe sleeping space from their comrades, or make do in chicken coops and livestock pens. This, of course, was Asteria's lot in any case.

That night, Xenophon sent out a squad of scouts to reconnoiter the enemy's position. After searching all night for the fires we had seen earlier, they returned exhausted and empty-handed except for one surprising bit of plunder they had captured: a Persian light-armored regular, the likes of whom we had not seen since leaving Tissaphernes behind weeks before. This sent the captains into a great deal of consternation at first, wondering whether the wily satrap had somehow outwitted us and marched a course parallel to ours this whole time in an effort to entrap us in the wilderness.

It took us several hours of searching before we were able to find an interpreter, as the few Persian speakers that had previously marched among the Hellenes had been killed or lost in earlier engagements. We finally came across an old man of the village, one who had served in the Persian army decades before in Ionia and spoke broken, rusty versions of the two languages, besides a half dozen others. The old lout was rousted from bed, half drunk or dotty and swearing up such a storm in every language he knew, plus several he was most likely inventing on the spot, as to make our own Spartans blush like virgins. When Chirisophus saw him, he was much put off with the man's spouting and refused to have anything to do with him, accusing him of being mad. Xenophon, however, prevailed on him to use the old fellow, pointing out that there might be some residual wisdom in his madness, and claiming that we are all mad to a greater or lesser extent. Chirisophus stared at him a long time, and then walked away in disgust.

The prisoner was not difficult to interrogate. He was simply told that if he did not cooperate he would be stripped and left to die in the nearest snow drift, and this was enough to make the loose-lipped Persian sing like a nightingale. As it turned out, our fears regarding Tissaphernes were unfounded. Our prisoner was a mercenary working for Tiribazus, and had been foraging for provisions when surprised by our scouts. Tiribazus, apparently, had a large force of mercenaries, Chalybians and Taochians, so large, in fact, that he could prevent our passage without technically breaking his truce—which was that the *Armenian* army would not impede us. The mercenaries, said the prisoner, had skirted our position along the back trails of the mountains, picking up local irregulars along the way, and were planning to fall upon us in ambush in the narrow places and canyons along the route, blocking our retreat and annihilating us in the snow.

Upon hearing this the officers were outraged. "Do we need a fucking lawyer to negotiate a simple truce with these barbarians?" Chirisophus asked in disgust. "Do we need to insert clauses to cover main troops, Chalybian mercenaries, farmers with pitchforks, and housewives throwing dirty dishwater at us?"

Furiously, Xenophon ordered the army into battle formation, amid much protest, but the measure was nevertheless necessary. Sitting there immobile, we would soon exhaust all our provisions, and would be allowing Tiribazus and his mercenaries time to collect additional forces and fortify their positions. The grumbling main body of the army marched at once with the prisoner as guide, leaving guards at the villages under the command of Sophainetos the Stymphalian.

The men, in an evil mood, were ready for murder, if not of the enemy then of Xenophon and Chirisophus, but they soon gained satisfaction. The light-armed troops, including Nicolaus' Rhodians, who were plowing through the snow in the lead, surprised a large body of the enemy in their own camp, with their shields down. The Greeks pelted the mercenaries with a withering fire of arrows and sling-stones without even bothering to wait for the heavy troops to arrive, killing dozens at the first volley, then rushing upon them with shouts and further shooting. Asteria, who did her best to make herself useful by distributing spare bullets and offering water, told me that the whole skirmish was like a dream: The attackers ran and floundered through the deep drifts as if flailing through clouds, while the terrified enemy attempted a retreat equally slowly, falling down in the soft snow, slowly rising and again attempting to run through the waist-deep powder. The scene was unreal and nightmarish, with even the combatants' shouts muffled in the silence of the snowy woods. Life only returned to concrete, material reality when the Hellenic troops physically caught up to those of the mercenaries who dared to stay and defend themselves, and the contact of the ghostlike figures suddenly resulted in screams of agony and the spray of blood and limbs across the fluffy, virginal whiteness.

The enemy fled with many killed, and the Rhodians even captured Tiribazus' tent, filled with slaves and gold and silver utensils, proving that the treacherous satrap was directly involved in the proceeding. To us, however, the gold was worthless. More valuable were the twenty purebred cavalry horses left behind, not sufficient to make up for those lost on our previous foray into the mountains, but welcome nonetheless, for the troops were hungry.

II

THE PRESENCE OF EVIL in the air was like a stench or a cloud, as I slipped over to Asteria's hut the next evening in an attempt to clear the poisoned atmosphere that had intruded between us. It was not like the constant tension of an army in retreat, an army besieged, which is something different, a background irritation like the distant roaring of a river, or the faint smell of a dead animal that one has not been able to find and bury, but to which one eventually becomes accustomed. The feeling that evening was distinct, a sharp wrenching of the gut, a bristling on the back of the neck, the sense that something was terribly wrong or dangerous in the world, the feeling that one is being watched by an evil deity, or worse, that the evil is in oneself.

Approaching the low doorway of the stone beehive structure, I gave my customary whistle to let Asteria know I was there, and was mildly surprised that she did not answer. Still, this was nothing—she might have been sleeping, or away, and so I stooped low at the waist and entered.

The phosphorescent white drifts reflecting through the door illuminated a sight for which I was not prepared, the consummation of the evil portent I had been sensing. Even before my eyes registered the sight, my ears were assaulted by the muffled, heavy breathing, the barely stifled grunts. Asteria was lying flat on her belly in the dirt, her legs spread out straight behind her, while a large, muscular figure kneeled above her buttocks, his knees digging painfully into the backs of her thighs. His left arm was stretched out toward her neck, and in the faint light I could see in that hand the evil gleam of metal, Asteria's own dagger, while his right hand fumbled clumsily at his groin as he worked at untying and loosening the loin straps under his tunic. He was facing away from me and had not even heard me enter for all his caprine snorting, and all I could see was his smoothly arched back and legs, the dolphinlike dorsal ridge of his spine straining at the skin of his back. What transfixed me, however, leaving me momentarily frozen in astonishment, was the sight of the enormous, pink, puckered burn scar on the brute's right shoulder, as cracked and ugly as the last time I had seen it twelve years before. Asteria had craned her head back over her shoulder to peer at me, her eyes pleading with mine in silent desperation.

Fifty years later I can still recall the snapping of my nerves, the feeling that whether he were man or god he had only minutes left to live. Despite his skills at hand-to-hand combat, Antinous did not stand a chance. Having burst into the hut at his most vulnerable moment, I reacted almost instantly, seizing him by the hair with a roar, lifting him bodily into the air and slamming him back against the wall with all my strength, in one motion. I noticed that if anything, he was bigger than I had remembered, but I too had grown, and was now more than a match for his bulk. His face registered a series of emotions: first shock and surprise, followed by pain at being hurled so brutally against the wall, then a glint of recognition and a narrow, evil smile, as he made my face out in the darkness. His loosened clothing had fallen off, exposing his obscene and tumescent nakedness, and in my rage I forced my knee up between his thighs and rammed it three times into his crotch with all my strength. He screamed and rolled his eyes back in his head in pain. When I let go his hair, he collapsed in agony to his knees, then onto his side, gasping for breath, where I left him retching and glaring at me with watery, hate-filled eyes, as he mourned the ten seconds of my rage that had resulted in the permanent loss of his manhood.

I turned back to Asteria without a second glance at Antinous. She had pushed herself up onto her knees and crawled over to the far wall where she now huddled, her arms wrapped around herself, looking at me with eyes as horrified as those of the writhing creature across the floor. As I crouched and reached my hand out to her, she reflexively flinched, as if afraid of me as well, then immediately came to herself, and burying her face in her hands began sobbing frantically.

"He . . . he was waiting for me when I entered the hut . . . caught me by surprise, he said he would kill me if I didn't do it . . ."

I let her sobs run their course for a moment, while the bleeding Antinous rolled and grimaced, all the while staring at us with his face contorted in fury.

Suddenly Asteria's shuddered convulsions stopped, and she was silent for a second, before slowly turning her face to look straight at the man who only moments before had held her life in his hands. She stared silently, as if considering his fate, before whispering to me, in a low, constricted voice, "He will survive."

I must have muttered some comforting platitude to her, about his having learned a hard lesson, but she stopped me with a finger on my lips. I then understood her meaning, and my blood ran cold. Asteria continued to stare at me, and I realized from the silence that Antinous, too, was now lying still, quivering like a freshly caught hare, watching me intently through the penumbra.

My heart sank as I realized what had to be done, and Asteria slowly stood, keeping her eyes fixed on me the whole while as if willing her strength into my backbone. Antinous began muttering at me as I approached him.

"You killed my brother," he grunted, "and now you've destroyed my offspring as well. Have you not taken enough from me?"

I paused for a moment and stared at him, searching his face, but his eyes glared back at me in hate, without a glimmer of remorse. Without further hesitation, I stuffed his filthy loincloth into his mouth and lifted him roughly by the hair. Shoving his dead weight through the low door into the snow outside, I followed immediately behind and then half dragged, half carried him to the dark copse several hundred feet behind the low outbuilding, where I dropped him onto the frozen crust of snow. Antinous lay on his belly, motionless and panting, a dark stain radiating out from his pelvis. As I stepped over his back with one foot to straddle him from behind, my mind flooded with memories, and I wondered that this pathetic creature was the same man who had forced Aedon into such a position years ago in his sadistic training regimen. "You'll live," he had said then, though I would not offer him now this same meager assurance. As I grasped his hair to jerk his head back and expose his pulsing throat, he gave a deep, wrenching shudder. I saw a reflection in his eyes, the disembodied head and shoulders of a man I did not recognize, and I paused for a moment to consider whether this truly was part of the gods' plan.

Antinous held his breath, waiting in agony, as I stared down at him; and then almost against my will, I released my grip on his hair. His head flopped back down onto the crusted snow and I heard him heave a great, convulsive breath. I did not wait to see what he would do next; I felt drained and empty, incapable of even wondering whether he would live or die. I trudged slowly to the hut, without looking back.

The agony of hate, the agony of love. This time there was no separation of the elements.

III

THE TROOPS' MORALE had dropped like a stone. Thus far we had spent over a week in these villages, accomplishing nothing but losing huge numbers of our men and animals to the bitter weather, exhausting our able-bodied troops by relentless forays into the mountains to attack local fighters who seemed to melt into the woods. Xenophon made endless rounds among the huts at night, dispensing what cheer he himself was able to muster, rewarding those who themselves took responsibility for furthering the march, and setting a strenuous example by working harder than the lowest battle squire. The man was exhausted, and I worried constantly for his sanity; yet still he pushed on.

The army finally marched, a forced effort beginning in the predawn darkness, in a final race to prevent the enemy from collecting themselves and occupying the narrows north of us. This time, upon our departure Xenophon looked at me with a more confident, or perhaps resigned, expression.

"You're more at peace with your decision to march this time," I noted. He looked at me curiously.

"I'm always at peace with the orders I give. I don't always know the results, and that's what worries me."

"Last time we were turned back by the snow," I said. "What makes you so confident of the outcome this time?"

I need not have asked, however, for the acrid stench of the black smoke, and the surprised shouts of the men outside our hut gave me all the answer I needed.

"I've ordered the villages torched," he said, "both in retribution for Tiribazus' treachery, and to eliminate any temptation we might have to return once more."

That night we reached the heights from which the barbarians had meant to attack us, and were able to pass through without a struggle. In their ignorance, Tiribazus' troops failed to realize that had they occupied the impregnable position instead of we, it would have meant the destruction of the entire Hellenic army in the frozen snows below.

We continued on, six miserable days to the upper Euphrates, so different from its warm, placid offspring downstream, and then another six over a wretched, windswept plain, across which a north wind whipped mercilessly, blowing directly into our eyes and burning us as if by the rays of the sun, leaving our exposed skin dry, parched, and cracking. Xenophon's face, as well as those of Chirisophus and the others, had become faces I no longer recognized, all of them melding into one, with fierce, staring eyes, sunken cheeks and ragged, infested beards that erased all traces of personal features that had once been the marks of their humanity, blurring their individual identities and reducing them to a mere species. We forgot everything but the need to keep constantly moving, to take one more step forward, and because each day was so like the day before, each gray night so like each drab day, time no longer mattered. We communicated in grunts of gestures. True speech took too much effort.

The snow had no structure, no bottom. Men sank into it to their waists or their chests, causing us to lose countless animals and supplies and dozens of soldiers, many of whom simply vanished from sight forever, falling on their faces and disappearing in their exhaustion, unable to rise again. Even the most able-bodied were faint with hunger and cold, and Xenophon realized that part of the problem stemmed not from frozen feet but from empty stomachs. He personally made the rounds of the army, scavenging stores and supplies and sending the strongest runners back along the trail and out on either side. He sought those who had fallen and given themselves up to die, forcing them to eat a bit, even if of stale bread or raw horseflesh unfit for maggots, and urging them, sometimes at the cost of blows to the face, to rise and stagger on. I saw him pull a tattered Rhodian boy from the snow, slapping his face and shaking him like a rag doll until the youth finally shouted in protest and choked down some cold oats soaked in milk which in better times would have been used as fodder for the asses. Xenophon watched him closely until he saw him begin lurching along toward the rest of the wraithlike troops, and then he moved on to the next dark patch he saw lying forlornly in the snow under a thin cloak, to begin the process over again. I didn't have the heart to tell him that as soon as he was out of sight, the Rhodian boy again lay down in the snow while the troops passed silently by. If a man was going to die in any case, this was the easiest and most painless way. He just lay down and waited, doing nothing, patient as the Fates, until sweet death came in the form of a gentle, frozen sleep, and his heart simply slowed down and stopped. To men bearing excruciating pain, hunger, and exhaustion, the notion of such a respite from suffering, such an easy welcome into the gods' embrace, was a seductive siren song impossible to resist.

Those who did have the will to live, but simply not the strength to keep up, suffered the most. Unable to make it to the night's campsite with the main body of troops, they would spend the night foodless and fireless where darkness finally overtook them. It was rare that any of these men survived until morning. Small parties of the enemy were constantly following like vultures, picking off stragglers and robbing them of their pitiful belongings, carrying off disabled animals that we ourselves were not sufficiently quick to butcher for food, harassing us at every turn.

Men who had the fortitude to walk miles even after losing their toes to frostbite would be stricken down by an unexpected calamity: blindness by snow, which rendered them helpless, even when led by a kindly companion by a leash or belt, because the depth of the snow and roughness of the terrain made walking without vision impossible. Those astute enough to realize the problem improvised eyeshades, or simply marched holding a black object in front of their eyes, but it was too late for others. These men we saw kneeling piteously in the snow as we passed, their eyes swollen shut, fluid streaming from the corners, as they implored their comrades, who themselves could barely stand, to lead or carry them to safety.

Our feet were the worst problem, however. Good leather sandals, with heavy oxhide soles, will serve a man well in battle, even allowing him to tread through fire, but will last only a couple of months under marching conditions, even with nightly repairs, and the troops' footwear had long past outlived its usefulness. The absence of oxen and camp followers to tan the leather and manufacture the footwear meant that the men had to improvise their own, most often with the newly flayed hides of mules that had fallen by the wayside. These the troops would skin even without waiting for the pitiful animal to completely die, to gulp down the meat and blood while still warm, and obtain a precious supply of hide before the enemy or their other colleagues arrived. Unless it froze solid first, a dead mule would be stripped of everything within minutes, leaving the carrion birds nothing to pick at but bloody bones. At the next campsite the men would be seen diligently trading scraps of leather among themselves, improvising needles from bone and thread from sinew, making crude sandals from unscraped hide that had been the cover for living flesh only hours before. It was difficult to tell, looking at the men's feet, whether the blood that stained them red was from their own blisters and missing toes, or from the freshly flayed hides. Anyone who did not take care to make the straps much looser than he otherwise would have soon learned a painful lesson, as the fresh hides shrank at night when they dried, cutting deep into a man's numb flesh, then freezing solid if he stood still for more than a moment or two. More than one able-bodied man lost his life when his mule-hide sandals lamed him and forced him to stay behind, weeping in the snow.

Because of the harshness of the journey, the army was spread out for miles, making communications between the van and the rear guard difficult. One night, after fighting the north wind all day, Xenophon's troops arrived at the camp hours after dark, only to find that the earlier arrivals had gathered every bit of scarce firewood available, and refused to let our frozen soldiers near their fires unless bribed with wheat or any other eatables they might have. When I reported this to Xenophon, his tired face darkened in anger, and he marched furiously over to Chirisophus' fire to confront him.

"Chirisophus!" he sputtered, "My men arrive after yours because they were *assigned* to the rear guard, to cover your ass! Yet when they arrive they find no food or shelter, while your men are comfortable. Are we one army or two?"

Chirisophus looked up calmly from the hunk of dried meat he was gnawing, his irritation at being interrupted readily apparent. He deliberately allowed the smile on his face to fade slowly, and coolly met Xenophon's angry stare.

"My men arrived and scavenged for firewood themselves," he said in measured tones. "They built shelters and *made* themselves comfortable. Yours can do the same. My men will be up and marching before dawn as the vanguard. Why don't you just let your poor tired boys sleep late in the morning, General?"

Xenophon stared at him in astonishment. "We don't have a vanguard and a rear guard," he said after a pause. "We have two separate armies. And since that is the case, I'll take your advice. I'll tell my troops to sleep late, and then join either army they wish, and if they all wish to join yours, I'll march alone." Chirisophus stopped chewing and looked up at Xenophon with frank interest.

"We'll give you a head start in the morning to be out of your way," he continued. "Naturally the Rhodian slingers will stick with me, as will the cavalry. All of Proxenus' old troops will stay as well, I imagine, both Thebans and Spartans. That would be fifteen hundred hoplites and five hundred light infantry. Since I took over Proxenus' command, I'll also keep his remaining supplies. Naturally I'd expect you to be fair and allow any Athenians and other Attics in your brigade to transfer to my army—I'd hate to see my countrymen marching under duress with Spartans."

Chirisophus' face reddened and his eyes bulged in anger. He stood up and faced Xenophon, their chests almost touching, though the leathery old soldier stood half a head shorter than his younger colleague. Xenophon did not flinch, but continued ticking off tasks like a shopping list:

"Perhaps the easiest thing to do would be to simply call a meeting of the joint forces, and allow everyone to walk over to whichever side they wish. I will, however, be happy to leave you with the sledges and wagons, Chirisophus, as well as any remaining camp followers that have sneaked along with the troops, to ensure your comfort . . ."

Chirisophus snorted in disgust and looked away. "By Zeus, General," he said resignedly, "can't you take a joke? I had no idea you were so sensitive about your men sleeping late." He sat down again by the fire and began poking at it sullenly. "Perhaps my men have been a bit too eager about settling in for the night after they arrive. I'll have a talk with them and order them to clear a space for your stragglers from now on. Try not to drag so far behind, though, will you?"

Xenophon assented silently with a nod of his head, and wheeled around to return to his troops. "That old son of a bitch is going to have to be dealt with sooner or later," he muttered, to no one in particular.

The next day, Xenophon saw, would be a test of his settlement with Chirisophus, for the weather and the marching conditions were even worse, if that was possible. We were traveling in a long, straggling line, each man and animal fending for himself. As the provisions were depleted, each empty wagon was abandoned, to conserve our strength. A few of the soldiers who had wandered off the path ran across a black patch in the snow where it seemed to have thawed, and indeed it had, because of a tiny hot spring welling up from the ground beneath. Twenty half-dead soldiers crawled and crowded their way into it, soaking their feet and legs in the steaming soup, neglecting even to scrape away a small side-hole from the main spring where they could mix the near-boiling sulfur water with snow to bring it to the proper temperature. These men, their feet already numb from the freezing temperatures and frostbite, and their skin already loose from gangrene, were horrified to see skin and flesh slough off of their own accord after dipping their limbs in the hot water, defying their frantic attempts to save their feet by tightly binding the loose meat to their bones with rags.

When I told Xenophon what had happened, he waded through the snow to the spring and ordered them, then begged them, to get up and continue walking, imploring them in the name of their mothers and wives to make an effort to move on, threatening them with abandonment at the hands of the enemy. He even resorted to brutality, forcing them up by beatings, but the men simply went limp. "Cut my throat if you wish," one said, "but I will not march." In desperation at the gathering darkness, he determined that the best strategy was to make one supreme effort to frighten away the marauding enemy bowmen who were picking off our stragglers and remaining supplies. Gathering those able-bodied men of his rear guard he could find, he set off through the woods on a noisy, crashing chase, floundering and smashing through the snow, while the disabled soldiers dying at the hot spring did their best to contribute to the ruckus themselves by shouting as loudly as they were able and beating their spears on their shields as they lay prone in the water. The astonished enemy, who for the most part were hotheaded local adolescents and farmers untrained in warfare, were terrified that a pitched battle might be falling upon them, and dove for cover or ran for their lives.

Xenophon spent the entire night tramping up and down the line as I accompanied him, assisting stragglers through the deep snowdrifts, posting guards where he was able, pleading with the strongest of the light troops to search with us, pulling out from the snow those too weak to march, forcing those who still had strength to keep moving so as not to freeze to death, distributing any minuscule rations still available. Chirisophus, meanwhile, who was two or three miles farther on, had encountered a village, a collection of fifty ancient huts scattered about in an irregular circle, with other villages nearby and within sight. As soon as he had secured the area, he sent his own hoplites, as well as men from the villages themselves, to assist us in bringing up the rear guard, assuring Xenophon that space would be saved in the villages, selected by lot, for all those able to survive the remaining miles of the march. Glad we were to see these men, too, for by now a good part of the rear guard had given up hope and had simply lain down to die. It took Chirisophus' tough Spartans most of the day to haul them, dead and alive, walking and staggering, into the miserable collection of little stone structures, which to us looked like heaven itself.

Except for the wisps of smoke curling lazily out the chimneys, the huts were scarcely visible until one was practically on top of them. To retain heat, they had been dug underground, with a low, rounded roof scarcely rising above the surface, and one had to tramp down a wooden ladder inserted through the very chimney, closing one's eyes to the smoke and hopping deftly over the small peat fire, to even enter—there were no front doors. Inside, thank the gods, the structures were warm and cozy, with shelflike bunks along the walls and mats on the floor in front of the hearth, each room capable of sleeping twelve or fifteen soldiers in a pinch. Tunnels and adjoining rooms had been built for the people's livestock, which gained access to the huts through separate entrances dug through the snow and which were fed all winter with forage stored from the harvest. Gutters carved at an incline into the packed earthen floor allowed the animals' urine to be carried away from the immediate living quarters to a crude drain at the far end of the house, but there was little that could be done about the droppings, short of shoveling them daily into a slop basket and climbing the ladder to pitch them out the roof hole. On snowy days, they were simply left to accumulate inside, in a far corner, contributing their essence to the rank atmosphere.

The stench from the smoke, the unwashed people, and the animals mixing freely in the living quarters with humans was almost unbearable, and the first time I entered one of the steaming, reeking shelters I thought I would pass out; but the warmth and comfort, from both the small fireplaces and the surprisingly good-natured Armenians residing there, soon brought me around. I began to actually look forward to descending into the dark, womblike pit in which Xenophon and I were billeted, to rest and gather my strength for the ordeal ahead, and to ponder the nature of the people, and especially the shelter and food they offered, that had saved our lives.

And ponder I did, most often the food, during those long, smoky hours of recovery and healing. The gods know my travels have allowed me to feast on both exquisitely prepared delicacies and the coarsest of military fare. I have found that, depending upon the circumstances, both can deliver ecstasy of almost equal proportion, for there is no food so rancid, no soldier's hardtack so wormy, that I have not marveled that after entering my body it is transmogrified into blood and muscle, ambition and courage. But here in this strange, barbarian village of earth and stone, we were presented with parts of animals that in my former life, even during the worst of Athens' famine, I would not have fed to dogs, cooked in unidentifiable oils or served unspeakably raw—all of which we consumed with the greatest of relish. The chewy sphincter muscle of the sheep, boiled for hours to a rubbery consistency and then marinated in oil for hunters to chew on to assuage their hunger, was a source of great hilarity to the troops. The tribe's special brain sausage, roasted roots and tubers stored in enormous communal cellars, and copious quantities of fermented goat and sheep milk, were greatly comforting.

Eight days we stayed in these villages, eight days for which I was more grateful than any in my life. On the day of our departure, the villagers showed us how to pack our supplies and prepare our animals in the Armenian style, with bags wrapped round the feet of the horses to prevent them from sinking in the snow. They improvised snowshoes and litters for the worst off of our men, of wicker cut from the sides of woven baskets, and showed us how to guard against snow blindness, by peering through flat slats of wood loosely tied together and attached to our faces, with only narrow slits to allow our eyes to see. If ever I had the opportunity, I would return gratefully to that village and kiss the feet of the grandsons of the people who so kindly helped us and fed us as we lay dying in the snow that winter.

IV

FUCKERS NEVER LEARN, do they?" Chirisophus muttered in disgust, chewing on a slice of sphincter and staring up at the surrounding heights. "The troops are starving and this shit-hole has to be taken, but I don't relish the idea of charging women and children."

In the past two weeks of bitter cold we had covered barely ninety miles, harassed by thieving tribesmen the entire way, until after fording a small river we had entered the barren land of the Taochians, a warlike people as hostile as any we had encountered thus far. Provisions had failed us, for the locals had removed or destroyed everything of value in their villages, and we feared we would starve if we did not find suitable supplies soon. Through harsh interrogation of prisoners we had captured along the way, Xenophon had determined the location of the Taothian stronghold, to which all the people of the country had retreated, bringing with them their provisions and livestock.

The place was a mountain fastness, barely habitable except in times of emergency such as these, and it could scarcely be imagined that women and children were holed up on that cruel rock; for a rock it was, a flat, frozen, windswept plateau, surrounded on three sides by a sheer drop of hundreds of feet. The surface was bare of snow, the result of the constantly whining and biting wind, and accessible only by a long, inclined approach consisting of a broad field, unbroken except by several ancient oak trees, and overlooked by a flat-topped ridge on which the defenders had placed a huge arsenal of boulders, logs, and rocks. These they were prepared to roll down on anyone attempting to cross the field to gain access. The stronghold fortifications themselves were of little consequence, nor did they need to be, given the site's natural advantages. The access was protected merely by a low stone wall. Inside the compound, parts of which we could make out from a distance when we stood on an adjacent height, could be seen several thousand people, refugees from the abandoned villages in the region, milling about on the bare rock in apparent randomness. They were sheltered from the wind and inclement weather by only the rudest of stick-and-hide structures.

When we arrived with the rear guard, Chirisophus was already waiting, in some perplexity, and Xenophon looked thoughtfully at the surrounding hills.

"We should have this routine down by now," he said. "Wait till nightfall, then set up a diversionary attack here against the stronghold with the bulk of the army. Send a few squads of infantry and light troops back down the road the way we came, then have them steal up onto the mountain to the enemy's rear. Take them from behind—your Spartans' favorite position, Chirisophus. It couldn't be simpler. The only thing I'm concerned about is when I'm going to get my breakfast."

Chirisophus complimented him sarcastically. "A fine tactic, General—I couldn't have hoped for better from an educated Athenian. Speaking of Athenians: Care for some sphincter?"

Noticing that Xenophon was about to offer an appropriate gesture in response, I quickly interrupted. "So the only question is who gets the honor of stealing up onto the mountain behind them. That could be a bloody affair if the barbarians have finally learned their lesson and posted guards along the back routes."

Xenophon again eyed the barbarians, and decided to take a different approach. "Why not take an interpreter and try to negotiate? Convince them that we're not a conquering army and don't intend to stay."

Chirisophus grunted through his wiry beard. "I already tried to talk to them. There's the entrance, the only one. We shouted that we meant no harm, that we only need supplies and wouldn't kill anyone. But whenever we tried to approach they rolled stones down on us. That's the result." He pointed to a half dozen litters nearby, carrying battered and bleeding men, one with both legs shattered, another with half his rib cage staved in. "They won't even let us collect the injured. They just keep dumping their rubble on us."

Up on the ridge, the Taochians stared down at us in fierce contempt, their levers and boulder carts ready for the Hellenes' next attempt to cross the field. "Let me try something," Xenophon said. "Theo, remember that Pisidian boy, the one we thought was an imbecile? If he only knew how much he taught me."

He called Callimachus, the captain commanding the rear-guard that day, as well as Agasias and Aristonymus and a few other officers, all of whom he knew were deeply competitive, and he walked to the grove of trees at the edge of the field, just out of range of the enemies' stones. There he waited in full view of the Taochian defenders, and shouted at them, to be sure that they had taken good note of him and were ready. Then taking a deep breath, he leaped from the shelter of the trees and raced across the field, zigzagging like a rabbit to prevent the slingers and javelin throwers above him from taking aim, and dove to the ground beneath the first of the massive oak trees. Eight or ten cartloads of heavy stones and boulders slammed into the tree and rushed by either side of it in an avalanche, inches from his head. He glanced back over his shoulder at the rest of us standing in safety at the edge of the field, and I could see even from this distance that his face was as white as a priestess' gown. Without giving the enemy time to collect itself, however, he jumped up and raced to the next tree, diving under it and again narrowly missing a lethal shower of boulders. Then leaping away once again, he fled back to us through a hail of arrows and missiles, arriving at the grove breathless and trembling. Chirisophus was furious.

"What the hell kind of a lame-ass stunt was that to pull?" he roared. "You're a fucking general, but you have no more brains than the chief ass-wipe for the goat herd, risking your command like that. Ignorant son of a bitch, I ought to chain you up and . . ." His voice trailed off in disgust as he saw that Xenophon was simply grinning at him. The other officers stared at him wide-eyed.

"In three minutes of running, those idiots on the ridge wasted twenty cartloads of boulders and a hundred arrows on me," Xenophon retorted. "Do you think their supply of ammunition is unlimited? With two or three hotheads out there attracting their fire, we can deplete their entire supply by this afternoon. I could probably ask for volunteers . . ."

His words were interrupted by the crash of another enormous load of stones that had just been sent racing down the hill and slamming into the tree. Looking over, we saw that Callimachus was already cowering in the first spot to which Xenophon had raced, and was preparing to run to the next tree. When Agasias saw him moving toward the stronghold, with the entire army watching, he could not bear the thought of his rival's attaining glory by being the first in, so he too rushed toward the tree, nimbly avoiding the shower of boulders and tagging Callimachus, who in turn rushed to the next way station. In dismay Aristonymus leaped out to the field and ran past them both, followed by another officer, Aeneas, drawing a deafening thunder of stones from the ridge top above.

Amazingly, not a man of them was touched, and within ten minutes of the captains' racing from tree to tree they were met not by the crashing of boulders from above, but by cries and shouts of consternation from the enemy. They had dropped over a hundred cartloads of stones on the Hellenes down below without hitting a single target, and now had no more heavy ammunition left.

Chirisophus did not waste time. Shouting to his hoplites to advance, they immediately began a brisk charge in formation, picking their way across the rubble-strewn field, while Callimachus, Agasias, Aristonymus, and Aeneas sprinted toward the unguarded entry to the stronghold, to the cries of terror from the women and children inside, certain they were to be murdered in cold blood by the filthy, long-haired attackers.

For decades I have tried to forget what I next witnessed. The women and old men inside the compound, hundreds of them, in their desperation and fear, rushed to the edge of the cliff—and simply jumped off. Not a moment of hesitation. It was as if they had practiced the maneuver their entire lives. Those with children or babies ran to the edge, paused for the space of a breath, then dropped the infants over the cliff first, before following behind. The entire army could see this from our vantage point, and we raised our voices in horror, shouting at the women to stop. The pitiful mothers, however, were mad from fear of being dishonored in front of their husbands watching up on the cliff, with their children skewered or taken as slaves, for such is the custom of the local tribes in warfare. They took our strange-sounding shouts as a cry for blood, and redoubled their efforts to commit mass suicide, some of them slitting the throats of the terrified and screaming children to spare them the agony of the long drop, others leaping into the abyss clutching their offspring or their aged parents to their breasts in a last embrace of death.

The four racing captains, their triumph at being the first to enter the stronghold turning to shock at the sight that met their eyes upon their arrival, rushed to the edge of the cliff themselves, shouting at the women and old men to turn back, that they meant no harm. They drew their swords and swatted at the terrified Taochians with the flats of the blades, beating them back from the edge, but this only threw them into greater panic and they began swarming in attack over the officers themselves. Aeneas spotted an elderly man, who by his dress appeared to be a headman, running furiously to the edge to throw himself over, and the Greek captain leaped to tackle him from behind. At the last moment, however, the frantic old wretch tripped over his vestments, throwing Aeneas off balance, and with his strong arms locked around the man's waist they both went hurtling off the precipice to the distant rocks below.

Chirisophus' Spartans finally arrived and were able, with difficulty, to put a stop to the carnage, but not before terrible damage had been done. Of the several thousand human beings huddled in terror on the boulder just minutes before, hardly a hundred remained. Our troops wandered the smooth, icy surface of the mountaintop in an agony of remorse that they had been the cause of this tragedy. The only sounds were the whimpering of the few children who had escaped the carnage, their mothers' arms being simply too full with their other babies, and the bleating and mewing of hundreds of head of cattle, asses, and sheep that had been left behind. My stricken mind could not even comprehend the emotions of the Taochian defenders watching on the ridge top, those silent men whose families were all dead by a meaningless suicide. We had no way of contacting them. Xenophon ordered all the local prisoners to be released, hoping they would make their way to the defenders in the hills, and tell them that the few children left alive would be taken to the nearest village and deposited with the residents there, with a full store of provisions.

. . .

That night, the entire army camped silently in grief for wives and children not even theirs, in the small enclosure of the flat mountain top. When I stole away from my duties to seek out Asteria, I had difficulty finding her. After searching for a time among the Rhodians' camp, I finally asked Nicolaus discreetly if he had an idea as to her whereabouts, and he pointed me in the direction of the cliff face behind the camp.

I soon found her, wedged into a dark gap between two large boulders, overlooking the site where the Taochian women had dashed themselves and their children onto the rocks. The sides and bottom of the cliff were now lit by flickering shadows cast by the enormous funeral pyre built below by the Cretan mountaineers whom Xenophon had assigned to collecting and burning the bodies and arranging for an appropriate marking. Asteria looked drawn, and acted nervous and uncommunicative.

"I brought you something," I said, trying to inject a note of consolation into my voice. I paused, waiting for a reaction that did not come, and unable to think what else to say I unwrapped from an oilcloth rag a bit of stale bread dipped in honey, which had been one of her favorite treats on the march. What simple things now satisfied her, after the rich existence she had once lived.

Asteria winced when she saw the food, and turning suddenly I heard her retch into a small cavity in the rock behind her, gasping for breath when she was done and then slowly turning around again to face me. From the close smell I noticed when I sat beside her, I realized she had been in here for some time.

She looked at me in a way that reflected, if not outright dislike, something only slightly more than indifference and far less than I had expected. She quickly composed her features into an expressionless mask, but the barren glance I had seen in that instant before she did so had said everything. I sat in silence, gazing out into the darkness.

"I'm not well, Theo," she finally murmured. "My belly is churning. Female problems." She cringed involuntarily when my shoulder brushed against hers, as if her skin had become overly sensitive, as after a severe sunburn.

I wrapped the bread and offered to bring her something more soothing. "Soup? The Rhodians have just killed a goat and are boiling it up . . ."

Asteria blanched and turned her head away. Again I remained silent, wondering what words I should use, then finally decided to simply unburden myself, for with her I had said everything, and had nothing left to hide.

"Asteria, I've accepted your services to the Rhodians. I've acknowledged your skills. I've violated my duty to the army for you, destroyed a fellow Greek for you. Yet still you shrink from me—are you truly so burdened by this betrayal of your father? I need to understand."

She paused for a long time, and I struggled to see her eyes and face in the growing shadows cast by the rocks in which she sat. Her voice came from far away, so softly I had to lean forward to hear, and she spoke almost without moving her dry, cracked lips.

"I'm far beyond concerns of my father. I mortally betrayed him and could never return to him. He knows what I've done, he's cursed me, and he's punished me by proxy, through the deaths of those close to me."

"Who? How do you know these things if he is not here? How can he even know of such a betrayal, or you of his punishment?"

"You cannot see the distant sniper in the dark, yet you feel his silent intent when the arrow buries itself in your throat. You cannot see the plague, yet you witness men swelling and turning black. So it is with my father."

I peered at her again in puzzlement. Still unable to make out her expression, I extended my hand to touch her face, thinking perhaps she herself was suffering from a fever, wondering at the changes I had seen in her recently. She shook my hand off in irritation with a brief wince as if from some deep pain.

"Theo, I don't expect you to understand—but I must be alone right now, rather than in the company of . . . men. I'll be fine for the march tomorrow."

I nodded. How can anyone know what passes in the hearts of women? They are more fickle even than the gods. Though Zeus is lord of Olympus, who is it that rules his actions, if not Hera and her rivals? As I began picking my way back down the path to the encampment, I turned back once more to look at her. She had already returned to her own thoughts, pushed me far from her mind, as if my feeble attempt at reconciliation had never taken place. I was struck by the fragility of her thin, bare legs extended in front of her without so much as a blanket for warmth, by the vulnerability of her defeated posture, in sharp contrast to the shorn hair and rough tunic of a Rhodian slinger.

In the light of the pyre, I saw in her face an ineffable sadness, even a longing, as she gazed down at the burial party tending to the dead mothers and babies below the cliff, and I watched as with tense and tormented fingers she clutched at her own burning belly.

BOOK ELEVEN

WHEEL OF FATE

For two urns stand upon the floor of Zeus's palace
Which hold his gifts to us, the one filled with evils, the other blessings.
When Zeus Lord of Thunder mixes his gifts between the two,
A man meets now with good fortune, now with ill.
But when Zeus bestows gifts from the jar of sorrow only,
That man becomes a pariah—cruel famine and madness
Pursue him to the ends of the earth,
And he wanders without aim, damned by gods and men alike.

—HOMER

I

BLIND HABIT WAS THE ONLY reason we were able to continue moving day after day, the only explanation for being able to endure and even ignore horrors which, in earlier times, would have thrown us into despair. Ignore, yes—but not forget. We forgot nothing. So long as we kept moving, surrendering ourselves to habit, we could push our wretchedness and the constant presence of death and disease to the backs of our minds. Fear can be endured if it is blunted and beaten into the dull form of a habit. But if we ever allow it to emerge, to take the keen edge of its true form, it will kill us as surely as a Scythian blade.

The army had fought its way step by step through hostile territory for almost five months since Cyrus' death at Cunaxa, and by now we had settled into a routine, though one of resignation rather than inclination. Morale had stabilized at a sullen, resentful but dutiful level. Each day the men simply trudged in silence, pushing from their mind all thoughts but that of surviving to the end of the day, stepping up their pace and lifting their sight only when necessary to defend themselves against attack, an almost daily occurrence. Finally, however, the weather began to break, with whole hours, then days on end when the weak sun strengthened sufficiently to begin melting the snow, and the icicles glittering on the stunted trees dropped their essence lazily, almost reluctantly, into slushy pools below. The wind, though still biting as it whipped through the narrow defiles and mountain passes, now carried a subtle scent of new vegetation, and of clean moisture rather than of sterile, frozen death. Descending out of the mountains we marched a hundred and fifty miles in a week, contending each step of the way with the Chalybians, a vicious tribe that was prepared, even eager, for hand-to-hand combat against our emaciated forces. The tribesmen wore linen corselets reaching to the groin, as well as greaves and stout helmets, unlike any of the other tribes we had seen. They carried enormous spears, and in their belt long daggers like the Spartans. We lost dozens of men to their lightning-swift raids and attacks before at last we were able to repel them in one of the many battles which have now become too tiresome for me to recount.

We were told by our guides that the sea, and safety, was scarcely more than two hundred miles distant, half a month's march, though Xenophon was reluctant to give credit to this information and unnecessarily raise the hopes of the exhausted troops. Word nevertheless spread rapidly that we were approaching our final stage, and the men's pace perceptibly quickened, their limping seemed to recover somewhat, and they carried their shields with slightly more aplomb.

And then we came to the River.

The recent snowmelt had raised the icy waters of the Harpasos to a level far too high for a safe crossing. After all the rivers we had successfully crossed in the past half year, this flow, which was not even shown on the crude maps devised for us by our seers, stopped us dead in our tracks. The silt in the water was so thick it was impossible even to determine the river's depth. Xenophon sent scouts on horseback in both directions to try to identify a passable ford, and by sunset both parties had returned. The team that had scouted south failed to find a crossing, and in fact reported that the river was joined by another tributary several miles downstream, widening it further and rendering it even more dangerous. The squad that had traveled north was slightly more fortunate, having encountered a hunting party of local Chalybian tribesmen, whom they had quickly run down and pressed into service.

Their leader was a morose and surly individual, a hunter with the unlikely name of Charon, who was familiar with the river and agreed under duress to guide us to a point he said would be passable, though not without a certain degree of difficulty. With Charon guiding the main party, the heavy troops slashed their way upstream for two days over rocky ground and through brushy ravines. Xenophon trailed behind with a smaller contingent of light-armed troops to protect our rear and what little provisions remained in the limping wagons and sleds. Finally arriving at Charon's objective, we saw that the water still appeared as fast and as deep as before, though the man swore that here it could be traversed by the army, with proper precautions. Gazing due west in the direction we were to ford, the low sun had turned the sky blood red, reflecting its hellish color into the murky water and the yellowish foam of the rapids, and my stomach knotted. I again felt the massed, unintelligible chanting and dark, minor chords of the Syracusan chorus surging up from my bowels, like magma throbbing underground, threatening to burst.

The hills on this side of the river were heavily wooded, and while half the troops made camp, collected firewood, and threw up defensive palisades and trenching, Xenophon ordered the rest to venture into the forest to cut light trees and lash them together for rafts. He had no illusions that we would be able to build a sufficient number of vessels for all the men and beasts—most of them would have to make do with their soon-to-be-developed swimming and floating skills—yet still, he hoped that with at least a few rafts we would be able to ferry across some of the wounded and most of our supplies, without further endangering our own lives.

For three days we were occupied in this task, under intermittently pouring and freezing rain that caused the river to swell even higher. Those among the soldiers who could not swim, which is to say most, kept to their work with a grim determination, though even tough Spartans, who would not hesitate to leap into pitched battle against a charging Scythian horseman, were as nervous as children at the thought of crossing the raging torrent they now faced. Spartans are land creatures and hate water crossings, though by this point of our journey one might have thought they would be accustomed to them. This roaring, murderous flow, however, carried in its silt the fear and fury of unknown lands hundreds of miles upstream, the ice and mystery of uninhabitable regions, perhaps even fearsome creatures and strange gods lurking beneath its surface. A man at the age I was then, burning with life, can normally no more foresee or contemplate his death than he can the lives of his descendants a thousand or two thousand years in the future. If death were to overtake him, it would be a complete surprise, unanticipated, with hardly a thought or reflection as to its meaning or impact. During those three days of staring at the river, however, I aged fifty years, and devoted as much thought to my death as I do now in my old age, when surrounded by it I can hardly escape reflecting on it.

On the appointed day the weather had cleared somewhat, but the skies still glowered. The seers sacrificed the two youngest sheep still remaining to us, in lieu of the lambs that would have been more pleasing to the river gods, slitting their throats so that the blood would flow into the water. Without waiting even for the priests to divine the gods' response, or perhaps purposely ignoring it out of fear, Xenophon ordered Charon to lead the first flotilla of small ferries across, each stacked high with our precious grain, the arms and armor remaining to us, a few bleating sheep and the terrified wounded men. The sides of the rafts were held fast by soldiers, those who could swim grasping the downstream side and shouting encouragement to those who could not swim, who were pressed by the current, panic-stricken, against the upstream sides of the rafts, praying to the gods for strength to be able to maintain their grip in the icy water. I had heard as a child that smearing the body with oil would help a swimmer retain body heat, so after quietly reminding Xenophon of this, he ordered the precious oil casks opened, which we had been carrying for anointing the dead, and every man was given a cup of it with which to coat his body. Each swimmer had small sections of split logs strapped precariously to his chest and back, in an effort to keep him afloat if he became separated from the raft, at least long enough to be washed ashore downstream before he died of cold or drowning.

As was their custom, the soldiers entered the water naked, save only their sandals, and each carried a silver coin or two, what little they had left from their last stipends, held in their cheeks for safekeeping. Chirisophus joked grimly that this measure would also save the survivors the expense of placing an obol in the mouths of the dead to pay their final toll, if the crossing was not successful. As the first rafts and soldiers entered the water, those on shore watched the progress of their comrades with hope, then busied themselves with their own preparations.

About a third of the army had entered the river, with the vanguard three-quarters of the way across, when a frantic clamor arose from the craft just behind Charon's, and we looked up to see the vessel standing almost vertically on its side, the torrent rushing up against it on the upstream side and forming a wall of froth, with the arms and legs of an upstream solder flitting out here and there as he struggled to maintain his grasp. On the downstream side the raft was braced firmly against a huge boulder unseen before in the rapids, but now visible behind the half dozen men standing hip-deep in the frigid water. They clumsily wrenched the raft back and forth, their strapped logs hindering them at every step, frantically trying to force it out of the jam. Another raft was quickly bearing down upon them, with its retinue of bobbing heads along three sides shouting in panic and attempting unsuccessfully to steer away from the boulder. The second raft, caught in the same vicious current, slammed into the first, both of them splintering like children's toys, overturning the provisions, and sending thirty men screaming into free-float in the frigid river, grasping at boulders, raft fragments and each other as they were swept downstream out of sight.

Even at this distance I could see the horrified look on Charon's face as he watched part of the army he claimed he could safely guide across the river disappear downstream without a trace. He frantically signaled to those in the water to stop their wading across the river, and to move directly upstream a hundred yards, to avoid the treacherous boulder that had destroyed the two rafts. We could all see the logic to this solution, yet those already in the water had been there for some time now, their bodies had become numb from the chest down and some were experiencing convulsions. The thought of remaining in the water for the additional time the detour would take was almost too much to bear. Those still on land quickly ran upstream to the newly designated crossing point, dragging the wagons and supplies with them, and then the soldiers slated to cross next strode into the water toward their predecessors, tossing them short ropes, blankets, branches, anything they could find to help their frozen comrades cover the last stretch.

When the entire army had shifted upstream to the new crossing point, we noted that Charon had unloaded his craft on the far side, and with several of the strongest swimmers from the troops had again entered the river and was returning toward the bulk of the army, swearing in his incomprehensible barbarian tongue and pulling into the ferry any soldiers he encountered midstream who were on the verge of going under.

Despite his efforts, a dozen more men were lost, as were two more rafts with their priceless cargo of supplies, while crossing the river.

Men straggled into camp on the other side for the next two days, naked and blue with cold, their feet bleeding from the icy and thorny ground on which they had walked miles from the point they had made landfall, others dragging broken limbs battered from the thrashing they had taken against the river boulders or the rafts themselves. Not a man was without serious bruises, myself included, and we remained in camp for three days nursing our wounds and trying to warm our frozen bodies, while search parties were dispatched downstream on both sides in an effort to find any further survivors who might have lost their way. One of the search parties never returned, and we guessed its fate from the gleeful taunts of the fur-clad tribesmen who mockingly waved their spears at us from across the river on the second night of our stay. In return for Charon's dubious services and inept guidance Chirisophus ordered that his head be removed and sent across by a catapult improvised from a springy young sapling, to his jabbering compatriots on the other side of the river. After they had retrieved the carefully padded bundle from where it had landed on the river bank and examined it, they set up an outraged chorus of lamentations and insults, but in the end, troubled us no more.

That night I slipped off alone under a moon as livid and cold as the eye of a blind man, wrapped in a borrowed wolfskin, spurning or spurned by Asteria, as I had been for weeks. I walked until I came upon a vast, barren plain covered with low plant growth. I had no fear of the darkness, that glowering sky of the Homeric epics, for there was no greater night than the darkness I felt inside me. As I walked, my chest constricted with a long-suppressed shudder, and I breathed deeply, taking in the redolent night air. Of all the scents most capable of eliciting emotion and memory—the smoke of a wood fire, a woman's sleep-warm body under a blanket, chalk on a child's tablet—there is perhaps none so simultaneously comforting and threatening as the scent of the moon. The scent of the moon. I ask the reader to reflect, to turn inward and carefully, slowly, inhale the still night air: one cannot help but notice that the night's scent is different by moonlight. The moon comforts in the light that it sheds on the darkness, yet threatens by emphasizing that very darkness and the mystery that still remains in the shadows beyond the moon's reach. Even a blind man unable to perceive light is confident in noting that the moon is shining, and will feel simultaneously both an inner comfort and a sense of foreboding at this knowledge. It is really only a question of breathing.

I strode through the frigid night for many hours, immersed in my thoughts, my rage at the needless losses of the crossing, and at my own, personal loss of Asteria, for she had remained as cold and distant to me as a flickering star since our encounter on the cliffs weeks before. Finally, in a state of exhaustion of both body and mind, I threw myself face foremost into the fragrant leaves, the asphodel of Xenophon's dream. Lying as if dead, I let my spirit wander through my former life, the hours spent sitting quietly in my mother's lap, Aedon's ethereal singing, the pride I saw reflected in his father's face as he heard Xenophon's praises touted by the other nobles of the city, his fury when informed of his son's departure.

The grandeur, the warmth and gaiety, the exuberance of my past, the exhilaration of life in Athens, the guileless joy of youth, were overwhelming in their contrast to my current state, and it was only with great effort that I forced my mind elsewhere. It is a weakness in a man to let his thoughts slip thus into needless melancholy, yet I did not have the strength to move from my position, nor even to open my eyes. My body was exhausted, it is true, but even under the harshest of circumstances, during times when I have been near death, I have always been able to move my physical being. This, however, was different, something I had never experienced—a complete emotional exhaustion, a draining of my very will to live, a crushing of the spirit so complete that my body, hardened and lean as it was from the months of campaigning, was completely immobilized.

After a long while I found the will to turn onto my back and open my eyes, and I gazed in wonder at the clear and frozen night sky. On the vast, treeless plain on which I lay, with the vault of the heavens stretching from horizon to horizon, the light from the millions of stars was overwhelming. When I moved my head to the side I saw the stars' light reflected again in a billion bedazzling drops of frozen dew that had formed on the blades of grass and flower leaves, eliminating the horizon line that gives people their bearings and balance, their sense of proportion and of their very place on earth, leaving me floating in the ether. I felt as though surrounded by infinite specks of light on all sides, supporting me from below and suffocating me from above, quivering and flashing, throbbing closer and closer in rhythm with the beating of my heart, while the ancient Syracusan chorus from my childhood welled up from the very depths of my bowels, irrepressible, threatening to burst out at any minute and completely stifling my thoughts and my existence. I felt as if I were drugged, or mad, for the lights around and above and below me were spinning and pressing me down, as if into the vortex of Charybdis, while the unintelligible chorus inside swelled to a deafening roar. I would go insane if I did not put a stop to this, and mustering all the strength left in me, or given to me in my desperation by a passing god who took pity on me, I sat up and screamed with all my life, a frantic, throaty, stentorian bellow, which after seconds left me gasping and hoarse.

As my cry died away, the maddening terror of the inner music stopped instantly and the fragrant night air rushed furiously back into my lungs. The stars returned to their normal places, and the sparks of frost fell back into formation, lined up neatly along the horizon and no longer threatening to break rank. I sat as if paralyzed, gazing around at the plain, as if in the Land of Dreams where the burnt-out wraiths of mortals dwell. I listened to the silence in wonder, as intently as I had listened to the impending rush of madness, daring it to return, forcing my will to face it and defy it, even trying unsuccessfully to bring again to mind the hellish harmonies that had filled my being so completely a moment earlier. My soul had returned to me, and was again firmly attached to those murky recesses in a man's body where it lurks, like a bat roosting in the darkness, eyes glittering in watchfulness.

Strangely, sitting there in the vast silence, a soft sound became evident: so soft I thought I had not heard it, and yet so near that the hair bristled at the back of my neck. I froze, and listened more closely: again it came, the same almost imperceptible rubbing sound, the slightest scraping, not inches from where I sat. I lay silently on my side and placed my face close to the ground, at the point from which I thought the sound had come. It stopped for what seemed a lifetime, as if its maker were considering what meaning to ascribe to this large-headed being that had placed its shaggy, sweat-drenched body so close to it. Slowly emerging beneath my eyes, softly reflected in the glittering blackness, I could make out the translucent gleam of an earthworm, carefully, blindly feeling its way out of the tiny hole it had spent its life digging. The minuscule particles of dirt it shoved aside as it slowly moved made the softest of scraping sounds to my overly sensitized ears, and as a comrade worm emerged from its own hole a few inches away, I heard yet another soft scraping sound, made by the tiny cap of dirt being pushed away from the top of its hole.

To this day, I am not sure what effect this stealthy consideration of a microcosm had on my spirit; for after my soul's wandering to its past, and the almost fatal crushing of my being by the revolving heavens and earth, this tiny dose of the most tactile reality—a vibrant, gleaming earthworm pulsing with life, pushing a speck of dirt from its hole into the starlight—seemed to be the antidote to my precariously balanced sense of proportion. I watched the worm almost without stirring for the rest of the night, slowly regaining my strength as my spirit rested and my mind emptied itself of all its fears of the past day and worries for tomorrow. I observed the worm and thought of nothing but how it busied itself with pushing insignificant quantities of dirt to and from its hole in its search for a dead thing for nourishment, and I took pleasure in this, as if it were a secret, known by no other being in the world—just myself and the worm.

As I watched, I marveled at the fact that even this insignificant creature, toiling anonymously, Sisyphus-like in its dark confines, was somehow able to make a small difference in the world; and it occurred to me that this tiny worm, rather than being a confirmation of death and decay and futility, was actually an affirmation of the persistence and stubbornness of life.

Though the mysterious music often returned to my mind for brief spells, like the lingering sleeve-tugging of some ancient deity afraid of being forgotten, it never again tormented me to madness.

II

COLLECTING OURSELVES ONCE again after the disastrous crossing, we set out across the plain, heading endlessly, unremittingly north. We were a day removed from the river when we were met by a small group of horsemen in ceremonial garb, among them the governor of the land through which we were passing, who entreated us not to harm his villages and livestock. Xenophon and Chirisophus, having been through this routine many times before, scarcely looked up from their trudging to address these nobles. They merely muttered their assurance to the barbarians that our only intention was to reach the Greek colonies along the Black Sea as quickly as possible, and that in passing through their land we would take only the provisions we needed to survive.

The governor and his envoys looked on in astonishment, though whether in response to Xenophon's weary rudeness, or to the army's overall aspect of complete exhaustion it is difficult to tell. Perhaps he felt pity for us, or mistrusted our ability to prevent the men from plundering, or possibly he felt that in our ignorance and weariness we might stray from our path and thereby tarry longer in his land than was absolutely necessary. In any event, after watching for an hour as the army limped slowly past his horses, he exchanged quick words with his advisors and then galloped back up to the vanguard, where Xenophon was marching this day in company with Chirisophus, and offered us the use of his chief advisor as guide. He explained that though our destination was not far ahead, no more than a hundred miles, the road passed through lands hostile to his own tribe, and that it would behoove the Greeks to have a reliable guide and interpreter for our own safety.

"We haven't had much luck with volunteer guides in the past," I pointed out to Xenophon, not even bothering to keep my voice low out of politeness. "What assurance do we have that this man will lead us to safety, and not into ambush?" Xenophon straightened up and eyed the governor suspiciously.

The barbarian snorted, overhearing my complaint. "I don't see that you're carrying anything worth taking," he noted observantly.

"Neither did the tribesmen in the interior," Xenophon snapped churlishly, "yet that didn't seem to dissuade them."

The governor softened his expression. "We bear you no ill will; in fact we often trade with the Hellenes along the coast. But if you insist on assurance, take my advisor as a hostage. If you do not spy the sea within five days, you have my permission to kill him."

The fixed smile on the advisor's face wavered briefly at this. Shrugging his shoulders, Xenophon merely grunted his assent and told the advisor to lead on. First, however, he gestured to me to seize the man's horse. I calmly walked over and grasped it by the reins.

"We don't ride horses in the army when on the march," I told him sternly. "We have too many sick and wounded in need of them. You're able-bodied; you can walk like the generals."

The guide glanced in dismay at the governor, who simply nodded as the man reluctantly climbed down and stood in the mud in his thin slippers. Xenophon sidled up to me where I stood, about to walk the horse back to the baggage area.

"Rather than loading it with gear," he said softly, his eyes steadily holding my gaze, "you might check with the Rhodian slingers. I understand they have some sick among them who would probably benefit from riding in a litter."

I gratefully nodded yes, and trotted off to find Asteria.

The guide proved true to his word, leading us not only on a direct route, but also showing us shortcuts and easier paths which we would have never found by simply using our crudely drawn maps. As soon as we passed over the boundary of his country on the third day, however, the man noted that we had entered the territory of his tribe's traditional enemies, and began urging that we burn every grove and field in our path. This, then, was the true motivation for the governor's kindly volunteering of his advisor as a guide. Xenophon refused the bait. Not only did he not wish to incur any further enmity on the part of the local inhabitants—a famished army of ten thousand marching through one's country is bad enough—but he was unwilling to delay the army's journey any longer to engage in mere plunder, or otherwise distract us from our one overriding goal—reaching the sea.

On the fifth day we reached the foot of the mountain known by the locals as Theches. It was surrounded by other formidable peaks, but this one stood out both for its overall height, towering above its brethren, and for its aspect: a smooth, cone-shaped slope rising to a flattened top, with sides of loose gravel and boulders, heavily wooded at the bottom and with the trees thinning out near the summit. The road meandered back and forth along the mountain's flank and through the trees, rarely affording any glimpse or view from the side of our approach, and requiring that the army climb in a single file, two abreast at the most, because of the roughness of the terrain. The road wound directly to the top of the mountain and down the other side.

This approach made the officers nervous. The troops would be stretched out for miles, unable to properly defend themselves in the event of an attack. It increased the likelihood that we would lose stragglers and the sick and wounded, and it would be virtually impossible to push and pull the bulk of our provisions and equipment up the steep, loosely graveled trail.

"We have no choice," Xenophon told his captains in resignation. "Leave the remaining wagons and supplies; we'll drive the livestock and pack animals between companies, with the sick and wounded to follow. We're vulnerable to attack; every soldier marches armed, in full panoply."

The next morning Chirisophus' soldiers led, as usual. The army was slow to move, marching singly or in twos, and it was almost three hours later that the rear guard was finally able to assemble in marching order. Shortly after the last scouts had pulled up their spears and begun climbing, we heard faint shouts from miles ahead, echoing through the ravines between the mountains. Xenophon's eyes narrowed.

"What are they shouting? Is it an attack?"

I could not distinguish the words, nor even the tone of the voices, but twenty minutes later the shouting had become more distinct and ever louder. We could now make out the clashing of weapons on shields.

"It's an attack," shouted Xenophon. "Double-time!" Then muttering more to himself than to anyone nearby, "I knew the sons of bitches would be watching our formation."

The men began trotting, groaning as they strained up the steep ascent in their gear, dreading the thought of yet another battle, and fearing for their safety in an extended, strung-out column. The troops' stepped-up pace created a ruckus all its own as the captains shouted orders and the armor and weapons clanged noisily, and for over an hour this obscured from us the source and quality of the sound we had heard. The men eyed the summit nervously, but it gave us little indication of what we were facing, for as each company ahead of us crossed over the lip and onto the flat plateau, they simply disappeared from our view. Chirisophus had sent no word back to us on the army's status or his needs for reinforcement, and we expected the worst.

Xenophon could finally bear the suspense no longer. Racing back to our makeshift cavalry, still headed by Lycius but now serving more as an ambulance and transport squad than as a fighting unit, he seized a horse and told Lycius to cut the provisions and litters loose from the animals. Lycius' face beamed at the thought of finally engaging in true cavalry action again.

Xenophon and twenty riders went trotting up the hill, forcing aside the ranks ahead of us to pass, as the shouting and clanging ahead grew louder. Suddenly reaching the lip and climbing over onto the flat of the mountain top, we encountered a sight that burst the heart.

The entire army that had arrived thus far, perhaps two-thirds of the total, was in complete and utter disarray; some of the troops had gathered in circles and were kneeling in the mud, their arms encircling each other's shoulders, praying to the gods. Others were maniacally slamming their shields against those of their comrades, like boys playing at combat, or pounding with their fists on each other's shoulders, even running aimlessly in circles. Still others simply stood as if transfixed, staring at the horizon to the north. Above all was the noise—deafening, steady, relentless shouting, a mixture of chants combined with sobbing and wails, the whole melding together, transformed into an orderless, indistinguishable, indescribable mass of sound. The words were incomprehensible, until one looked into the faces of the soldiers and saw tears not of desperation and fear but of rapture, and until one realized from their gestures that those praying were not beseeching the gods for deliverance but praising them in thanks, and until one read the lips of those quiet ones simply standing still and weeping, their mouths forming those words so long denied us in our terrible march across the deserts and over the mountains: *"Thalatta, thalatta!"*—"The sea!"

Men seized Xenophon and lifted him high onto their shoulders, laughing and bellowing his name in the chant they had cried when they had first acclaimed him general so long ago. They pummeled his back as he gazed proudly around at his warriors, a broad smile creasing his face and flashing through his thickly grown beard. I stood alone, watching in a daze, a mixture of ecstasy and ache, as the men that had been marching behind me continued to pour over the crest of the mountain to their own first, rapturous view of the sea. After a moment, however, I sensed a presence I had long given up hope of encountering again, and turning around I found that I was not alone, for Asteria stood silently facing me, her eyes hollow and tear-filled, her cheekbones prominent on her gaunt face, but with a gentleness to her expression that stopped my heart just as surely as if a goddess had appeared before me. I opened my arms and she stepped into them as if she belonged there and had never left.

I looked up and there, just visible in the smoky, distant haze, shimmering like the blade of a sword catching the light of the sun, was the narrow blue line of the sea. So true it is, that tears belong to joy and sorrow alike.

III

THIS, OF COURSE, is the dramatic climax of my tale, the point at which, had it been a drama enacted on the stage, the audience would be settling back into their seats, hoarse from cheering, wiping the tears from their eyes, while the play concluded with some feeble spoken epilogue recited by the story's narrator, or a closing hymn chanted by the chorus. If the gods had any sense of proportion or balance, or even artistic awareness, this is what they would have permitted, and indeed the feeble epilogue will be coming soon enough, for those readers who would not feel my reminiscing to be complete without it; but the gods had one further plot twist in mind.

There is a dramatic device often used in our Greek plays, which I consider as being a sign of intellectual laziness, or perhaps excessive piety, on the part of the playwright, and it very well may be that the two are the same thing. Just when the protagonist's circumstances appear to be as dire as can be imagined, with no possible way to escape his impending doom, an actor representing a benevolent and all-powerful deity is lowered by ropes and pulleys from the top of the stage. He then proceeds to emit lightning bolts to destroy the enemy, or cast a spell to reconcile the young lovers, or perform whatever other sorcery may be required to enable the drama to be satisfactorily resolved and to tie up all loose ends in the remaining moments. We refer to this as a "mechanical god," a means of putting back to rights all that is unresolved, in a way not otherwise humanly possible.

To my knowledge, no playwright has yet considered the opposite phenomenon of, shall we call it, a "mechanical Nemesis," though language and Greek dramatic tradition fail me here. The image I mean to convey is one of a grubby, smirking little satyr that clambers unannounced from where it had been lurking beneath the stage floorboards and proceeds to immediately undo all satisfactory outcomes that have been rendered. In the final minutes of the play, he throws into chaos all instances of victory, reconciliation, and happy endings that were on the verge of being so painstakingly wrought. But in the drama of human life, is not this phenomenon more common than the former? Is it not truly a more realistic example of the actual behavior and performance of the gods, either through clumsy blundering or willful spite? It is no wonder, therefore, that I have lost faith in the benevolence of our guardian deities.

The Wheel of Fate turned. Just as a cat tortures and plays with a mouse before finishing him off, so the gods toyed with us. The deity often takes pleasure in making the small great and the great small.

For months we had sacrificed to the gods daily, in entreaty, in thanksgiving, for guidance. Down to our last starving goat we had sacrificed to the gods. Libations of water had been poured in the absence of wine, stale bread crumbled in the absence of animals. Never had Xenophon neglected his duties to Zeus and Apollo, in fact he had insisted on their faithful exercise, even in the face of Chirisophus' clear exasperation. Never was there a more faithful or exacting acolyte to the gods, until the day of our arrival at the summit of the mountain. But there, in our excitement at finally arriving within view of the sea, in the troops' ecstatic promotion of Xenophon from mere general to hero, we innocently, though apparently not forgivably, forgot to sacrifice to the gods in thanksgiving.

In return, they sent us honey.

A great deal of honey, hundreds of hives of the stuff, heaps of the sweetest, stickiest, most nourishing and delicious gobs of golden dew we had ever tasted, which we looted from an enormous apiary in the mountains after easily routing the last hill tribe standing between us and the sea, the Colchians. The fact that it was stolen made it even sweeter, and the famished men hooted and danced like children as they tore into the lightly constructed hives, ripping them with their spears, driving the bees away with blackly smoking pine-pitch torches, ignoring the feeble stings of the few brave little insects who remained behind to defend their property. The men, already near delirium from their awareness of the nearby sea, gorged on the stuff. They wandered among the hives in blissful content with honey smeared on their faces and hands, congealing in their hair, tossing handfuls of honey mass and sticky comb at each other out of pure mischief after they were sated. Their pleasure was so pure, their delight after the suffering they had endured over the winter so innocent, that none of the officers had the heart to even attempt to maintain discipline, and in fact were hard pressed themselves to keep from jokingly smearing a wad of the bounty into their fellow captains' faces out of sheer delight.

There is an old story of the Thessalian King Knopos, who was advised by his priestess Enodia to select the largest and finest bull, and then drug it with her potion. The maddened bull escaped and was captured by the enemy, who accepted it as a good omen, sacrificed it and ate it in a feast. Upon consuming the drugs, they went mad and were slaughtered by Knopos' troops in a brutal attack. Whether the Colchians had poisoned our honey in their retreat in the manner of that ancient king, or whether the starving bellies of our troops were simply unaccustomed to the richness of this dessert, within hours all who ate of it fell violently ill, leaving their senses, puking and retching, an astringent greenish diarrhea running uncontrollably down their legs. Men who merely tasted the honey appeared as if they were drunk. Those who ate a great deal ranted like madmen, raving and feverish, lying about in heaps and sometimes even dying, recalling the days of the plague in Athens. Men rolled on the ground in pain, their bellies distended, their faces contorted and their swollen tongues turning blue as they bit their own flesh in agony. The stickiness on their hands and faces, which they had not even had time to wash off before being stricken, collected dirt and leaves from the ground, as well as the filth being ejected from their bodies. As they lay in agony, their eyes pooled in horror and disbelief at the realization that after months of bravery and hardship, the seemingly invincible Greek warriors could be brought to defeat and collapse by such innocent sweetness.

Not a man, Xenophon and the other officers included, could stand on his feet, and it is a wonder that the Colchians did not return and slaughter us all in our wretchedness. Indeed, many of the troops would have thanked them for putting them out of their misery. The fact that the Colchians did not return is perhaps the truest proof that they had not, in fact, knowingly poisoned the honey, and I should probably be thankful to the gods for that, though I cannot help but think that if I were to praise the deities for such an empty gift, I would only be encouraging them in their puerile games. Had I seen such a scene as this in a play in Athens, I would have scoffed at the playwright's clumsy and heavy-handed treatment of irony, bringing the most valiant and long-suffering fighters on earth to their knees by a pleasure as innocent as a mouthful of honey. No doubt the audience, too, would have been offended at the author's apparent insult of the gods. The fact that this was no mere stage drama made the deities' betrayal all the more damning.

Most of us recovered within a day or two, and stumbling to our feet as if dazed and drugged, we staggered back into formation, burying the dead and attempting to regain our threadbare dignity. Asteria, however, a lover of honey since childhood, had gorged on the substance, and when I was finally able to locate her among the miserably retching groups of Rhodians, I found her lying unconscious, scarcely breathing, her bile-encrusted lips turning blue with cold and her bare legs under the short tunic caked with the filth in which she had been lying untended. Weak and trembling as I was, I struggled to pick her up and was startled to find that her body felt as light and fragile as a bundle of dry twigs, bereft of any muscle or fat after the long march and the purging of the last two days. All remaining softness had disappeared from her limbs and torso, and her feverish face was hollow with huge, darkly circled, watery eyes, which had rolled back into her head with only the whites showing beneath the bluish lids. I carried Asteria's body in my arms along the path down the last range of coastal foothills, and I felt certain that my own life had ended.

IV

THAT DAY, A YEAR AFTER their glorious departure from Sardis, something under ten thousand starving, half-naked, bushily bearded Greek troops, wearing full, battered armor and bearing triumphant expressions, limped in perfect formation out of the foothills before the incredulous townspeople of Trapezus. Grime filled every pore and fold of their skin, and traces of the dried vomit from their most recent misadventure were still visible in the corners of their mouths and under their chins. Their teeth were rotten or missing, and they hawked great phlegmy gobs on the earth which were trampled under the thickly horned, bare feet of the men marching heedlessly behind them. Their dented helmets were slung from their shoulders by the nasals, or simply perched carelessly on the tops of their heads, the empty eye sockets peering blackly at the sky, like masks on their pegs. The men told unbelievable tales of walking a thousand miles overland from Babylon, and they bore only half as many toes and fingers as an army that size should have. The troops around me bellowed out the paean to Apollo in their weary gratitude at having finally arrived among friends and allies, and the townspeople looked on in wonder and awe at the men's matted hair and tattered scarlet cloaks, but I was deaf and blind to all around me. In truth I was hardly in worse shape than when I had started, with the exception of the physical toll I had suffered, which would fade with time. Still, I had had a taste of glory and fullness, I had desired Xenophon's peach, and once having known a hint of such richness, even for an instant, its absence made me feel infinitely poorer.

I broke ranks without informing a soul, and entered the first miserable inn I encountered, kicking in doors with my feet until I found a room with a vacant cot, where I deposited Asteria's body before turning to arrange settlement with the astonished innkeeper. I had no money, not an obol to my name, so I left my battered and still blood-begrimed shield and helmet as surety, gave instructions that I was not to be disturbed except for a simple meal once a day, and entered the room with Asteria, closing the door behind me on the innkeeper and on the army, on Xenophon and on the man I was up to that day.

I am no physician, certainly no Hippocrates, and I doubt that any but midwives and witches would have been available in that wretched town in any case. To tell the truth, I was more concerned with finding an undertaker than a physician, though often in such places the same august personage would fill one and the same role, conflict of interest notwithstanding. The army surgeons I had seen among our troops and even in Athens invariably had but one remedy for hemorrhage: further bleeding. If the woman survived that, she would survive her illness; if not, then so it was ordained by the gods. The Hippocratians would put on an impressive show, to be sure, taking samples of the patient's vomit, blood, tears, snot, uterine fluid, sweat, urine, runoff from festering wounds, ear wax, and any other bodily emissions they could extract, then analyze them by tasting them, or if the patient were cogent, having her taste them herself. But I would have no such indignities performed on Asteria. I would care for her my way.

During one of the long evenings, as I sat silently on the edge of her cot watching her fitful and feverish sleep, I fetched a bowl of cool water and proceeded to sponge the perspiration off her body, trying despite the filth of our surroundings to keep her in some semblance of cleanliness. I absentmindedly murmured her name, "Asteria," more to myself than in any hope she might answer me. The word passed through the long, vast wilderness of her consciousness, enveloped in darkness and inhabited by shades, meandering through the lonely byways of her mind and lingering for eons, it seemed, before finally reaching its destination; whereupon it slowly elicited a response, which traversed the tortuous path back through the shades to the outside as the mists slowly dissipated and her tongue moved laboriously, her eyes still closed: "Theo." The word was spoken so softly it startled me, and I wasn't even sure I had heard it, for her expression had not changed, nor had her eyelashes even fluttered. I had almost resigned her whisper to a figment of my imagination, perhaps a truer assessment of my existence than I had ever realized, when she spoke again, with an infinite effort: "Forgive me."

I looked up and saw her struggling to speak, gasping silently, her lips and tongue working thickly. Some inner surge of energy had welled up within her, and she would not be put down. Her lids lifted half open, and she looked at me strangely, feverishly, with glassy eyes that alternated from steely gray to pale blue as my flickering light reflected off them, only to become suddenly very dark, the color of the ocean depths or of the grave, if touched by even so much as a hint of shadow.

"Theo," she struggled. "You loved Proxenus as a brother, as you love Xenophon." I nodded silently, my astonishment at hearing her speak tempered by the fear that it was some awful disclosure that was prodding her to do so. I begged her to be silent, to rest.

"I'm sorry, Theo," she gasped again, and then lay panting, her eyes closed, struggling to regain her breath and her calm. I did not interrupt her effort, except to tighten my grasp on her racing pulse, and to pad away the beads of perspiration that had sprung out on her forehead in her feverish striving.

"Asteria," I said finally, "you have nothing to be sorry for. Proxenus was a soldier, he died as a soldier, and he is with the gods."

At this her eyes fluttered wide open, and her expression was absorbed by an inexpressible sadness and torment. "I—I killed him," she said, looking straight into my eyes, and then repeated it over and over, in a voice drained of strength and emotion, fading away from me again. "I killed him."

Oddly, I felt a relief at this, knowing full well that she had done nothing of the sort and that she was merely being taunted by a grotesque dream, some savagery of the gods who were not satisfied with torturing her body, but sought to torment her mind as well.

"Asteria, sleep. You killed no one, it is only a dream." She was still agitated and shaking, still trying to say something, which I knew would be only further hallucination. I sought to dissuade this useless expenditure of her depleted strength by repeating the calming words. "You did not kill Proxenus. Tissaphernes did. You are innocent."

At this she gasped and nearly sat up in her frustration at being unable to make me understand, and her desperation to speak. "You foolish man!" she blurted, in a voice rasping and whispery, her face contoured with pain. "*I* am Tissaphernes!" Thus having spoken she collapsed back down onto her flat, sodden pillow, panting and wretched. I sat wide-eyed, astonished at the strength of her outburst, but at length I resumed my calming litany of platitudes, and was finally rewarded to see her shallow breathing return to normal, and her tensed limbs begin to relax.

She looked up at me once more, her face bearing an expression of profound sadness. Her lips worked silently, and I thought she might again try to give voice to words better left unsaid and unpondered, but then, slowly closing her lids, she reentered the land of shades and dreams which she had inhabited for so many days. Dreams, those torments, desires, false and true portents—that larval, ghostly world inhabited by an even greater abundance of jeering, irrational beings than may be found in our waking existence. She disintegrated as if descending down an ever darkening well, each level more constricting than the last. I was beyond her now, she was fighting her own battle, entirely alone with her little life and the memories of her meager sins, and even when sleeping she occasionally wept hot tears because both her years and her memories were quickly departing.

Later that night, I carefully rolled her into a fetal position in an attempt to relieve the unremitting fire in her belly. I then gently stroked her neck and back hairline, that soft, magical place on a woman's body where the smooth curve of her nape becomes as downy as a child's and then transforms into the line of soft, feathery wisps along the curved edge of her locks, those tiny hairs that defy all attempts at taming, even when the rest of the woman's hair is subject to the most elaborate binding. Wondrous little cilia they are, which when backlit by a lamp, shine and glow like a sort of aurora, undying remnants from the woman's childhood, as visible and as beautiful and as unmanageable on the richest Persian queen as on the poorest peasant maiden, the first hairs to appear as an infant, guardians of her sweet, female scent her entire life, the last wisps to remain on her head in her feeble dotage, defying time and space. I lingered there with the cool sponge, emptying my mind and thinking of nothing as she sighed and murmured in her sleep.

I had just leaned down to lift her back to the center of the cot when I noticed a small mark or spot, just at her back hairline. I had never noticed it before, for prior to her illness I had never seen Asteria's body in daylight, and before that, when Cyrus was still alive, her neck had never been exposed due to her long hair. Bringing the oil lamp closer and bending down slowly, I could make out the faded outlines of the traditional infant tattoo she had been given after her birth in Sardis, to identify her father and family origins in the event of a disaster. I peered at it carefully, trying to make out the faint lines and distinguish between shadow and ink, when suddenly I caught my breath and sat up as if stung by a scorpion, jostling her roughly and causing her to moan in her sleep.

The symbol on her neck was one I had seen and trembled at many times, one that had haunted my dreams for nights on end, one I thought I had left behind me forever months before—the winged horse of Tissaphernes.

I was horrified, and shuddering, I stood up and backed away from her cot to the far wall, where I stood motionless, staring at the shriveled, miserable creature lying unconscious across from me. Coming to myself, I paced the room for hours, pounding my fist at the stone wall until the knuckles bled, bellowing my rage and defiance of the gods, willing myself, against all better judgment, to ignore what I had just seen, to remain constant toward Asteria as if she had not been so savagely defiled by the tiny mark, more polluted than she could ever have been by foul Antinous in the hut. The effort I made was supreme, perhaps more exhausting than any I had experienced on the entire march, for this was a battle within myself, against the very gods, and one that I fought bitterly in my mind and my soul until finally, utterly depleted, I collapsed on the floor and slept a sleep of death, but the sleep of a victor.

Hours later I awoke, and listened for Asteria's breathing, and was at peace. The trap of the gods had not defeated me, for unlike one that strikes at one's health or that threatens one's safety, this was a strike at the mind, and at my mind alone, one that I had in myself to accede to or to defeat. The gods force men to love those whom they should not, and to disrequite those whom they should. Answerable only to their own devices, which are unknowable to mortals, they let perish those who should live, and spare those who should perish. But this time the gods' comedic timing was off. The annoying satyr that had been dogging my tracks for weeks had made this one further cheap attempt to play the clown, but had flubbed his lines, fatally delaying his entrance until far beyond the point when the maximum impact could be felt. Rather than meriting a standing ovation from his fellow deities at the cleverness of his stage pranks, he elicited nothing more than a bored yawn. My state of mind was now such that I could think of no better vengeance on Tissaphernes than this. The classic elopement scene, the showdown between the enraged father and the grinning and triumphant son-in-law. The nasty, hairy-eared little demon who had been pursuing me made a quick exit from the stage in embarrassment, and did not return.

I buried her in the hills outside the town, in a hole scratched into the earth using my sword and bare hands. No marker or monument did I erect, for Asteria's very presence in this city was unknown to all but myself and the Rhodians, and I had no need of such a token. The only possession of hers I retained was a small, battered feather I withdrew from her matted hair just before winding the sheet about her body.

I lay on the ground beside the grave and slept, a deep, dreamless, exhausting sleep, devoid of vision or meaning. Waking in the middle of the night with my tongue dry and my head aching, I stood and walked numbly to the Greek camp, passing unchallenged past the guards to the hut which I knew Xenophon would be occupying, from the pennant flying above. Stumbling in, I found him at work, writing at a crude table by lamplight. He looked at me without surprise or reproach, his eyes bearing dark circles and his cheeks still gaunt from the harsh journey and the even harsher suffering he had experienced since his arrival. He nodded quietly in greeting and welcome, glanced to the cot in the room that had long lain empty, awaiting my return, and quietly went back to his work. It was many years before we ever spoke of Asteria or the events of those weeks, when I was not myself.

So long in my internal exile, it had never occurred to me that he too might be suffering, for his loss had been double, and I cannot think about it even now without a shudder of regret. Self-preoccupied as I was at the time, I did not realize until much later that this was the first time since Xenophon's birth that he and I had ever been apart.

BOOK TWELVE

GOD AND MAN

Self-born, untaught, motherless, unshakeable,
Giving place to no name, many-named, dwelling in fire . . .
All-seeing ether . . .

—INSCRIPTION FROM A TEMPLE WALL IN LYCIA

IT WAS HIS EYES I first noticed: sightless, watery orbs clouded an opaque creamy color from the thick cataracts covering them. He was as blind as a worm, yet his sightless gaze bored through the passersby on the crowded street as he peered straight into my face.

Listening carefully, I could hear his strange song rising above the background din of the street. The lyrics were faint, hardly more than a mumble, a repetitive chanting under the breath, but their effect was immediate and terrible. Trembling, I shouldered my way across the dusty street and seized the tottering old man roughly by the arm.

"Where did you learn that? Who are you?" He stared at me as I hissed at him, his blank expression slowly creasing into a grin, and he began laughing, the laugh of the deranged or the desperate. I thought perhaps he didn't hear me, or couldn't understand, so I brought my face closer. "Who are you?" I pleaded again, slowly and deliberately. My fingers gripped his surprisingly firm bicep in a kind of desperation. Despite my harsh grasp, no wince passed across his face—merely a vague stare, of amusement perhaps, even of triumph, though the strength of any emotion he might have been feeling was not sufficient to halt his mindless chuckling. I despaired of an answer, and stood there trembling in frustration, one old man tormenting another on a noisy street corner in Sparta.

Again he began his rhythmic, mournful chant, swaying slightly in time to his mental chorus, his face turned toward me expectantly.

The words to his song, which had remained latent for decades in my memory, in a misty corner of Mnemosyne's regions to which I rarely traveled, now echoed and rolled through my mind once again, taking on thoughts and shapes and a life of their own. A faceless, black-haired young woman leaning over me as I rested on her lap, singing a song—a lullaby?—in a low voice, an exotic, primitive melody that was more a chant than a tune, and which over the years had lent itself to endless variations in my inner thoughts. The words themselves were unintelligible to me, a language I had never spoken and do not understand. It is not the familiar Doric of Syracuse, nor even the obscure Elymi or Sicani, for I have spoken with many Sicilian merchants and soldiers in my life, and none, during my discreet queries, recognized any of the words I attempted to parrot from the recollections of my infancy. A Phoenician mapmaker I once asked told me the sounds were like those of his language, though he recognized none of the words. Is memory such an ephemeral thing that even my earliest and most sacred impression, that of my own mother, has been unrecognizably corrupted?

I loosened my grip on the old man's arm, and dropped a handful of obols into the small clay bowl he was carrying, probably more money than he had ever held at one time in his life. The insane cackling ceased immediately, and he wrenched his arm away from my clench with a strength that was astonishing for one seemingly so frail. It was only with great effort and much coaxing that I was able to soothe him from his mindless babbling and elicit from him anything approaching lucidity.

"My little song?" he asked, and as he bobbed his head and resumed his chuckling, I feared I had lost him completely. He recovered his concentration, however, as quickly as it had eluded him seconds before, and my heart began alternately stopping and racing as his attention ebbed and flowed. "Those words . . . ," he rasped, "Those words mean nothing! Ha! Ha! A nonsense rhyme I learned from my grandfather in Syracuse a century ago, who learned it from his grandfather . . ." He began losing his focus again as this counting of the generations broke down into more hoarse laughter. I glimpsed in my mind the faint shadows of his forgotten ancestors and mine, ancient Sicilian warriors who had lived when the gods still walked the earth, and I saw them slowly recede back into the mists from which they had just been unexpectedly summoned. Like those very deities, who once could effortlessly cross the line of mortality, assuming human form or godlike essence at will, they were dead.

I emptied my purse into his clay pot, again halting his mindless chortling when he felt the suddenly increased weight in his hand. Peering up at me with his rheumy eyes, he blessed me by nodding gravely, and as he clenched my forearm I was startled to note that his gnarly, bent fingers belied a grip forceful and unyielding, like that of a warrior with strength yet remaining for battles to be fought. His gaze locked on mine, and he recited again, in a low, cracking voice, the precise words I remembered my mother chanting from so many years before. The hair stood up on the back of my neck and then my knees weakened and I wept openly in the street, the passersby averting their eyes in embarrassment.

After a moment I stood up shakily and walked away in silence, convinced I had wrung everything from the old man that he was capable of giving. I had returned across the crowded street, my vision still a blur, when it occurred to me how singular it was to have seen a beggar here. Under this city's harsh administration, vagrancy was punishable by, what?—death? imprisonment? No reasonable man would even attempt to beg in Sparta. Panicked at the danger the old fool would face if caught, I whirled and raced back across the street, dodging the carts and mules passing in front of me, to the corner where he had stood a moment before.

It was empty.

My family: two lines of ancient and forgotten song recited by a tramp. I later taught them to Xenophon's sons, in a fruitless effort to keep them among the memory of the living.

EPILOGUE

Character is destiny.—HERACLITUS THE OBSCURE

After a month's time spent gathering provisions and looting the surrounding Colchian countryside of its stores, the army and Xenophon made arrangements to continue back to Ionia, by ship and by foot, much to the relief of the overwhelmed townspeople, and the troops departed early one sunny spring morning. Several months and many deaths later, we arrived in Byzantium bereft of any plunder or even of those belongings with which we had started our long journey. Though poor in coin, however, Xenophon was rich in reputation and guile, and after campaigning with distinction for ten years more with the Spartan king Agesilaus, he retired wealthy to a large estate at Scillus, hard by Sparta itself, to spend the remainder of his years hunting and writing and observing from afar the affairs of Athens, which had banished him for life.

Accompanying him, as always, I too lived at Scillus. Philesia, his plain and uncomplaining Spartan wife, served him admirably in his daily care. Xenophon continued to sacrifice to the gods daily, and became closer to their world as he advanced in age, even at times maintaining running conversations with one or another of them when he thought he was alone. I, on the other hand, participated in the sacrifices not to seek omens or to entreat the gods' favor, but merely to appease them in order to avoid their notice of me one way or the other. "Pain," my countryman Epicharmus said, "is the price the gods demand we pay for all our benefits." If that is the case, I preferred their indifference.

Sparta's defeat by the Thebans at Leuctra changed our lives, driving us from beloved Scillus and forcing us to Corinth, a city without the beauty and grandeur of Athens, or the simplicity and nobility of Sparta. This move, I am certain, cost ten years of Xenophon's life. He aged as I watched him, becoming an old man before my very eyes. Even more disconcerting, he told me that I did the same. As I write this, a fanfare of trumpets and beating of drums can be heard in the distance, as Corinthian youths train for their never-ending military campaigns. Hearing such sounds revives long-dormant emotions in an old soldier, like watching a beautiful woman pass by, when there is nothing remaining to him but the memory of desire. The sway of her hips, the quiver of her breasts make the man's stomach knot. Yet though the woman beckons, her eyes filled with desire, though the trumpets brazenly summon to war—still the old man remains rooted to his chair, unable to rise.

Xenophon's two sons, who did act on such calls, died in the battles raging across Attica and the Peloponnese, and this was his final burden. Not having a son to follow one is difficult to bear, to which I can attest in my own acarpous life, though this was small comfort to him. In vain did I try to assuage his and my regret on this score. *Hous hoi theoi philousin, apothneskousi neoi,* I told him: Those whom the gods love die young. The minute these words left my mouth, however, I regretted them, for like most simplistic, pithy sayings this one was dual-edged, and of particularly small solace to those of us who die old.

I wax maudlin and sentimental, and it is with increasing effort that I try to keep my pen on the straight and narrow path of my tale. A Gallic sorceress named Yourcenar once said that no man is a king to his physician. To this I would add, nor is he a general to his squire. Both the physician and the squire, in order to be successful in caring for their wards, must be skilled to some degree in professional prevarication, omitting the bad news while yet retaining the recipient's full confidence. In the end, however, the truth must be laid bare and though neither party may quite wish it, social niceties and conventions must finally be set aside for the sake of precision.

And thus, seventy-five years after his birth, I again find myself in the position of caring for my alternately incontinent and strangurious ward, wiping his nose and cleaning his bottom as I did when he was an infant. It is a quiet role, and a not unsatisfying one, no doubt the last one I will play. But I err—for in hastily scribbling these leaves, in contemplation of my twin, my student, my benefactor, my very self, my last role will be not that of a nurse or an undertaker, but rather of a midwife, even of a god, as I strive, through these writings, to bring his true life to light.

Through this poor threnody I hope and trust that my goal will have been achieved, and that I will have shed some small bit of enlightenment on even one reader, even a hundred or more generations from now. The father of history wrote his masterpiece "in order that the memory of the past might not be erased from among men by time." Although I have no ambition myself to aspire to Herodotus' literary glory, I note nevertheless that a mere child sitting on the shoulders of a giant may see even farther than the giant himself. Perhaps purely by dint of my difference of perspective, I may be capable of seeing farther than my more worthy predecessors.

Let this, then, be the end of my narrative. I sign this document with the remnant of a songbird feather, which I have carefully saved for fifty years in a small pouch of oiled fabric; and I use my full name, to which as a man finally free and at peace, I am now entitled. Someone else, perhaps, will complete what I have left undone.

Themistogenes of Syracuse

1st year of the 105th Olympiad,
in the archonship of Callidemides
Corinth

AUTHOR'S POSTSCRIPT

Xenophon was born in Athens in approximately 426 B.C., and joined Cyrus' army on its fateful march in 401 B.C. He later served many years as an officer in the Spartan army under King Agesilaus, for which he was banished by Athens under penalty of death. After retiring from the military, he spent the remainder of his life writing works of philosophy and history, a memoir of Socrates, and treatises on household and farm administration. Although the Athenian government eventually repealed Xenophon's banishment, he never returned to his home city. He died in Corinth sometime after 356 B.C.

The most famous account of the March of the Ten Thousand, the *Anabasis,* was written by Themistogenes of Syracuse, which most modern scholars agree was the pseudonym of Xenophon himself.

ACKNOWLEDGMENTS

Since a re-creation of a historical figure and the era in which he lived always contains large elements of conjecture, the author need not formally substantiate the evidence for the historical facts that it does contain. The meaningfulness of such a novel, however, is greatly enhanced by closely adhering to the actual events, and when all else fails, the author must make an honest and determined attempt to remain within the bounds of what "could have happened."

Hence, one of my heaviest debts in researching the historical events and background in this work is owed to the primary sources, most importantly to Xenophon himself. His *Anabasis* is a first-rate report of the odyssey of the Ten Thousand and is a gripping adventure story in its own right, even absent any feeble enhancements I may have added to it. I also relied heavily on some of his other works—in particular, the history he wrote of his times, the *Hellenica.* Thucydides and Herodotus were also indispensable for their background information on events immediately preceding the time this novel takes place, and Plato, Plutarch, Philostratus, and Diogenes Laertius for personal information on certain of the protagonists which may be found in no other sources. Homer, of course, stands alone for being the source of much inspiration. As Robert Burton, in his persona of Democritus Minor, noted: "The matter is theirs most part, and yet mine . . . yet it appears as something different from what 'tis taken from; that which nature doth with the aliment of our bodies—incorporate, digest, assimilate—I do dispose of what I take."

Modern-day scholars were also of great help, and I can cite the works of J. K. Anderson, Edouard Délebecque, Simon Hornblower, and A. M. Snodgrass as being just a few that contained penetrating insight into certain arcane areas of Greek arms and *Xenophontia.* Likewise, several modern-day historical novelists and memoirists, even those not dealing directly with ancient Greece, served as sources of inspiration, though more often of despair at my ever being able to rise to the heights of poetry and historical insight they attained. Most notable in this regard were Robert Graves, Erich Maria Remarque, and Marguerite Yourcenar.

There are others to whom an even greater debt is owed, most especially friends and acquaintances, several of whom had never even known me before I began pestering them for information and advice relating to their specialties. They dedicated many hours of time and burned untold quantities of synapses attempting to drill the necessary historical accuracy, literary technique, and plain good sense into my head, with mixed levels of success, and any failures to do so are attributable solely to my own obtuseness. (The Earl of Shaftesbury, in his *Characteristics of Men, Manners, Opinions, and Times* of 1711, bewailed the practice of his day whereby an author "pathetically endeavors . . . to reconcile his reader to those faults which he chooses rather to excuse than to amend." Clearly, very little has changed in this regard.) Here I would specifically like to thank my editor, Pete Wolverton, for his professionalism and patience; my agent, Bob Solinger, for his constant encouragement; Nicholas Sterling for his inexhaustible knowledge of Xenophon and his times; and especially my friend and teacher Mark Usher, who reviewed every page of the early manuscript for historical verisimilitude and commented copiously and invaluably. All of them gave me permission to mention their names, which I consider as being most indulgent on their part and for which I am grateful.

Naturally, unbounded gratitude is due to my parents, who from my earliest childhood have instilled in me a love of study and learning, and who were ever encouraging and understanding in making allowances for my flights of fancy and quest for travel, far beyond, I am sure, what their finances and patience could comfortably bear.

Finally, and most importantly, the greatest debt is owed to my wife, Cristina, who for many months tolerated my "graveyard shift" writing habits (and the resulting crankiness the following day), and who never flagged in her encouragement and belief in me. Her taste and skill as a critical reader (and as an expert in pancration) I trust implicitly, and her quiet and loving qualities as a Muse are unparalleled even by Calliope and Clio. It is impossible to imagine being able to write even a single page of this book without her.

M. C. F.

ABOUT THE AUTHOR

Michael Curtis Ford, a native of Washington State, worked for many years as a consultant and banker. He currently lives in Oregon, working as a translator and helping his wife, Cristina, educate their two children at home. This is his first novel.

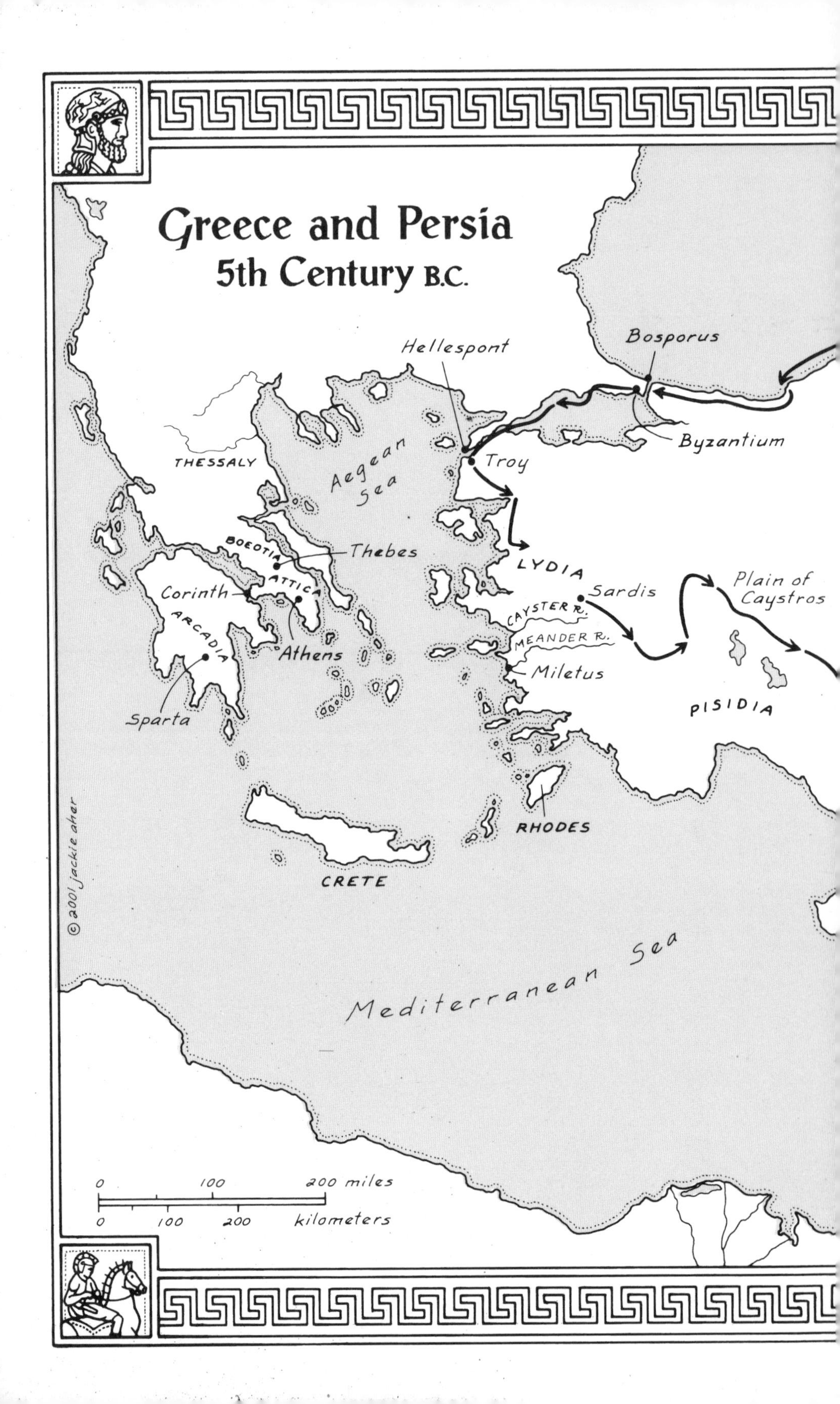
Greece and Persia
5th Century B.C.
Hellespont
Bosporus
Byzantium
Troy
THESSALY
Aegean Sea
BOEOTIA
Thebes
ATTICA
Corinth
ARCADIA
Athens
Sparta
LYDIA
Sardis
Plain of Caystros
CAYSTER R.
MEANDER R.
Miletus
PISIDIA
RHODES
CRETE
Mediterranean Sea
© 2001 jackie aher
0
100
200 miles
0
100
200
kilometers